Ilsa Evans lives in a partially renovated house in the Dandenongs, east of Melbourne. She shares her home with her three children, two dogs, several fish, a multitude of sea-monkeys and a psychotic cat.

She has completed a PhD at Monash University on the long-term effects of domestic violence and writes fiction on the weekends. *The Family Tree* is her seventh novel.

www.ilsaevans.com

Also by Ilsa Evans
Spin Cycle
Drip Dry
Odd Socks
Each Way Bet
Flying the Coop
Broken

ILSA EVANS

The Family Tree

Pan Macmillan Australia

First published 2009 in Macmillan by Pan Macmillan Australia Pty Limited
1 Market Street, Sydney

Copyright © Ilsa Evans 2009

The moral right of the author has been asserted.

All rights reserved. No part of this book may be reproduced or transmitted by any person or entity (including Google, Amazon or similar organisations), in any form or by any means, electronic or mechanical, including photocopying, recording, scanning or by any information storage and retrieval system, without prior permission in writing from the publisher.

National Library of Australia
cataloguing-in-publication data:

Evans, Ilsa.
The family tree / Ilsa Evans.

ISBN 978 1 4050 3903 1 (pbk.).

A823.4

Typeset in 11/15 pt Birka by Post Pre-press Group
Printed in Australia by McPherson's Printing Group

The characters and events in this book are fictitious and any resemblance to real persons, living or dead, is purely coincidental.

Papers used by Pan Macmillan Australia Pty Ltd are natural, recyclable products made from wood grown in sustainable forests. The manufacturing processes conform to the environmental regulations of the country of origin.

The Family Tree has its roots in a short story I wrote twenty years ago, when trying to come to terms with the death of my own father. As such, I would like to dedicate it to those who have spoken out for the right to die with dignity. I salute you all.

She saw the rifle, its barrel gleaming dully in the fading light, as soon as she turned into the passageway leading to her father's bedroom. She came to an abrupt halt and stared, disbelief shoved aside by mushrooming distress. For as long as she could remember that rifle's existence had been betrayed only by a flash of walnut stock or a glimpse of blackened metal deep in the recesses of her father's wardrobe; but now it was out in the open. And she understood the implications immediately.

The rifle was propped in the only corner of the bedroom that she could see from where she now stood, and she knew there was significance in the placement. To see the rest of the room she would have to continue up the passage and through the doorway, then turn to face the matching twin beds, and her father, and a choice that had clearly been made. But instead she remained where she was, unwilling to move forward in either space or time. And she suddenly reasoned that the events waiting to unfold could not begin without her, that she was the linchpin, and therefore as long as she remained on the periphery there could be no conclusion. But even as she clutched at this reasoning, the rifle casually mocked her with its presence. And she knew that, really, she was nothing more than a bit player. She could only postpone, not prevent, whether she liked it or not. But still, that first step was just so damn hard.

ONE

It was the loss of three whole months that finally opened Kate's eyes to the enormity of the problem. For quite a few years now she had been accustomed to losing a slab of time – usually during spring, which seemed to excel in a 'now you see me, now you don't' type of methodology. One minute she would be noting with pleasure that Christmas was soon approaching, and the next she would be standing, rather stunned, at the pointy end of the stick. With everybody else having long finished decking their halls and bowing their hollies, and now just becoming inebriated on a surfeit of Christmas spirit. And she would wonder frantically whether she had somehow slipped through a ripple in time, and whether there was any way of clawing her way back again.

But that year it wasn't just a few weeks that went by the wayside, but an entire season. It seemed that she tore August off the calendar only to reveal December lurking beneath, having used the cover of winter to do a little illicit queue-jumping. And at first she couldn't even *see* the track from where she was standing, let alone start planning how to get back on it. Because the time-warp issue wasn't the only concern. It was exacerbated by – or perhaps even related to – the fact that the very last remnants of her get-up-and-go had quite clearly got up and fled, and showed no signs of returning, even for a fleeting visit.

Somehow Kate did get through Christmas, probably because she'd done it for so many years it was almost second nature now. Making lists, fighting crowds, writing cards, wrapping presents, attending festivities, and sourcing the globes for Sam to light up, once more, the sputtering fifty-year-old Christmas-tree lights that his late mother had once bought in Coles for a few shillings. And which, apparently, sentimental grounds demanded couldn't be replaced even if their homicidal tendencies became more pronounced with every passing year.

But the traditional argument she mounted against the lights was largely absent this year. Indeed, it was difficult to muster up any level of concern, despite the obvious threat to life and the vicelike headaches brought on by spasmodic bursts of white light. Instead it seemed that, in a swift internal takeover, her get-up-and-go had been replaced by a lethargy that made each of her chores feel like climbing Mount Everest. Whilst dragging along the rest of her family in a sled tied to her back.

Strangely, as well as producing a desire to simply sleep each day away, despite a predominance of bad dreams, the lethargy also opened her eyes to things that she hadn't quite registered before, and they rankled. Like the way everybody sat on the couch watching television while she decorated the Christmas tree. And the way she devoted hours to finding that perfect present, while they all dashed out at the last minute and flew from shop to shop merrily grabbing whatever was left. And the way she spent the entire morning cooking Christmas dinner only to have Sam sit in pride of place carving the turkey and grandiosely handing out slices. With a largesse that suggested not only had he cooked the bird, but he'd also raised it from a chick and breastfed it each evening.

Then there were her presents. A new, very expensive vacuum cleaner from Sam that did everything bar toast bread, a pair of dangly beaded earrings from Shelley, a bottle of perfume from little Emma, an electric pancake maker from Jacob, and a book entitled *In Pride of Place: The fascinating history of garden gnomes* from Caleb. Complete with a free plaster garden gnome whose badly painted face gave him the appearance of the elephant man. And, as she opened each gift, the relevant giver spent several minutes extolling its virtues, and their cleverness in choosing it.

'I noticed your old vac wasn't very efficient last time I did the car,' said Sam proudly, putting on his glasses to read the hundred and thirty page instruction book. 'And it didn't have all those bits to get under the seats and that sort of thing.'

'You're always wearing *those*,' commented Shelley, pointing disparagingly at her mother's tasteful gold sleepers. 'So I thought I'd get you something a bit funkier.'

'This little beauty'll make *two* pancakes at a time,' enthused Jacob, running a hand lovingly over the shiny chrome surface of his gift. 'So you know how usually we have to wait ages when you make us pancakes? Not any more!'

'I know how much you love books,' said Caleb with a wave towards his mother's pile of editorial work. 'And you also like gardening, so when I saw this book I was rapt! *And* a free gnome! How cool was that?'

'Da,' dribbled little Emma, who was yet to utter an intelligible word, as she popped the perfume bottle out of her mouth and held it up, the atomiser showing clearly the amount of damage one tiny tooth can do in less than a minute.

And it wasn't just that the gifts weren't particularly thoughtful or, if they were, displayed a distinct lack of knowledge about her (for instance, she would *never* willingly choose vacuuming, pancake-making *or* gardening as a leisure activity), it was compounded by the fact that each person then demanded visual proof that she appreciated their particular offering. So Kate's Christmas morning was spent with *In Pride of Place: The fascinating history of garden gnomes* propped on the kitchen counter as she made piles of pancakes for breakfast while wearing the dangly earrings that, every time she turned her head too quickly, whipped around and threatened to impale an eyeball. Then she had to use the new perfume, which entailed removing the damaged atomiser knob and pressing the thin tube into her wrist hard enough to release the perfume, so that while she smelt nice, she also had a row of tiny indentations across her wrist that looked like a tribal tattoo. Finally, because Sam was looking rather put out, in between stuffing and cooking turkey, roasting pork, carving ham, baking copious amounts of potatoes, pumpkin and parsnip, and making gravy, she had to trial-run the new vacuum cleaner, which had such strong suction that it devoured some silver tinsel that had been trailing from the Christmas tree and very nearly brought the whole thing down.

But easily the worst present of all was the one which displayed the most insight and the one which she herself had placed under the tree. A hardback book from her father with a glossy black jacket titled, in vivid red lettering: *So you want to write? Then enough with the excuses – just do it!* And as Kate stared at the cover, knowing that her family's eyes were fixed upon her with concern, it was all she could do to hold her smile in place. And not let it slide away until she burst into tears and flung the hardback through the nearest window. Preferably a closed one. Let Sam vacuum up *that* mess with his one hundred and thirty page instruction, supersonic, super-strength vacuum bloody cleaner.

Then Christmas, too, was past, gone in a blur of tinsel and a flash of epileptic fairy lights, and it seemed like the seventeen hours she'd been awake that day had been condensed into three at the most. And she fell into bed on Christmas night with the sort of weariness that saps bones, and then opened her eyes on what felt like the next morning only to discover that it was New Year's Eve. Already. Because life wasn't just passing quickly, it was roaring past with a velocity that was downright terrifying. Like a hurricane that probably wouldn't stop until she was ready for a nursing home. Then time would go back to normal, and she'd sit at the window in her wheelchair with a crochet rug over her lap wondering where the years had gone, and why they were now limping past as if ancient themselves.

And when the elderly Kate tried to live in the past, there would be this huge black hole in the latter half, containing only a blur of momentum with occasional events standing out as atypical peaks in a flow chart. Like when Shelley announced that she and Daniel, her live-in partner of the past year, were separating and, oh by the way, she was pregnant. Or the day Jacob declared that he was giving university a miss in favour of becoming a professional Internet gamer and yes of *course* he had thought it through. Or like 18 June just gone when she'd stood in her father's bedroom and wondered, desperately, whether refusal was an option. Or whether it would simply leave her with a far larger burden of guilt, exacerbated by the understanding in his eyes.

But the main problem was the whirlwind. Definitely. And even if its momentum had increased post-June, the fact remained that it had been eddying before that. And, strangely, she seemed to be the only one affected. So that they were all busily *living* life, while she was simply providing sustenance, like bloody pancakes. And being the wind beneath their wings wasn't as fulfilling as it was cracked up to be. No, she wanted to *have* the wings. So that not only could she, too, fly, but she could also use them to beat everybody over the head until they started picking up after themselves, and feeding themselves, and generally caring for themselves so that she could get something done. Something for herself.

Like maybe write a book.

And that, she suspected, was the crux of the problem. Not her life itself, or even her father, but simple run-of-the-mill frustrated ambition. Because there had always been a book, or several, curled up somewhere within her, just waiting for extraction. Years ago they had been friendly entities, which lent her a sense of warm security with the knowledge that one day the time would be right for their birth. As a university student she had spent her spare time in smoky dark cafes with fellow literary souls pretending to be tortured by talent. Feeding off their collective angst to produce obscure poetry and agonisingly dark prose. And if somebody had told her then that she would end up editing other people's work, she would never have believed them. Because back then she never doubted that her drive was unstoppable and her destiny was assured. She *would* get that writing career started as soon as she finished university, and then it was after she had spent some time in Europe, and then it was after she had worked in the publishing industry for a while, and then it was after she and Sam had bought a house, and then it was after the kids were older, and then it was never. And never was now.

The bottom line was that she was Katherine Rose Painter, who lived at 23 Haverlock Lane in Lysterfield – a wife, mother, freelance editor and a failed writer. With no one to blame but herself. She could have paused at any point and made time for writing. But it seemed that whenever the chance arose, she went a different route. And it had been *her* who wanted to start a family sooner rather than later, and *her* who insisted on having another child when Shelley was only two, and then *her* uterus that hospitably made room for two eggs at the same time and therefore put an end to even the concept of free time for the foreseeable future.

So twenty-five years after Kate started working in the publishing industry as a stopgap until she wrote her first novel, she was still working in it. Only these days she worked from home, either editing or, more often than not, writing up reports on other people's manuscripts. Each one representing a stranger who was waiting, somewhere in Australia, to discover if they would be published. And no matter the standard of their work, they had each accomplished something she hadn't – they'd written a book.

But, along with the gradual acceptance that she herself was never going to join their ranks, there slunk a bitterness that underscored everything else. So that the shadows of what she had *failed* to achieve were now discolouring what she had, like her happy marriage and her reasonably affluent lifestyle – with spacious home, swimming pool, block of land in the country – until their edges were blurred. Once, she thought, she would have used humour to cope, but now it seemed as if everything was beyond a joke. And it was simply too hard to pretend there was nothing wrong. As if the months weren't flying past, and she wasn't the only one who was being left in their wake just staring at the calendar and fighting back the tears.

TWO

They had planned a low-key New Year's Eve that year, inviting only Kate's cousin Angie and her ex-husband, Oscar. Shelley was leaving the baby with them while going into the city for the fireworks, and both Jacob and Caleb had other plans also. So, like many other evenings, it was to be just the four of them, sitting on the decking by the pool, enjoying a barbecue and some nice wine. Then later, after Emma was put down for the night, they would relax even more, maybe play some cards or simply lean back and effortlessly allow the final minutes of the old year to slide past.

An hour or so before her guests were due, Kate smoothed the last of a mudpack around the curve of her chin and then peered at the mirror. Cracks were already segregating her crow's feet and creating a fault line between her eyes, the whites of which looked rather rheumy against the richness of the mud. Her light brown bob was pinned back but strands had adhered themselves to her skin in feathery clumps. Kate grimaced and the mud fissured even further. In the background she could hear Caleb playing his guitar, badly, while from the lounge room floated the sound of an early evening game show, complete with canned laughter and adenoidal compere.

Kate put a hand on either side of the basin and leant forward, noting that her eyes were now exactly the same shade as her skin, which was gradually resembling a *National Geographic* exposé of soil erosion.

Or an analogy for her life. Kate took a deep breath and consciously tried to relax. She had ten minutes to while away before a guaranteed glowing complexion so she sat down on the side of the bath, picking idly at the hardened mud on her fingers and flicking the flakes into the bathtub where they dissolved quickly into the puddles of soapy water. She watched the water turn brown and, with a sudden memory flash, recalled the mud pies she and Angie used to make as children. Clad only in knickers and dirt whilst patting their concoctions into containers and then scattering seeds on top before leaving them in the sun to dry. A rush of nostalgia warmed her, bringing a smile to her eyes. It had been an idyllic childhood, long on freedom and short on accountability: the despair of the neighbourhood women and the envy of their offspring.

It had also been an unusual upbringing, even by today's standards. After a complicated miscarriage led to the death of her mother when Kate was only three, her father had sold his Gippsland farm and moved back to Ferntree Gully, where he had been born and raised. The plan was for James to buy into his brother's profitable market garden and build on the property, thus giving Kate a sister figure in her two-year-old cousin, Angie, and a mother figure in her Aunt Sophie, a generous woman who was known to bend over backwards to help anybody out.

What was not general knowledge at the time was that most of Sophie's recent bending over had been of the extramarital variety. This involved a twice-weekly trip up behind the radishes to meet a neighbouring market gardener whose only claim to fame, until then, had been the tendency to pop out his glass eye after a few drinks and put it on somebody's shoulder whilst saying: 'Watch it, mate, I've got my eye on you.' Sophie clearly thought the joke had a certain longevity because, within a few months, she took off with her one-eyed paramour to places unknown.

In a time when a man bringing up a child alone was rather unusual, *two* men bringing up *two* children, both girls, was rare indeed. Nevertheless James and Frank decided to stick it out. While Kate and Angie were still small they simply tied a rope around each child's waist and then leashed them to the nearest fence post while they worked. As the girls grew, the market garden became their personal playground: acres of freedom where the only rule was not to harm the produce. Long, lazy hours spent playing by the creek or at the orchard or, more often than not, at That Bugger's neighbouring property where the blackberries had taken over much of the garden and the empty, echoing house was an ideal venue for fertile imaginations.

Neither father ever remarried, although Kate's Uncle Frank brought a procession of girlfriends home over the years. But, perhaps still scarred by his wife's particular brand of neighbourly largesse, he shied away from any meaningful relationship. Nor did Sophie ever return; even That Bugger's land was sold in the mid seventies and subdivided into house lots. It was the obvious success of this venture, followed relatively quickly by Frank's first heart attack, which led to the brothers doing the same with the market garden, making a tidy profit and retaining only the house and about half an acre to retire on. The tidy profit had also financed a year in Europe for Kate and the birth of *Fully Booked*, Angie's bookstore that was still thriving in central Boronia. And it was just after Kate had returned from Europe and was settling into her new publishing job that, while visiting her father one weekend, she started chatting with a young builder named Sam who was working next door. And the rest, as they say, was history.

'Mum! Angie 'n' Oscar are here! And can you hem up my black jeans for me?'

Kate jerked into alertness and jumped up, staring at her reflection in the mirror. Large sections of mudpack were now flaking forward and, with her facial muscles firmly plastered into position, she couldn't have answered Shelley even if she wanted to. Kate picked up her watch from beside the basin and read the time. And then read it again. Five twenty-one. How could that be possible? Even now it seemed the thin gold hands had a speed out of sync with reality. Five twenty-two, five twenty-three.

Kate dropped the watch and turned on the tap, filling her cupped hands with cold water and splashing it onto her face. Flakes of mud pack fell into the basin, their edges quickly melting as they leaked a rich chestnut-brown. After the water finally ran clear, Kate groped for a towel, dabbed her face dry and stood back to examine it. Predictably enough the promised glow was simply a dull crimson sheen, like old beetroot, especially around her nose. She sighed as she clipped her watch back on, without looking at it, and then unpinned her hair, brushing the mud residue out before disguising her new sheen with moisturising foundation.

'Mum! Didja hear me? I need my jeans hemmed before I go out!'

'Here, Shell, let me do them.'

The low, *rescuing* tones of Angie mellowed out Shelley's demands and then their voices faded into the background of music and television. Kate wrapped the towel around her and took a deep breath before padding quietly down the passage to the master bedroom. There were clear signs that Sam had already changed, as a T-shirt and overalls were abandoned by the bed with grey-white socks sticking out from the pant legs. Kate knew that if she picked up the overalls a pair of jocks would also fall out. Because her husband had the rather odd talent of being able to shed his clothing like a snake's skin and, like a snake also, he'd dump them wherever they fell.

Feeling a shaft of annoyance out of all proportion to the deed, Kate collected the bundle and threw it into the clothes hamper. Then she dressed herself, neatly but casually, in a khaki layered skirt and a loose crushed-cotton cream shirt. For once, contemporary fashion was ideal for women in their late forties with a slight spare tyre, less than slim thighs and an almost pathological hatred of ironing.

Kate flicked off the game show on her way through the lounge room and then continued into the kitchen where she poured herself a glass of water and then gazed through the scrim-covered window at the decked area outside. The decking abutted the entire rear of the house, with the barbecue at one end near the sliding door and the cedar outdoor setting. Three wide steps led down to a forked path, one side heading straight towards the hinged, childproof gate in the swimming-pool fencing, and the other meandering off to the right until it reached

Shelley's bungalow at the far corner of the garden. The bungalow itself was mostly obscured by a high jasmine-covered trellis, but the dark green Colorbond roofing was visible, juxtaposed against the cobalt blue of the sky.

It had been a beautiful day, warm without being overly humid and with a light wind that carried the scent of the jasmine up to the house. Threads of smoke came from where Sam was firing up the barbecue; Oscar stood next to him, leaning against a pillar. Apart from the fact Sam was slightly taller and a little more solid, the two men were very similar looks-wise, both with olive skin and short, dark hair that had not yet receded but was beginning to sport flecks of grey over the ears. The type that looked distinguished on a man, but unkempt on a woman. Their personalities, though, were *very* different. Sam was a quiet man, self-contained and easygoing, yet a hard worker who enjoyed manual labour so much that, years before, he had thrown in an architectural degree in favour of a career as a builder. On the other hand Oscar loved nothing better than a deep philosophical discussion in which he solved the ills of the world by pontificating about each and every political or social dilemma. He was saved from complete pomposity only by a keen intelligence and the occasional ability to laugh at himself.

As Oscar passed Sam a beer and waved his hands in the manner he had when explaining some pertinent point, Kate transferred her gaze to her cousin Angie. Her best friend, her surrogate sister. Who was sitting at the cedar table bent over Shelley's jeans, her hand rising and falling as she pushed a needle through the denim. Angie was only a shade shorter than Kate's five foot five but was, and always had been, a good deal plumper. Kate thought it suited her, softening her features and creating an overall *roundness* that was charismatic in itself.

Oscar and Angie had separated five years ago, soon after their daughter Melissa left for university. Like many, they had declared their intention of remaining friends for the sake of their child but, unlike most, they had managed, almost effortlessly, to achieve this. In fact, if anything, they were better friends now than they had been during the last years of their marriage. Whilst giving some credit to Oscar, Kate attributed this mostly to her cousin, and to the neutralising effect of her serenity.

If Angie could best be described as serene, then the person sitting next to her and tapping one foot impatiently on the decking was her polar opposite. Michelle was a tall, thin girl with straight, almost waist-length nut-brown hair and a rather hyperactive edginess. No matter what she was doing, whether working or resting or playing, one foot would be tapping, or a hand fidgeting, or her eyes blinking as a million thoughts whipped through her mind. And she had been like that since infancy. Always on the move, always edgy, always demanding.

At the moment, though, Shelley's outfit was more striking than her personality. A filmy, spaghetti-strapped number on top, and a pair of pink polka-dotted pyjama pants on the bottom. Together with full make-up and gold beaded earrings that sparkled between the strands of flowing hair and brushed against her shoulders as she turned. On her mother's pyjama-clad lap, and getting a free jiggle, was little Emma. Seven and a half months old and adorable as only a baby could be. A perfectly symmetrical head covered by sparse blonde waves that were currently secured in a waterfall, huge blue eyes, button nose and a coral-pink rosebud mouth.

'What're you doing, Mum?'

'Watering the plants,' said Kate, immediately pouring the remaining contents of her glass over a few potted herbs on the windowsill before turning to her eldest son.

'Well, if you're not doing anything, can you drive me over to Box Hill? I want to have a few drinks tonight.'

'Ditto. And do you happen to know where your brother is?'

'Already left. But can't you drive me over *before* you have a few drinks?' Caleb raised an eyebrow and gave her his most winning smile, which may well have worked but for the fact her guests were already sitting on the decking. Kate pointed wordlessly and Caleb leant in closer to have a look. He was a tall boy, an inch or two over six foot, and well built in the bargain. The best-looking of Kate's children as well as the most easy-going and the most popular. At one stage, of all the phone calls received each day in the Carson–Painter household, about three-quarters would be for Caleb. With the advent of mobile phones, Kate was at least saved from having to continually take messages from laconic boys and eager, breathy girls.

But she could well understand why Caleb was so well liked. He was a person without subterfuge, so that there was never any game-playing or point-scoring or sidelong glances. What you saw was what you got. A personable, educated, laid-back bloke with all the easy confidence that comes from twenty-one years of security and good looks. Everything, in fact, that his twin brother was not.

Caleb straightened and then grinned down at his mother. 'Okay, you're off the hook. I'll ring around and find someone who's heading in that direction.'

'Good idea.' Kate watched her son stroll away, already flipping open his phone. Why, she wondered with a flare of irritation, hadn't he just done that in the first place? Was it so much easier to persuade her to give up *her* time than it was to get organised in the first place?

The glass sliding door was sent shuddering across its tracks as Shelley bounded through, the finished jeans hanging over one arm. She glanced at her mother with an instant frown. 'Mum! What're you doing there? Doesn't matter, haven't got time. Gotta run.' And she was gone, heading rapidly towards the bathroom. Her perfume hung in the air; a musk aroma that felt thick and vaguely suffocating.

Kate took a deep breath and left the safety of her position by the sink. As she walked, she turned her head as far as it would go to the right and then to the left, feeling the tendons stretch with some satisfaction. It was an exercise she had read about which was designed to assist tension, and perhaps even lessen the headaches that beset her from time to time. Thus far it had achieved minimal success. She pushed the sliding door open with less gusto than her daughter and went through onto the decking, fixing a smile to her face.

'Kate! *There* you are!' Angie turned awkwardly, the baby on her lap having a firm grip on her black beads. 'I thought we'd have to send out a search party!'

'Just got caught up.' Kate sent a wave in Oscar's direction. The barbecue was in full sizzle now; marinated steaks hissed on the grill and a few chilli-speckled burgers browned beside them.

Angie peered at Kate. 'Have you got eczema or something?'

'No, just flushed with vitality.' Kate sat down beside her cousin and reached over to slip the hair tie out of Emma's hair before running her fingers through the blonde waves and smoothing them down. The baby chuckled approvingly.

'Vitality, hey? Sure you haven't got a head start on us?'

'I wish.'

'Well, you can catch up now then. Have a glass of this.' Angie wrapped one arm around Emma's waist so that she could use the other to push a bottle towards Kate. 'It's a very nice chardonnay.'

'From up near Seymour,' called Oscar. 'A great little winery that's off the beaten track. Superb place. Hardly anyone knows about it.'

Angie leant towards Kate. 'Unless they read the huge-ass signs along the highway, that is. And then follow the arrows.'

Kate poured herself a glass while she examined her cousin more closely. Her long, curly chestnut hair was pulled back into a plait from which a few tendrils had escaped to frame her face. Apart from the black beads, she was wearing a pair of thin linen pants and matching loose vest that covered a black T-shirt.

'Have you lost weight?'

'No such luck.' Angie paused with a dip-laden cracker halfway to her mouth. 'Why? Do I look like I have? I *am* on a diet, so maybe it's working.'

The sliding door bounced open again and Shelley emerged, her long legs now encased in tight black denim. Kate, who had pulled the salad bowl over to start tossing the salad, paused to eye her critically, deciding that she preferred the pyjamas. They made her daughter look somehow more vulnerable and less predatory.

'Thanks Auntie Angie, you did a *great* job. Much better than Mum would've.' Shelley leant down to give her daughter a kiss on the cheek. 'Bye, bye precious. Shoot, has Grannie taken out your pretty hair tie already?'

'If I'm looking after her I prefer the child not to look like an onion.'

'Grannie,' repeated Angie, with a grin at Kate.

Shelley gave Emma another kiss. 'Anyway, I'd better go. Running late.'

'Bye sweetheart,' called Sam, waving the spatula. 'Have fun.'

'I will. Bye all. Happy New Year and all that.'

After they had each echoed this sentiment, Shelley flew back through the sliding door and disappeared into the house. Shortly afterwards, her Astra could be heard firing up in the driveway and then reversing out with a high-pitched scream.

'She makes me feel exhausted,' said Angie.

'You and me both.' Kate took one of Emma's fat fists. 'Lucky you're a bit more relaxed than Mummy, isn't it?'

'Ker-*choo*!' spluttered Emma, her body shuddering with the effort as a fine spray of mucus and spit rained down on her grandmother's hand.

'Bless you!' said Angie as Kate retracted her now damp hand and stared at it.

Sam threw a roll of paper towel towards the table, striking his wife squarely on the shoulder. The paper towel bounced off, hit the side of the table and rebounded into a potted plant where it nestled amongst the fronds.

'Great catch!' Oscar toasted Kate while Sam held up his hand in apology, although with a grin that robbed it of any real sincerity.

As Sam turned away again, Kate glared towards the back of his head and then retrieved the paper towel, tearing off a piece to wipe down her hand. It still felt sticky, but rather than go inside and give it a good wash, she topped up her wine and took a deep sip instead.

'Are you getting a cold then, gorgeous?' asked Angie in a singsong voice. Kate passed over a piece of towel and Angie used it to dry the baby's face and nose deftly as Emma batted at her with chubby starfish hands, finally managing to strike herself on the nose. Her eyes widened with surprise and she stared at her hands, spreading and then clenching her fingers as if a clue lay just within their grasp.

'Ever smelt mothballs, Katey-loo?' asked Oscar suddenly, apropos of nothing.

Kate frowned at him. 'Don't call me Katey-loo. And of course I've smelt mothballs. What's that got to do with anything?'

'Then how'd you get their legs apart?'

'How did I . . . ?' Kate's frown cleared as she got the joke. She smiled wanly and took another long sip of wine.

'Good one, huh?' Oscar slapped his thigh happily and turned back to Sam.

'Idiot,' said Angie. 'Can't believe I stayed with him for twenty years. Are the boys here tonight?'

'Are you kidding? New Year's Eve? No, Jake's already gone and Caleb's inside waiting for a lift. Or he might have left by now.'

Angie readjusted Emma and then straightened the baby's candy-striped rompers. 'So Jake's gone out? That's a good sign, isn't it?'

'Who knows?' Kate shrugged. 'If I try to ask him anything, he just gives me this *look*. As if I'm being amazingly intrusive.'

'I *know* that look. Melissa's an expert at it.'

'But you're lucky. I mean, Mel's so sensible.' Kate petered off as she took another sip of wine. 'How is she anyway? Have you heard from her lately?'

'Well, I told you she'd renewed her contract over there, didn't I? I suppose it's great career-wise, but I do miss her.' Angie looked rueful. 'And I think she's quite serious about that Brad guy she brought out. You know, for the funeral.'

'Grub's up!' announced Sam cheerfully, bringing a platter of still-sizzling steak and burgers over to the table. Oscar followed him with their beer.

'Looks great,' Angie sniffed enthusiastically and then looked down at Emma. 'And what do I do with the little princess here?'

'I'll just put her in the playpen.' Kate hefted her grand-daughter off Angie's lap as she stood up. As usual, the soft, pliable weight of the baby brought a rush of affection so Kate lifted her even higher and kissed her gently on the soft curve of her cheek. Delicious.

'Where'd you get your meat, mate?' asked Oscar, sitting down next to Sam and piercing a piece of steak with a fork. He lifted it up and examined it critically.

'Dunno,' replied Sam equably. 'Ask Kate.'

'At the local butcher.' Kate lowered Emma into her playpen with its scattering of brightly coloured toys. The baby immediately grabbed an interlinked set of red, blue and yellow rings and tried to shovel the entire lot into her mouth.

'Oh, you should go to this bloke up in Bayswater. Can't get any better. Big thick steaks that melt in your mouth. I'll give you the name. Tell him Oscar sent you.'

'And if I want big thick steaks, I'll keep him in mind,' said Kate, sinking back into her chair. 'But I find that when you intend *marinating*, thin is the way to go.'

'Doesn't matter. He does everything well,' replied Oscar, unperturbed.

Kate piled some of her thin, beautifully marinated steak onto her plate and then used the servers to collect a portion of tossed salad. Everyone else had already begun eating, both Sam and Angie opting for the steak while Oscar had now made himself a rather overloaded burger, which he was attempting to wrap his mouth around. It occurred to Kate suddenly that he looked exactly like Emma with her plastic rings. She laughed.

'What's funny?' asked Angie before following Kate's gaze. 'Oh, him. Believe me, it's only amusing in small doses.'

'As with perfection,' replied Oscar, removing some lettuce from his burger.

Angie took a sip of wine and contemplated him quizzically. 'Personally I don't find perfection all that amusing. In small *or* large doses.'

'Clearly. Otherwise you'd never have let me go.' Oscar pressed the heel of his hand down on his burger to flatten it. 'Where'd you get these buns, Katey-loo?'

'I made them,' replied Kate shortly, slicing up her steak and ignoring the amazement on her husband's face.

Angie chuckled. 'You'll have to give me the recipe.'

'Sorry, no can do. It's a family one, passed down through generations.'

'In case you've forgotten. I *am* family.'

'On my mother's side, I mean. She wrote it out with her last breath.'

'What? Like on a fogged up window?'

'Hey, they're really good.' Sam spoke thickly, as he was now chewing on one of the perfectly round, sesame-seed buns that came from the local hot-bread shop. 'Can you make more of them? I might start taking them to work. Taste a bloody sight better than the bought stuff.'

'Sure. In my spare time.'

'Thanks, sweetheart.'

'How's the permit going for the development?' asked Oscar, putting his burger down and breaking a small crescent of meat from the middle. He popped this in his mouth and turned to Sam questioningly.

'On track,' replied Sam, glancing across at Kate and then shaking his head imperceptibly at Oscar.

'You'll be rolling in it soon. And the kids,' Oscar beamed across at Kate and Angie, neither of whom beamed back. He frowned. 'What? What did I say?'

As nobody answered him, Oscar shrugged his shoulders and went back to picking at his burger. Kate glanced across at Sam and he smiled at her, a smile that both apologised and sympathised but did nothing to ease her.

A rustling movement underneath the bottlebrush heralded the gradual emergence of Hector, their fifteen-year-old Labrador-cross. The dog stood at the bottom of the steps for a moment, as if hoping some alternative form of ascension might materialise. Then he sighed heavily and began the climb himself, one paw at a time. Finally reaching the top, he swayed melodramatically and wandered slowly over to Sam's chair, where he gazed up at his master.

'How's it going, mate?' Sam reached down to ruffle the thick grey-black fur of Hector's neck.

'Don't feed him,' said Kate, turning to Angie to explain, 'Vet's orders. He needs to lose a bit of weight.'

'Him and me both,' commented Angie, finishing off her steak.

'Actually, it's not so much his weight as the flatulence,' added Sam, rather unnecessarily in Kate's opinion.

'Uncanny,' said Oscar, looking from the dog to Angie and then back again. 'The similarities keep building. Wasn't that one of the reasons we got divorced?'

'Very funny. I think you're projecting there, sport.'

Hector continued to stare at Sam for several minutes, but when it became obvious that a neck ruffle was the best he could hope for, he wandered over to Oscar instead.

'Have you started reading that book yet?' asked Angie, pouring some more wine.

'What book?'

'You know exactly what book. The one about writing.'

Oscar held up a hand as he swallowed some burger. 'I know what you should do. You should go to one of those retreats.'

Kate raised her eyebrows. 'Really? Like to practise my yoga?'

'No, I'm serious. You see them in the paper sometimes. Writers' retreats.'

'That's actually not a bad idea,' said Angie, staring at him.

'Don't sound so surprised.' Oscar took another bite and chewed contentedly.

Kate allowed her mind to entertain the prospect for a moment. A writers' retreat, perhaps set on a mountain amongst towering trees and meandering paths, where everybody was totally self-sufficient and dedicated to their craft. And the only sound was the tapping of keyboards and the occasional whisper as ideas were explored. Then at night, all the occupants would recline on the balcony overlooking the blue-grey clefts of the mountain range as they discussed Proust and Plath and the merits of differing narrative techniques.

'Maybe I should have given you one of those for Christmas instead of the vacuum cleaner,' said Sam with a smile. Then he elaborated hurriedly, 'I mean like a weekend there, not the whole place.'

'Glad you made that clear.' Kate smiled back, rather flatly. With some effort she recaptured the balcony scene again, but this time all her companions were much younger with smugly superior smiles and could actually talk about Proust and Plath and know what they were talking about. She was totally out of place.

'You gave her a *vacuum cleaner?*' asked Oscar, lifting one eyebrow.

'Hey, come on. It was the latest model. You should see it!'

Emma chose that moment to start complaining rather noisily, so Kate jumped up before Sam could offer to fetch the vacuum cleaner and show it off. The baby was holding tightly to the wooden rails and straining as she tried to lift herself, but her bottom barely left the ground. Kate hefted her up and snuggled her koala-like against her chest as she carried her back over to the table. Emma chortled happily.

'So any chance of Shelley getting back together with that Daniel?' asked Oscar, his eyes on the baby.

'Can't see it,' Sam leant back with a sigh, the vacuum cleaner forgotten. 'I'd like to say it's his fault, but . . .'

The sentence was left hanging as Kate sat down with Emma on her lap. The baby immediately hooked a damp finger underneath her grandmother's watch strap and then ducked her head down with determination, mouth open and reaching. Angie slipped off her necklace and, clicking the beads against each other to attract Emma's attention, passed them over.

'Thanks, Ange.' Kate manoeuvred Emma back into a sitting position as the baby crammed beads into her mouth. Oscar sighed happily, pushing his plate away as he patted his stomach with exaggerated satisfaction. Next to him, Hector seemed to be looking just as content. Kate frowned. 'Oscar, did you feed that dog?'

'Someone had to,' replied Oscar sanctimoniously. 'Poor ole bugger. Food's one of the few pleasures he's got left and you won't even let him have that?'

'It's for his own good!' protested Kate crossly, jiggling Emma. 'And it's not like he's being starved, you know. He only had his dinner a couple of hours ago.'

'Don't get excited. It was just one of those chilli burgers.'

'For god's –'

'New year's resolutions!' interrupted Angie brightly. 'Who's got one?'

'First a refill, I think,' said Oscar heartily. 'Especially for you, Katey-loo. You seem a bit on edge tonight.'

Kate watched Oscar narrowly as he refilled her glass and then emptied the chardonnay into Angie's, finishing off with a showy twirl of the bottle. She was just using her mental thesaurus to describe him fittingly when she felt a distinct nudge against her ankle under the table. At first attributing the nudge to Hector, she was a bit surprised to see that the dog was still sitting by Oscar's chair. Kate glanced across the table at Sam. He winked sympathetically, but instead of the action soothing her, it only honed her irritation. A reaction which, in turn, made her feel even worse.

'Okay.' Oscar passed Sam another beer from the esky and sat back, looking at them all with an air of self-satisfaction. 'I'll start, shall I? My new year's resolution is to sell the house.'

'Really?' Kate glanced at Angie and could tell she already knew.

'It makes sense. I've hung on to it mainly for sentimental reasons. You know, that's where Mel grew up and all. But driving into town each day for work is pretty stupid, especially with petrol skyrocketing now. So I've decided to put it on the market and buy one of those apartments at the Docklands.'

'He offered it to me first,' added Angie. 'But I like my unit.'

'So you'll be a yuppie, then?' asked Sam, grinning.

Kate regarded him thoughtfully. 'I think you'd make a good yuppie.'

'I agree,' Oscar nodded. 'And the good news is that if you ever need anywhere to stay in town, like after a play or something, you'll be right. But it means I'll have my work cut out getting the house ready. I need to retile the bathroom, stuff like that.'

'I'll give you the name of an excellent tiler,' said Sam. 'Top bloke.'

'Thanks, mate. Appreciated. So what's yours then? Your resolution?'

Sam glanced fleetingly across at Kate and then shrugged. 'Don't really have one. Just that this year's better than last.'

'Here, here,' said Oscar, raising his beer slightly as everybody fell silent.

Kate stared out across the backyard and suddenly, as if a shutter had clicked in her mind, she clearly saw her father's doorway, up at the end of the passage. Frozen in time. She blinked, and forced herself to retreat. Back towards the balcony at the writers' retreat where, judging by the faces of the others, *nothing* was expected of her.

'You next then,' said Angie, taking a sip of wine and then looking at Kate quizzically. 'What's your new year's resolution?'

Everybody on the balcony waited for her answer. She shrugged. 'I don't know.'

'Come on, Katey-loo. You need something to focus on. Put last year behind you.'

'Well, how about you leave me till last,' said Kate lightly. 'Give me time to come up with something.'

'Okay then, me,' Angie sat up straighter. 'Mine is that I'm going to take some positive steps to move forward. Last year *was* dreadful, but now it's over.' She paused for a moment before continuing quickly. 'So for starters I'm going to do something I've been thinking of for a while, ever since Mel went over to London in fact. I'm going to clean her room out and get a boarder.'

'You're *what*?' Kate's mouth stayed slightly open as she stared at her cousin. Emma, fascinated by this turn of events, stuck a damp finger inside her grandmother's mouth and giggled.

Sam nodded approvingly. 'That's a great idea. Give you some company.'

Kate removed Emma's finger and closed her mouth. It tasted like soggy plastic.

'You want to watch who you get,' said Oscar pragmatically. 'There's some weirdos out there. Haven't you ever seen *Fatal Attraction*?'

Angie stared at him. 'What on earth has that got to do with having a boarder?'

'Hang on,' Oscar clicked his fingers. 'Wrong film. I meant the one with the psychopath who moves in with Kate Hudson. *Single White Female* I think it's called. Anyway, the point's the same with both films. Women can be very dangerous.'

'And men can be idiots,' commented Angie. She turned to Kate. 'So? What do you think?'

Kate was still thinking about what Angie had said. *Now it's over?* She felt resentful that Angie could even sum it up like that. Then she thought about her cousin sharing her unit with someone else. Cooking meals, watching television, sitting in the spa enjoying a bottle of wine. Each of the images flipped forward, crowding on top of each other until the stack of them gave her a headache. She drained her glass and then stared at the empty chardonnay bottle as if it might refill by sheer strength of willpower. Oscar reached over into his esky and pulled out an identical one. Using a corkscrew, he levered the cork out with a dull plop, and then passed the bottle over.

'Thanks.' Kate refilled her glass and took a long sip. The wine gave her a pleasant fuzziness around the edges that made Angie's news slightly more palatable. She repositioned Emma and turned back to her cousin. 'Do you have someone in mind?'

Oscar suddenly frowned. 'Male or female?'

'No, and female. Preferably non-psychopathic,' Angie grinned. 'Although you must admit that'd inject some spice into my life.'

'Why do you *need* any spice?' asked Kate. It came out like a whine, so she cleared her throat before continuing. 'I mean, you always said you liked the solitude. Having your own space.'

'I *do*, but it'd be something different. And right now different's good.'

'Not necessarily,' said Oscar darkly.

Kate drank some more wine, aware that Sam was watching her, puzzled. But instead of feeling warmed by his regard, she felt annoyed. As if sensing tension, Emma let go of the beads and started to fidget restlessly. Kate automatically took her by the hands and helped her stand unsteadily on her lap, where she rocked from side to side happily.

Angie was looking at her quizzically. 'What's up?'

'Nothing.' Kate kept her eyes on Emma, now giggling happily. There was another nudge against her leg under the table but she didn't want to look in Sam's direction. Emma's knees strained and then folded, the baby sitting down with a thud, so Kate took advantage of having a spare hand to have another sip of wine. Emma grabbed the hand back as soon as it was free and then used it to lever herself back up again. She laughed proudly.

'So what about you, Katey-loo?' asked Oscar. 'What's your resolution then?'

'Write a book, I suppose,' replied Kate distractedly. 'Same as it was last year, and the year before that. And don't call me bloody Katey-loo.'

'Maybe this year you should make a definite plan,' said Angie. She glanced across at Sam. 'Putting *specific* time aside.'

'Yeah, that'll work.' Kate stared over towards the bungalow. She knew that Angie meant well but she wished she would stop trying to be encouraging; it just made her feel worse. Emma crouched down once more and then paused, giggling, before shooting upwards and connecting with the underside of Kate's chin, which made a distinct cracking noise that echoed all the way up her jawline. Tears sprung into her eyes, while Emma collapsed into a heap and started crying.

'Christ!' Sam jumped up and lifted the wailing baby off Kate's lap to examine her head. 'Are you okay, sweetheart?'

'I'm fine thanks,' said Kate through gritted teeth as Emma continued to howl. She felt her chin gingerly, half expecting to find a split in the skin weeping copious amounts of blood. But it just felt tender. *Very* tender.

'That was some whack!' said Oscar admiringly.

'Here, Sam, give her a cracker.' Angie pushed the dip platter over towards Sam, who sat back down with Emma on his lap. He took a cracker and waved it in front of her. 'Here you go, sweetie, want this?'

Sweetie obviously did, as her sobs immediately receded and she reached out a fat, damp fist to grab the cracker, shovelling half of it into her mouth. Hector left his post by Oscar's chair to pad back to Sam's, clearly hoping to share in the spoils.

'You okay, Kate?' asked Sam, finally.

'I'll live.' Kate moved her jaw from side to side tentatively and then let go of her chin as she turned back to Angie. 'So are you going to advertise? For this person?'

'I suppose so.' Angie shrugged. 'Unless you know someone?'

Kate shook her head. She took a sip of wine and tried to come to grips with her reaction to Angie's news. She knew, instinctively, that it was made of many parts but felt as if the wine had blurred each so that they leached into one another. Making them impossible to interpret.

'I've got an idea,' said Sam, suddenly breaking the silence. He turned to Oscar. 'Why don't you and I go and put Buggerlugs here to bed and we'll watch something till she goes off?'

Oscar jumped up quickly. 'Good thinking, mate.'

'Say goodnight then.' Sam brought Emma over to Kate and bent down so that she could kiss the baby on her cheek, still sticky with half-dried tears. Then he hoisted Emma up over his shoulder so that her head dangled slightly and the remains of the soggy cracker fell from her mouth and onto the decking. The baby stretched out her hand after it but laughed anyway. Hector watched them go and then wandered over to devour the soggy cracker before crawling underneath the table by Kate's feet.

'I can't believe you didn't tell me,' blurted Kate, almost accusingly, before Sam and Oscar had even reached the bungalow. 'Not even a hint!'

Angie frowned at her. 'I don't know why you're taking this so personally. It's not that big a deal, really. So I get a boarder? So what?'

'Sharing your home's not a big deal?'

'Hang on.' Angie flipped her plait back and stared at her cousin for a few moments. 'Are you feeling threatened or something?'

'Don't be ridiculous.'

'Then why are you being such a bitch about it?' Angie spoke mildly, which took some of the sting out of her words. 'I just want to do something to shake up my life a bit. Help me move on. You do realise that I'm in pain too, don't you? He wasn't just my uncle, he was almost a father. And I know nothing will fill that void, but I'm trying to be pro-active. And maybe you should too.'

'Hang on!'

'Or at least support me,' continued Angie as if Kate hadn't spoken. 'Acknowledge that I'm making an effort.'

Kate held Angie's gaze for a moment and then dropped her eyes until she was staring at the double row of stitching along her neckline. Her chin throbbed. Angie was right. She *knew* Angie was right, but she still couldn't get past the feeling of resentment, as if she was the one being left behind. And suddenly Kate realised that was *exactly* how she felt. Abandoned in her current state of ambiguity.

'Listen, Kate –'

'Shhh, I'm thinking.' Kate raised her eyes briefly to her cousin's face before flitting off to stare under the table at the dark mound of Hector. She used her foot to stroke him absentmindedly while she followed her train of thought. And she decided that if Angie had announced the news hesitatingly, as if unsure or needing approval, then she, Kate, would have reacted quite differently. But it was her air of certainty, of decisiveness, that had set her teeth on edge from the very beginning. And why? Well, because she was . . . jealous.

'Are you not talking to me now?'

'Of course I'm talking to you.' Kate frowned as her thought processes fractured, leaving just the one word lit up in neon – jealous. Jealous. JEALOUS.

'You've got a funny way of showing it.' Angie pushed her chair back so that she was facing Kate full on. 'Do you want to tell me what's going on?'

'Nothing's going on.'

Angie put a hand on her cousin's arm. 'It's Uncle James, isn't it?'

'Of course not!' Kate emptied her glass and the wine helped. The slight fuzziness around her periphery had added a kaleidoscope effect, so that whatever she looked at was instantly framed within a mobile border. It was quite disconcerting. Kate looked across at Angie, trying the visual effect around her cousin's face and was pleased to see that it gave Angie's curly hair a Medusa-type look, with a halo of snake-like tendrils, each waving independently of the other. She smiled.

'At last!' Angie smiled. 'The mask cracks!'

'There was no mask,' said Kate, concentrating. 'Just concern, that's all.'

'I appreciate it. Really. It's just –'

'And whoever moves in with you is going to be very lucky,' Kate nodded, agreeing with herself. 'I mean it. You're very easy to live with.'

'Well, thank you. But don't forget you haven't lived with me for a long time,' Angie laughed. 'I think I've picked up a few foibles along the way. Still, I don't think I'll have too much problem finding someone. I mean, the unit's nice and central. And they'll have plenty of time to themselves, what with me at the shop most days.'

'Sounds perfect.' Kate smiled stiffly and reached out for the wine bottle to refill her glass. She knew it'd be a good idea to slow down, but she just couldn't summon the willpower. Instead, the thought of the kaleidoscope actually taking over her entire being was rather appealing. To hide behind it and lick her wounds, and only emerge when everything was back to normal. Or was *normal* the problem?

The bungalow door could be heard shutting very softly and then Sam and Oscar came into view past the trellis, strolling up the path towards the decking.

'Hey girls,' said Oscar, bounding up the steps and throwing himself into his chair. 'Absolute crap on TV. Just a bunch of idiots already counting in the new year.'

Sam set the baby intercom down on the table and checked the volume as he sat down. He smiled across at Kate and she was able to frame him neatly, but with less visual success than with her cousin. Instead his face remained steady, and only the background became blurred and indistinct.

'Christ, what's that smell?' Oscar leant back with a grimace.

'I can't smell . . . yes I can,' Sam looked accusingly down at Hector, who had the grace to look embarrassed as he slunk from underneath the table.

Kate glared at Oscar. 'Chilli burger, hey? Well done.'

Angie waved her hand in front of her face and laughed. 'That's rank.'

'It'll pass,' said Oscar airily, turning to Sam. 'So this tiler of yours then. Does he do paving as well? I need some of that redone before it goes on the market.'

Kate tuned out as Sam replied. She knew that once Oscar latched onto a subject he would worry at it from every angle, which meant that her input would not be needed for at least the next half hour or so. Instead, she found her thoughts veering towards Angie's unit. Its *ambience*. No dropped clothing, or abandoned books and magazines, or plates of congealed food slid underneath the coffee table, or soggy dummies behind the couch cushions, or flatulent dogs, or dirty fingerprints, or . . . anything that required constant menial tasks that sapped one of strength and – *essence*. Yes, essence. Kate nodded to herself righteously. It might sound melodramatic, but it was how she felt.

And she had meant it when she said that Angie's flatmate would be a fortunate person. Because, as she knew from personal experience, Angie was terrific to share with. Considerate, generous, liberal, virtually unflappable and *neat*. Very neat. And they would have this room, in this lovely unit, with this lovely *neat* person, and they would have it all to themselves for each and every day except Sundays, which was the only day that Angie had off. Even then she was usually out socialising or whatever. So there was this room, this whole *unit*, empty and peaceful and neat and just begging for someone who would appreciate it. Like her.

If it had not been for the alcohol, this last thought probably would have occurred to Kate a lot sooner. But also, if it hadn't been for the alcohol, she probably wouldn't have taken it so seriously. Instead, her eyes widened as the idea blinked into being, and then took hold, blossoming outwards until any and all objections were enveloped within its folds. It was like an epiphany, a revelation, which answered everything and glistened with potential. Kate shook her head and smiled with amazement.

'You look like the cat that's got the cream.' Angie was looking at her curiously.

Oscar glanced over and laughed. 'Told you it was good wine.'

'Oh my god.' Kate was still in wonder at the brilliance of her idea. 'I've had a *brainwave*. A resolution of my own! And it's perfect! You need a flatmate, and I – I need somewhere! For peace and quiet. To see if I *can* write a book. Give it a chance.'

'Hang on,' Angie stared at her. 'You're not saying that –'

'*I* move in with you! You get your boarder and I get space! It's brilliant! Perfect!' Kate beamed around the table, her excitement blinding her. 'And even if I *don't* get a book written, then at least I know I tried. But I've got a great feeling about this. I really do. It's the answer to everything. And it means I'll be able to move on as well. It's absolutely, one hundred percent perfect!'

There was utter silence for a few moments, and then Hector broke wind.

THREE

Kate opened her eyes slowly and stared at the fluorescent green numbers on the bedside clock: 8.15 am. She could hear the drumming of the ensuite shower, which was probably what had woken her, and could feel the emptiness beside her that meant Sam was no longer there. She took a few minutes to allow the events of last night to filter through, and flinched when she came to the moment when she had made her euphoric announcement.

Surprisingly enough she did not feel as ill as she deserved. She was tired, but it was that same intrinsic tiredness she had felt for months now, the one that seemed to colour everything in shades of grey. Apart from that, there was just a sore spot on her chin, a dull ache around her temples, and a slightly nauseous feeling in the pit of her stomach. But it was difficult to say whether the latter was due to overindulgence or the lingering reaction to an evening that had been less than pleasant.

Kate pulled up the pillow and pressed it against her face. She felt like crying, and she also felt like screaming. Now she clearly remembered the stunned silence, the embarrassment. And, from Oscar, a barely disguised amusement that had done more to sober her up than the stillness emanating from her own husband. The shower stopped with a rumble of the water pipes, and she pulled the pillow off her head quickly before flopping over to face the ensuite doorway. She opened her eyes a trifle so that she could observe through her lashes.

The door opened and a large quantity of steam issued forth to dissipate against the ceiling. Sam emerged, drying his hair with one towel, another wrapped around his waist. He stopped by the bed and looked down at her for a moment before heading over to the wardrobe. The sound of coathangers jangling followed, so Kate rearranged herself quietly. Sam, now totally naked, was standing at the foot of the bed with his back to her while he chose an outfit. Kate opened her eyes fully and admired his buttocks. They really were rather impressive for a man of his age. Nice, firm, and showing just the slightest effect of nearly a half-century of gravity.

'I know you're watching me.'

Kate didn't answer, mainly because he had now bent over to fetch his runners and words failed her.

'That was Pete on the phone before. There's been a break-in at the Berwick job and they've trashed the place. Kids most likely. Anyway, I've got to go assess the damage. Make a police report.'

'Okay,' said Kate, watching his back and trying to guess his mood.

'I'll probably be a few hours.' Sam pulled on a pair of jocks and then jeans and a polo shirt. He turned and looked at her, holding her gaze for a few seconds, before sitting down on the edge of the bed and tugging on his socks and runners.

'So how's with Oscar selling the house?' asked Kate brightly. 'About time, hey?'

'I suppose.'

'I think it'll be good for him. I mean, all that travelling into town, and a family house for just one guy . . .' Kate petered off and waited for a response. When none was forthcoming, she swallowed the nauseous feeling that always rose to meet the silent treatment. She glanced back towards Sam, who was now dressed and fixing his watch onto his wrist. Suddenly it seemed important to say something – anything – before he left, so she blurted out the first thing that came into her head. 'I might go out for a while.'

'Fine.'

'Okay.'

'See you later then.'

Kate watched him leave the room and then pulled the pillow back over her head miserably. She had no real intention of going out, but she didn't want to stay home either. And remaining in bed allowed too much opportunity for thought, and she really didn't want to think. Not yet.

The ensuite was still steamy and Sam's boxer shorts lay half in and half out of the shower cubicle. Nor were there any towels, as both the clean ones now lay crumpled at the foot of their bed. With some relief, Kate allowed irritation to counter her guilt while she fetched one of the damp towels and showered before dressing casually, in a pair of navy tracksuit pants and a white T-shirt. Then she headed for the kitchen, and some much-needed coffee.

Out on the decking were the remains of last night's get-together: charcoaled barbecue, dirty plates, empty beer stubbies and two chardonnay bottles. The former contents of which, she felt fairly positive, were mostly now sitting heavily in her gut busily transforming themselves into calories. On top of the outdoor table lay Hector, fast asleep with his head lolling over the remains of the dip platter. No doubt the dog would be a mobile gas emission for the entire day.

It took her over an hour to clean up and stack the dishwasher, after which Kate sat down and stared out at the glistening surface of the pool. In the centre, where the sunlight danced along the water, it looked like a patchwork of royal blue and white sequins. Picture perfect. Kate shook herself and made a mental note to put some chlorine in later.

She got up and went inside just as the front door slammed noisily. Jacob appeared, looking furtive, but as this was his standard expression Kate ignored it and smiled at him brightly. 'Did you have a good night?'

'Nah, not really.' He slopped down into a chair and stared at the table top as if it might offer him some answers.

'That's a shame. Do you want a coffee?'

'Yeah, okay. Ta.'

Kate didn't bother trying to make conversation because she knew it would be both frustrating and futile. Of her three children, Jacob was the one she understood the least. Moody, difficult and, she strongly suspected, not very happy. She had always assumed twins would share similar characteristics, but from the moment they emerged, her two boys could not have been more different. And not simply because one was extroverted and the other introverted, but also physically. Where Caleb was tall and muscular, Jacob was barely five foot five and just plain skinny. All over. Then there was Caleb's smooth dark brown hair compared with Jacob's unruly sandy mop that had not one but *two* crowns as well as a retarded cowlick.

As Kate poured coffee into two mugs, Shelley could be seen making her way from the bungalow and up onto the veranda. She was dressed in her pastel pyjamas and was carrying Emma, clad in a Wiggles T-shirt and disposable nappy. The sliding door shot open and they came through into the house.

'Coffee?' asked Kate.

'God, yes,' replied Shelley with feeling. Her hair, still stiff with whatever hair products it had been lathered with last night, bunched up on one side and waved back on the other, so that she looked like she'd been caught sideways in a tornado. Then there were her eyes, with dark puffy bags and the pink tinge of an albino rabbit.

'Good night?' asked Kate sardonically.

'Not bad. Not bad at all,' Shelley grinned and lowered Emma into the highchair kept near the kitchen bench. Then she pulled out a chair opposite her brother and sat down, looking at him for a few moments. 'What's up with Shorty?'

'I told you not to frigging well call me that.' Jacob abandoned his perusal of the table surface to glare at his sister.

'Don't swear.' Kate brought the two coffees over to the table, giving Shelley the one she'd prepared for herself. Then she put the kettle back on. Emma, who had been playing with the beads set into the edge of her highchair tray, soon bored of this activity and started trying to climb out of her seat. Kate went over and strapped her in.

'Thanks, Mum.'

'You need to do this straightaway, Shell. She's too big now just to sit. Too adventurous. Aren't you, honey?' Kate gave Emma a kiss and then got the toaster out for her grand-daughter's breakfast. The kettle boiled so she got another mug ready.

'You never use my pancake maker,' said Jacob accusingly, staring at the toaster.

'I do so. Just not today.'

'Listen, Mum.' Shelley tried to run her fingers through her hair, but when they got stuck in the bird's nest at the side, she abandoned the attempt with a grimace. 'Could you do me a huge favour? See, I've been invited to a New Year's Day lunch thing but Daniel's picking Emma up at twelve. Could you just hand her over for me?'

'I'm going out,' said Kate. She poured out her coffee and avoided Shelley's frown. The toast popped up so she buttered it and cut it into triangles before putting it on a plastic plate featuring cross-eyed farm animals. Emma chortled and immediately grabbed one piece to thrust deep into her mouth. After blinking and gagging slightly, she managed to get the exact distance right and started sucking happily.

Shelley was tapping her fingers on the table. 'Well, what's Dad doing? Or Caleb?'

'Dad's at work and Caleb must be still out. So it looks like you'll have to make other arrangements.'

Shelley ceased the finger-tapping and took a sip of coffee, deep in thought. Her face cleared and she glanced across at her brother. 'Um, Jake . . .' She chewed her lip and then grimaced. 'Nah, doesn't matter.'

'That's right, you wouldn't want *me* looking after her, would you?' Jacob sneered. 'It's not like I'm *responsible*, or even *dependable*, or –'

'Terribly mature,' finished Shelley smoothly.

'Get stuffed!' Jacob drew himself up and pointed across the table at his sister. 'Anyway, look who's talking! *I'm* not the one trying to offload my frigging kid!'

'Kid! You?' Shelley looked at him scornfully. 'The only kid *you'd* have is some sort of virtual offspring. Otherwise you've got –'

'That's *enough*,' snapped Kate furiously, her head starting to pound.

She glared from one child to the other. And suddenly she realised that this was a scene that had been replayed so many times she already knew exactly what would happen next. Now that she'd intervened, they would limit themselves to narrow glances and hissed abuse whenever her back was turned. Nothing had changed in years. She could replace this image with a ten-year-old Shelley, her hair in pigtails, and an eight-year-old Jacob, with glasses and skinned knees, and the basic script would be exactly the same. The actual *words* might be different, especially their vulgarity, but the discourse remained identical. As she registered this, Kate glanced over at the table with a sort of sick wonder, and watched as Shelley treated her brother to one of her slow up-and-down sneers. And he retaliated with his middle finger.

Enough was enough. Kate took a sip of her coffee and then plucked her handbag from the end of the bench and walked out of the room, without even a backwards glance. Through the lounge room, out the front door, down the steps, into the garage. She slid into her car, started it up and reversed out without waiting for it to warm up. And, as she shot out onto the road and changed gears, she glanced back at the house and saw Shelley, standing at the lounge room window and looking down, rather stunned. Kate had the sudden urge to proffer her *own* middle finger, but instead she put her foot down on the accelerator, quickly leaving the house, the children, the bickering, the *weight* of it all behind her as she drove away.

She breathed a sigh of relief as she reached the Wellington Road roundabout without meeting Sam's car coming the other way. Then she veered right and drove, with growing contentment, up the winding road towards Belgrave. She had no idea where she was going, and didn't much care as long as it was away. And it was a lovely day for a drive. Warm and still, with a few puffs of cloud threaded across the sky.

Kate found a car-park on the side of Belgrave's winding main street and got out to stretch. New Year's Day tourists clustered around the various shops that were open, or sat outside the Puffing Billy café, enjoying coffee and cake and public holiday sunshine. Kate joined in, window-shopping her way along the anonymity of the touristy town.

Here she wasn't anybody's wife or mother, she was just Kate. Stealing back a few hours in which she came first. And whenever a sliver of guilt uncurled, and her mind touched on the work she'd intended getting done today, or Sam arriving home to find her absent, or Jacob's obvious unhappiness, or even Shelley now having to find somebody else to look after Emma, she would jerk it away. And summon up a sense of self-righteousness that lent her support.

At the huge bookshop at the end of the main street, Kate stopped to peruse the piles of books in the window display and wasn't at all surprised to see the distinctive shiny black cover of *So you want to write? Then enough with the excuses – just do it!* She walked back to the car slowly, her hands deep in the pockets of her tracksuit pants, and then drove out of town and down the mountain, through Tecoma and past Upwey before coasting by the national park area and into Ferntree Gully. By the time she put her blinker on and turned off the highway, she knew exactly where she was going, had probably always known, but still felt better to have not gone there directly. Less childish, less maudlin.

His house was the oldest one in the area by many years. All the other original residences had been bulldozed when their land had been sold off for residential developments. Even That Bugger's house next door had been razed many years ago to make way for a block of units, and the radish patch where Angie's mother had frolicked with the forbidden fruit was now a row of carports. But Kate could still point to each and every landmark she had grown up with. The red-brick house to the left was built over what had once been an apple orchard, and the white-rendered two-storey nearby covered the dirt area where the old Ford truck had been parked, next to the huge corrugated-iron shed. With its white paint so flaky that she and Angie had been able to peel off large sections to develop their own works of art. Employing paints made from mushed grass, or the glassy red sap from the gum trees, or the brown pigments they would extract from the crumbly clay dirt that surrounded them.

Kate parked her car by the kerb and walked up the driveway past the weatherboard house. The old gate protested as she pushed it open, and she passed through into the backyard, where she closed her eyes for a moment and imagined that when she opened them she would see her father in the vegetable patch. He would be dressed in his dun-coloured overalls, over a white singlet that had seen better days, while on his head would be a broad-brimmed hat that would be better placed on a cricket umpire. His stooped posture would emphasis his lack of height but his wiry physique would be carrying not a spare inch of flesh. Just suntanned wrinkles and ropy muscle.

He would be working steadily. Up one of the regimented rows and down the next. Perhaps armed with his spray bottles, with which he would dose each plant after careful examination. And her internal conflict would be instantly soothed by the repetitive nature of his labour – repetitive not just in the sense of what she was watching, right then, but in that these were the same actions she had seen him perform for as long as memory served. It would be like looking at the stage that had set the scene for the entire spectrum of her life. Giving her tacit permission to regress, and to shed all her different adult personas and just be his daughter. More selfish, more simple, more secure.

Kate opened her eyes and the backyard was empty. And although she had known it would be empty, it couldn't be anything *but* empty, nevertheless his image had been so strong that she was pierced anew by a sense of loss that brought tears to her eyes. She blinked, recognising that it had been a mistake to come but also acknowledging her lack of real choice. The house and its empty backyard were like a magnet whose power only grew as their numbered days were counted off.

Kate wiped her eyes roughly, almost angrily, and pulled the gate closed before taking a deep breath and walking over to the wrought-iron setting. With only one chair remaining, it sat between a dull pewter-coloured Hills hoist and a large lemon tree with a trunk so gnarled that it seemed to be growing in several directions at once. Ignoring the thin covering of dirt that blanketed the wrought iron, Kate pulled out the chair and sat, facing away from the house.

She stared at where the vegetable patch had once spread its way across almost the whole backyard and, with an ache that felt like molten lead, registered the fact that it could barely be seen now. This, more than anything she might see in the house itself, forced her to acknowledge that he wasn't there, and hadn't been for quite some time. Because her father would never have let it reach such a state. Weeds now as high as the winder on the Hills hoist, with only their undulation indicating the corrugated nature of the earth beneath. Apart from that, a few straggly silverbeets at the end closest to the gate were all that could be seen of what was once a thriving garden. With rows of crisp lettuces, and golden-orange carrots, and snow peas, and celery, and turnips and a patch of dirt-encrusted potatoes just beneath the ground up in the top corner. The same corner where, on a chilly morning last June, her father frowned as he flexed his left arm and then, moments later, grabbed desperately at the paling fence as a shaft of vicelike pressure gripped his chest.

At least that was the way Kate would have liked it to have happened. Short and sharp. Just as it had been with her Uncle Frank long before. Bitterly, Kate turned away and stared down towards the swirling patterns of the wrought-iron table top. She prodded roughly at the dirt that filled the centre umbrella hole until it caved in, falling in a solid lump that shattered as it hit the ground below. Then she started picking at the paintwork, sliding a nail underneath one section and flaking it upwards to reveal a solid knob of red-brown rust, while wondering, not for the first time, why she kept coming back here. It was macabre, as well as masochistic. But it was also an option that would soon be gone, just like her father. Because now that the permits had all but gone through, within a few months the old weatherboard would be razed and the remains of her father's vegetable garden concreted over to provide foundations for the block of twelve units to be built here. By Sam.

Kate stopped picking at the table and brushed away the tiny flakes of paint, revealing a brown circle that now surrounded the rusted protrusion. She wondered absently whether, if vital enough when alive, if *needed* enough when alive, a person could leave some part of themselves behind. Then maybe if someone close concentrated harder than they had ever concentrated before, maybe that person could call the other into being. And a dreadful emptiness could be filled, if only temporarily.

Kate lowered her head slowly down onto the table, feeling the metallic coolness of the wrought-iron press against her cheek. She stared at the flaked brown circle, now so close that, with only a bit of effort, she could actually visualise it as a face. With close-cropped grey-white hair and fine lines punctuating the features, ageing them well beyond their seventy years. She reached out a finger slowly and traced it along the side of the face, down to the jawline.

'Tell me what to do, Dad. *Please* tell me what to do.' Kate closed her eyes, still keeping the image alive. 'I really need your help, because I'm suffocating here.'

The silence that followed stretched until it became unbearable, and it *had* to be filled. So finally the words came. '*You're* suffocating? Try being buried six feet under!'

Kate smiled, despite herself. 'But Dad, I don't know what to do. At all.'

'I take it you found my book?'

'Yes. When I was packing up the house ... afterwards. Angie said you bought it for me for Christmas. So I kept it till then, put it under the tree.'

'That was a bit maudlin, wasn't it?'

'Exactly what Sam said.' Kate traced his jawline again, gently. 'But I thought it'd make it seem like you were still here.'

'Did it?'

She sighed quietly, the breath warming her cheek. 'No.'

'Ah, girl. You've got to stop with all this, you know. Doesn't do you any good. And you know why I bought that book? Because you need a kick up the you-know-what. If you want to bloody write, then just do it.'

'It's not as simple as that. I mean, there's not even anywhere for me *to* write, and then there's all the interruptions, and everybody wanting –'

'Here we go again. Christ, just read it. Maybe it'll give you some ideas to make time. And I'll tell you something for nothing, if you *don't* do something soon, you're going to drive the rest of us nuts. Or yourself.'

Kate fell silent as tears built up behind her eyes. She swallowed and then clenched her lips together, waiting until the tears abated before opening her eyes slightly and whispering across the table: 'But . . . well, don't you think I've left it too late? I mean, I'm forty-seven years old. I think I've missed the boat.'

'Christ! You talk like you've got one foot in the grave. And, believe me, you don't want to do that before it's time. There ain't much in the way of entertainment there. Anyway, what's forty-seven? Some of the greatest writers in the world didn't do their best stuff till they were near ancient! But what the hell, it's your choice.'

'Yes, I suppose it is.' Kate shifted her focus so that her father's face softened. She thought about the vacant room in Angie's unit, quiet and peaceful and undemanding. 'Dad? Did you hear about Angie getting a boarder?'

'You mean how you'd like to *be* her boarder?'

Kate rested her finger on her father's chin. 'Yes.'

'Well, go for it, girl.'

'Really?' Kate felt a bubble of excitement. 'But I can't just shift out . . . can I?'

'Why not? You lot can afford it now, what with flattening my house. I mean, you're going to make a killing on all these units here, aren't you?'

'Oh god, Dad. I didn't –'

'Doesn't matter, love. Do what you have to. I owe you that much. But the point is, this is your chance. I don't know whether you can write or not. I reckon you're good at it, but then I'm your father. By the way, you get that from your mum, you know.'

Kate smiled at the gift. 'Yes, so you've said.'

'But anyway, I'll tell you something for nothing here – *you* need to find out whether you can write a book or you'll never settle. If that means moving out for a bit, then so be it. If Sam's got any sense, he'll see it's a small price to pay to stop your . . .'

'Whining?'

'Yes. And it's not like you're splitting up or anything. Not like Angie did. No, just look at it like it's your office. You don't even have to sleep there, just spend the days, and see what happens.'

'My office,' repeated Kate softly, scratching a fingernail absentmindedly at the paint that rimmed her father's face.

'Exactly. Although sleeping there mightn't be a bad idea either, maybe even get rid of those dreams you've been having. Besides, it won't do that lot of yours any harm to have to fend for themselves a bit. Especially the kids. They run you ragged.'

Kate grimaced defensively. 'They're not that bad.'

'Sure they are – basically nice *and* spoilt rotten. But right now you need to get back to them. Sort your life out. And I've got to skedaddle.'

'I don't want you to go.'

'Tough, you've got no choice. By the way, sorry I couldn't go the same way as your uncle. It was hard on you, love, I know.'

'Yes, it was. Still is.'

'Wasn't your fault, you know. It was mine. Should never have involved you. But that's life, and if this helps you, then I say go for it. Now, for Christ's sake, stop picking at my damn table.'

Kate opened her eyes fully and her father's face vanished. She stared across the wrought iron for a moment before sitting up and pulling a sleeve over her hand to wipe down her face and then press hard against her eyes. When she removed it, the tabletop had turned into a kaleidoscope of images, all in sparkling greys and browns. Slowly, her focus came back but the face was still gone. Along with his understanding, and compassion, and reliability. All that was left was a circle of lumpy brown surrounding a knob of darkened rust. Which, from this angle, just looked like a rather well-used nipple. Despite herself, Kate smiled as she put a finger out to run gently over the areola. Perhaps she would be better off forgetting about the writing and instead harnessing her creative side into sculpture and using this as her first piece. She could call it 'Corroded Motherhood' and sell it for a fortune.

FOUR

'So you see it wouldn't be a separation at all. More like a . . . well, long service leave. Six months tops. A *hiatus* of sorts.'

Expressionlessly, Sam walked slowly along the tiled lip of the pool, dragging the leaf catcher through the water to skim curly-edged brown leaves and the odd twig off the surface. Kate, from her position perched on the steps of the decking, watched him carefully and waited for some sort of response. Anything.

'And the unit would be like an *office*. Where I do my work.'

Sam lifted the leaf catcher out of the water and swung it through the air like a celebratory banner. A sparkling spray of water followed its arc until he banged it against the fence, hard. The leaves tumbled damply into the garden and then he hefted it back up again, splashing it down into the pool to continue his methodical progress.

'And this would still be *home*. I mean, I'd be coming back here all the time.' Kate waited patiently for an answer but none was forthcoming. Hector wandered slowly up the path and then stood hesitantly for a few moments before lurching up beside her where he collapsed across the step, panting. She put out a hand and ruffled the pouched fur around his collar, then turned back to Sam. 'You know, staying over, and coming on Fridays to do your books. Like usual.'

Sam lifted the leaf catcher up slightly and watched as a bee clambered drunkenly up the rim. Once clear of the water, it spread its wings several times, trying to dry them. Sam brought the leaf catcher over to the edge and tapped it gently on the concrete, letting the bee fall to the ground in a scattering of leaves. After a moment, where it couldn't be seen, the tiny insect crawled clear and then stopped by the pool gate, unwilling or unable to make a definitive bid for freedom.

'I know you don't understand and I am really, *really* sorry about that. But it's something I need to do. And I just can't do it here. I need to get . . . away.' Kate spoke slowly and without looking at Sam. Instead, she stared at the bee, mentally urging it to flight. *You can do it, just give it a try.*

'You know what really pisses me off?'

Kate's gaze flicked upwards, to her husband's face, staring at her impassively as he leant against the leaf catcher.

'It's that I *built* the bloody bungalow.' Sam jabbed a finger accusingly in the direction of the bungalow, behind the jasmine-covered trellis. 'All because you wanted somewhere to do your bloody writing. So you've had plenty of chances to do whatever it is you *need* to do. But no, you wait till now. And don't think I don't know why. It's because you're trying to punish me.'

'Punish you?'

'Don't play the innocent, Kate, it doesn't suit you. You're trying to punish me for building the units, it's as simple as that.'

'What!' Kate sat up straight and stared at her husband, taken aback by the accusation. 'That's ridiculous!'

'You reckon I railroaded you into the whole thing; you've made no secret of that. So now it's payback time, hey?'

'That is the stupidest thing you've ever come up with. As if I'd –'

'And what *also* pisses me off is that you're not taking it out on Angie, are you? Yet she was just as keen about the whole plan!' Sam picked up the leaf catcher and thrust it down into the pool, turning away from Kate as he began slapping it through the water, sending the leaves away on waves rather than collecting them.

Surprise transformed into anger, measured by the tightening of Kate's lips. She pushed Hector off her lap and spoke curtly. 'The fact that you feel driven to raze my father's house to the ground has absolutely nothing to do with my wanting to write. I have *always* wanted to write, and you bloody well know that. As for the bungalow, it's not exactly *empty*. In case you haven't noticed, it's got –'

'I know it's not empty!' Sam stopped punching the leaf catcher through the water and stared at her again. 'I'm not a bloody idiot. But you're acting like you're some sort of martyr. I mean, I built the damn thing for *you*!'

'For me? Or just to shut me up?'

'What's the damn difference?' Sam punctuated his words by swinging the leaf catcher through the air again and slamming it against the fence with a thud that echoed along the palings. Clearly gaining some sense of satisfaction, Sam arced the catcher backwards and then walloped it against the fence once more. This time the thud was followed immediately by a crisp snapping sound and the head of the leaf catcher fell into the garden bed.

Kate clapped twice, slowly. 'Well done.'

Sam stared at her thin-lipped, the leaf catcher pole still grasped within his hands like a weapon. After a few moments he turned and javelined it into the garden bed where it impaled the earth at an angle, the broken end quivering gently. Sam watched it for a moment and then turned back. 'I spent three months building that bungalow in my spare time. Three bloody *months*! Every weekend, every spare minute! And do I get any thanks? No, of course not. Instead, you just go and give it away!'

Kate jerked back, affronted. 'Hang on a damn minute! You act like I just handed it over on a whim. For god's sake, Shelley was –'

'Without even *discussing* it –'

'Pregnant! And didn't have –'

'With me! Or trying to –'

'What the *hell*!'

Kate whirled around to face the sliding door, which was where this last rejoinder had come from. Standing there was Caleb, looking from one parent to the other with amazement. Kate opened her mouth to explain but Sam spoke first.

'Sorry mate. We're just having a bit of a chat.'
'Some chat. I'm surprised the neighbours haven't rung to complain.'
'It wasn't that bad,' said Kate defensively.
'And we're finished anyway.' Sam picked up the leaf catcher head and tossed it into the pool, where it floated into the middle, the net dangling deeper in the water.

'Whatever.' Caleb cocked an eyebrow at his mother and then went back into the house, leaving the sliding door half open. He was followed relatively quickly by his father, who slammed the pool gate shut and passed Kate on the steps without even a glance.

She watched as he slid the door closed and disappeared from view. Then she turned to face the pool and took in a huge lungful of air, which she let out again in a rush. Hector, perhaps sensing that she was in need of comfort, edged his way closer again and laid his head down in her lap, looking up at her mournfully.

The half-drowned bee had now disappeared from sight. Kate wanted to believe that it had made a successful bid for freedom, but thought it more likely that it had finished its life on the bottom of Sam's runners as he strode angrily away from the pool. The moral being that you only have a brief period of time to break free, otherwise you'll be flattened.

She sighed and tried to muster up the energy to follow Sam inside and try to explain, again. But instead she leant backwards against the pillar supporting the steps and stretched her legs out, forcing Hector to rearrange himself. Maybe she could write things down? That way she wouldn't be distracted by incidentals and could state her case clearly and concisely. This thought cheered her, so she occupied herself by mentally constructing a dot point series of excellent reasons for her plan to take place.

Kate had just reached dot point number seven (*it'll be an excellent opportunity for enhanced bonding with your offspring*), when the sliding door opened and Sam came through, carrying two glasses of red wine. Without speaking, he placed them gently on the outdoor table and then sat down on one of the chairs, facing her.

'Is one of those for me?'

'Obviously.' Sam stretched a leg out and gave the opposite chair a push with his foot. 'Come on, let's talk. Without yelling.'

Kate was washed by a wave of relief, which gave her the momentum to push Hector off her lap and get up. She crossed over to the chair while the dog followed, settling himself underneath the table. Kate sat down, watching Sam. 'I thought you weren't speaking to me.'

'I wasn't. Then I thought we can't just leave it like that.' He looked at her expressionlessly for a moment. 'You're really serious about this, aren't you?'

'Yes.'

'So let me get it straight. You want to rent Angie's room and move in for six months to write a book. Then you'll move back and everything'll be the way it was.'

'Except then I'll have done it. Or not done it. But at least I'll know.'

'Maybe.' Sam stared over her shoulder for a few moments, and then sighed. 'Look, I won't pretend to understand why you can't write here. If you can do your editing here, I don't see why you can't write as well.'

'There's too many . . . distractions.' Kate stared into her glass, the red wine glimmering like liquid rubies. She tried to be honest. 'Or maybe I'm just using them as an excuse. I don't know.'

'But you want to find out.'

Kate looked up, nodding. 'Yes! That's exactly it!' She felt washed by a wave of relief that he might understand. 'And about the bungalow –'

'I know.'

'I didn't have a choice, did I? I mean, Shelley needed us. But I thought you knew how much I appreciated it. And I really did. Enormously.'

'I know,' repeated Sam, glancing towards the building in question. 'And I also know you *had* to give it over to Shell. But that doesn't help things here, does it?'

'No, not really.'

'Listen, I have to ask. Has this got anything to do with your father? I don't mean the units, I mean like a . . . you know, a sort of reaction to his –'

'No,' replied Kate shortly. 'Certainly not.'

Sam held her gaze. 'Look, I'm not trying to belittle the fact you've always wanted to write. I *know* that. But it just seems to me it only started becoming . . . well, an *obsession* last year. Which makes me wonder if –'

'Nothing to do with it. Totally separate.'

'Oh. Okay.' Sam gave a slight shrug. 'Well then, I'm pretty well stuffed either way, aren't I?'

'What do you mean?' Kate injected a questioning tone into her voice but really, she knew exactly what he meant. And she sympathised, just not enough to show it.

'Well, I either agree and go along with all this, or I don't – which means I force you to make a choice.' Sam paused, looking at Kate searchingly. When she didn't respond, he smiled grimly and nodded, as if confirming something to himself.

The silence lengthened uncomfortably as Kate searched for something reassuring to say. Something that would let him know that her feelings for him were unrelated to this. Absolutely divorced. But she couldn't find the right words, and the only ones that came to mind rang with meaninglessness, even before they were spoken.

'So go for it.' Sam spoke offhand, but with an edge of bitterness that made Kate flinch. He turned back to her. 'But I want one promise in return. If you're still unhappy after the six months are up, whether or not you've written a bloody book, then I want your word you'll go and see someone. Okay?'

Kate felt a flare of irritation but forced herself to nod. 'It *is* the writing though, Sam. And I *have* to know. Do you see that?'

'Oh, I don't doubt the writing's important. It's just I still –' Sam broke off abruptly as the sliding door rattled open again and Caleb came through with a can of beer. He pushed the door shut with a foot and then flopped down into a vacant chair, his long limbs arranging themselves with a sort of rag-doll effect, and held up the beer.

'Hair of the dog.'

For a moment Kate wondered what he meant, and then her eyes widened as she realised, with a jolt, that it was still New Year's Day. That it was only yesterday when everybody had gone out partying, and she had come up with her brainwave.

Sam cleared his throat. 'Did you have a good time then, mate?'

'Yeah, not bad. What about you two?'

'Well, it was different, I'll say that.'

'Cool. Then what's for dinner?'

'Whatever.' Sam waved a hand dismissively. 'Listen, can you go get your brother and sister? I think I heard Shelley's car get in just before. We need to talk to you all.'

Kate stared at him with surprise. 'No! Not yet!'

'This sounds interesting.' Caleb raised an eyebrow at them both and then, leaving his beer on the table, headed back inside.

'You could have waited until we sorted *ourselves* out,' hissed Kate.

Sam shrugged. 'We have. You're leaving and I'm staying. That's it, isn't it?'

'It's not so simple,' Kate glared at him. 'Now you're trying to punish *me*.'

Sam smiled at her, without humour. 'Not me.'

Kate turned away, picking up her wine glass and taking a sip. It tasted acidic and she grimaced as it settled in the pit of her stomach, emitting sour fumes. She was just pushing the wine away as Caleb came back out onto the decking, followed by his sister, who still looked very much like an advertisement for the pitfalls of the morning after. Her heavily-made-up eyes actually emphasised her pallor rather than disguised it. She flung herself down into a spare chair and closed her eyes tiredly.

'Where's Jake?' Sam asked Caleb, who had made himself comfortable again.

'He's coming.'

Kate looked over at Shelley. 'And where's Emma?'

'I told you before, she's with Daniel today. He's dropping her off after tea.' Shelley opened her eyes and stared at the table for a few moments before suddenly glancing at her mother with more interest. 'Hey, could you do me a huge favour?'

'What?'

'Well, I really need some sleep because I have to work tomorrow.'

Shelley paused for a moment to roll her eyes, reminding everybody, rather needlessly, that she hated her waitressing job. 'So could you have Em this evening and just bring her down to the bungalow later? I'd really appreciate it.'

'Anyway, what *is* for dinner?' asked Caleb, finishing his beer and crushing the can. 'I'm starving.'

'Where's bloody Jake?' asked his father irritably as, right on cue, Jacob emerged from the house. If his sister looked like an advert for the benefits of abstinence, then he seemed more like a poster boy for the homeless. Sandy hair cowlicked in several directions, while his face bore clear creases from the pillow he had evidently just been lying on. Leaving the sliding door open for a quick getaway, he leant against the side of the house and peered at the gathering suspiciously.

'What's up?'

Kate looked at them all brightly. 'Why does anything have to be –'

'Just thought we'd fill you in on a few things,' interrupted Sam. 'Firstly, your Uncle Oscar is going to sell his house because it's too big.'

'About time,' said Caleb with little interest.

'Where's he going?' asked Shelley, tucking a leg underneath herself and yawning.

'Town. He's going to buy an apartment there.'

Shelley nodded. 'Cool. So was that it? Can I go to bed now?'

'Not quite yet,' said her father with rather theatrical grimness. 'And maybe this next piece of news might get your attention. Your mother's leaving too.'

This announcement had the effect he was obviously hoping for as all three recipients gazed at him in surprise and then, almost in unison, turned to stare at their mother. Shelley opened her mouth and then closed it again.

'That's not quite true,' snapped Kate, glancing crossly at her husband. 'I'm not *leaving* . . . well, that is, I *am* leaving but not . . . not –'

'Not *what*?' Shelley's black-rimmed eyes stood out even more.

'Not really *leaving*,' finished Kate, trying desperately to remember the words her father had used that sounded so *right*. 'It's not like a separation. Not like Uncle Oscar and Auntie Angie. More a time-out, a sort of long service leave. A hiatus.'

Caleb cocked an eyebrow again. 'A who ate what?'

'I thought a hiatus was a type of hernia,' said Shelley, frowning.

'No, it's not medical,' explained Sam helpfully. 'Psychological perhaps. A form of escapism. Like going AWOL.'

'But *why?*' Jacob's evident confusion shaved years off his age and made Kate's heart lurch. 'Oh, frigging *hell*! You're moving in with Uncle *Oscar*, aren't you?'

'Mu-*um*!' wailed Shelley, sitting up straight.

'Don't be ridiculous!' Kate frowned at them all, and was even more annoyed to see the slight smile on Sam's face. 'It's got nothing to *do* with Uncle Oscar!'

Shelley sneered. 'So you're saying it's just a coincidence?'

'Of *course* it is!' Kate paused, taking a deep breath. 'See, you know how I've always wanted to write?' She waited for some acknowledgement of this, from anyone, but when none was forthcoming, closed her eyes briefly and then continued regardless. 'Well I've finally realised that I can't do it here. There are too many distractions, and I'm not saying it's your fault because it's mine too, but the thing is it's not going to happen. Not here. So I've decided to take Mel's old room in Auntie Angie's unit and give myself a few months to see if I really *can* write. Then I'll be back again.'

'So you're moving into Auntie Angie's place?' asked Shelley, clearly relieved.

'Yes. And it's not like I won't ever be here. I'll still be doing your father's books and dropping in and staying over and all. It's just that I'll have this place where I can go and see if I can write. Like an office.'

Caleb leant back again, nodding approval. 'That makes sense.'

'*What?*' Sam stared at him.

'Good on you, Mum.' Shelley stood up, stretching. 'Now can I go to bed?'

Kate smiled at them both as a surge of relief warmed her. She turned to Jacob. 'What about you then?'

'Yeah, cool,' Jacob nodded also. 'Whatever. I mean, good idea.'

'I'm so glad you all understand.' Kate relaxed, beaming. 'And I have to say it makes me feel proud of the lot of you. Really proud.'

'Great,' Caleb grinned. 'Now what's for dinner?'

'I'm skipping dinner in favour of sleep.' Shelley yawned again as she rose, pushing her chair in. '*Some* of us have to work tomorrow. Goodnight all.'

Kate watched her daughter head down the little path towards the bungalow, her stilettos dangling from one hand. Then she snuck a glance at Sam, and almost grinned when she saw his set expression. Checkmate, she thought with satisfaction.

'I might go get a pizza.' Caleb looked at his mother hopefully for a moment but, when she didn't offer any other meal choices, sighed exaggeratedly and headed inside.

'Can you grab me one?' Jacob followed, shutting the door behind him for once.

With the smile still hovering around her lips, Kate sat back and watched Sam, waiting for him to speak first. He sipped his wine slowly, gazing over towards the pool.

'So when do *I* get long service leave?'

Kate let her smile finally settle. 'When I get back. First come, first served.'

'I'll do that,' replied Sam firmly, still without looking at her. 'And after a few months with this lot, I'll probably need it.'

'Fair enough,' Kate spoke lightly.

Sam finally looked at her. 'So what are you going to tell everybody?'

'The truth. That I'm going to try my hand at writing.' Kate contemplated this for a moment and then grinned. 'Actually, maybe I should just tell them that we've separated. It'll be less embarrassing if the book never eventuates.'

'Tough. Or if you *do* tell everyone that we've separated, then I'll find myself a little blonde floozy to keep in the wardrobe.'

'It'll have to be on my side, your side's too messy.'

'That's okay. She can clean it up while she's waiting at my beck and call.'

'I don't think they make floozies like that nowadays. Besides, she'd probably exhaust you inside a week.'

'Probably,' Sam grinned lasciviously. 'But, oh, what a week.'

Kate smiled back, feeling so many different levels of relief that it was almost impossible to entangle them. Relief that the conversation had lightened, relief that Sam was no longer overtly annoyed, relief that the kids had taken it so well. And amazing, overwhelming relief that it looked like it was all going to happen, and soon.

'This wine's pretty foul.' Sam examined his glass critically and then, standing up, flung its contents briskly into the garden. Hector immediately crawled out from underneath the table and loped off to give the wine a second opinion.

'How about a cup of tea instead?' Kate pushed her chair back.

'Good idea.'

Sam took her glass with his and then led the way inside, kicking off his damp runners just outside the sliding door. Before she entered, Kate had a sudden thought. She bent down to flip them over and examine the underside for any signs of the bee that had disappeared earlier. Suddenly it seemed important to find out the insect's fate. But both soles were bee-free, with not even an errant leg or wing stuck between the herringbone tread. This, of course, did not guarantee that the bee had survived, but Kate chose to take it as a good sign. And a very good omen for her.

FIVE

'Hi, Angie, it's me. Listen, could you give me a ring when you get –'

The phone suddenly clicked as it was picked up. Then came the sound of some rather heavy breathing before finally Angie spoke: 'Hi, Kate. I'm home.'

'And rather excited about it too, by the sound of you.'

'Ha, ha. Actually I was up in Melissa's room, cleaning and packing.'

'How's it all going?' Kate spoke more seriously, trying to strip the lilt from her voice and infuse it with compassion.

'God, Kate!' Angie sounded surprisingly irritated. 'I don't have cancer, you know. My daughter's staying in London and I'm getting a boarder in, that's all.'

'Hey, I was just trying to be sympathetic! I thought it might be hard, packing up all her stuff.'

There was silence for a moment and then Angie sighed. 'You're right. Sorry, I'm just being touchy. And yes, it is a bit hard. I thought I'd accepted her staying over there, but . . . I don't know.'

'Do you want some help?'

'Actually, I wouldn't mind. It'd be fun then. And we can have lunch together.'

'Sounds great,' Kate spoke firmly, turning her back on the state of the lounge room behind her, and the pile of editing still waiting on the desk. She flopped down onto a lounge chair and put her feet up on the coffee table. 'I'll be over in about an hour. But first, let me tell you my news.'

'Can you grab lunch on the way over?'

'Sure. Now listen –'

'Something nice to give me energy. But don't forget I'm on a diet.'

'Okay already!' Kate tried not to snap. '*Now* can I tell you my news?'

Angie laughed. 'Sure.'

'Well, guess what? You've got yourself a tenant!' Silence greeted this announcement. A silence that stretched for several moments until Kate's smile slid slowly from her face. 'Angie? Are you still there?'

'I'm here.'

'Well? Aren't you going to say anything?'

'Um . . . I take it you mean yourself?'

'Of course I mean myself!' Kate's frown deepened as the silence stretched once more. Then she had a horrible thought. 'Don't tell me you've already found someone!'

'No,' Angie sounded hesitant. 'It's just . . . is this like a trial separation?'

A surge of relief eliminated Kate's frown. 'Of course not. I'm simply taking a few months off, like long service leave, to see if I can finally write that book. It's a hiatus of sorts. That's all.'

'A hiatus, hey? And Sam's okay with this?'

'He's not exactly ecstatic, but he understands. Sort of.'

'I see.' Angie sighed quite clearly. 'So you want my spare room?'

'Yes! Although I must say you still don't sound too happy about it. In fact . . .' Kate laughed lightly in an attempt to take the accusation out of her words, '. . . I'm beginning to get the feeling you don't want me there at all.'

'No, it's not that.'

Kate picked up on the cautious note of her cousin's voice and interpreted this as an attempt to avoid offence. Yet her desire to be cautious itself spoke volumes. She took her feet off the coffee table and leant forward, speaking tightly. 'What is it then?'

'It's . . . it's not that I don't *want* to live with you. It'd probably be kind of fun but, see, it's so out of the blue that I can't help thinking this is all, well, like some sort of post-traumatic thing.'

'Well, it's not.'

'But, Kate, look at it from my perspective,' Angie spoke almost pleadingly. 'There's no denying that last year was the year from hell. From the diagnosis onwards. Then there was . . . what happened at the end. *Nobody* can go through something like that without some repercussions. And you have to admit that you've been rather . . . well, withdrawn since. Gone into your shell.'

'That's only because it's neater than this place. More cosy too.'

'And every time someone says anything about it you make a joke,' continued Angie smoothly. 'To try to head things off.'

Kate felt an instant bubble of anger. 'Your point is?'

'Well my point is . . .' Angie hesitated again and then continued in a rush. 'I don't want to feel responsible if your marriage goes belly up because of this. To be brutally honest, I don't think you need to move out as much as talk to someone. And stop using humour as a shield.'

'I see.'

'I've offended you, haven't I?'

'Good heavens, no. Why would you think that?'

'Because you're talking in that constipated way you get when you're annoyed.'

Kate stood up and stared unseeingly towards the lounge room windows. 'So now I'm constipated as well as mentally unstable. Thank you very much.'

'I didn't *say* that. I said –'

'Never mind. And don't worry about the spare room, I'd hate to put you out.'

'Kate! Come on!'

'I've got to go, Angie. Speak to you later.' Kate pressed the End button and then flung the phone down onto the couch. It bounced against the armrest and fell back into the gap between the couch cushions, its emerald-green light flashing like an SOS beacon. She stared at it for a few moments and then stalked into the kitchen where she filled the kettle from the tap and thumped it down onto a hotplate. Why did everyone keep linking what happened to her father with her desire to write? It wasn't as if this was something new, she had *always* wanted to write. And she *couldn't* do it here.

Kate glanced angrily around the room to underline this last thought. The usual haphazard mess. And although the house was quiet at the moment, she knew this wouldn't last. Jacob would surface to play either loud music or loud computer games, or both, while his brother would most likely rouse himself just as friends arrived, and then they would spend the day lazing on the decking. The females standing up to stretch their lissom bikini-clad bodies, while the males watched through half-lidded eyes and, every now and again, launched themselves into some rough *loud* game in which something always ended up getting broken.

Kate strongly suspected that Angie actually had no idea what it was like to exist in such a household. *Her* daughter was so undemanding and independent that she probably cut the umbilical cord herself. And she was now settled in London, with an excellent job, an excellent partner, and all the other excellent incidentals that came from being a perfect offspring. Life was a bit different with three not-so-perfect children, and a husband whose organisational skills were left at the building site each day. It had nothing to do with her father or her inclination towards humour. What Angie didn't seem to understand was that humour was keeping her *sane*. Without that she wouldn't just have crawled into her shell, she'd have filled it with concrete and then flung it, and herself, off the nearest mountain. Maybe one near the writers' retreat so that all the young up-and-coming authors could get some new material.

Kate stared down at the unlit hotplate and her anger suddenly evaporated, leaving behind a void that made her feel slightly nauseous. She closed her eyes and felt self-pity begin to trickle into the space and, while it didn't make her feel less ill, it at least gave her something to focus on beside the reality of her situation. It just wasn't *fair*.

This last thought was still resonating bitterly when the phone rang, its sound slightly muffled by the couch cushions. Kate stayed where she was and listened while the phone rang steadily three times and then the answering machine cut in.

'Hello Kate?' Angie's voice came with a metallic echo as it was routed through the answering machine. 'Are you there?'

There was a long, whirring silence as Kate walked slowly out from the kitchen to stare at the phone, still blinking away amidst the cushions.

'C'mon, Kate. We need to talk. There's important things at stake here . . . like my lunch. Does this mean I have to make my own?'

'Damn right,' said Kate towards the phone.

'Look, I've been thinking about it and actually I'd *love* to have you move in. It was just you took me by surprise before and . . . well, I suppose I worry about things. Although you must admit . . .' Angie hesitated for a moment. 'But that's beside the point. Because if that's what you want, then let's go with it. And it's your choice after all. In fact, when I think about it, this could be really great. Living together again, after all these years!'

Kate nodded, because she wholeheartedly agreed.

'Come on, it'll be like we're kids again!'

Kate finally smiled, with both affection and relief, as she moved across the room to pick up the phone and press the button. The answering machine immediately turned itself off with a loud click.

'So?' asked Angie with echo-free clarity. 'What do you say?'

'I say . . . are you sure?'

'Absolutely!'

'And am I allowed to make the occasional joke instead of exploring my feelings?'

'As long as they're good ones.'

'Then let's go for it!' Kate sat down on the couch and hugged her spare arm across herself. 'Because you're wrong, you know, this is something completely separate. And just imagine! It *will* be like we're kids again. Except I'll try to be better at sharing. But think about it . . . no responsibilities, no noise, no demands,' Kate took a deep breath and then let it sigh out. 'Bliss. Complete bliss.'

SIX

In the end, it was a lot easier to leave than Kate had imagined. Even though she knew she was being melodramatic, every time she had laid her head down on her pillow over the last few weeks she had been immediately diverted by a steadily less realistic fantasy. It had started relatively low-key, with her walking to the door with a suitcase in either hand, while five pairs of eyes stared at her expressionlessly from the lounge room. Then, just as she was turning away, she would notice a small but significant tear trickle down Sam's cheek. From this rather inauspicious although relatively heart-wrenching prospect, she had graduated to an Oscar-winning epic that included integral wires being removed from her car so she couldn't leave, Jacob running away to join the army, little Emma suffering from an obscure medical problem (which turned out to be infantile depression), and everybody forgetting to feed Hector, who wasted away with an accusing look in his eyes. And of course, as she finally left, she glanced back to see a small but significant tear trickle down Sam's cheek.

Reality was nothing like this. Instead, Sam went off to work as usual, without betraying by a single word, or action, or small but significant tear, that he knew what was happening that day. Shelley wished her good luck, Caleb offered a hand, and both Emma and the dog ate a hearty breakfast and showed no signs of either depression or neglect. The only one who gave any cause for concern was Jacob, who still hadn't emerged by the time Kate was ready to leave. But closer examination revealed that the boy wasn't so much unable to face his mother leaving as reluctant to face the day full stop. Kate left him sprawled across corrugated sheets in his darkened room, which smelt vaguely of perspiration and leftover food, and then she continued absconding, not only minus any heart-wrenching farewells, but minus any audience at all.

Admittedly the entire process was made considerably easier by the fact that this was only a temporary move and therefore required no division of furniture and other things. Indeed Kate took very little, not only because she didn't need to but also because, with guilt heightening her awareness, she sensed that the less she took, the more reassured Sam would be about her return.

She was also fortunate in that her father's worldly goods and chattels were still stored underneath her house. With Caleb's help, she had extracted his old walnut desk and, over the course of a week, sanded it back and then restained it. Then it was simply a matter of delivering it to Angie's unit together with the few boxes of personal effects that she was taking, and she was in. And out.

So, on a rather humid Monday morning at the start of February, after having spent the past three days in a whirl of cleaning, Kate picked up her handbag and a plastic carrier containing a few last-minute oddments, including the now-read *So you want to write? Then enough with the excuses – just do it!*, and then closed the door on an almost obsessively tidy house. Twenty minutes later she was parking outside the unit in Boronia, leaving just enough room for Angie to manoeuvre into the carport when she got home from work.

Kate got out of the car slowly, trying to savour the moment so that in the future she could picture this arrival like a snapshot that heralded a new phase in her life. A new phase that was all about *her*, and what *she* wanted. And maybe, years after she was gone, there would be a tasteful brass plaque on this ordinary suburban unit that read *Katherine Rose Painter lived here*, or even *KR Painter lived here*. Then some enterprising builder would, in the inimitable fashion of builders everywhere, purchase the now ageing units and try to bulldoze them to make an obscene profit. And the KR Painter fan club would mobilise in protest, picketing the building site, waving placards, organising a petition and maybe even chaining themselves to bulldozers in desperation.

A grin spread over Kate's face and then she shook her head slightly. There were four two-storey red-brick units, set out in two pairs sitting in an L shape, with each unit separated from its twin by a double carport. Edged grassy areas contained a variety of plants and shrubs, with bottlebrushes clearly in the ascendancy, and a lovely yellow-tipped wattle sagged cheerfully over the bank of letterboxes by the road. Angie's unit was at the rear, right in the corner of the L shape, and promised a privacy and seclusion that was exactly what Kate needed.

A nearby bird started a loud, undulating warble that seemed to echo in the silence surrounding the units. Using her key, Kate let herself in and closed the door behind her, immediately shutting off the birdsong in mid-warble. Where the silence outside had been pleasant, the silence inside was almost uncanny. Kate took a deep breath, the absolute stillness making her feel light-headed. And it tasted wonderful. She dropped her things in the foyer and looked around with new eyes.

Kate had been to the unit many times since Angie had moved in, and had even stayed there overnight on several occasions, but this was different. She suddenly realised she was smiling rather foolishly, and was grateful that she had chosen to move in while Angie was at work. She decided to begin with a tour. As if she had never been there before, or just needed to mark the unit with her presence.

She started by going up the staircase that sat to one side of the small, tiled foyer. At the head was a small landing with three doors. The one on the right, and towards the middle of the house, led to the small study that now housed all of Melissa's possessions, packed neatly into boxes. The other two rooms were bedrooms, with an ensuite in between. Kate walked eagerly into her own room. Here Melissa's bed dominated, with the built-in wardrobe and ensuite sliding door on the inside wall and a dressing-table on the other side. Against the far wall with the window was her father's desk, its glossy walnut almost as reflective as the mirror.

For a moment Kate stood staring at the desk, picturing her father sitting there and writing up the meticulous account books he had kept for the market garden. Her Uncle Frank, with his oft-stated motto 'We'll cross that bridge later', had quickly been relieved of any book work when it had become obvious his bridge-crossings were always going to be more turbulent than the family could afford. Instead her father had spent part of each evening transcribing receipts and forecasting expenses before filing everything away neatly in the deep, beautifully dovetailed drawers.

Kate realised that, consciously or subconsciously, she had replicated the desktop as it had been during her father's use. A framed photograph of her children sat on the left-hand side, just where the gilt-edged one of her parents' wedding had lived during his time, while on the right was a green-glass banker's lamp almost identical to the one he had owned. The only real difference was her laptop that sat front and centre ready to be put to use. This last thought shook Kate out of her reverie and she closed her eyes briefly. Then she moved out of the room, leaving her father behind.

Back downstairs, past the tiled entrance, was a small but cosy lounge room. The entire unit had been painted in a functional cream that matched the speckled cream carpeting and allowed any splashes of colour to stand out in bold relief. The lounge room led directly to the dining area and the kitchen, which were separated from each other only by an island bench. Two stools edging the bench matched the Baltic pine table and chairs which, in turn, matched the kitchen cupboards. Both rooms were much sunnier than the lounge room, courtesy of the large window by the table and the sliding door unit that led directly to the backyard.

It was easy to imagine lazy Sunday breakfasts here, or even late-night mugs of hot chocolate sipped in semi-dark silence. Kate smiled again and moved over to the sliding doors to gaze outside, where the small yard had been cobblestoned and largely contained within thick Merbau pillars, jade-green trellis and clear rippled perspex roofing, to give it a courtyard effect. This had then been filled with clematis climbers, luxurious bird's-nest ferns and, the pièce de résistance, a partially in-ground octagonal spa.

Kate tried to control her smile, but soon gave up. Because everything was perfect, unbelievably perfect. The entire unit, from its soft colour scheme to this beautiful courtyard, seemed to be filled with a natural simplicity that promised in abundance the one thing she craved the most – time. Here there would be no interruptions, no dependencies, no neediness. And no excuses either.

'*There* you are!'

Kate opened her eyes and smiled lazily at her cousin, who was framed within the open sliding door. She stretched out one hand and pressed a button on the side of the spa, cutting off the throbbing jets. The bubbles dissipated, leaving an airy froth across the surface of the water. Kate picked up a glass of riesling that sat by the spa and held it aloft. 'Welcome home. Cheers!'

Angie shook her head. 'It doesn't take you long to settle in, does it?'

'Not at all.' Kate took a sip of wine and then put the glass back down before leaning against a cushioned backrest and grinning at her cousin. 'So, how was your day? Sell many books?'

'Bit slow actually. But that was okay, gave me a chance to catch up on some shelving. I won't ask how your day was, it looks pretty obvious.'

'Mmm.' Kate stretched her arms out on the rim of the spa and allowed her legs to float up towards the surface. 'Why don't you join me?'

'Maybe later. Don't suppose you did anything about tea?'

'I most certainly did, you doubting Thomas. There's a casserole of honey chicken in the fridge. Just needs to be heated up.'

'I'm impressed,' Angie smiled. 'In that case, I'll pop it in the oven and get changed. Then I might have a glass of whatever you're drinking.'

'It's a particularly nice drop,' Kate mimicked Oscar's voice. 'From a wonderful little winery that's off the beaten track up Seymour way. Superb place, m'dear.'

Angie grinned. 'Don't be mean. And try not to overindulge while I'm gone.'

Kate watched her cousin close the sliding door. She had turned the spa temperature down earlier but now, with the onset of early evening, the water was starting to feel cool. She took a deep breath, letting it out slowly before gathering the energy to get out.

Kate dried herself off as best she could and then shrugged her terry-towelling dressing-gown on and, underneath, awkwardly shed her wet T-shirt. Leaving it spread out on the trellis with the towel to dry, she picked up her glass and went inside just as Angie came into the kitchen, now dressed casually and with her hair in a ponytail.

'Nice outfit,' commented Angie as she added some rice to a pot of boiling water.

'Thanks.' Kate tucked her dressing-gown securely around her and sat down at the table, immediately feeling the dampness of her knickers soak into the terry-towelling.

'So how'd Sam take you leaving today?'

'He's fine,' replied Kate airily. 'I mean, he's not *happy* about it, but I think he understands. And I'll make it all up to him down the track.'

Angie glanced over at her expressionlessly. 'And I take it we didn't start writing our masterpiece today?'

'I don't know about you but *I* didn't. Today was settling-in day.'

'Mission obviously accomplished.'

'You're not going to turn into a nag, are you?' asked Kate mildly.

'Sorry,' Angie sighed, then smiled wryly. 'I'm just tired. Back-to-school rush.'

'Well, you can relax now. Have a glass of wine.' Kate looked around and took a deep breath. 'God, I *love* this place. There's no *clutter*. No piles of crap needing to be put away. No music blaring, or socks to be sorted, or dishes to be washed. And no bickering either.'

Angie stirred the rice. 'Give us time.'

'You know what I mean. Anyway go on, have that wine. I'd get it for you but my dressing-gown isn't terribly secure and I don't want you to lose your appetite.'

'Believe me, *nothing* ruins my appetite. You could dance naked on the tabletop and it wouldn't make any difference. Although I'd probably disinfect it afterwards.'

'Are you saying I'm not clean?'

'I'm just saying that I prefer to eat my meals on surfaces that haven't been contaminated by naked females going through a midlife crisis.'

Kate leant back in her chair and regarded Angie thoughtfully. 'Is that what you think I'm doing? Going through a midlife crisis?'

'Well, aren't you?' Angie opened the fridge and took out the bottle of wine, pouring herself a glass and then refilling Kate's. 'I mean, don't see it as some sort of derogatory label, but you *are* middle-aged, and you *are* going through a crisis. Ergo, you're going through a midlife crisis.'

'But it makes it sound like I'm about to buy a red sports car or pick up some blond toy boy.'

'You wish.'

'Not really.' Kate grimaced. 'Firstly, I don't find the wind-blown look terribly flattering. I just end up looking like a stunned mullet with beehive hair. As for the toy boy, I'll take quality over quantity any day. Young guys are like rabbits.'

'Interesting comparison.'

'What about you? Planning on replacing Oscar any time?'

'Believe me, he's irreplaceable.'

'What happened to that guy you went out with last year? The one with the nose?'

Angie shrugged. 'He was okay, but did I tell you he collected Disneyland memorabilia? Not that there's anything *wrong* with that, but it was all through his house. And opposite his bed was a poster of Goofy saying "aw, shucks",' she glanced over at Kate expressionlessly. 'Which, without going into details, could be rather disconcerting at times.'

'Oh, details please!'

'Not a chance.'

'Spoilsport. So tell me about the other people here then. In the units.'

'Well, next door is Mrs Jarvis, she's an older lady. Very nice. And up the front is Terry but she's in Tasmania for a while, so her daughter's looking after the unit. The guy next to her is away as well, he's some type of actor and he's in a play touring Australia. So his unit's empty. And that's it. Not terribly exciting, I'm afraid.'

'Not terribly exciting is exactly what I want.' Kate took a sip of wine and watched Angie as she stirred the rice. 'What about you? Is *exciting* what you're after?'

'Not necessarily.' Angie hesitated, as if in thought, and then began stirring again vigorously. 'Melissa wants me to move over to England.'

'What!'

'Just for a year or so,' added Angie quickly, still stirring. 'She reckons I could afford to take a year off now that . . . you know.'

'I know.' Kate waved a hand dismissively over that part of the equation. 'But don't tell me you're thinking of it seriously? What about *Fully Booked*?'

'Well, that's the point, isn't it? There's no way I'd find a manager I could trust enough for me to flit over to the other side of the world. Except maybe you, and you're not interested.'

This last was said almost as a question so Kate shook her head emphatically to lay the idea to rest. Then she looked at her cousin curiously. 'But would you have considered it? If I'd been willing?'

'Not really,' Angie shrugged, lifting the ladle out with a few grains of rice clinging to it. She blew on them lightly. 'I've got to sort myself out here first.'

'Maybe you could go over on a holiday? A month or so?'

'Maybe. I'll play it by ear.'

'And in the meantime, do find yourself a toy boy. Reclaim your youth.'

'Reclaim it? I don't even remember it.'

Kate ran her fingers through her damp hair to fluff it up, and then tucked it behind her ears. She took another sip of wine and smiled contentedly. It felt very strange to be sitting and watching someone else prepare a meal, with nothing to do but engage in light conversation. And every so often a stray thought would sidle away to wonder what was happening at home. She had left a casserole there also, but had anybody thought to put it in the oven? Had Jacob emerged from his room? Was Emma being strapped securely into her highchair? Was Sam just now getting home, tired and dirty, only to be confronted with the reality of her absence? Would she ever find somewhere to store her residual guilt so that it was unable to seep out and infect her enjoyment?

'I suppose we should really work out something about cooking.' Angie carried the pot of rice over to the sink and poured it into a colander. 'I mean, it's not fair that you should do it every day just because you're home.'

'I don't mind.'

'Well, you should. You're supposed to be working, and you need to treat it just like you would if you were at an office.'

Kate thought about this and then nodded. 'You're right. Well, what about taking it in turns?'

'Okay, but don't forget I'm on a diet.' Angie banged the colander sharply against the side of the sink and then spooned some rice onto two plates. She waved a hand dismissively at Kate, who had just started to rise. 'Sit down. It's under control.'

'You sure?' Kate remained half out of her seat as she looked at her cousin questioningly. It wasn't just that she felt she *should* help, but she actually *wanted* to. It wasn't an altogether pleasant feeling merely sitting by.

Angie waved her down again as she set the table briskly. 'Anyway, so when does the masterpiece begin?'

'I wish you'd stop calling it a masterpiece. It makes me feel weighed down by expectations before I even begin.' Kate smiled to lighten the words.

Angie ladled chicken and thick honey-soya sauce over the rice and then brought the two plates over to the table. 'Actually it's a bit pretentious of you to assume I was serious. But no problem, how's this? When does work on the mediocre opus begin?'

'Ha, ha.'

'Mediocre opus,' repeated Angie in low, sombre tones, as she sat down opposite Kate. 'See, it'll be your MO. And if you aim for mediocre, you can't fail, can you?'

'Actually, yes. I could finish up with *below* average, or just plain lousy.'

'A real positive thinker, aren't you?'

Kate didn't bother answering, instead she picked up her fork and began eating.

'So what's your MO going to be about anyway?'

Kate looked up. 'I don't really know yet.'

'No ideas at all? You're just going to sit there and wait for divine inspiration?'

'Something like that.'

'Great plan.'

'I thought so.'

Angie rolled her eyes and went back to concentrating on her meal. Kate popped a piece of chicken into her mouth and began chewing pensively. It *was* true that she didn't know what she wanted to write, but it was also true that inspiration was one thing she had never had to worry about. Ideas about plots and characters and story-lines had always appeared, even at the most unlikely of times. Like while waiting in the car for the kids, or during rather average sex, or while reading through other people's manuscripts. One of her most memorable had even come to her during the long and painful labour with Shelley. Something to do with a reproductive breakthrough that involved implanting the embryo just beneath the flat skin of a male stomach and then providing special medication that would enable the baby to grow steadily, until the male could no longer see his own toes, and then have the child burst forth. Sort of like that scene from the movie *Alien*, complete with all the screaming and wailing and rending of flesh.

However, now that she really thought about it, when was the last time she had dashed off to write down a really great idea? When was the last time she'd reached out to grasp a half-baked notion, and then gradually fleshed it out until it throbbed with the oh-so-sweet promise of a fully fledged story? Kate thought, but wasn't exactly sure, that it had been quite a while. And this realisation gave her a sense of righteousness over what she had done. It was a rescue mission, to peel away the layers built up over the years and uncover, once more, all those embryonic ideas that had been forced to lie dormant as her creative side had been smothered by everything else.

Kate smiled to herself, both at this concept and its inherent melodrama. Then she let herself be warmed by the fact that tomorrow morning she would begin writing. A series of words that would turn into sentences and then paragraphs and then chapters. An achievement that would then raise her up and propel her forwards. And it didn't matter that she hadn't had an idea for a while, because the desire to write was still as strong as ever. So given the right circumstances, and these *were* the right circumstances, then inspiration would occur naturally. It was just a matter of sitting back and letting it come.

SEVEN

Title

By KR Painter

Kate stared at the cursor, which was blinking cheerfully two rows below her name while it waited for her to type something. Anything. She narrowed her eyes and quickly typed *Screw you, cursor*. The cursor paused as soon as she finished and, clearly not offended, immediately started blinking again from the edge of the full stop. Kate hit delete and erased her suggestion before it embedded itself like a virus. Then she put both elbows up onto the desk, lowered her chin into her cupped hands and went back to staring at the screen. It had been two and a half hours since she had called out goodbye to Angie and danced up the stairs to begin her career. Two and a half hours in which all she had accomplished was a rather unimaginative working title and the decision to use her first two initials rather than her full name.

The problem was that she had absolutely no idea what she wanted to write about. She ran through all the ideas that she could remember ever having had, even including the vengeful one with the embedded embryo, but nothing seemed right. None of them demanded to be written, none of them filled her with any sense of passion. And the situation was made even worse by the fact she hadn't slept well at all. It was strange sleeping alone, and not altogether pleasant. And the bad dreams had come regardless.

At just past eleven, Kate went downstairs and fetched a couple of biscuits from the cupboard. She wandered into the lounge room while she ate them, absentmindedly fluffing up some pillows and straightening the magazines on the coffee table. She thought about vacuuming but the carpet didn't really need it and, besides, she recognised that as classic procrastination. The doorbell rang just as she was rather reluctantly walking upstairs again. A delivery man stood on the porch, holding a small, very colourful flower arrangement. He smiled at her.

'Kate Painter?'

'Yes, that's right.' Kate stared at him with surprise as she took the flowers.

'Someone likes you,' said the man, still smiling. He held out an electronic pad with a style-pen and Kate signed awkwardly.

'Thank you.'

'Have a lovely day!'

Kate closed the door and then carried the flowers through to the kitchen, where she put them on the island bench. She slipped out the attached card and read it quickly. *To Mum. Good luck with the writing! Lots of love from Shelley, Emma, Caleb and Jacob.*

Kate stared at the flowers with amazement. It was a modest arrangement, a few orange gerberas and purple irises set amongst some vivid green fronds. But the size was immaterial, because it was the thought that was bringing tears to prick behind her eyes. So absolutely unexpected. Although it would have been even better if Sam's name had been there also.

After one last smile towards the flowers, Kate went into the lounge room to the telephone. First she tried ringing home, and then she tried each of the mobiles, but was unable to reach anyone. Instead she left messages of effusive thanks and then went back into the kitchen to gaze at the flowers once more.

The only problem with such a gesture, she eventually decided, was that they were like Angie's use of the word 'masterpiece'. Carrying with them expectations that were cumbersome in themselves. However, this last thought broke her reverie and sent Kate back upstairs, determined to accomplish more than simply the word *Title*. She sat down at her desk, stared at the computer for a while and then picked up the copy of *So you want to write? Then enough with the excuses – just do it!* She flicked through the pages slowly until she got to where the author advised yoga as a method of channelling ideas. Kate threw the book onto the bed and watched as it fell open at the page containing the author's picture with his smug, yoga-induced smile. She turned her back, staring at the computer screen again and praying, without much hope, for inspiration.

Kate took a deep breath and then let it out in a rush. It seemed ironic that the problem had been the rapidity of time, yet now time seemed to be almost standing still. She gazed out of the window. Perhaps she should just give up for now, go for a drive or do *something*. A small blue hatchback drove slowly down the shared driveway and parked outside the neighbouring unit. The driver's side disgorged an elderly lady, her thin figure clad in a coat despite the warmth of the weather. Kate leant closer, trying to ascertain if this was actually their neighbour or a visitor, but the angle of the porch roof cut her vision and the lady disappeared from sight.

As she straightened again, Kate noticed another two elderly women walking down the driveway. They were dressed more comfortably, and one even wore a royal-blue visor perched on her head. As the women reached the porch, the visored one turned and waved to something or someone behind her. Shortly afterwards, yet another older lady came into view and then the three of them stood for a while, talking animatedly, before moving up onto the porch and out of view.

Kate sat back again and amused herself for a while by imagining all the different reasons that a group of elderly ladies would get together. Perhaps it was a bake-off, or a knitting circle, or something more sinister like a coven. Or maybe they simply got together once a week to strip off and share a spa, where they played show and tell with their bunions. Most probably, though, it was just lunch. Which seemed like a good idea.

Kate went downstairs and fixed herself a ham omelette, with grated cheese sprinkled over the top. While it was cooking, she moved her flowers around, finding the best angle to catch the sunlight. Then she took her lunch into the lounge room and switched on the television before settling herself on the couch. She flicked through the channels with the remote control until she found a talk show where the male host seemed to be solving each of his guest's problems between fairly constant ad breaks. Kate ate slowly, as a man with a self-diagnosed sex addiction was followed by a mother and daughter who couldn't be in the same room without resorting to physical violence. As the daughter launched herself across the stage, and security rushed forward, Kate decided that even if one of the upcoming guests didn't have a problem like writer's block, she was justified in watching it as other people's issues counted as potential material. Grist for the mill, even if the mill was stuffed.

At about one o'clock, having decided that residual guilt might well be blocking the creative flow, Kate drove to the Lysterfield house. There were no cars there so she let herself in and then stood just inside the doorway, breathing in the familiar smells for a moment before getting to work. She started in the main bedroom, where Sam's clothes from yesterday lay across the carpet, and entrails of bedding trailed from the unmade bed.

The lounge room wasn't as bad, with only evidence of last night's occupation scattered around. Coffee mugs, a few magazines, some baby toys, Sam's reading glasses tucked between the couch cushions. Kate worked quickly. She wondered what her family were having for dinner that evening but, when she checked the refrigerator, could find no meat being defrosted. Afterwards she went outside to the shed and, with some difficulty, located the cardboard box containing her old writing. She dusted it off perfunctorily and then carried it inside to the kitchen sink where she gave it a more thorough clean. Corners of the box curled upward, revealing a honeycomb of cardboard and dust. Just as she put the box down on the table, Jacob materialised in the doorway and made her start.

He stared at her blearily. 'What're you doing?'

Kate took a deep breath to regulate her heartbeat. 'Just fetching this box, that's all. What about you? I didn't see your car in the driveway.'

'It's gettin' fixed. Blew the muffler.' Jacob shuffled over to the table and sat down. 'Any chance of a coffee?'

'Sure. No problem.'

From the laundry came the sounds of the washing machine hitting the spin cycle mode with a high-pitched whirr. Kate put the kettle on and then prepared two mugs of instant coffee while waiting for it to boil. Jacob yawned and laid his head down on his arms, watching his mother tiredly as, with one hand, he picked idly at one of the curling corners of the cardboard box. Thin but relatively hairy legs stuck out from his boxer shorts and his toenails badly needed trimming.

'So how's the writing going?'

Kate glanced back up and nodded. 'Good. Really good. And thank you *so* much for the flowers. I've left a message on your phone.'

'The flowers?' Jacob stared at her for a moment before his face cleared. 'Oh, yeah. That was Shelley's idea. D'you like them?'

'I *love* them.' Kate switched off the kettle and poured boiling water into the mugs. She added a dash of milk, brought them over to the table and sat down.

Jacob pushed himself up and ran a hand through his hair, which then remained vertical, much like an unkempt mohawk. He pulled a mug towards himself and, closing his eyes briefly, took a deep sniff. 'God, thanks Mum.'

'My pleasure. Were you up late last night?'

'Yeah, a bit.'

'So . . .' Kate fiddled with the handle of her mug. 'No jobs on the horizon then?'

He stared at his coffee. 'Nah. Nothing.'

'That's no good.' Kate mustered up a sympathetic smile. 'But I'm sure something will be just around the corner. And how is everyone then?'

'What d'you mean?'

'Just . . . how are they?'

Jacob looked up and started to grin. '*I* see. You want to know if they missed you.'

'Certainly not. I just wanted to know if they were all okay.'

'Yeah, sure.' Jacob's grin remained in place for a moment and then he yawned again, giving a good display of the two back fillings he received when he was twelve.

'Hand over your mouth,' snapped Kate automatically.

He closed his mouth abruptly. 'Why? Is this a stick-up?'

'Ha, ha.'

Jacob yawned once more, this time with his hand ostentatiously over his mouth, and then rose with a languid stretch. He picked up his mug. 'I'm off to my room then. Thanks for this.'

After he had vanished, Kate stood up and emptied her coffee down the sink. Then she washed the mug out before picking up her box and heading out. On the way, she made a detour past Jacob's room and knocked softly. Taking a muffled response as an invitation to enter, Kate pushed the door open with the box and peered into the semi-gloom where the bright white of a computer monitor was the only illumination. 'I'm off now.'

'Oh, okay. See you later.'

'Yep. Be good.' Kate hesitated. 'And cut your toenails, they're disgusting.'

'Yeah, thanks for that.'

'Well then. Bye.'

'Bye.'

Kate felt an oddly liquid mix of regret and resolve as she left the house, but this time it was untempered by the overwhelming relief she had felt the day before. Instead she had a strong feeling that this entire visit had amounted to no more than the procrastination she had been wary of earlier. Except, that is, for the cardboard box.

Accordingly, as soon as she got back to the unit, Kate sat down on the couch and placed the box on the coffee table before her. Then, with 'Judge Judy' on the television in the background, she prised open the cardboard flaps and started to delve through the contents. It was like a somewhat self-indulgent time capsule. There were handwritten stories with multicoloured titles and, later, more mature works with greying pages splodged by correction fluid, their corners secured by rusting staples. Most with two-word titles like *Tangled Webs* and *Alien Deception*. There were sheets of half-fleshed ideas and some bleak poetry, dripping with an angst that now seemed merely trite. And then there were the creative writing essays, with assignment covers scrawled with advice from tutors: *Excellent use of synonyms here. You're on the right track, Kate. Keep it up!* Except, of course, she hadn't.

Just as she had started on the university assignments her mobile rang and she scrabbled for it inside her handbag. 'Hello?'

'Hi.'

'Hi.'

'It's Sam.'

Kate grinned. 'Yes, I did realise that. After all, it's only been a day so I'm not likely to forget quite so soon.'

'Yeah, well.' Sam cleared his throat. 'Listen, did you come by the house today?'

'How did you know?' Even as she asked the question, Kate glanced at her watch and was amazed to find that it was past five o'clock. Judge Judy and her tight-lipped smile were long gone and the news was on. She had been reading her own fiction for well over two hours.

'Because it's pretty obvious, that's how.'

Kate suddenly realised he was talking about her little clean-up. She leant back in the couch and smiled. 'Just thought I'd pick up a few things while I was there. You know, help out.'

'Well, don't.'

'Pardon?'

'I said don't. Look, no offence but we're more than capable of picking up after ourselves. We are all adults, you know. And if you come round and start that sort of caper while we're all out, it's like you're the *maid*, for Christ's sake. Anyway, wasn't your whole idea to get *away* from all of that?'

'I suppose,' replied Kate rather begrudgingly. She felt hurt.

'Besides, you left a load of washing in the machine and now I have to go and bloody well hang it up.'

'Hey, didn't you just say that –'

'So I'd really rather prefer it if you didn't.'

'Fine then,' snapped Kate as she sat up straight. 'I'll just stay away, shall I?'

'That's not what I meant and you –'

'You're just trying to pay me back.'

'Me pay *you* back! Christ almighty! Talk about the pot calling the kettle black!'

'What's *that* supposed to mean?'

'You know exactly what that means!' Sam's voice was rough and edgy. 'But you can't have it both ways. You can't demand your own space and then come around here and clean up after us as well. It just doesn't work that way, sweetheart.'

'Fine then! Have it your way!'

'Good!'

Kate listened to the dial tone in shock. Sam had never, in all the time she had known him, ever hung up on her before. She flicked her phone shut and tossed it across the couch where it hit *Tangled Webs* with a dull thud.

Even through her anger Kate recognised the silliness of the argument. Being forbidden to clean up after her own family? If only that had happened years before! Then her anger bubbled up again and drowned out any humour. How *dare* he hang up on her!

A key scrabbled in the lock and then the front door swung open and closed again. Angie came into the lounge room carrying a stack of three Chinese takeaway containers. She looked slowly at the cardboard box and the spread of papers surrounding Kate and raised her eyebrows questioningly.

'Sorry,' Kate started to gather the pieces together. 'I was looking through some old stuff for inspiration.'

'Finding it hard to get going?'

'Yes. Very.'

Angie reached down with her spare hand and plucked a stapled sheaf of papers off the couch. She raised her eyebrows again. '*The Yellow Eyes of Darkness?*'

'I know,' Kate laughed, but only because it was expected.

'God, you'll give yourself nightmares.' Angie scanned through the first paragraph or so and then put it back down. 'Now I *definitely* need a drink.'

'You realise that's probably where the yellow eyes come from in the first place?' asked Kate rhetorically as she tossed the papers she was holding into the cardboard box and followed her cousin towards the kitchen. Angie put the containers down on the dining room table and then stared at the flowers on the island bench.

'You're getting flowers *already*? My, don't we work quickly!'

'They're from the kids.' Kate picked up a gerbera and laid it across her fingers. 'They sent them for good luck. With the writing.'

'How lovely!' Angie smiled at Kate, clearly pleased for her. 'Kids are amazing, aren't they?' Angie started to set the table perfunctorily. 'Just when you wonder why you bothered, they do something that blows you out of the water.'

'Tell me about it.' Kate poured two glasses of wine and carried them over to the table. She sat down and prised open one of the takeaway containers. The nutty smell of satay chicken overlaid both the flowers and her anger at Sam as her stomach tightened in anticipation.

'Couldn't be bothered cooking,' Angie sat down opposite and peeled the lid off the fried rice.

Kate grinned. 'I thought you were on a diet.'

'I am. That's why I got Chinese.'

'But these are all loaded with calories.' Kate waved a hand at the rice. 'Why do you think that's called *fried* rice?'

'Well, I could have got deep-fried chicken and chips, couldn't I?'

'Yes, but –'

'So these are by far the better option. Now, eat up before it gets cold.'

Kate looked at her cousin with some amusement, but her mind was really elsewhere. She ate in silence, only pausing to take the occasional sip of wine or to send a fleeting smile of appreciation towards Angie whenever they caught each other's eye.

'Oscar said to say hi,' said Angie after a while, scooping up some more rice. 'He dropped in at the shop to give me two boxes of his old books. I think he's trying to make the house look less crowded.'

'Do you know, I really admire you two. You've got such a good relationship. Almost like brother and sister.'

Angie raised her eyebrows. 'Which would make Melissa what?'

'You know what I mean. Although I did think you might get back together for the first few years. Not now though.'

'*He* would have liked to.'

Kate looked at her with interest. 'Really?'

'I have a hypothesis.' Angie used her fork to punctuate the words. 'Men cope less well with change, mainly because they're lazier. So while the idea of freedom sounded great to Oscar in theory, the reality wasn't as appealing.'

'So did he actually ask you? To get back together?'

'Well, yes. In an offhand way.'

'Maybe that's why he kept the house all this time.' Kate plucked a tiny curled prawn off her plate and popped it into her mouth. 'Hoping he'd wear you down. That you'd end up back there simply because you didn't want to hurt his feelings.'

'Not a chance,' said Angie firmly, scooping up the last of her rice. 'I'm very fond of the guy, but not *that* fond. And I love being single.'

Kate laid her cutlery across her plate and patted her stomach. 'That was delicious, Ange. Thanks.'

'My pleasure.' Angie picked up her wineglass and stared at her cousin thoughtfully over the rim. 'So, moving on from Oscar and my magnetic attractions, you're having problems getting started, then?'

Kate picked up her fork again and pushed a snow pea around her plate. 'Yes. Very much so.'

'Well, you know what they say. Write about what you know.'

'*And* I've managed to have an argument with Sam.'

'When did you see Sam?'

'I didn't.'

Angie took a sip of wine and looked at her quizzically. 'So . . . it was a telepathic argument then? Like he sent you the finger via thought transmission?'

'He rang. To tell me to stop cleaning up after them.'

'I can see why you'd be upset. What a bastard.'

Kate grinned weakly. 'Doesn't matter, I'll sort it out.'

'Excellent. Then back to the MO. Did you hear what I said before?'

'Write about what you know?' Kate dropped the fork with a clatter and sighed again. 'If only it was that simple.'

'Well, why isn't it?' Angie regarded her for a few moments and then, when no answer was forthcoming, continued regardless. 'I mean, I'm no expert but every writer I've ever listened to has always said the same thing, so there must be something to it.'

'Yes, but what *do* I know?' blurted Kate. 'My life has been full of absolute *nothing*. Happy childhood, happy marriage and now miserable middle-age. That'll make for *fascinating* reading.'

'You're hopeless.' Angie rolled her eyes. 'Everybody has *something* to write about somewhere. You've just got to dig it out.'

'Yeah? Like what?'

'Like . . . something. It doesn't have to be earth-shaking. It could be even about raising kids, or suburbia, or what about when you were overseas? Maybe, somewhere, there's the tail end of a mystery that you could pad with imagination. Use what you know and turn it into fiction. That's what they say.'

'Good for them.'

'Well, I'm going to go and watch some television.' Angie pushed her chair out and rose. 'Your turn for the dishes. And please feel free to join me when you've finished being so negative.'

Kate closed up the takeaway containers and stacked them on top of the two plates. Then she moved them to one side, put both elbows on the table and rested her head on her hands. Write what you know! It was easy for those pretentious writers with their oh-so-full lives. Living in exotic countries, or sitting on balconies with other literary souls whilst they discussed existentialism or whatever. What was *she* going to write about? How to make an edible school lunch? How to survive a family holiday with all members of the family still intact? How to make a teenager clean their room?

Kate got up and carried everything over to the sink. She knew Angie was right, that she was being far too negative, but she couldn't seem to find the energy required to lift.

As if on cue, Angie came into the kitchen with her empty wineglass in hand. She opened the fridge and took out the bottle, holding it up. 'Do you want another?'

Kate turned and shook her head. 'I think I need to stay sober.'

'Not necessarily. Some pretty good writers were drunks, you know.'

'I think that only works if you're male. Like Hemingway.'

'You could be right.' Angie refilled her glass and then replaced the bottle in the fridge. She looked at Kate pensively. 'This is really getting to you, isn't it?'

'Yes, it is. It's like I kept blaming the fact I wasn't writing on my circumstances, when it was really me all along.'

'God, Kate! It's only been one day!'

'Yes, and all I managed to write was one bloody word – *Title*.'

'*Title?*' repeated Angie, trying, without much success, to smother a grin.

'Hysterical, isn't it. I think I will have that drink after all.'

Angie moved out of the way. 'What about what I said before? Write what you know. And stop trying to measure your life against all those others, which you seem to think are so full. That's just the grass always being greener. You know, even a happy childhood makes for interesting reading. And ours wasn't exactly conventional. Just start with memories and build from there. Or you could even . . . no, doesn't matter.'

Kate looked at her curiously. 'What?'

Angie sucked her bottom lip for a moment, as if in two minds about continuing. 'Well, I was just going to say that the issue isn't about getting published at the moment, is it? I mean, you just want to get into the swing of things, so you could even use it in a sort of *therapeutic* sense. Maybe write about what happened last year . . . you know, Uncle James and all.'

'And why do you think I need that?'

'*Anybody* would need that after –'

'Do you know what?' Although Kate's tone was quite friendly, her gaze was not. 'I am heartily *sick* of everybody assuming that I have ongoing issues over all that. My father died. Fathers die every bloody day. And, yes, mine died in a particularly . . .' Her voice petered off for a moment. 'But that doesn't mean I need to bloody well *write* about it. God, next you'll be suggesting I *do* publish it, and make money off his death.'

'Hey, that's not what I –'

'You know what?' Kate gazed at her cousin narrowly. She put down her glass. 'You know how you suggested I find a little mystery to write about? I just thought of one. How about your mother? How about that?'

'You can be such a bitch.' Angie picked up her wine and walked out of the kitchen.

Kate stared after her balefully but then, as her cousin disappeared, she closed her eyes and gulped in air, letting it out with a huge sigh. She felt tears hovering and rubbed both eyes. Then, with lids still closed, she watched the jewelled effect play across the insides like one of the kaleidoscopes she used to have as a child. She sighed again, opened her eyes, and then went after Angie to try to make amends.

In the lounge room the television was still on but Angie was no longer watching it. Kate walked slowly up the stairs and, from the midway point, looked up towards her cousin's firmly closed bedroom door. She hesitated and then went back down the stairs and stood at the lounge room window, staring out towards the communal driveway. She did her neck exercise and then, when that didn't work, started massaging her temples. What on earth had got into her? Angie was only trying to help. And she, Kate, had launched into full attack, spearing straight towards the jugular.

A slim elderly lady emerged from the next door unit with a dog on a lead beside her. It was a rather handsome cocker spaniel of the blue roan variety. Kate watched the pair head off up the driveway at a rather spry pace. The thought suddenly occurred to her that, really, she should run after them and pick a fight. About anything. That way, what with having already alienated Sam and Angie, she could make it a hat-trick.

EIGHT

> *Dear Dad, I've been sitting here trying to think of some memories, but they're slippery little things, aren't they? And a lot of them are in black and white, which makes me think they're from photos anyway. Or maybe colour just leaches over the years. But did I ever thank you for a great childhood? In a way it feels like it really only ended last year, when you died. That some part of me was able to remain a child because I was someone's child, until you were gone. So, you see, you were my buffer in more ways than one!*

Kate pushed her chair away from the desk. She read through what she had written and then quickly highlighted the whole lot and deleted it. She sat back again and stared at the blank screen, with the cursor now blinking accusingly. Minutes ticked by and she did not move, then finally she leant forward and reinstated the words.

Angie was right, anything was better than nothing. And maybe some fragment of memory, or just random thoughts, would lead her somewhere.

Kate laced her hands across her stomach and stared up towards the ceiling. She decided to work backwards, from now, until she tripped over something that inspired. The last year was out of the question, and before that was a two-decade expanse of family life. Marriage, kids, suburbia. And although many a good book had been written around these themes, she knew instinctively that it wasn't what she wanted to concentrate on. Not now, not yet.

A small grey spider tiptoed slowly along the edge of the cornice, pausing every so often to lift a leg and wave it gently in front, as if testing the waters before commitment. Eventually it arrived at the corner, where it flattened itself into the plaster joint. Kate looked away and then back again, marvelling at the way the spider was now hidden. If she hadn't seen the journey, she would never have guessed it was even there.

There was always the year she spent in Europe, which held *definite* potential. With a smile, Kate let her mind skip along the same path her feet had trodden so many years before. But it wasn't long before she reached certain detours that made her eyes widen, and her smile deepen, and she realised that writing about that particular year might be a mistake at the moment. Later maybe, when Sam was feeling less threatened.

Just then the doorbell rang and Kate ran downstairs to answer it. Somewhat to her surprise, Shelley stood on the threshold with Emma in her arms, already struggling to be put down. Kate grinned with pleasure. 'Shell! How *lovely* to see you!'

Shelley looked slightly taken back at her mother's enthusiasm. 'You too, Mum.'

'And aren't you gorgeous!' Kate took one of Emma's flailing arms and the little girl immediately stopped wriggling and began to shake hands with gusto.

'Can we come in?'

'Of course!' Kate let go off Emma's hand and stood back, shutting the door behind them as they came through. 'Well, this *is* a surprise. Do you want a coffee?'

'Yeah, sure. Thanks.'

'Follow me.' Kate led the way towards the kitchen. She put the kettle on as Shelley lowered Emma with a sigh of relief, placing the child next to the dining room table with a couple of plastic toys that she pulled from her oversized handbag. Then she sat down at the table and crossed her legs, looking over at her mother curiously.

'So, how's it all going?'

'Good. Very good. Did you get my message? About the flowers?'

Shelley glanced over at them, still sitting on the bench. 'So you liked them?'

'I *loved* them. And I know it was your idea,' Kate smiled at her daughter. 'It was really thoughtful. Thank you.'

'No worries. So your book's off and racing then?'

Kate busied herself with preparing the coffee. 'Well, it's not as simple as that. Let's just say I've made a start.'

'Great.' Shelley started drumming her fingernails against the table. 'What's it about, then?'

'I'd prefer not to say just yet. Don't want to jinx it.' Kate brought the two mugs over to the table and sat down herself, trying to ignore the steady tapping. 'Nothing personal. It's just a superstition that writers have.'

'Really? I've never heard of it.'

'Well, that's probably because you're not a writer.'

'Fair enough.' Shelley stopped tapping and reached down to steady her daughter, who had hoisted herself up on the side of the chair and was standing, albeit with quite a wobble. After a few moments, during which the wobble increased in intensity, she let go of the chair and then folded, sitting back down on her padded bottom with a thump.

'So . . . how're things going at home?' asked Kate casually.

'God!' Shelley rolled her eyes. Then she sighed for added emphasis.

'Oh? What's up?'

'Dad is driving us *nuts*. Either he's walking around like a bear with a sore head, or he's nagging us to pick up, or wash up or whatever. I usually just go out to the bungalow after tea so as I don't have to listen to it. God! I thought *you* were bad!'

'Really? Well, that doesn't sound like –'

'As for that damn vacuum cleaner. *Shoot!* All you have to do is take a bag of chips into the lounge room and he's got the vacuum out all ready to go.'

Kate smiled ruefully. 'I could always take it, I suppose. After all, it *was* my Christmas present.'

'You're as bad as he is.' Shelley stopped tapping as she gazed at her mother with disbelief. 'Why on earth would you want something like that for Christmas?'

'What makes you think . . . no, doesn't matter.'

Emma pulled herself back up onto the chair and this time, after stabilising herself, took an unsteady step sideways. This was clearly more than her tenuous balance was capable of because for a moment she swayed there, with legs apart, and then, with a surprised expression, went backwards and landed on her padded posterior once more.

'Good try, Em!' said Kate encouragingly, before turning back to Shelley. 'I feel like I've missed so much. I mean, she's trying everything now.'

'You're talking like you've been gone for months!' replied Shelley, rather disparagingly. 'It's only been a couple of days!'

Fortunately Emma saved her having to answer by crawling rapidly around to her grandmother's chair and trying her standing up trick with this clearly more appreciative audience. Kate leant over and put a hand supportively on the baby's back as she pulled herself upright again and then stood proudly.

'Listen, Mum, what're you doing on Friday?'

'Why?' asked Kate, immediately suspicious.

'It's just I need a babysitter. And, yes,' Shelley held up a hand as her mother's mouth opened, 'I *know* that you're trying to work on your book. But I wouldn't ask if it wasn't important.'

'I thought you took Emma with you on Fridays?' Kate lowered the baby to a sitting position and turned back to her daughter curiously. Shelley had a part-time job as a waitress but also worked every Friday and the occasional Saturday morning at Angie's bookshop. On these days she usually took Emma with her as there was a portable playpen set up in the storeroom.

'Yeah, I do. But this Friday we're doing a bit of a stocktake so I'd *really* like to have her looked after. Please?'

Kate knew that she should politely refuse, because if her family were ever to grasp the equal importance of *her* time, then she would have to make a stand. But it was easier said than done. Mainly because she *missed* her contact with them, even though it had only been a couple of days, and she wanted to feel connected. She didn't want the fence she was building between them to be six-foot paling, she just wanted a small picket divider that made a statement but could still, if needed, be easily stepped over. Besides, a day with the baby would be *fun*.

Kate took a sip of coffee to disguise her willingness. 'Well . . . okay. But just this once. You have to understand that —'

'Thanks, Mum! You're the best!' Shelley gave her mother an appreciative smile which was almost immediately replaced by a frown. '*God*, I wish I could work at the bookshop full-time. Then I could tell the restaurant to shove it.'

'I know.' Kate tried to muster up some sympathy but, as she had been hearing this refrain since soon after Shelley had started waitressing nearly four years ago, it was getting quite worn. Besides, she was fairly sure her customers felt the same way. 'At least it's only three days a week now. It could be worse.'

Shelley gathered her long hair together over one shoulder and ran her fingers through it broodingly. Then she flipped it behind with an impatient gesture and sipped her coffee. 'If only Auntie Angie tried to build the business up. Advertised or something.'

'But she's happy with it the way it is.' Kate was also heartily sick of this conversation, which invariably followed the other. 'She gets a good living, so why expand? Then she'd just be run off her feet.'

'Well, she *wouldn't* be run off her feet if she hired me full-time, would she?'

'Take it up with her, then,' Kate shrugged.

'God, thanks for your support.'

'If you mean the fact that I'm babysitting for you on Friday instead of working, then you're welcome. Do you want another coffee?'

'No thanks. Got heaps on today.' Shelley bent down so that she could gather Emma's toys and shove them into her bag. She stood, smoothing down her jeans.

Kate hoisted Emma up onto one hip. 'Who's going to spend the day with me on Friday then, hey?'

Emma's eyes crinkled as she grinned back and reached out one finger to touch her grandmother's lip gently. The grin faded as she concentrated and then, quite suddenly, she thrust the finger into Kate's mouth and hooked her lip neatly, pulling it outwards and downwards with surprising strength. The baby laughed gleefully.

'Damn!' Kate grabbed the finger and disengaged it before rubbing her lip. 'That really hurt!'

Shelley glanced across casually. 'Oh, yeah. Sorry, I should have warned you. She's been doing that lately. Thinks it's funny.'

'Well, it's not,' Kate passed the baby over to her mother and then sucked her bottom lip, which was throbbing painfully. 'And you need to cut her fingernails.'

'Bad girl,' Shelley said to her daughter, in a voice that could just have easily said 'well done' or 'next time go for her nostril and see if you can deviate the septum'.

Still sucking her lip, Kate took Shelley's bag from her and led the way to the front door. She opened it and preceded them out into the sunshine. It was a bit warmer today than it had been for a while, and the forecast was for steadily building temperatures until they reached the high-thirties by the weekend. Kate shaded her eyes and looked up the driveway for Shelley's car. 'Where did you park?'

'Out by the front.'

'I'll walk up with you.' They walked companionably up the concrete driveway, Emma busily flexing and un-flexing her fingers.

As they reached the row of letterboxes, a young woman of about Shelley's age turned into the driveway pushing a large three-wheeled stroller. She was a Nordic-style blonde with a statuesque figure that was emphasised by a denim miniskirt. Inside the stroller was a baby of about a year and a half who could easily be used as evidence that cloning was already in practice. The young woman frowned at Shelley for a moment and then her face cleared into a smile. 'Hello, what are you doing here?'

Shelley grinned. 'Just visiting my mother.' She waved a hand in Kate's direction. 'Kate. She's living in one of the units for a while.'

'Really? So am I!'

'Get out. Are you? How funny!'

The young woman smiled over at Kate. 'My name's Bronte.' She gestured towards the stroller, where the baby sat placidly. 'And this is Sherry.'

'We go to mother's club together,' said Shelley. She turned back to Bronte. 'So which unit are you in?'

Bronte waved towards the one at the front. 'That one. It's actually my mother's and I'm house-sitting. She's in Tasmania for a while.'

'Lucky you.'

'Pardon?' said Kate, rather taken aback.

'The house-sitting,' said Shelley quickly, with a grin. 'Not the Tasmania bit.'

'Look, Sherry, here's your friend Emma.' Bronte bobbed down by the stroller, took hold of one of her daughter's plump hands and pointed it towards Emma. Sherry responded with a supreme indifference.

'She's a lovely baby,' commented Kate politely. 'How old is she?'

'Nineteen months. But she's rather big for her age. And advanced.'

Kate glanced down at the occupant of the stroller who, although a large-ish baby, did not seem to be displaying any significant signs of advancement. In fact, she had barely moved a muscle since they had arrived, obviously content to sit and watch events docilely. Emma, on the other hand, was wriggling determinedly in her mother's arms, trying to get her hand loose.

Bronte stood up again. 'Hey, I've got an idea. Why don't you come in for a bit? I'm sure the girls would *love* to play with each other.'

'Okay, great!' agreed Shelley with some enthusiasm, getting control of Emma's hand again and clearly forgetting that she had so much to get done that day.

'Oh, and you too of course, Kate,' added Bronte with a courteous smile.

'No, but thanks anyway. I'll leave you to it. And I'm sure we'll meet up again at some stage. See you Friday, Emma.' Kate waved and then headed back down the driveway. She felt suddenly ancient. Because it seemed impossibly long ago that she had met with other mothers like that. Where the only thing they had in common were their babies, but that was all they needed. And with a jolt Kate realised that it *had* been a long time. Twenty years, in fact.

It was a rather depressing thought, even though she didn't really want to be that age again. Rather it was the passage of time that was disheartening, and what she had accomplished in the meantime. Kate shut the front door behind her and then hesitated, gazing up the staircase to where her computer awaited. She sighed, and abruptly decided to go for a drive instead. Clear her head, get the thinking cap on, find some inspiration. Get started on something, before another twenty years passed and she was still no further.

Shelley and Bronte had disappeared by the time Kate reversed her car up the driveway, but Sherry's stroller could be seen neatly parked outside the front unit. Kate took off down the street until she reached the main road. Then it was just a matter of about a few kilometres. She pulled up outside the weatherboard house and turned off the ignition.

After a few moments Kate got out and locked the car. She walked up the driveway and through the gate to the lemon tree and the old wrought-iron setting, where she settled herself, dropping her handbag down on the ground. *Corroded Motherhood* was still there, just slightly less brown than it had been at the beginning of the month, as the lack of rain had left it baking in the sun each day.

She laid her head down on the tabletop and, blurring her eyes, tried to conjure up her father once more. But this time the image refused to formulate, and the harder she tried to recall his features, to put them into place, the more difficult the task became. Her eyes became teary with the effort and she blinked and closed her eyes.

'Dad?' she whispered, her breath seeping through the lacework. 'Are you there?'

'As always.'

Kate relaxed as relief surged through her. 'I thought you were gone.'

'Actually I am. You of all people should know that.'

'I didn't mean . . . I meant here – for me.'

'I'll always be here for you, girl. That's a given.'

'Good. Because I need you. I can't work out what to write about.'

'And you think I can? Well, I'll tell you something for nothing, you're not going to get any help from a dead man, are you?'

Kate's eyes flashed open and she stared across the table towards the overgrown backyard, viewing it as if on a plate. She stared blankly for a few moments and then sat up straight, rubbing her eyes. The backyard glittered blurrily and then slowly came back into focus, still overgrown and still empty. She tried to imagine what the property would look like when everything was replaced by Sam's block of units. Concrete driveways, neat crisp brickwork and identical façades. It was impossible to picture. Impossible to accept. Apart from the year she had spent overseas, and maybe the odd other exception, she had visited this house every single weekend throughout her adult life. It had *always* been here. But then again, so had her father.

Kate let this notion permeate for a moment, almost enjoying the shaft of pain it brought. Then she pushed it away with frustration. Why couldn't she let go? Not erase, never that, but just let *go*? Isn't that what normal people did? Move methodically through the stages of grief instead of being stuck somewhere in between like a psychological wedgie. Kate thought back to her uncle's death and wondered whether Angie had ever experienced anything like this. With a jolt, she realised that she had never asked.

Uncle Frank's death had been so sudden. Even though there had been that minor heart attack the year before, no one had seemed to take it all that seriously, mainly because *he* hadn't taken it seriously. Still always with a hand-rolled cigarette in his mouth and a few beers in the afternoon. Strong and fit and *there*, but then suddenly gone. Just a blink between life and death. Now, in middle-age, Kate knew that the doctors must have given him some warning, or at least some preventative advice that he had chosen to disregard. For starters, even in those days they would have strongly encouraged that he give up smoking. The fact that he hadn't changed his lifestyle at all filled Kate with a sense of fond irritation, but at least it had been his choice. And she both admired and envied him that.

She had a tapestry of memories from that time, but two in particular stood out. The first was the night before the funeral, when she and Angie had sat together in their bedroom and talked until the early hours of the morning, just as they had as girls. But this time there had been no smothered giggles, only a hoarse conversation of loss punctuated by ready tears. And Angie, who was then midway through her business degree, told of her decision to move in with her mother's sister in Ballarat for a while. To get away from it all, and maybe learn more about that side of the family.

Then she had gone on in a half-embarrassed whisper, not quite making eye contact, to tell of the fantasy she had developed in the three days since her father's death. That at the funeral, now only hours away, she would feel a hand on her shoulder and would turn, only to be enveloped within the arms of her mother. Returning to the fold when she was needed the most. Kate could still see Angie's face clearly as she had said this. Pale, with red-washed eyes and a sheepish smile that already acknowledged the inevitability of disappointment.

The second memory was of the weekend after the funeral, when she had come back to keep her father company. The house had been so incredibly empty. Each room larger than it had ever seemed before, and more stifling. Just her father left behind, working all hours in the garden to avoid spending time inside. And for the first time Kate learnt that the absence of a voice has an echo of its own.

She stared out at the backyard, remembering how it had been and realising that as empty as it had seemed then, it was now infinitely worse. A small starling swooped over the back fence and flew up to the washing line, where it settled on one of the sagging wires, looking beadily down into the weeds. Kate watched it for a while as she wondered whether, as in Angie's case, the echo was even louder when there was ambiguity surrounding the absence. Like with her mother. How on earth must that *feel*? At least with Kate's mother she had known exactly what had happened and, because her father had so many stories, it had been almost like she was still there. Or at least would have been if she could. But to not even know whether your parent was alive or dead, or even whether they paused, every now and again, and spared a moment to think about you. To have such obscurity shadowing your childhood, and then still *never* have it resolved.

Slowly, as she mused over this, the nucleus of an idea formed and then gradually enlarged. Kate's eyes widened. It had been there all along – a full-blown mystery with all the trimmings. Angie's mother. The actual disappearance, framed by the past and the future. Maybe told from the perspective of a relative, or just an onlooker, or even a child. She could use the structure to build a fictional story, or go for broke and make it factual all the way through. Regardless, she now had her idea. And it was *inspired*.

Furthermore it had been Angie herself who had suggested that Kate write about what she knew, maybe even find, somewhere, the hint of a mystery. And there it was – tailor-made. She grinned at the irony and then the grin faded as a worm of doubt raised its head. But would Angie be in favour? Or would she flatten the proposal at the outset? Kate thought about their argument yesterday, when she had angrily thrown at Angie the very idea that she was now exploring seriously. But then she had used it as a weapon, almost unthinkingly, and it had not been so much the concept as the *intent* that had been designed to wound. Surely Angie would have recognised that? Because why, after all, would she object to having her mother's story investigated? Maybe she would still get that hand on her shoulder, even after all this time.

Nevertheless, after some thought, Kate decided that she would keep it to herself for now. The story might turn out to be a dud, in which case there was no point concerning Angie at all. And besides, even though she was quite sure her cousin would not object, Kate simply didn't want to take the risk. So she'd first do some preliminary research, start to understand the background, and *then* present Angie with her discoveries and ask permission to continue. After that, and only after that, would she begin the actual writing. Develop the story-line, build the book. And she knew, already, that she'd found exactly what she needed, and it was going to be great.

NINE

> *Dear Dad, I'm excited. I'm* very *excited! Which has made me realise that I haven't been really excited about anything for a long time. It feels almost clumsy! What frustrates me, though, is that if I had started writing this a year ago, I could have just come to you for information, but I've left it too late. Typical. Or maybe it would never have occurred to me then? Anyway, I still haven't decided how to write it – as a pseudo-memoir? A tragic romance? A mystery? I keep seeing lines, like:* From where she sat, amongst the radishes, she could see the roofs of both houses and knew she had a choice to make. Smoke rose from a chimney, wafting across the sky in what seemed a beckoning gesture. Was that a sign?

Kate hit save and then took a deep breath as she pushed her chair back from the desk. It had been a week since she had come up with her brilliant idea and she had been unable to move much further than just the essence. A phone call from the main publishing company she freelanced for had forced her to prioritise a backlog of work and it had taken her all this time to work through it.

The only day she took off was Friday, when she babysat Emma at the Lysterfield house and worked her way through Sam's paperwork instead. At least that meant meeting up with Sam himself, and whilst their scrupulously polite conversation hadn't repaired any bridges, it had at least retained the connection. But it took all her willpower not to straighten the cushions or at least unload the dishwasher.

She had also managed to renew connections with her sons, as both Jacob and Caleb had been sprawled across the lounge room floor when she arrived, playing some strange 3-D game on the Playstation. One which apparently required frequent yelling, the occasional muttered obscenity and a large amount of fist-pumping.

Nor, as with all their disagreements, was there much effort required to mend fences with Angie. There was too much history between them to let a few harsh words do a lot of damage. Kate just made an especially nice meal for the following evening and slid an apology into the conversation relatively quickly. Then they moved smoothly on, chatting about children and life in general. The one thing they hadn't touched on, mainly because Kate hadn't raised it, was her epiphany.

This in itself had been quite frustrating. Because she would have loved to discuss it with Angie. But the worm of doubt ensured her silence. She simply couldn't take the risk, small as it might be, that Angie would refuse permission.

But this morning marked the end of her frustration. With all extra commitments taken care of, she was now able to start her research. She began by making a list while drinking her morning coffee. Avenues of exploration, directions of research, people to question. A priority, she decided, were names. All she had at the moment was Sophie Painter, but she also needed a maiden name, in case she had reverted, and also the real name of That Bugger she had run off with.

Accordingly she spent some time at the computer, first checking that the name of Sophie Painter didn't appear anywhere in cyberspace. Once she had established that it didn't, Kate turned to title searches to best discover the identity of That Bugger. However, as the land had been subdivided, this proved rather complicated. Finally, after a few frustrating phone calls, she contacted a firm which specialised in title search and commissioned them to do it for her.

There was one obvious place to start looking for background

information but the thought brought with it a mix of feelings. Excitement because she would definitely find some clues; dismay because it would be a long and dirty job; and trepidation because it meant facing something she had been putting off since last June. Which was going through all of her father's worldly goods and possessions.

It wasn't just his possessions, either. When her uncle died, his furniture and personal effects had simply remained in place. Nobody had ever asked or offered to change matters and it wasn't as if her father needed the space. It had simply been understood, tacitly, that everything would be sorted after his death, when she and Angie would be equal beneficiaries. So, after the events of last June, came the distress of not only clearing out his bedroom, but also Uncle Frank's, which was a virtual time capsule.

Oscar and Sam had done most of the work, packing and storing everything under the Lysterfield house for the time being. And, except for the desk that Kate had recently extracted, that's where it all remained. She knew she had a choice now. Move forward, face a few demons and hopefully get some results, or forget about the whole thing right now. If she made up her mind quickly, she could even phone the title-search firm to cancel her payment.

Kate sat up and massaged her neck. The truth was there *was* no choice. It had been so terrific to stumble across a concept that actually excited her, there was no way she was giving that away at the first hurdle. She would just have to rely on motivation to help her get through. Tomorrow, or maybe even the following day. But definitely one day this week. Definitely.

Later that day, while passing the lounge room window with her third cup of coffee, Kate happened to glance out and see the elderly lady from next door setting out on another walk with her dog. To postpone returning to her computer, where she was trying to establish a half-fleshed family tree, she leant on the back of the lounge chair and watched the pair walk briskly up the driveway and turn right towards the little park at the end of the road.

It suddenly occurred to Kate that a good source of information would be contemporaries of Frank or Sophie or even That Bugger, who could perhaps fill in some of the background. School photos would be of no assistance because, even though she knew both Frank and her father had attended local schools, class photos of the time did not include the names of students. And the odds were fairly good that That Bugger had possessed both eyes as a youth, so he wasn't likely to stand out. Other records, such as town meetings or sporting clubs, would contain many names, but no clue as to whether there was a connection. It would be different if they'd any hobbies, but all she knew for sure was that her Uncle Frank would get dressed up every now and again to, as he used to put it, 'go hit the town'.

But it may not even have been his town he was hitting. The local area hadn't exactly been known for its nightlife, even when *she* had been a teenager. So it was more than likely Uncle Frank had been venturing further afield, going to pubs or clubs or local dances; an anonymous man in a crowd looking for a good time. As for her own father, his social life had ended with the death of her mother. He'd say, with a smile, that she had ruined him for anyone else, but because of the smile, and the matter-of-fact way he spoke, Kate never truly grasped the tragedy behind the words until she was much older.

For a moment, she stared blankly at the flickering sunlit patterns across the lounge room floor and thought about her father, living for forty-three years after the love of his life had died. *Forty-three* years. Raising a child alone, never really going out, never really moving on. Just going to bed each night alone, through the doorway at the end of the passage. She shook her head to put an end to this line of thinking.

Instead she turned back to his elusive peers, who would have spent their childhoods in the shadow of the Second World War. Where did one go to look for the elderly? Retirement homes, or bowling clubs, or bingo? Perhaps she could infiltrate, ideally by ingratiating herself with someone of the right age group. Kate grinned – the answer was right in front of her. Or at least would *soon* be right in front of her, walking briskly down the driveway with a well-behaved cocker spaniel on a lead. Kate estimated that the elderly lady from next door would be in the right age group and, even if she herself was a dead end, she seemed to have a lot of visitors; surely *one* of them might know something. Or know of somebody else. And so on.

There was a slight risk that starting her enquiries so close to home, in fact right next door, would mean it got back to Angie sooner rather than later, but that was a risk Kate thought worth taking. She could always claim to have just been making polite conversation that was misunderstood. And now was as good a time as any.

Still deep in thought, she left the unit and walked slowly up the driveway. It was a gorgeous summery day, with very few clouds and absolutely no breeze at all, just steady sunshine. When she got to the row of letterboxes, she shaded her eyes and looked up the road in the direction of the park, but the woman was nowhere in sight. How far could someone of that age walk? And, more to the question, how long could she stand there before her contrived casualness turned into suspicious loitering?

A car could be heard approaching from the opposite direction but Kate didn't pay much attention until it slowed to pull into the driveway behind her. She turned, out of curiosity, and was somewhat surprised to see Shelley's Astra come to a halt next to the letterboxes, its engine idling. The front passenger door opened to reveal the blonde girl from the front unit, Bronte.

'Hi . . . um, Kate,' grinned Bronte as she got out, clearly pleased at her recall.

'Hello.' Kate nodded briefly at Bronte and then turned her attention to the car, where Shelley, with one hand on the steering wheel, was leaning across the front passenger seat and smiling up at her mother. Kate glanced into the back seat where Emma and Bronte's daughter Sherry lay sprawled in their car seats, both fast asleep with sweat-slicked hair clinging to their foreheads.

'We've just been to the zoo,' said Shelley by way of explanation. 'Long day.'

'Sure was,' agreed Bronte, rather superfluously, as she opened the back door and unstrapped her daughter, gently lifting the baby out of her seat. Sherry stiffened and her eyes flew open for a second, before slowly closing again as she settled koala-like against her mother's chest.

'What about you?' asked Shelley curiously. 'What are you doing skulking out here? Touting for business?'

As Bronte chortled appreciatively at her friend's humour, Kate looked at her daughter narrowly and then gestured downwards at her T-shirt and baggy tracksuit pants. 'That's right. But I'm targeting those with a fetish for slobs.'

'Well, I don't think you'll find them around here, dear,' said an elderly voice from behind Kate. 'Not really the ideal area.'

Kate took a deep breath and slowly turned around. Her target stood underneath the shade of the wattle tree, smiling broadly. As Kate had assumed, she *was* around the right age group, with short white hair and pouchy jowls, which looked out of context with her very thin build. The cocker spaniel stood by her side and, although it was panting, it seemed to be grinning at her discomfiture too.

'Hi, Mrs Jarvis,' said Bronte in a low voice so as not to wake her sleeping baby.

'Hello, Bronte. You're looking well as always.' Mrs Jarvis turned back to Kate with interest. 'And you must be Angie's cousin, Kate? Moved in next door?'

'Exactly,' replied Kate rather stupidly.

'Lovely to meet you.' Mrs Jarvis gave another genial smile all around and then set off down the driveway, the spaniel trotting along at heel.

'And I'd better be off too,' said Shelley. She jumped out, leaving the car idling, and unhooked Bronte's car seat. Then she carried it up to the unit and left it on the porch. Bronte followed, sending a wave towards Kate as she left. Emma slept on in the car, her face flushed.

Shelley ran back and clambered into the car again. She leant over and waved at Kate cheerfully. 'See you Friday, Mum.'

Kate frowned, but before she could ask what she meant, Shelley had straightened up in her seat and was reversing out of the driveway. She pulled into the road and drove off with a slight crunching of her gears.

Kate winced, then glanced quickly down the driveway, but Mrs Jarvis was long gone. She cursed, under her breath, and childishly scuffed a foot against the ground with irritation. Not only had she missed her opportunity, but the woman probably thought she was some sort of deviant. Kate took a deep breath and then checked her letterbox so that the whole thing wasn't a complete waste of time. She fished out an elastic-banded bundle of letters and started walking back towards her unit, slapping them against her thigh in irritation.

As she neared the end of the main driveway, where the concrete narrowed and veered off towards the corner unit, Mrs Jarvis's front door suddenly opened and the elderly woman came out, walking quickly towards Kate with a smile.

'Went right past the mailboxes and forgot to check mine!'

Kate laughed politely while she tried to think of a good conversational gambit.

'And I didn't introduce myself properly before either, did I?' Mrs Jarvis stopped by Kate, still smiling. 'The name's Dawn Jarvis. And I know you're Kate. Well, it's very nice to have a new neighbour. We're such a settled bunch here that it doesn't happen too often.'

'Oh, you've been here long?'

'Long enough. And they'll only be taking me out in a body bag, believe me.'

'I'm sure that won't happen,' said Kate, trying to be courteous.

Mrs Jarvis looked at her. 'Well, unless some vampire gets me and I become the *walking* dead, then it'll have to. Because, believe me, I ain't leaving here alive.'

'Oh.'

'But the chances are probably slim about the vampire.' Mrs Jarvis paused, seemingly rather disappointed. 'I mean, even if one happened by, he's not likely to go for me when he's got young Bronte nearby, or even you. Much nicer necks all round.'

'Um. Thanks.'

'And he'd probably give up anyway because my veins are *notoriously* hard to reach. The nurse down at the health centre always has a dreadful time getting my blood. They've all sunk, see. My mother was the same. So it'd definitely be your necks on the chopping block, so to speak.'

'Oh.'

'Don't look at me like that, dear,' Mrs Jarvis laughed, her jowls quivering, and laid a hand lightly on Kate's arm. 'I'm not crazy. Just watch too much Buffy, that's all. You know, "Buffy the Vampire Slayer". A veritable font of information, that show.'

'Of course,' Kate nodded, rather bemused. She wondered how she could segue neatly from vampires to Sophie Painter. Perhaps via the commonality of nocturnal cavorting?

'Anyway, I'd better let you go.' Mrs Jarvis dropped her hand and smiled. 'I'm sure I'll see you around. Nice to meet you.'

Kate decided to just go for it. 'Listen, I wonder if I could ask you something?'

'Certainly, dear.'

'It's like this. I'm doing some research for a book I'm writing and –'

'You're an *author*?'

'Well, not . . . yes. Yes, I am.'

'That's amazing.' Mrs Jarvis looked very impressed by this revelation. 'Really *amazing*.'

'Um, thank you. Anyway, I'm doing some research on a woman who used to live in this area about forty-five to fifty years ago. And I was wondering whether, by any chance, if maybe –'

'I knew her?'

'Ah, yes.' Kate nodded, rather embarrassed.

Mrs Jarvis patted Kate's arm apologetically. 'Sorry dear, but I only moved here after my husband died about ten years ago. Lived over at Blackburn until then.'

'Oh, well. I just thought it was worth –'

'Asking? Absolutely. And I'll tell you what,' Mrs Jarvis paused to think, 'I've got an idea. You need to come over to one of my poker days and ask the ladies there.'

'Poker days?'

'Yes, every Tuesday. They start at ten sharp and you'll really need to be there before then because once the play starts no one's going to pay you the least attention.'

Kate thought back to the stream of elderly visitors that first Tuesday. 'Ah, I see.'

'Yes, and I know for a fact that at least two of my regulars have lived around here all their lives. I'll introduce you to them. And even if they don't know your woman, they'll be able to ask around.'

'That would be absolutely marvellous.' Kate smiled, amazed by this sudden turn in fortunes. 'Thank you so *very* much.'

'My pleasure. But tell me,' Mrs Jarvis increased the pressure on Kate's arm and leant in a little closer. 'What did this woman do? Was it juicy?'

Kate's smile widened. 'That would be telling. But, if this pans out, I'll put you in the acknowledgements. *And* make sure you get one of the first copies of the book.'

'It's a deal!' Mrs Jarvis finally let go of Kate's arm. '*Lovely* to meet you, dear. And I'll see you next Tuesday. Don't forget, ten sharp!'

'I'll be there.' Kate waved as the elderly woman turned and strode briskly up the driveway. She watched her go, still marvelling at such positive results, and then walked towards her unit feeling reinvigorated. She had *leads*. She carried the mail into the dining room and dropped it on the table before pulling out a chair and flopping down into it.

The results of her little stroll up the driveway could not have been better. Not only did she get to meet the next door neighbour, but it seemed she now had a willing accomplice. Mrs Jarvis might be a trifle odd, what with her sunken veins and her penchant for vampires and geriatric poker games, but she was definitely entertaining. And, most importantly, she was a conduit to the local elderly.

Kate slid the bundle of mail towards her and levered off the elastic band. She leafed through the envelopes and, rather to her surprise, found one with a computerised label addressed to her. There was no return address on the reverse. Kate slid a fingernail underneath the flap and tore the envelope open, then unfolded the single sheet of buff-coloured paper within. It was an invitation.

*The presence of Katherine Rose Painter
is requested for dinner this Friday*

At: 23 Haverlock Lane, Lysterfield

Dress: preferred (as there will be small children present)

Kate read through the invitation the first time with surprise, and the second time with a smile. Her day just kept getting better.

TEN

Dear Dad, I was thinking about when I started school and you used to walk me all the way to the corner and then watch me go the rest. Remember? Then the next year Angie started as well, so Uncle Frank would sometimes walk us. But instead he'd stroll right up to the gates, amongst all the mothers, and he'd say, 'Good morning, ladies!' If any of them were dressed in tennis gear or netball skirts, he'd clap his hand to his heart and say something like, 'Oh, my dear lady, haven't you just made my day!' But the point is, somehow I realised that while he wasn't fazed by their company at all, you hated it. And that was the reason you didn't go any further than the corner – because you wanted to avoid them. En masse. Maybe you found them intimidating? But for the first time I saw you as vulnerable, although I wouldn't have been able use that word.

PS: How's this: Somehow Sophie had always thought that the choice she made on her wedding day was the last life-changing choice she would ever be asked to make. It was only now that she realised how young she had been. How naive.

The entrance to the under-the-house area was festooned with spiders' webs, but fortunately none seemed to house any still-living occupants. Kate flicked on the light and then, using a twig, wound the more obvious webs up like fairy floss and flung them away before continuing. The area was in the front of the house, predominantly beneath the main bedroom and lounge room, and alongside the garage. Particle board had been installed to separate this high-ceilinged section from the remainder, where the ground sloped dramatically upwards. At the same time Sam had also concreted it, so that it now formed an easily accessible, large and very functional storage area.

Over the years, it had become the repository for all the flotsam and jetsam spun from their lives. But last year an enormous clean-up had taken place and now everything was either boxed or stacked neatly along the interior wall of the area, with bicycles and other wheeled toys hanging from hooks set into the overhead joists. Leaving ample room for the household of goods that had arrived after June.

It was towards these goods that Kate was now moving, picking her way carefully past the concrete stumps of the house. The furniture was stacked at the far end, wrapped in plastic sheeting; a dimly-lit mountain range of odd shapes and sizes. Slightly more uniform was the brickwork-stack of tea-chests and boxes that lined the wall to her left. Kate stopped at the point where the stack began and manoeuvred a tea-chest off the top row, lifting it down to floor level.

She had been putting this task off ever since she realised the necessity of it. Possibly the only reason she was finally here now was that, having had to come over to Lysterfield for Sam's paperwork and then for the invited dinner, it was difficult to justify *not* doing it.

So Kate took a deep breath and levered the cardboard flaps open with a spray of dust. She retrieved a spiral notebook from within. Each of the notebook pages was numbered, in Oscar's meticulous handwriting, with every number corresponding to a box. Then underneath was printed a list of contents right down to the incidentals, such as *stationery oddments* and *ugly white eggcup with scalloped edge*.

The vast majority, including the *ugly white eggcup with scalloped edge*, was destined for the local charity shop. But last June neither Kate nor Angie had been up to the task of sorting so, rather than risk discarding something sentimental, Sam and Oscar had simply packed the entire contents of the house and stored the lot. And Kate knew she had Oscar to thank for the fact that everything was so beautifully itemised. If it had been up to Sam, she would now have had to trawl through each box, and each memory. Instead, she had merely to consult the notebook, which itself was included in the contents for box number one, and her search was finetuned considerably.

Kate ran her thumb quickly down each list of contents, flipping pages until she reached box number six, which contained *assorted paperwork from James's desk*. She made a mental note and then continued until she came to *manilla concertina file* in box twelve and then, finally, *shoebox with papers from Frank's wardrobe* in box sixteen.

Kate moved slowly down the row of boxes, checking the numbers that were marked boldly with texta on the sides. Number six was one of the smaller boxes and was, of course, securely wedged into the centre of a stack. Kate had some difficulty extricating it, especially as it was heavier than it looked, and then even more difficulty rearranging the others without it. Finally she wiped a grimy hand across her forehead and then, with her foot, pushed box number six in short dusty bursts until it was midway to the doorway.

Box number twelve was on a top row so Kate lifted it down and thumped it onto the dust-strewn concrete. She stared at it for a while, wishing she had kept the spiral notebook out so that she could read what else was in the box. Then at least she could have been prepared if the file was tucked beneath something that would bring memories crashing down around her, like a favourite book, or his bone-china coffee-mug, or that chequered dressing-gown.

'Hey! Whatcha doing?'

Kate jerked her head rapidly towards the doorway, straining a muscle in her neck. Leaning in with a hand on either side of the frame was Jacob, his features unreadable with the sunlight at his back.

'Would you stop *doing* that!' she snapped, massaging the base of her skull.

'What'd I do?'

'Sneaking up on me! Giving me such a fright!'

Jacob stepped inside. He was grinning. 'Who me? Never.'

'Humph,' retorted Kate, displaying a fine grasp of riposte as her scowl slowly slid into a grin itself. She turned her head as far as it would go to the left, and then the right, and felt the muscle loosen with relief. 'You'll regret it when I have a heart attack and you have to look after me while I recuperate.'

'Only if you survived,' replied Jacob, a little too matter-of-factly for his mother's liking. 'Anyway, so what *are* you doing?'

'Just looking for some stuff.'

'In *Grandpa's* things?'

'Yes. Some papers I need . . .' Kate trailed off for moment and then she looked back up at Jacob. 'Listen, want to give me a hand?'

'Not really.'

'Well, you can anyway. It won't kill you.'

'That's the last time I come investigate when I hear noises.' Jacob frowned at her accusingly. 'This is what you get when you try to do the right thing.'

'Good god, Jake! I'm not asking you to build the Taj Mahal,' snapped Kate crossly. 'I only want you to get a couple of things out of a couple of bloody boxes. You won't even raise a sweat!'

'Why didn't you just say so, then?' Jacob's voice immediately became, for him, relatively cheerful. 'Whatcha want me to do?'

Kate closed her eyes and counted to ten quickly. Then she took a deep breath and opened them again, only to find Jacob looking at her expectantly. She took another breath and then spoke evenly: 'I'd like you to find box sixteen and look through it till you find a shoebox full of papers. Then put that box back neatly and look through this one here,' Kate kicked a foot at it. 'And find a manilla concertina file.'

'A what what?'

'A manilla concertina . . . just look for something that might hold papers.'

Jacob looked at her curiously. 'So what's all this in aid of anyway?'

'A bit of research, that's all,' said Kate airily. She moved past Jacob and started pushing box number six up to the doorway, leaving skid marks of dirt across the concrete. Outside it was far warmer than it had been under the house, and by the time Kate had half carried, half pushed the box down to the driveway and manoeuvred it into the back seat of her car, her face was shiny with perspiration.

Back under the house again, she took a moment to enjoy the lower temperature and the feel of it tightening her skin. Further up, Jacob had already located the shoebox and was now squatting down, methodically removing items from number twelve. He glanced up as he heard his mother approach.

'Hey, do you reckon I could use this lamp?' Jacob carefully held up the green banker's lamp. 'It's just going to waste down here.'

Kate stared at the lamp. 'I don't know. You might break it.'

'I'd be real careful. Promise. It reminds me of Grandpa.'

'Oh.' Kate glanced at her son but he was gazing at the lamp, almost reverently. 'Well, I suppose so. But you *must* be careful.'

'Yeah, no problem.' The reverent expression disappeared instantly. He laid the lamp down across the shoebox and then continued taking items from the box, clearly enjoying himself. Next was the two-pronged brass candelabra that used to sit on top of the lounge room bookshelf, and then the square carriage clock that sat by it, with the minute hand that had to be tightened every few months, otherwise it would dangle loosely at half-past whatever. Unable to move forward at all.

As he removed each item, Jacob glanced up at his mother with a smile that spoke of shared reminiscences. *Remember where Grandpa had this? Or that?* Kate smiled back, tightly. Siren-like, the memories beckoned with promised warmth, but the thickness of her pain kept them at bay. She massaged her temples lightly. Jacob laid the carriage clock gently by the banker's lamp and then pulled out the medi-alert that she had given to her father. It fitted in the palm of his hand and he stared at it for a moment before laying it aside. Then he drew a stack of framed photographs from the box. He rocked back on his haunches and grinned at her as he lifted the first photograph and examined it. She could see that it was the sepia-toned portrait of her paternal grandparents that had always sat, with a collection of other framed photos, by her father's bed. In the room at the end of the passage.

'I'm going back,' said Kate suddenly. 'Could you just bring the things in with you when you're finished?'

Jacob held the photo up. 'I was going to ask you . . .'

'Later, okay? I really need a shower.' Kate gave him another tight smile and then left before the questions started. Because it was just too damn hard to find the answers.

'Can someone pass the salt over?'

'How do you know you even *need* salt?' asked Shelley, looking at Jacob's plate critically. 'You haven't tasted anything yet.'

'I just know, okay?'

'Here you go.' Caleb picked up the salt shaker and tossed it underhand across the table, a spray of salt marking its flight path. Jacob caught it deftly and flicked a sneer across at his sister. She, however, was now staring at her plate in horror.

'You idiot! Look what you've done! You've got salt all over my food!'

'Come on, Shell,' said Sam mildly. 'There's barely anything there.'

'There's enough! Do you *know* how much fluid retention salt causes?'

'Pity it doesn't cause verbal retention,' muttered Jacob, liberally sprinkling salt over his meal, and the area surrounding his plate.

'You think you're *so-oo* smart, don't you?'

'That's enough!' Sam banged a fist down on the table and glared at his offspring. 'Christ, I am *sick* of you two!'

'Quite like them myself,' commented Caleb. Then he grinned. 'You know – U2, the band? Get it?'

Kate didn't bother responding. She turned to Shelley. 'Apart from the fact this is getting *very* old for the rest of us, have you ever asked yourself what sort of example you're setting for Emma?'

Shelley opened her mouth, and then closed it as she glanced across at her daughter, who was sitting next to her in the highchair and watching

Sam's clenched fist with fascination. Sensing everybody's attention, she lifted up her own hand, made a fist and then thumped it down on the tray several times. The sound it made was nowhere near as loud as Sam's, but it clearly met her expectations because she chuckled gleefully. As she raised it once more, Shelley leant over and took her daughter's hand, spreading out the fingers with some effort.

'No, Emma. No banging. No.'

'God, they copy things quickly, don't they?' asked Caleb cheerfully.

Shelley picked up the bowl of roughly chopped vegetables that was on the table near Emma and held it up. 'Dinner, Em? Yum, yum.'

Kate watched with a mix of frustration and fondness as Shelley started to feed the baby, pausing every so often to take a mouthful of her own meal. They were all seated in the dining room, which in itself was a fairly rare occurrence nowadays. While sit-down meals had been the norm as the children were growing up, over the years they had gradually been replaced by a type of counter service. Where dinner was announced, and collected, and spirited away. Then once a week Kate would demand the return of her crockery from various rooms and the dishwasher would groan under the weight of the load. She knew it wasn't terribly family friendly, or even very hygienic, but it was easy. And sometimes easy was all she had.

But Sam had excelled himself tonight. Not only had he managed to gather everybody together, but the meal itself was delicious. Fettuccine with a garlicky tomato sauce and slivers of parmesan, a tossed salad with Italian dressing, and an alfoil-wrapped loaf of garlic bread, dripping with melted butter. The airconditioner hummed steadily in the background, taking the edge off what had been a very warm day.

'So what's it like living with Auntie Angie, Mum?' asked Caleb, tearing off a piece of garlic bread. 'Must be like being a kid again, hey?'

'Not quite.' Kate smiled at the thought. 'She was easier to push around then.'

'I can't imagine her like that,' said Shelley. 'I mean, at the shop she's so organised and in charge.'

Sam grinned across the table at Kate. 'I think it was more a case of your mother *thinking* she was pushing Angie around, when really Angie was just smiling and nodding, then doing exactly what she wanted anyway.'

'True.' Kate returned the grin, and it felt personal. Like it was saying much more than just the words being uttered.

'So how's the writing going then?' asked Sam casually.

'Good, good. Getting there.'

Caleb looked at her. 'What're you going to write about? Us?'

'You can write about me if you like,' suggested Shelley generously, winding fettuccine around her fork. 'You know, girl desperately seeks meaning in life.'

'But girl limited in choices due to earlier impregnation,' added Jacob.

Shelley bounced up out of her chair and jabbed her fork in his direction, pasta sliding off onto the table. 'Christ, I've *had* it with you!'

'Enough!' snapped Sam, although his glare was centred on Jacob.

'Well, this is fun,' commented Caleb. 'We should do it more often.'

Shelley sat down again, staring angrily across the table at her youngest brother, who blithely ignored her.

Silence fell as everybody concentrated on their meals and the hum of the airconditioner seemed even louder. Kate surreptitiously glanced around at her family, glad to be there but also glad that she wasn't going to be there for too long. The knowledge that the unit was waiting, with its tidiness and peace and *stillness*, transformed any flickers of irritation into a wry amusement. It was like watching a play, without having to actively play a part. Or even stay till the end.

'So what did you want with Grandpa's stuff?' asked Jacob suddenly.

Kate blinked, caught by surprise. 'Um, just some bits I needed. For research.'

The others were now staring at Kate too, each wearing an identical look of surprise. Sam was the first to speak: 'You went through your father's boxes?'

'Not all of them,' said Kate, feeling inexplicably defensive. 'Just a couple.'

'What for?' Sam paused as he made an effort to school his expression towards indifferent curiosity. He pushed some fettuccine around his plate and shrugged. 'I'm just interested, that's all.'

'Me too,' added Shelley.

Caleb grinned. 'Me three.'

'She got a shoebox and a folder thing full of papers and a whole box. I dunno what was in that,' said Jacob helpfully.

'For goodness sake!' Kate fanned her defensiveness into annoyance. 'Do I have to explain my every move around here? If you *must* know, I'm just doing a little family history research. And I needed some of his papers. Is that okay with everyone?'

'Shoot, Mum, calm down.' Shelley put up a hand as if to ward off her mother's psychopathy.

'Do you mean like genealogy?' asked Caleb.

'Something like that.'

Caleb looked interested. 'Show me when you're done, okay? That stuff's great.'

'And let me know if you discover I'm adopted,' said Shelley, staring at the ceiling as if bored with the whole proceedings. 'I'd really like to know.'

Sam sent her an irritated glance. 'I think your mother would have already had an inkling, don't you?'

'Yeah, but we live in hope,' said Jacob.

'That's *it*.' Shelley stood up, thinning her lips almost to the point of absence, and hefted her surprised daughter out of the highchair. Emma immediately began to struggle, reaching a chubby, orange-smeared hand down for a piece of vegetable.

Sam looked at her wearily. 'Come on, Shell.'

'No, I've had it with him. And you *never* tell him off. It's bloody ridiculous.' Shelley glared accusingly at her father and then stalked across the room to the sliding door, which she wrenched open with a force that sent it shooting back on the tracks after she passed through. Jacob got up and helpfully closed it all the way.

'Why do you have to do that?' asked his father evenly.

'Coz otherwise the flies'll get in.'

'You know what I mean.'

Jacob shrugged an answer and then stood behind his chair, staring down at his near-empty plate. 'Okay if I go now?'

'You might as well,' replied Sam sardonically. He watched him leave. 'And thanks very much.'

Caleb, who had taken no notice whatsoever of the preceding events, laid his cutlery across his plate with a clatter and then beamed at his parents. 'That was *delicious*.'

'My pleasure,' replied Sam, looking at him rather nonplussed.

'And lovely to see you here, Mum. Been missing you.' Caleb stood up and leant forward to drop a kiss on the top of his mother's head. She felt her hair part softly under his breath. 'I'll have to come round and visit soon, won't I?'

'Absolutely. Whenever you like.'

'Cool. I'll be in my room if you need me.'

Kate watched him as he walked off, and then turned to her husband. They looked at each other for a few moments and then both started laughing at the same time.

Sam shook his head. 'Maybe they're *all* adopted.'

'No such luck. I'm afraid we're totally responsible.'

'Bugger.'

'And it's probably too late to adopt them *out*, as well.'

'Double bugger.'

Kate grinned across at him, warmed by their rapport. 'Listen, Sam. This was lovely, really lovely. Thank you.'

'Even with the entertainment?' He sighed and then shook his head. 'I don't know what's up with those two. They just can't seem to get on, can they?'

'Not at all,' replied Kate pensively. 'I think it's because they're both frustrated at the moment. Shelley with her job and Jacob with where he's going. So they take it out on each other. Easy targets.'

'What's wrong with Shell's job?' asked Sam with surprise.

'She's been telling us that she hates being a waitress for years!' Kate smiled, rather amazed. 'Don't you ever listen?'

'Not when I can avoid it.' Sam continued to push the fettuccine around his plate and then looked back at Kate. 'So what about Jake then? If he's so unhappy, why doesn't he just get a bloody job himself?'

'Because he doesn't want a bloody job himself. He wants a career.'

'In *computer* games?' asked Sam, his voice husky with disdain. 'Well, good to see he's got his feet firmly planted. Why the hell can't he be more like his brother?'

'Ssh!' Kate automatically glanced behind her to make sure that Jacob hadn't heard this last exchange, and then she turned back to Sam with a frown. 'That's half the problem, dimwit! He'd *love* to be more like his brother!'

Sam nodded slowly and then sighed again. 'Yeah, I know. It's just frustrating, that's all. And don't call me dimwit.'

Kate smiled with casual apology. She looked across the table, which was scattered with plates and cutlery and errant pasta and garlic bread crumbs. 'Shall we?'

'We shall.' Sam pushed back his chair and stood. Then he paused as he glanced across at Kate. 'You staying here tonight?'

'Do you want me to?'

Sam shrugged. 'I just thought it'd be easier. You know, if we wanted to take a bottle of wine out onto the decking and continue the evening.'

'That's true.' Kate pretended to mull this over. 'But you still haven't said if you *want* me to.'

Sam laughed and rolled his eyes. 'God, woman, you make it hard!'

'Ah! Then in that case it *would* be easier if I stayed.'

Grinning, Sam reached across the table and grabbed Kate's hand, raising it up to his mouth and giving it a quick kiss. 'Then it's settled. You're staying.'

'Seems that way.' Kate reclaimed her hand, feeling the skin cool quickly where the kiss had landed. They started to gather the dishes together in companionable silence and Kate realised that she wasn't just doing Sam a favour by staying, she was also doing herself one. She *wanted* to stay for the night, to enjoy his company and his partnership, but the choice was made easy by the fact that it *was* a choice. And escapism was only twenty minutes away.

ELEVEN

> *Dear Dad, I've given Jacob your green banker's lamp. They all miss you, you know, but I wonder if he misses you the most. Maybe because he spent so much time with you last year. Sometimes I think he'd like to talk to me but I always change the subject. It's just too hard right now. Maybe soon. Remember when I asked you about my mother? Not about the stories you used to tell, but how she was when she died. That sort of thing. So you took me for a walk along the creek, and you showed me how to skim stones. And I'm sure we talked about her because I remember that's why we went for the walk, but I don't really remember what was said. So maybe you did what I'm doing now. Changing the subject. Deflecting.*
>
> *PS: How about this:* She paused by the child's bed for a long time that night. So long that she was in danger of being too late. Wondering if that was a choice in itself.

It was the following Monday before Kate was given the chance to start sorting through the things she had reclaimed from underneath the Lysterfield house. But even then, with the unit to herself, she hesitated. The main problem was that the purloining of her uncle's shoebox had reawakened her worm of doubt, now swollen with guilt as well. Because this had belonged to *Angie's* father, not her own, and she knew that by taking it she had stepped over an invisible line. She soothed the worm by assuring it, and herself, that her appropriation of the shoebox was more in the nature of a *loan*, so temporary that it barely counted. Besides there would probably be no need to even open it; instead she'd find what she needed elsewhere.

Nevertheless, even after she decided to ignore the shoebox for now, Kate sat on the couch and simply stared at the cardboard box and concertina file on the coffee table before her. It occurred to her that this little trip into history might be like driving slivers of bamboo down behind her fingernails, into the puckered mass of nerve endings, and then lighting them and letting the flames cauterise what feeling she had left. Or like childbirth, which was even more painful. And maybe her search might net her some facts she didn't really want to know. Like maybe there never was a Sophie Painter, maybe Angie had been adopted. Or even stolen.

Kate grinned and then lifted up the concertina file before she could analyse the moment any further. She flipped open the plastic catch so that the compartments all fell open, forming a semicircle across her lap. Each section was alphabetised and it did not take her long to realise that the contents all related to vegetables. Receipts for fertiliser and insecticides, instructions for assorted grafting methods, newspaper clippings showing ridiculously large produce, flyers from rural shows, accounts from nurseries for various purchases.

Smiling again, but this time at the irony, Kate went through each section methodically, just in case something important had slipped in amongst the vegetable-related matters. But her father had been meticulous and, unless she wanted to start her own vegetable patch, the concertina file was basically useless.

She pushed the file back together and put it down next to the couch, then turned to the cardboard box. Dust sprinkled around like fine powder as she opened it. She peered inside, confused for a moment at the expanse of maroon leather, and then her breath caught as she recognised it. It was her father's leather desk set. A rectangular mat with brassy-gold corners, a matching envelope vice and a cylindrical pen holder. She lifted each object out and placed them gently on the floor, resisting the memory of her father sitting at his desk, accounts spread before him as he reached for a pen.

Underneath the desk set was a metal tin that had once held assorted chocolates. It rattled interestingly as she lifted it out but, when she prised the lid off, held only a large assortment of biros and pencils, some still in their packaging. Kate put it down with the desk set, returned to the box and took out the gilt-framed black and white photograph of her parents that had always sat by the lamp on her father's desk. She wiped the glass down with an edge of her T-shirt. They were standing on the steps of the courthouse after their wedding, her mother in a full-skirted white dress and holding a bouquet of long-stemmed lilies. Standing close, but not quite touching, was her father, and he seemed so impossibly *young*, squinting in the sunshine with one hand in the pocket of his baggy, high-waisted trousers.

Kate blinked, and then squeezed her eyes shut for a second. Photos of her mother at around this age brought a dull sense of loss, but no great sense of nostalgia. Because Kate had no real memories of her, she always perceived her as if frozen in time and, as such, photos like these seemed rather apt. But her father was different, *these* drove the bamboo slivers in further. Especially when her mind juxtaposed this image of youth and health and hope with the man he had become at the end. The expression on his face. *That* was shocking.

Nevertheless she was going to place this photo where it belonged, back on her father's desk. She reached over and laid it carefully against a couch cushion so that it was facing her. Then she turned her attention back to the box, and hit paydirt. Layer upon layer of papers filled the bottom half. Some loose, some stapled, some in large, mustard-coloured envelopes with addresses crossed out and her father's fine cursive script printed over the top.

Before she could change her mind, Kate started with the envelopes. She plucked each out, straightened them into a pile on her lap and then started flicking through. Irrelevant ones, like *Petrol receipts: 1971 – 1979* and *Gas & Fuel: paid accounts*, she placed with the desk set and soon she was left with just one envelope *Certificates: assorted*, which she tossed over onto Angie's armchair. Next were the loose papers.

Three-quarters of an hour later, Kate had checked each paper in the box and still had not come up with anything that would help with her research. She found plenty of personal items, like her own childhood drawings, report cards, and even letters that she had written from overseas. After the first few of these, when she felt her emotions begin to swarm uncomfortably, Kate forced herself to adopt a purely clinical approach. Check for relevance but ignore detail, then put to one side. Over and over. When she finally finished, Kate collected everything together, except the framed photo and the envelope of certificates, and repacked the box. Then she sat back and stared at it with a frown.

Where were all the private papers? Like letters to and from her mother whilst they were courting, or cards from special occasions, or her mother's own papers. Diaries, or postcards from relatives, or even the death notices from the newspaper when she died. Instead it seemed that her father had religiously kept every article regarding deformed vegetables that he could possibly find, and yet not one single newspaper clipping mourning his wife's death.

Kate shook her head with disbelief, and then her expression cleared as it all began to make sense. Obviously he had been too distressed. And he had deliberately chosen not to keep any reminders of her life and, especially, her death. Which, of course, had also been the death of his second child. Perhaps it had simply been easier that way. Swallowing painfully, Kate looked down at the shoebox on the floor. It was a burnt-orange colour with diagonal black stripes across the lid and the words: *Dobsons! Over 200 stores nation-wide!* The bottom four corners had all been scuffed, with the orange peeled back to reveal soft grey cardboard, and one entire side had come loose, being only held in place by the snugness of the lid. It looked so innocuous, sitting there, that Kate reasoned it couldn't possibly hold anything terribly personal. In fact the chances were that it was exactly the same as her father's, and the mystery was in the concept rather than the contents.

She lifted it onto the coffee table and continued to stare at it, waiting while her guilt was steadily eroded by the very *ordinariness* of the box and the fact that, so far, she had found nothing of real note. Finally Kate took a deep breath and gently prised the lid off, the split side immediately opening like a drawbridge and spilling papers out across the coffee table. Without moving, Kate cast her eyes over them and was immediately and uncomfortably reminded that her extroverted, flamboyant, jovial uncle had been a very different man from her reticent, self-contained father. Because this man had kept everything. She could see tiny dog-eared photographs, and thin-papered letters, and certificates, and postcards. An entire life contained within an orange-striped shoebox.

And Kate also realised that it was too late to go back now. Her curiosity alone would not allow it. Besides, she had already stepped over the line so she might as well see what it had to offer. She reached forward and delicately plucked a letter from within the pile and held it up to read the spidery script that filled half the page.

Dear Frank,
I hope this letter finds you well. Your father and I are both well. I must tell you that I have written to the Padre there to request he encourage you to write to us. I have sent you three letters and have not heard back once. We would like to hear that you are well or not. Also we need to know when you will be getting out as your father wants to look for some good land but not if you no longer wish to go into partnership with him. Write back soon.
Your loving mother.

With a shock, Kate realised that the letter was from her paternal grandmother, who had died when she was only a baby. She read through the letter again, searching for clues as to where her uncle had been when the letter had been written but there was no address or date. She put it down on her lap and peered at the other papers across the coffee table, soon finding another with the same writing.

Dear Frank,

I hope this letter finds you well. Your father and I are both well. I received your letter yesterday and was v. pleased to hear from you after so long. Now I can sleep easy. First I must tell you some good news. Your father has found some v. reasonably priced land in Ferntree Gully that he says will be excellent. There is a house already there but it needs fixing. James has come down from Mt Isa and is willing to help until you get out. If all goes well, we should be living there when you return.

Here is all the news from here: Jean Tapscott from next door has had another baby girl, which makes five girls with no boys at all. They called her Patricia, which I am not v. fond of. Your auntie Val visited last week and they are all well there. She tells us Thomas is now engaged to Sophie Wharton. Last week James ran over poor Bessie with the truck but fortunately little damage was done and he managed to straighten the fender himself. That is all the news from here. Please write back soon as I do not want to be forced to contact the Padre again.
Your loving mother.

Kate stared at the letter, hoping fervently that poor Bessie had been a dog or a cat and not one of Jean Tapscott's numerous daughters. The threatening tone of the last sentence was also slightly disturbing. *I do not want to be forced to contact the Padre again.* She tried matching it to the sepia portrait that had sat by her father's bed, with her grandmother staring balefully at the world with tight, narrow features, and found that it fitted. Perhaps it was just as well the woman had not lived long enough to pen some of these missives to either her or Angie. Therapy had not been widely available during her childhood.

Kate laid the two letters down and fanned out the other papers across the coffee table, searching for more of the same. But it seemed that her uncle had only kept these two letters from his mother. Could these possibly have been the pick of the bunch? But, more to the question, where had he been? Twice his mother mentioned him 'getting out' from somewhere, which, if Kate didn't know her uncle better, she would have thought suggested incarceration. But that was patently ridiculous.

Leaning forward, Kate collected a handful of documents and dropped them in her lap before going through them. These were mainly certificates. Angie's birth, her baptism, various school certificates and a marriage certificate. Between Francis Vivian Painter (b. 1935) and Sophie Marie Wharton (b. 1940) on 3 March 1958. Kate's eyes flew over the bride's name one more time and then she scrabbled by her side for her grandmother's letters again. She quickly scanned through the second, pausing when she came to Thomas and his engagement – to Sophie Wharton. It *had* to be the same girl. So it seemed that Sophie had been engaged to somebody else before she had married Uncle Frank. And that someone had been well known to the family; perhaps, judging by his seeming familiarity to Auntie Val, even a relative.

Progress at last. Kate smiled with satisfaction and, putting the pile of certificates by her side, took another handful. These were odds and ends. Small white-framed photos of smiling men in shades of grey, broad-hatted women, one of a baby she thought might be Angie propped against a wooden walker and smiling broadly at the camera. Kate flipped through them and laid them aside. But the last one caught her attention. It showed her uncle as a young man, wearing some type of coveralls and standing in front of a high concreted wall, the top of which was made up of circles of barbed wire.

Kate stared at it, her smile now gone. It had to be an institution of some type, most likely a jail. Which, together with the letters, meant that her uncle most probably *had* been incarcerated. *This* was what he needed to 'get out' from, and this was where his mother had written, receiving no answers. Until she had been forced to write to the padre. And this was why Kate's own father, James, had returned from Mt Isa to help out. It was almost unbelievable. Uncle Frank just didn't seem the type. Certainly he had been a bit of a reprobate at times, but *jail*?

Angie was going to be devastated. Still holding the small, incriminating photo, Kate leant back and stared up at the ceiling, imagining how it must have been for Frank's parents, and for his brother James. A son, a brother, a criminal. But maybe the crime had been relatively minor. Like running over poor Bessie, or one of her sisters. Maybe he had even been innocent. People were wrongfully convicted, after all. Sometimes. Whatever it was, it can't have been *too* bad because soon afterwards Sophie Wharton had thrown over her fiancé and married Francis Painter instead.

Kate sat up again and, after one last look, dropped the photo and then pushed everything off her lap onto the couch. Then she set to the remainder of the papers with a vengeance. Somewhere there had to be an explanation, maybe even a summary of charges or a sentencing report. But after twenty minutes of searching Kate was forced to admit defeat. There were other photos and letters, some scribbled notes, a couple of postcards, even a valentine's card from someone called Margie – but there was nothing else that referred to Frank's sojourn inside, or even to Sophie Wharton.

Carefully, Kate replaced all of the papers into the shoebox and, pressing the split edge in, fitted the lid back on tightly. It looked like it had never been touched. But she reasoned that it was even more important to continue the research now, for Angie's sake. Find some answers. Kate got up and crossed over to the armchair, picking up the dull-gold envelope containing her father's certificates and then sliding them out. As expected there was her own birth certificate and her mother's death certificate, together with a certificate registering the business name of *Painter Bros. Fruit & Vegetables*, a roadworthy certificate for a long-deceased Bedford truck, and her parents' marriage certificate. This document was considerably less decorative than her uncle's, but Kate read the names with even greater fondness: James Edward Painter (b. 1934) and Rose Anne Kimber (b. 1938), joined together in matrimony on 21 January 1960.

It took Kate a few moments of staring at the certificate with the niggling feeling that something wasn't quite right before the penny dropped. Her parents were married on 21 January 1960, and she was born on 30 April the same year. Three months, one week and two days later. It was a shotgun wedding, and a rather sluggish shotgun at that.

Kate sat down on the armrest of the chair slowly. She had been brought up on stories of love at first sight at a local dance, and a joyful white wedding, and how they had hoped for a baby as soon as possible. Well, it seemed that the latter had certainly come true. No wonder they had married at the courthouse. After procrastinating for several months, there had clearly been no time for anything else. And no wonder her mother was clutching those enormous lilies, they hid the swelling evidence of their inability to contain themselves. Kate read the certificate through again, but the date remained the same.

She slid all the certificates back into the envelope while she tried to work out why she was so upset. It wasn't like she and Sam hadn't jumped the gun with their own premarital activities. Or even that those particular premarital activities were the first she had ever indulged in. But the issue wasn't really about her parents having hit third base prior to their marriage, or even a reluctance to marry at all, it was more about the wondrous tales her father had told her while she was growing up. Where her mother was like a beautiful princess whom Kate had always imagined in Cinderella-at-the-ball type clothes: silver-edged, snow-white chiffon floating as she danced. And then there was her father, young and handsome, and determined to woo her and win her despite the odds.

How did one reconcile that with the image of the two of them, huffing and panting in the back seat of some old car, with the chiffon dress hiked up and the windows cloudy with the rapidity of their breathing? It was probably that Bedford truck, which wouldn't even have *had* a back seat. Just an ancient suspension being put to the test.

So if he was able to turn *that* story into something that sounded wonderfully romantic, then what else might have received similar treatment? What else wasn't quite what it seemed? What else, of him, had she never known? And, worst of all, how was she ever to find the answers now that he wasn't even around to ask?

TWELVE

> *Dear Dad, remember when I was trying to save up for those rollerskates and I asked you to buy them for me and I'd pay them off? But you just gave me this big lecture on 'deferred gratification'. Well, that seems a little hypocritical now, doesn't it? I must admit when I found out yesterday I was pretty floored, but I've slept on it now and it doesn't seem quite so earth-shaking. Maybe it just makes you both seem more human. Fallible. Although I do find it hard to imagine you being so rash – maybe my mother was more the impulsive type and you went along for the ride (no pun intended). And what's all this with Uncle Frank being in jail? Then pinching someone else's fiancée? Talk about the swinging sixties. And what about your mother? If she got so nasty over a few missed letters, what did she have to say about all* these *shenanigans?*
>
> *PS: I'm thinking now that I might write the book as an investigation. Maybe with flashes of Sophie breaking through as the story unfolds. It's less personal then, and I won't feel as much like a usurper. That sounds better, doesn't it?*

'I'm off now.' Angie picked up her handbag from the dining room table. 'Any ideas what you'd like for dinner tonight?'

Kate shrugged. 'Whatever. I'm not fussed.'

'Okay then. How about Indian? I *love* pappadams!' Angie put up a hand. 'And before you start going on about my diet, it's under control. See, it's not so much *what* you eat, as the portion sizes. That's the key.'

'Sounds fair.'

Angie looked at her cousin searchingly. 'Are you okay? You were very quiet last night and you don't seem much better this morning.'

'I'm fine.' Kate wrapped her hands around her coffee mug and tried to appear relatively normal. 'I'm just a bit frustrated, that's all.'

'And here was I thinking Friday night put paid to that little problem.'

'Ha, ha. I meant with the writing.'

Angie grinned. 'I know. Just trying to inject a little levity. Tell you what, I'll bring heaps of Indian food home with me and we'll talk about your writer's block all evening. Come up with some solutions. How does that sound?'

'That's fine,' said Kate quickly. 'I'm sure I'll think of something today.'

'Okay, I'll keep my fingers crossed.' Angie held up two crossed fingers as a demonstration. 'But I'll still bring lots of Indian home just in case.'

Kate mustered up a smile as she nodded. Then she watched her cousin bounce out of the room and, shortly afterwards, the front door slammed behind her. It was true that she had been rather quiet the previous evening but that had not been so much to do with what she had discovered, as the inability to discuss it. As long as she could remember, they had discussed anything and everything. No secrets. So to hoard these incredible nuggets of information, and not be able to show them, was very difficult.

Kate finished her coffee and went upstairs to shower and dress before it was time to head next door. It was now even more important that she get some answers from Mrs Jarvis's poker cronies because, instead of answers, all she had succeeded so far was to collect more questions. Like who was Thomas? Why had Sophie Wharton thrown him over? When, where and why had her uncle spent time in jail? Had her parents even *known* each other before their little roll in the hay, or the vegetable patch, or the Bedford? Had there even been any love at first sight involved?

Forty minutes later Kate was freshly showered and dressed casually in khaki-green pedal pushers and a sleeveless shirt. After a warm night the temperature outside was already in the low thirties, promising a very hot, humid day. Kate shut the door behind her and walked along the edge of the driveway over to the next door unit. The front door was already open and she could see through the screen door, which was made up of swirls of white iron-work and matching mesh. She pressed the door-bell and listened to the sounds of Edelweiss play out from within. Footsteps could be heard approaching and the screen door swung open.

'Kate! Come in! I was hoping you hadn't forgotten, dear.'

'Not a chance.' Kate smiled at Mrs Jarvis and moved inside. The unit was similar to Angie's, with a tiled entry and carpeted stairs leading up to the second floor. The décor, however, was very different. Where Angie had opted for relatively neutral tones, Mrs Jarvis had gone with the predominant theme of orange. A lot of it. A burnt-orange couch with brown vinyl armrests, a sturdy orange-tiled coffee table, mission-brown curtains flecked with orange, a walnut standard lamp with an orange shade. Even the three ducks flying diagonally up the wall had bright orange beaks.

Kate followed her host into the dining room, where an extension table surrounded by many chairs filled the room and a low overhead light glowed through orange glass, casting fiery highlights even into the corners that had managed to escape the colour scheme. Three elderly ladies were already sitting at the table and they looked up curiously as Kate entered.

'And here's the reason I asked you three to come early,' announced Mrs Jarvis, waving a hand proudly towards Kate. 'This is Kate. She is A Writer.'

'Well, sort of,' said Kate, feeling awkward under their impressed gaze.

'And she has some questions to ask you. For her Next Book.'

'Are we going to be interviewed?' asked one of the ladies, who was wearing a transparent lime-green visor.

'And is there any payment involved?' asked another, much shorter one, clearly sizing Kate up for potential profit.

'I'm afraid not,' replied Kate apologetically. 'But I'll definitely put you in the acknowledgements.'

The short mercenary one looked unimpressed with this offer. She pursed her lips. 'What about a free book?'

'Just ignore her,' suggested the third lady, who appeared younger than the others, but that may have been because she was also the plumpest, and her wrinkles were more padded.

'Kate's writing a book about a lady who used to live in the area,' explained Mrs Jarvis in a proprietorial tone. 'And she needs people who lived here way back then.'

'Well, that's us!' laughed the plump lady. 'Way back then is our speciality!'

'What was her name?' asked the one with the visor curiously.

'Sophie Wharton.' Kate held her breath, but all three looked back at her blankly and then at each other.

'Does that ring a bell with either of you two?' asked the plump one of the others. 'You've both been here since birth, whereas I only came as a teenager.'

The mercenary one frowned pensively. 'Well, do you know what year she was born?'

'Nineteen forty,' replied Kate.

'Hmm, I don't recall her. Is that her married name?'

'No, she married a man called Frank Painter.'

'Frank Painter!'

While Sophie's name had brought not a flicker of recognition, Frank's met with a variety of reactions. The plump lady started laughing, one hand across her ample bosom, while the visored one turned to the mercenary one with a grin. 'Well, Bev, do *you* know Frank Painter?'

'I know *of* him.'

'That's terrific!' Kate smiled with relief. 'Then you'd have also known his wife, Sophie?'

The plump one nudged her mercenary companion. 'Not as well as she knew Frank. Would that be right, Bev?'

Bev pursed her lips. 'She was a bit before my time.'

'Just as well!' chortled the visored lady, wiping her eyes.

Kate looked from one to the other and realisation dawned. With it came the unwelcome visualisation of her much-loved uncle and this short, rather sharp-featured, fiscally-focused elderly lady. She held her grimace within and tried to look sympathetic. 'I gather you, um, saw him sometimes.'

'Sometimes,' she answered reluctantly, steadfastly ignoring the amusement on either side of her. She pursed her lips again. 'But that was a while after his wife left.'

'So you never knew her then?'

'Not really. Saw her around of course, but that was about it. So it's Sophie *Painter* you're writing about then.' She paused, thinking. 'She wasn't raised here, you know. Only came when she married Frank.' She turned to the visored lady. 'Do you remember the scandal, Margie?'

'Margie?' repeated Kate, staring at the visored lady with surprise as she recalled the Valentine's Day card that had been tucked in her uncle's shoebox. Surely it couldn't be *this* Margie?

The lady in question smiled at her and then turned back to Bev. 'Didn't she run off with an old boyfriend?' She looked around the table as she continued. 'Left her baby behind as well. A little girl.'

'How terrible!' said Mrs Jarvis, clearly shocked.

'And was never heard from again,' added Bev rather melodramatically.

Margie took off her visor and polished the perspex with her sleeve. 'Poor Frank.'

Mrs Jarvis frowned. 'Are you sure it wasn't a case of . . . Foul Play?'

'Or maybe even vampires?' asked the plump lady, with a sidelong look at Mrs Jarvis. '*That* seems fairly logical.'

'Nonbeliever,' scoffed Mrs Jarvis with a smile. 'You wait. You just wait.'

'I went to primary school with Frank,' said Bev, staring off towards the orange island bench. 'Lord, he was a handful then. A real little daredevil.'

Margie refitted her visor and smiled. 'Yes, I remember. I was in the next grade up with his brother. What was his name?'

Kate's breath caught. Although she wasn't sure why she was so surprised. If these ladies knew Frank, then it was only to be expected that they also knew her own father.

'James,' said Bev with certainty. 'James Painter. Jimmy. He went out with my sister a few times. But then he went up to Mt Isa to work in the mines and she married Fred Armstrong instead. I don't think they were serious.'

'Then why did she marry him?' asked the plump lady, looking confused.

Bev sighed crossly. 'Not Fred, you numbskull. *James*.'

'I think he died last year.' Margie turned to Bev. 'Did you tell me that?'

Bev frowned pensively. 'Mmm. I think there was some sort of tragedy about it. Can't quite remember.' She paused for a moment. 'He married the Kimber girl.'

'You're right. So he did.'

Kate felt her throat constrict and she coughed to clear it. 'Um, what was she like? Rose Kimber, I mean.'

'Good lord,' said Margie flatly.

'They say never speak ill of the dead,' added Bev, pursing her lips piously.

Kate frowned, trying to make sense of this. Edelweiss suddenly sounded out from the front door and Mrs Jarvis hurried off. The plump lady picked up a pack of cards and started shuffling them with an anticipatory smile.

'Horrid woman,' said Margie with a grimace. 'Couldn't stand her.'

'Never had a nice word to say about anyone.' Bev had clearly forgotten her never speak ill edict. 'Not even as a child. Sly little thing, she was.'

Kate stared from one to the other defensively. 'Hey! But –'

'Couldn't understand why on earth that nice man married her.'

'She trapped him, that's why. Got herself . . . you know. Poor Jimmy.'

'No wonder he never married again. A few years with Rose Kimber would have turned anyone off.' Bev shook her head and then spied Mrs Jarvis leading two more ladies into the room. 'Esme! Raine! Hope you two brought plenty of money!'

'This is Kate,' Mrs Jarvis announced to the newcomers, her jowls wobbling proudly. 'She is A Writer.'

'And she's been interviewing us,' added Margie. 'For her new book.'

'We'll be getting a free copy,' Bev chimed in, as she emptied a Tupperware container of small change onto the table. A few coins rolled away from the pile and she slapped them down. Kate pulled herself together, managing to nod politely towards the new ladies, who were placing clingwrap-covered plates onto the island bench. Then they took their seats around the table, greeting the others cheerfully.

'You ladies can get started on the first hand while I talk to Kate,' instructed Mrs Jarvis, taking Kate by the arm and ushering her into the kitchen.

'Okay then, enough chatter. Dealing 'em up!' The plump lady fanned the cards out expertly and then palmed them before flicking them downwards until they formed a neat pile which she immediately scooped up and started dealing to the others. They were all ready, with coin piles before them and avid eyes watching the cards as they slid smoothly across the table.

'Well, that went well, didn't it?' Mrs Jarvis let go of Kate's elbow and switched on an electric kettle. 'Told you I'd know someone who knew her, didn't I? Cuppa?'

Kate shook her head. 'No thanks. I'd better be getting back. But thank –'

'And I'll write their names down for you. For the acknowledgements.'

'Absolutely,' Kate mustered up a smile. 'Look, I really can't thank you enough.'

Mrs Jarvis nodded proudly as the kettle started to hum. She turned away, pulling over a large silver teapot and an orange-lidded canister.

Feeling a little like she was in shock, Kate watched her for a moment and then looked back over at the group clustered around the dining room table. Each of their faces was a study in concentration, their cards held up in a five-pointed fan. Bev was the first to move, pursing her lips as she plucked three cards from her hand and tossed them disdainfully down on the table.

'Oh, will you look at that?' One of the new women tutted at her cards and started to rearrange them. 'I'm backwards!'

Margie shook her head without looking up. 'No, dear. Just a little slow maybe.'

'Very funny, Margie. We'll see who's laughing in a minute, shall we?'

'I just wanted to say thanks again,' interrupted Kate, although she no longer felt as indebted to them as she had earlier. 'And good luck.'

'You're welcome.' Bev looked up briefly to smile, whilst the others nodded in Kate's direction. But it was clear that their minds were now elsewhere. There would be no more information coming from this quarter, even if Kate could have handled it. Which at this point she quite definitely couldn't.

The telephone was ringing as Kate let herself back into the unit, but she let Angie's answering machine pick up the call.

'Hello? Kate? It's Sam. Are you there?'

Kate was lighting the gas ring underneath the kettle. At the sound of Sam's voice, she dropped the lighter and went back towards the telephone but, by the time she lifted the receiver, he had hung up. Kate replaced the receiver with some annoyance. She would have liked to speak to him, even if she didn't share, just yet, the newly discovered information that her mother may not have been the shining light she had always been painted. She thought about ringing him back but decided against it.

She walked back into the kitchen and made herself a cup of coffee. Then stood by the sink, staring at nothing in particular, with her hands wrapped around the steaming mug for warmth. She was aware of a change around her, but wasn't sure where it had come from. The absolute stillness of the unit, which had been almost blissful, now seemed impersonal. And her solitude, instead of being luxurious, felt rather leaden and onerous. Kate took a sip of coffee and then put the mug down on the bench just as the telephone rang again. She hurried back into the lounge room. 'Hello?'

'Katherine Painter?'

'That's right,' said Kate, disappointed.

'Hi, it's Nigel Redfern from Redfern Titles Search. I'm just ringing with the information you requested. About the property in Ferntree Gully.'

Kate frowned, but only for a second, before remembering her request for details regarding That Bugger's property. She brightened up, eager for answers. 'Excellent!'

'We'll also be mailing you out a summary, for your records, but we like to give a courtesy phone call. Just in case time is important.'

Kate nodded. 'It is.'

'Well, the property that you enquired about was actually sold in 1974, to a firm of property developers, who subsequently subdivided it. But I believe your main interest was the name of the gentleman who owned the land prior to the 1974 sale?'

'That's right.'

'It was a Thomas James Painter.'

'Painter?' repeated Kate, frowning.

'That's right. He purchased the land in 1957 and owned it right through until 1974. Now, as I said, we'll be sending this out in the mail. And if you have any further queries, please don't hesitate to give us a ring.'

Kate hung up the phone and stood with her hand on the receiver, glad to have this distraction. Then she walked slowly back into the kitchen. It was all becoming clear, in a most unexpected way. It seemed that rather than her uncle being the cuckolded one, who lost his wife to a usurper, *he* was the one who had been the original usurper. Sophie Wharton had been engaged to Thomas Painter, who had probably been that Aunt Val's son and therefore a cousin of Frank's. Then *something* had happened, around the time Frank was released from jail, and she had thrown over Thomas and married Frank instead.

Kate leant against the island bench, thinking about the dates in question. She knew for a fact that Frank had been working on the Ferntree Gully land around the time her parents married, because her father had often spoken of having the choice of working with his family there, but deciding to buy the farm in Gippsland because he did not get on particularly well with his own father. By the time he returned, in 1963 when Kate was three years old, his father had passed away and he had gone into partnership with his brother.

So, given that she now knew her parents had married in 1960, and that Thomas had bought his land in 1957, both branches of the family must have purchased the neighbouring lots at around the same time. Which would make perfect sense if it weren't for the fact that one cousin had just stolen the fiancée of the other cousin. Unless . . . when they had purchased the land, the fiancée hadn't been stolen, yet.

Kate took a sip of coffee and stared pensively into the courtyard. It all fitted. Her grandparents had probably even told Aunt Val, and therefore Thomas, about the reasonably priced, excellent land in Ferntree Gully. And the young man, about to be married, had decided to establish some roots. Then later that same year, 1957, the prodigal son returned from jail, moved onto the property next door and promptly took up with the teenage fiancée. Perhaps Thomas's missing eye had begun to be a bit of a turn-off. Or maybe she was just the type who found bad boys irresistible.

By March 1958 the errant couple were married and, late the following year, her own parents were testing out the suspension of the Bedford, with rather unexpected results. Kate shook her head as she tried to imagine how it must have been for Thomas, living alone in the house he had built for his bride, right next door to the newly married couple. How bitter the man must have been. How resentful. Bad enough to lose the woman you loved to a stranger, but to family? And family whose home you could see just beyond the nearest fence? He must have felt like poking out his remaining eye for some relief.

Yet clearly he had not given up. Because, five years later, when her only child was two years old, Sophie Painter née Wharton had wandered up to the neighbouring property and made the acquaintance of her ex-fiancé all over again. Eventually deciding that her original instincts had been right on the money and absconding with her new/old paramour to places unknown.

Kate took another sip of coffee and tried to imagine how Angie was going to react to this news. In one fell swoop, her mother had been transformed from a delinquent mother with loose morals, to a teenager who had made a bad choice, and so had become the major player in a quasi-tragic romance. While there was no doubt that Sophie's maternal instincts were still questionable, to say the least, she did at least appear in a more sympathetic light. Unlike Kate's own mother.

Kate sighed, unsure where to go with this information. Did she continue to believe her father, who seemed to have played a little fast with the truth, or did she accept the opinion of Margie and Bev? Maybe they both had an axe to grind. Who knew? But one thing was certain, rather than being a pillar of the community and loved by all, her mother was heartily disliked by at least two of her peers. Who saw her as a sly child who grew into a horrid woman without a kind word to say about anyone. Eventually managing to get herself impregnated by a local man who was clearly not thinking with his head at the time.

And if even *some* of this was true, would her father really have been so devastated when she died? Or was he, perhaps, just a little relieved? Kate finished off her coffee and put the mug in the sink. No wonder her father had kept no mementoes, just his marriage certificate and her death certificate. Perhaps for reassurance that she really was gone.

Kate stared blankly towards the dining room as, almost reluctantly, she visualised a slim young woman swirling around a parquetry dance floor, holding the silver-edged hem of her white dress up with one hand. Above her, suspended from the domed ceiling, a chandelier sparkled, sending lozenges of light to play against the faces of all those who watched. Amongst them was a young man, reclining against the wall with one hand thrust into the pocket of his high-waisted trousers, trying to appear nonchalant as he watched her dance. Grace in motion. Love at first sight.

Kate played the scene, well remembered from her childhood, for the last time. Then she pirouetted the solitary dancer over to the edge of the dance floor and watched as she metamorphosed into a plain, sharp-nosed woman in an orange-toned twin-set. Who determinedly grasped the young man by the hand and, with a knowing smile, led him out of the dance hall towards the gravelled car-park and an old Bedford truck, and a soon to be hijacked future.

THIRTEEN

Dear Dad, what's going on? Are those old women just malicious? Or were all your stories just fairytales? Or maybe (I'm trying to be fair), you started the stories and then I finished them. Embellished them with imagination. Because I wanted to see her, and my only points of comparison were princesses and fairies and beautiful Disneyland heroines. Or perhaps the truth lies somewhere in between. And I've remembered something that seems strange now. I know I used to talk about my mother a lot, not because I missed her as such but because I was proud of her, like as a point of reference. But I can't remember Uncle Frank ever mentioning her name. Why not? Didn't he like her either?

PS: I've definitely decided on the investigative angle. And with the flashes of insight, I shall collaborate with Angie so that it's not just me.

Birthday parties had not been terribly common when Kate had been a child, certainly not to the extent that they were nowadays. So whenever one was on the horizon, it became quite an anticipated event. Of all the parties she had attended, Kate particularly remembered one when she was about eight years old, for a girl with the unfortunate name of Agnes Poxleitner. From the moment she entered Agnes's house, in her lemon party dress with the built-in petticoat, Kate became fascinated by the pass-the-parcel, waiting on the sideboard. It was huge, bigger than any she had seen before. Layers upon layers of newspaper making up a bundle so big that it overhung the sideboard and cast a shadow of its own. And while all the other guests ran around playing and throwing balloons, Kate stood to one side and stared at it, wondering what could be within something so magnificent.

Finally, after a rather rough game of musical chairs, Agnes's mother announced that it was time for the pass-the-parcel. The excited children were organised into a circle, sitting on the floor, while Agnes's father put a record on. The sounds of Burl Ives filled the room, with 'Chim Chim Cheree', and the huge parcel was lifted down and placed on the birthday girl's lap. Kate felt like her heart was about to burst, and she had to clasp her hands together to prevent them from reaching out and grabbing at it before the game had even begun.

For what seemed like hours, but was probably only about ten minutes, the parcel made the rounds of the circle, each child tearing off a sheet of newspaper if the music stopped while they held it. Every time it reached Kate she would hold it tightly, her fingers leaving indentations in the newspaper, as she stared wide-eyed at Agnes's father and *willed* him to stop the music so that she could tear a sheet off. But Burl Ives continued without pause and suddenly her lap would be empty as she watched the parcel continue its bumpy journey.

By the time it had shrunk to a tenth of its original size, Kate began to feel physically ill. The other children started to accompany each unwrapping with cries of 'This is it!' and 'You've got it!' But the parcel kept shrivelling and, it seemed, the music got louder. Until 'Chim Chim Cheree' was battering at Kate's head like a hammer and she didn't think the parcel would ever reach her again before the end. And then it was with the boy to her right, who held it for what seemed like forever without being told off, and Kate looked pleadingly at the adults. *Say something! Say something!* Then suddenly the parcel was on her lap and, as the girl to her left clutched, Kate slowly, slowly, lifted it. And the music stopped.

She'd won, and it was hers. Kate pulled off the last sheet of newspaper and then stared at the lumpy, silver-wrapped gift. 'Open it,' said Agnes's mother, smiling at her. So Kate had, breaking her reverie to rip open the silver with eager hands and reveal – a bag of liquorice. So surprised was she by this that it took a moment to register and then, when it did, it took an effort not to burst into tears. She didn't like liquorice, had never liked liquorice. And how could that magnificent parcel, so mysteriously huge, have held nothing more than a bag of liquorice?

Kate spent the rest of the party in a crushingly disappointed daze. Then later on, she mulishly, and rather masochistically, decided that since she had won the liquorice and it now *belonged* to her, she would eat it anyway. So she sat down, in her lemony party dress, underneath a shrub in Agnes's backyard, and determinedly ate the entire bag. Fifteen minutes later Kate staggered into the lounge room, where all the other children were feasting on fairy cakes and chocolate crackles and wobbly little jelly squares. With her hands clenched over her stomach, she made her way across to Agnes's mother, opened her mouth, and threw up a copious amount of black-studded vomit all over the woman's best shoes.

The episode became known, in the Painter household, as the Liquorice Incident. But, as memorable as the embarrassment and humiliation still were, another recollection was even more vivid. It was her father, that evening in between her frequent trips to the toilet with dreadful diarrhoea, holding her tight and telling her that sometimes what you *think* you want, above all else, was the very last thing you actually needed. So it was important to recognise that, and to think twice before you went ahead. Her Uncle Frank had simply laughed and commented that it was also important to recognise what gave you the shits, and then avoid it.

To Kate, all of the new information about her family, and particularly that regarding her mother, was like the Liquorice Incident all over again. The feeling that she had held something good, only to peel the layers off and reveal an entirely different reality. One that couldn't be wrapped back up again, not in the same way. So that now that she'd started, she had no choice but to finish. Even if it made her feel ill.

The whole thing worried at her ceaselessly, throwing up even more questions and giving her an almost constant headache. She searched through her father's papers again, with the new information in hand, but was still unable to discover anything that either proved or disproved its validity. All she had was the memories of his stories, coloured by the veracity with which he had told them. And that was what hurt the most.

At one stage Kate even drove around to her father's house, hoping that perhaps answers would come there. But, for the first time ever, she was unable to get out of the car. Instead she sat with her hands on the steering wheel, as she stared over at the vacant weatherboard, with weeds sprouting amongst the gravel of the driveway and the curtains pulled in every window, especially the last.

In the end, her wake-up call came from a rather unlikely source. A message on the answering machine heralded a couriered package of urgent editing and Kate had no choice but to stop tormenting herself, in order to get the work done. So she wrapped up the issue firmly, within sheets and sheets of cerebral newspaper, and stored it away.

It took four days of solid work, interrupted only by a flying visit from Caleb and a three-hour babysitting stint with Emma, before Kate was able to courier the manuscripts back to the publishing company. By then her masochistic desire to revisit the issue of her parents, dissecting and analysing it over and over again, had largely dissipated and the whole thing simply made her feel weary. So she made a conscious decision to leave them for now. They weren't going anywhere, after all, and could always be dusted off when the time was right.

Instead, she opted to concentrate on her original mystery, that of Sophie Wharton. And neither her parents' marriage nor her mother's personality really had anything to do with Sophie's story. They were simply peripheral landmarks that had become visible as the panorama cleared.

Accordingly, Kate spent a full day on the computer writing up all of her findings thus far. She added summaries of relevant documents and also a transcript, from memory, of her interview with the poker-playing trio next door. Last of all she drew up a timeline with proven dates in bold, and assumptions, such as the timing of her uncle's incarceration, in italics. When all this information had been safely saved, Kate took all of the items she had removed from under the Lysterfield house and put them in the boot of her car. Then, determined not to put it off, she drove them back.

It was well past five o'clock by the time she pulled up by the kerb, so Kate was rather surprised not to see Sam's car there. Shelley, she knew, would still be at *Fully Booked*, so it seemed, by the cars in the driveway, that only the boys were home. She let herself in the front door expecting to hear some sort of noise, whether it was the television, or the Playstation, or even some loud music floating out from behind somebody's closed door. But there was silence.

Kate shut the door and walked into the lounge room, jingling her keys in her hand. It was surprisingly neat, with cushions in place and magazines fanned across the coffee table. She continued on into the dining room and glanced towards the kitchen. No dishes to be seen, island bench wiped down and tea towel hung neatly over the oven handle.

'Caleb! Jacob!' called Kate loudly as she went through the kitchen and down the passageway. 'Hello? Anybody home?'

She knocked on Jacob's bedroom door and then, when there was no answer, pushed it open. It was almost reassuring to see this room in its usual state of disarray. Floor covered with rumpled clothing, smudged glasses half filled with a partially solidified liquid, the bed a mass of tangled sheets and inside-out clothes. And the smell: a muskily unpleasant combination of perspiration, unwashed sheets and what was probably rancid milk. But there was nobody there.

Kate closed the door again and tried Caleb's room. This room was very similar, only minus the rancid milk smell. But it was also uninhabited. She closed the door and headed back to the kitchen, where she peered out of the window, scanning the backyard from the decking over to the pool. Apart from Hector, who was sleeping at the top of the steps, it was empty.

Frowning slightly, Kate turned and leant back against the sink. She realised she was actually rather disappointed, that she had looked forward to somebody, anybody, being home. Especially Sam. In fact, her decision to return the boxes at this time of day stemmed from the sure knowledge that he finished work at about 4.30 pm each day and was usually home by now. Kate let her breath out in a shallow sigh, and noticed that there was a note stuck to the fridge underneath a magnet spruiking the expertise of a local plumber. She reached forward, slid it out and read it.

Hi Shell, don't forget to feed Hector. His tablets are on the washing machine. We'll be back from Eildon late Sunday afternoon. Have a good weekend. Love, Dad.

Kate's frown deepened. Eildon? They hadn't been to their block of land for a quite a while, so why would Sam suddenly decide to spend a weekend there? And, judging by his 'we' and the empty house, it seemed the boys had gone with him. And nobody had even thought to ask her.

They had bought the block outside Mansfield, on the shores of Lake Eildon, shortly after Shelley was born. It was originally purchased as an investment, but soon turned into a favourite holiday destination. As a family Christmas present that year, her father had given them a second-hand caravan and they towed it up to the block as a permanent feature. A few weeks every summer thereafter, and the odd weekend during the year, had been spent up at the lake, where they were often joined by Oscar and Angie and Melissa and even, sometimes, by her father.

But in a strange parallel, as the kids had grown older and not as interested in family holidays, so too had Lake Eildon shrunk. Until the lake was no longer even near their land, but rather a twenty-minute walk over a dried honeycomb of cracks surrounded by grassy cliffs that were once shores. As the drought pushed the lake further away, the businesses that thrived around it had suffered also. The holiday units that had thronged the land alongside were now mostly empty, their boat ramps leading blindly down to the dry lake bed. Buoys, their bright colours long faded by the relentless sunshine, studded the expanse like odd vegetation. And the floating petrol station now lay grounded, a forlorn reminder of how vibrant the lake had once been.

Their investment, which peaked about ten years after they bought it, dried up alongside the water. So that even if they put it on the market now, it wouldn't sell. Too many similar blocks were on the books, at ridiculously cheap prices. So they had decided to simply hang on to it and see what happened. Occasionally one of the kids headed up there, with friends, to spend a few days in the caravan and enjoy the solitude and freedom. But each time she or Sam mentioned spending a weekend there, something always intervened and the trip was postponed.

Now it seemed that he had made the time, then followed through without even mentioning it to her. And that hurt. Although things *had* been a trifle strained, she'd really thought that last Friday night had gone some way to getting them back on track.

Kate pushed away from the sink and refixed the note to the fridge door. Then, trying to ignore the dull ache behind her eyes, she went down to the car and piled the concertina file and the shoebox on top of the cardboard box before carrying the lot around to the side of the house and then underneath. After she had put them all back in their correct places, Kate went back up to the house and locked it securely. She was just getting into her car when Shelley's Astra pulled up at the kerb behind her.

'Hey, Mum! Wait up!' Shelley stuck her head out of her window to call over to her mother and then opened her car door and got out quickly.

Kate closed her own door and walked over. 'Hey Shell. How's everything going?'

'Good, good. Listen, are you doing anything tonight?'

'Well, I . . . um,' Kate bobbed down and looked into the rear of the car, where her grand-daughter was fast asleep, her head lolling to one side of the car seat.

'It doesn't matter too much if you are,' said Shelley generously. 'Because Daniel's mum said she'd have her. I just thought you'd be easier. Closer, you know.'

'Well, maybe you should let her have a turn. She'll be looking forward to it.'

Shelley flicked her hair back and nodded. 'Yeah, I suppose.'

'Where are you off to?'

'This new club in Ringwood. Should be fun.'

'Oh, good.' Kate watched as Emma stirred slightly, her fingers splaying, and then settled again. 'Listen, what's up with your father going to Eildon?'

Shelley shrugged, her dangly earrings brushing against her shoulders. 'Just some sort of boys' weekend. Whatever. Hey, what are you doing for Easter?'

Kate frowned. 'A boys' weekend? And you weren't invited?'

'Correction. But I have a life. Would you believe tomorrow I'm taking Em to the Healesville Sanctuary? With Daniel? We're doing our bit to present a united front for her. Good idea, huh?'

'Yes, great idea. So when did they decide this then? About Eildon?'

Shelley shrugged again. 'I don't know. And what's with the twenty questions?'

'Just curious,' replied Kate casually. 'That's all.'

'Okay, well I'd better get going. I still have to get Emma ready and stuff. Were you coming in?'

Kate shook her head. 'No, just leaving.'

'Okay then,' Shelley opened the back door of her car and gently undid Emma's seatbelt. 'Come on, honey. We're home now.'

Kate watched as her daughter emerged slowly with the baby across her chest, her flushed little face leaning against her mother's shoulder. Shelley readjusted her load, putting one hand securely behind Emma's back as she straightened. Kate reached into the car and hooked Shelley's handbag, which she slipped over her daughter's arm.

'Thanks, Mum.'

'So . . . you've got the house to yourself then?'

'About time.' Shelley closed the car door deftly with her hip. 'Jacob's really driving me nuts. And Caleb's not much better. I wish your six months'd hurry up. They're much worse when you're not here. Even Dad.'

'Really?'

'Yes, absolutely.' Shelley was already heading up the driveway, the top of Emma's head just visible beyond her shoulder.

Kate took a deep breath and let it out with a slow sigh. She felt a slight throbbing at her temples and did her neck exercises, hoping to head it off. She wondered if Sam had already arrived at Eildon, whether he had finished work early to get a head start or whether he had waited until 4.30 pm before swinging by and collecting the boys. In which case, she had only just missed them. Would it have made any difference if she'd been fifteen minutes earlier? Would he have then asked her along for the weekend? And why, most importantly, regardless of missed timings, hadn't he invited her in the first place?

'Do you know, I'm really glad you got takeaway tonight.' Angie picked up a fat, golden chip and pointed it accusingly at Kate. 'You were beginning to make me feel guilty with your home-cooked meals.'

'So after all the effort I've put in, you'd rather I just get fish and chips?'

Angie nodded. 'Every now and again. So that I don't feel I have to cook.'

'You *never* cook.'

'Exactly.' Angie popped the chip into her mouth and then spoke around it. 'And I don't want to feel guilty about it either.'

Kate leant back on the couch and smiled. 'Glad to be of service.'

'Well you won't have to do anything for the next week or so. Not for me anyway.'

'What do you mean?'

'I've promised Oscar I'll stay at the house. He's been called over to Hong Kong, for business. Leaves on Monday and he's stuck over there for Easter. So he asked me to stay there, which means you'll have the unit to yourself. No excuse not to write now!'

Kate was not sure whether this was good news or not. 'But why do you have to stay there?'

'Oh, you know Oscar.' Angie waved her hand. 'He's got this bug in his head about houses that are on the market being greater candidates for burglary.'

'So *you'll* be the security?'

'No, apparently his theory excludes houses that are clearly being occupied. I think he's being paranoid but I owe him a few favours. Mind you, I didn't tell him I was going away for the Easter weekend anyway. I'm staying with Diane Weston. Remember her? My friend from uni? She lives in Bendigo now. But what he doesn't know won't hurt him. So anyway, I expect to see the MO almost finished by the time I get back. Though you still haven't told me what you're writing about.'

'Pardon?'

'Well, we had that conversation ages ago, about you having trouble finding something to write about. And I assume you've come up with an idea in the meantime because you haven't mentioned it since. So?'

'Well . . . I *have* come up with something,' acknowledged Kate slowly, tucking her feet underneath her. 'But if you don't mind, I'd like to keep it under wraps for a while. Writer's superstition.'

Angie shrugged. 'Far be it from me to jinx your creative flow. Want to watch the news?' She reached over and picked up the remote control from the coffee table, next to the grease-spotted butcher paper that held the few remaining chips. She flicked the television on and a beetle-browed gentleman immediately appeared, pontificating about the fact they were heading for the second hottest March on record.

'Why are the guys always the distinguished ones?' asked Angie critically. 'Don't females ever get older in TV-land?'

'I think it's against the law,' replied Kate absently, her mind elsewhere. They would have arrived in Eildon by now, without a doubt. Probably had fish and chips for tea as well. Lots of chips with a piece of battered flake for each of the boys and about three or four steamed dim sims for Sam, with plenty of soya sauce. Then maybe they'd go fishing at dusk, or just sit outside the caravan on folding chairs, having a few beers as they watched the sun set into the clear, smog-free horizon.

'What's on your mind?'

Kate blinked and looked at Angie, who was staring at her curiously. 'Pardon?'

'Well, *something*'s obviously up. You're staring at the curtains as if they've done you a personal injury.'

'Sam's taken the boys up to Eildon for the weekend.'

'And?' asked Angie, frowning. Then her face cleared. 'Ah, but he didn't ask you?'

'Yes. Don't you think that's odd?'

'Maybe they just wanted a boys' weekend.'

Kate shook her head dismissively. 'They never have before. Besides, they asked Shelley but she didn't want to go. And it's not just that he didn't *ask* me, he didn't even *tell* me.'

'Oh. Well, that *is* a bit odd then.'

'Thanks.' Kate plucked some fluff off her tracksuit pants and then looked back at Angie. 'Do you think he's trying to teach me a lesson?'

'A lesson? What about?'

'Well, you know. Like you don't want us, so we don't want you either.'

'Not a chance,' replied Angie without hesitation. 'That's not Sam's style.'

'I wouldn't have thought so either.'

Angie picked up the remote control again and turned the television volume down. 'Maybe he's trying to do what *he* thinks is the right thing. Leave you alone, let you get some writing done. I mean, it's not like he's been here every second day, is it?'

'I'm not sure that makes me feel better.'

'What I mean is, maybe he thinks the more he leaves you alone, the sooner you'll come back.' Angie leant back and tossed the remote onto the coffee table. It slid neatly across the polished surface and tumbled off onto the carpet. 'Besides, hasn't that always been the way he plays things? When things get uncomfortable, steer clear and wait for it to settle. You use humour to deflect and he uses avoidance. And he's not the only guy who worships at that particular altar. Mind you, *I* was married to a guy who liked to talk things to death. And then resuscitate them and start all over again.'

Kate nodded. It fitted, but it didn't alter her disquiet at not being invited. On the television, the weatherman was now holding the fort, a backdrop of fast-moving clouds behind him. The temperature for the next week flashed up on the bottom half of the screen so, even without hearing him speak, Kate could see that the hot spell was going to start easing in a few days. At last. She watched as the names of country towns scrolled across, with their expected temperatures, and then frowned as she turned back to Angie. 'Does your aunt still live up in Ballarat?'

'You mean Auntie Faye? Why?'

'Well . . . I was just thinking I might go away for the weekend myself. And I wouldn't mind dropping in and saying hello. Haven't seen her for ages.'

Angie stared at her, clearly puzzled. 'But you never really liked her.'

'Actually, I didn't *mind* her.'

'You called her Attila the Bum. To her face.'

'At least I wasn't talking behind her back,' said Kate piously. 'Besides, age gives one perspective. It'd be nice to see her again.'

'So you're going to go all the way to *Ballarat* to drop in on my aunt?'

'Of course not. I just thought I might say hi while I was in the area, that's all. But I'd be mainly going to catch up with friends.'

'Which friends?'

'Lord, who needs a parent when I've got you!' Kate laughed, then realised what she'd just said and her face stilled. She stared at Angie, trying to think of something that would skate over the moment before it stretched uncomfortably. Then Angie gave a rather artificial laugh, which immediately broke the matter into tiny fragments.

'Well, I must say you're full of surprises. Shall I give her a ring for you?'

'That'd be great,' Kate nodded, allowing an infusion of self-satisfaction. Angie cast her one more questioning look but Kate just smiled agreeably. Then, while her cousin started to dial, she picked up the butcher paper, scrunching the outer leaves over, and took it into the kitchen. She pushed the bundle inside the rubbish bin and then wiped her hands with a slapping motion. She could hear the low murmur of Angie's voice, falling silent every few seconds as her aunt replied.

Kate suspected that the woman would be a little astonished that she wanted to pay her a visit. Especially without Angie. Maybe she would be feeling irritated, pursing her mouth up there in Ballarat. If it went ahead, Kate resolved to pick up some flowers, or chocolate, before she arrived. She glanced into the lounge room and Angie gave her a thumbs-up. All systems go.

She lit the gas underneath the kettle and began preparing two mugs. The main point was that Sam wasn't the only one who could just go away for the weekend on a whim, who could just throw a few things in the car and head off into the wild blue yonder. And the beauty of *her* plan was that it was something that probably needed to be done anyway. An information-gathering exercise from one of the few primary sources left. It would be a *working* weekend, not like some.

FOURTEEN

Dear Dad, do you remember Angie's Auntie Faye? Of course you do. She visited a lot when we were young – maybe she thought it was her duty, given that her little sister had done a runner. I know I resented the way she seemed to examine us both, especially Angie. Maybe I was a bit jealous. I remember one time I made Angie hide underneath the old truck when we saw her car arrive. And you were all calling us over and over. Uncle Frank thought it was hilarious but you were really cross. Embarrassed, I suppose. I don't know why visiting her didn't occur to me before now, because surely she'll have a few answers. Perhaps she even knew my mother?

PS: I've decided against the flashes of insight. Better to avoid the subjective altogether.

The traffic over the Westgate Bridge was heavy, but it started to clear once Kate drove beyond the new housing estates that had sprung up on that side of the city. She had the airconditioner on already because the temperature overnight hadn't dropped below the mid twenties and was warming up quickly again. To her surprise, according to Angie, Auntie Faye had been delighted that Kate was about to pay her a visit. Even insisting that she come for lunch, and promising something delicious.

On the back seat were an overnight bag, her pillow, laptop and a box of liqueur chocolates. And Kate had chosen her outfit with some care. Conservative enough for lunch with an elderly relative-by-proxy, yet comfortable enough for a relaxed drive. Black strappy sandals, an Aztec-patterned layered skirt and a black silky singlet top. She reached forward and turned the radio on, the gravelly tones of Jimmy Barnes immediately breaking the silence. Kate smiled to herself because the weekend lay before her like a gift, full of potential. Apart from the lunch today, she had nothing at all planned. In the end she hadn't even contacted the friends casually referred to in the conversation with Angie. Infinitely more appealing, at this time, was a lack of direction and a night in a motel somewhere along the way.

Kate took the bypass into Bacchus Marsh and stopped for morning tea at a lovely little café, which had number plates from all over the world plastered to the walls. While she drank her coffee, she amused herself by imagining the steady stream of tourists who stopped here for sustenance, only to have their number-plates stolen by the unscrupulous hosts. Perhaps there was even a *Psycho*-style motel out the back. She paid for her coffee and returned to her car, grinning at herself as she automatically checked to ensure her own number plate was still intact. A little over an hour later, Kate hit the outskirts of Ballarat and pulled over to check the map that Angie had drawn. Twenty minutes after that, she reached her destination.

It was a fairly small house of white clinker brick, set back from the road and with louvre shutters adorning each of the windows. Much of the front yard was concreted and what little lawn left was mown to within an inch of its life, with far more grey patches than green. Roses of every size and colour, with an assortment of garden gnomes, ringed the lawn area and edged the driveway in a curve from road to house. An extremely ugly garden gnome, which looked rather like the one Caleb had given her for Christmas, sat by the front door. Kate knocked and stood back to wait.

'Coming!' The voice was accompanied by the sound of hurried footsteps and then the door was opened wide. 'Kate, honey! *What* a pleasure!'

Kate smiled at the elderly woman who was beaming at her with obvious delight. She looked very much as Kate had remembered, a large, big-boned woman with what her uncle had once rather rudely referred to as 'Neanderthal hips'. Facially wise, there was a vague resemblance to Angie. Similar brown eyes, wide mouth and round face. But her aunt's features had long since been wreathed with deeply bedded wrinkles and her hair was now short and snowy-white.

'Don't just stand there! Come in!' She reached forward and grasped Kate by the arm, assisting her somewhat forcefully over the threshold and then slamming the door behind her. 'Now then, let me have a look at you. Aren't you maturing nicely then!'

'Thank you,' replied Kate, keeping her smile in place. She wondered whether she should return the dubious compliment.

'I suppose you're wondering what to call me, huh? But why don't we just stick with Auntie Faye. That's what you always called me when you were little. Not so little now, huh?'

'No, unfortunately.'

Auntie Faye immediately frowned, letting go of Kate's arm at last. 'Don't tell me you're one of those ones who gets all hung up about their size? Don't be a fool, honey. If you ask me, a little bit of padding never did any harm. Be proud of your curves and to hell with anyone else.'

Kate smoothed her singlet self-consciously. 'Um, okay. Thank you.'

'Now, follow me!' Auntie Faye immediately strode away into a neat, compact lounge room and went straight up to a set of French doors at the side. These were flung open to reveal a sunroom, each wall lined with white weatherboard up to waist height and then with louvred-glass windows to the ceiling. More multihued roses, this time in pots, took up most of the space except for the very centre, where a table had been set for lunch. With the expanse of glass the room was like a sauna. Perfect for a hothouse, not so great for anything else.

'Lovely roses,' said Kate politely.

'Yes, aren't they? One of my hobbies. And I often eat out here, it's so lovely and cosy. Snug. Now make yourself comfortable and I'll be back in a bit with our lunch.'

As her host left the room, Kate got the chocolates she had bought out of her handbag and then sat down on one of the old-fashioned, thickly padded kitchen chairs. She saw that Auntie Faye had gone to some effort, with a single apricot rose in a crystal vase in the centre of the tablecloth and silver cutlery either side of what looked like Royal Albert tableware. Kate wiped her forehead and then stared down at her damp fingers, sending a brief plea skyward that the meal would not be a hot one.

At that moment, Auntie Faye came bustling in, bearing a tray with two bowls of steaming soup and a cane basket full of bread. She placed it on the table with a flourish. 'Here we go, honey. Just the thing after a long drive.'

'Oh, excellent,' said Kate weakly, the heat of the soup wafting up as it was placed before her. She remembered the box of chocolates on her lap and lifted them, her thumb immediately pressing down on one corner. 'Um, for you. Chocolates.'

'You shouldn't have!' Auntie Faye took the box gingerly. 'But thank you anyway. Perhaps I'd better put them in the fridge.'

'Good idea.'

Auntie Faye was back within seconds, closing the French doors behind her. Kate shook out a white napkin and laid it on her lap, staring down at the soup. It was a transparent dull-yellow colour, disturbingly reminiscent of urine, with small glutinous chunks of something pink floating on the surface.

'Well then, dig in, honey! Enjoy!'

Kate mustered up a faint smile and obediently dug in. While the soup didn't taste quite as bad as it looked, it didn't taste all that good either. After about four mouthfuls, Kate found herself glad that Angie *didn't* cook, because there was always a chance this sort of culinary ability was genetic. She laid her spoon down and sighed with exaggerated contentment. 'Lovely, thanks! Did you make it yourself?'

'Certainly did,' replied Auntie Faye, tipping her bowl forward and scooping up the last of her own soup. 'Family recipe.'

'Ah.'

'If you were going straight home, I'd give you some to take back with you. But Angie says you're going on to stay with friends?'

'That's right,' said Kate quickly. 'Otherwise . . .'

'Never mind, I'll send some down with her next time she comes up.' Auntie Faye stood up and collected the bowls. 'Ready for the second course?'

'Second course?'

'Coming right up!'

Kate watched the older woman leave the room again and then tucked her hair behind her ears and used her napkin to mop her forehead. It was very hot in the sunroom, and very humid. A throbbing had started at her temples, emitting vibrations that echoed around the eye sockets. She looked around, almost desperate enough to drink the water out of a watering can if she spotted one, but there was nothing except ridiculously healthy roses and a box of snail pellets in the corner. She stared at the warning signs plastered across the box, and wondered how many pellets would put her out of her misery.

Auntie Faye came back into the sunroom, carrying the tray again. She placed it down on the side of the table and to her immense relief Kate saw two long glasses full of iced water. One was immediately passed over, followed by a plate of meatloaf and vegetables. 'Here we go then. Eat up before it goes cold!'

Kate smiled her thanks and then forced herself not to act too eager as she drank some water, the iciness providing an almost painful bliss. Within seconds, the throbbing in her head lessened to a dull resonance that felt heavy, but bearable.

'So Angie tells me you're staying with her while you're writing a book?'

Kate picked up her cutlery. 'Well, yes. That is, I'm trying to anyway.'

'I'm sure you'll succeed. You always were a determined little bugger.' Auntie Faye paused for a moment. 'And I'm so sorry I couldn't make it to your father's funeral last year. I wasn't well myself at the time.'

'Yes, Angie told me, and we got the flowers. Hope you're much better now?'

'Of course,' replied Auntie Faye airily. 'Food poisoning, you know.'

Kate stared at her meatloaf.

'Just one of those things.' Auntie Faye deftly sliced her broccoli into bite-sized pieces. 'Unfortunate timing though.'

'Oh, well. It happens.' Kate surreptitiously pushed her meatloaf to one side and began eating the mashed potato instead.

'Dreadful business. I was shocked.'

Kate knew that she wasn't talking about the food poisoning, and she also knew that she needed to head this conversation off. 'This is lovely potato, Auntie Faye. Unusual taste though. Is it another family recipe?'

'Heavens, no. I'll tell you a secret, it's just powdered stuff with condensed milk. That's the trick.'

'I'll have to remember,' said Kate, nodding.

'I always liked your father. Lovely man. Made me so angry that it had to come to that.' Auntie Faye glared down at her plate. 'Should be a law against it.'

'There is,' said Kate expressionlessly. 'That's the point.'

'You know what I mean.' Auntie Faye looked at her searchingly. 'So how are you holding up then, honey?'

'I'm fine. Absolutely fine.'

'Did you know . . . beforehand?'

'Oh, yes.' Kate knew exactly what she meant. She kept her voice light, conversational. 'Well, I didn't know that particular *day*. But he never made a secret of it, from the time he was diagnosed. It was only a matter of time. Before things got too bad. I suppose Angie told you all that. Everyone knew.' Kate paused in an effort to stem the flow of words. She finished lamely: 'It was his choice, after all.'

'Yes, of course.' Auntie Faye shook her head. 'But still . . .'

'So what sort of things do you get up to? I mean hobbies and all that.'

Auntie Faye grasped at the change of subject. 'Oh, I keep myself busy. I'm the secretary of the community centre, you know, and then there's the bowls and my book club and pottery. Never a spare minute, that's how I like it.'

Kate took another sip of water and then continued eating slowly. If anything, it felt even hotter in the sunroom now than it had before, but she knew she had to swallow her growing lethargy and lead the conversation towards Sophie. She glanced across at Auntie Faye, who laid her cutlery down and looked at Kate's plate.

'Sure you've had enough, honey?'

'More than enough,' said Kate heartily. 'It was delicious, thanks.'

'My pleasure.' Auntie Faye stacked the two plates and put them both back on the tray. She stood up with a groan. 'Back in a minute with coffee and dessert. No, no, you stay there.'

Kate, who had half risen to assist, sank back into her chair and watched the older woman leave to fetch course number three. It would have been nice to let the food settle a bit, but her host clearly favoured the rapid-serve, speed-eat mode of dining. Accustomed as she was to a sandwich or two for lunch, and with her appetite already lessened by the heat, Kate had been full after the soup and bread. Everything else was now simply coagulating in her stomach. She drained her glass and resolved to segue the conversation before she was somehow ushered out the door with the same forcefulness with which she had been ushered in.

The French doors shot open again and Auntie Faye came through with the tray, this time bearing a coffee plunger, mugs, two shallow bowls of what looked like trifle and, to Kate's enormous relief, a glass jug full of water.

'I saw how thirsty you were.' She put the jug down by Kate's empty glass. 'Now, how do you have your coffee? Black? White?'

'White with one,' said Kate, refilling her glass. 'Thanks.'

Auntie Faye prepared the coffee and passed a mug over to Kate with one of the bowls of trifle. Then she pushed the tray to one side and sat down again. 'You're lucky, I hardly ever make trifle nowadays but I did some for the bowls yesterday and there was heaps left over. So when Angie rang and said you were coming, I thought *well*! How fortuitous!'

'Fortuitous indeed,' replied Kate, poking at the trifle with her spoon.

'Oh, I forgot the cream! Did you want some?'

'No thanks. It's lovely just as it is,' said Kate, finally breaking off a small piece and popping it into her mouth. It was surprisingly tasty. 'Listen, Auntie Faye, could I ask you a question?'

'Certainly, honey. Anything. Except about my love life of course!'

'Ah, of course.' Kate slammed that mental door closed quickly. 'It's actually about a relative of my father's. I was going through his papers and came across this name I'd never heard. So I was worried that it was someone I should have notified. Last year. And it just occurred to me that you might know.'

'I'll do my best. What's the name?'

'Thomas Painter.'

Auntie Faye paused, with a spoonful of trifle halfway to her mouth. A piece of jelly wobbled on the rim and then fell off onto the plate with a soft plop. She put the spoon back down, still full. 'Thomas Painter, hey? Yes, I know him. He was your father's cousin.'

'Oh, really?'

'Yes. He even lived next door to your father for a while. Back in the sixties, it must have been.' Auntie Faye looked at Kate pensively. 'There was a bit of a scandal, see. Did no one ever tell you?'

'No,' said Kate with absolute truthfulness. 'Could you?'

'Of course I could,' replied Auntie Faye without hesitation. As delighted as she had been to have Kate visit, she was clearly even more delighted to be the one to impart this piece of family gossip. She pushed her trifle away and leant forward slightly. 'Now, you wouldn't remember my sister, would you? Angie's mother? No, of course not. Well, this is where Thomas Painter comes in. You see, Sophie was engaged to him before she met your Uncle Frank. Broke it off about two months before the wedding and married Frank instead. I can see you're surprised.'

'I *am*.'

'And I can tell you it was a huge scandal at the time. Frank's mother, your grandmother, was absolutely furious. You see, it affected her relationship with her *own* sister, who was young Thomas's mother. And your grandmother wasn't the forgiving type. She made Sophie's life hell until the day she died.'

'*Sophie* died?'

'No, your grandmother. Pneumonia, I think it was. But I haven't got to the good bit yet.' Auntie Faye leant back, pausing as she relished the moment. 'I wouldn't be telling you all this, but we're all adults here now. You see, young Angie was born around that time and I came down for a while to help out. New baby and all. Anyway, soon's I arrived, I knew something was up. It was the way she was acting.'

'Oh?' encouraged Kate.

'I always could see right through Sophie. Hopeless liar, my sister, always wore it over her face. I took one look and said to myself, hello! *Something*'s up!'

'So what did you do?'

'Asked her straight out. When Frank wasn't there naturally. Just sat her down and wouldn't take no for an answer. So she admitted it.'

'What?'

'That she'd fallen for Thomas again. Was even visiting him up at his house every other afternoon. You see, they were having An Affair.' Auntie Faye smiled, rather smugly. '*Now* I've shocked you, haven't I?'

Kate nodded impatiently. 'You have. Then what happened?'

'Well, nothing. Not for a couple of years. That is, I let Sophie know what I thought of her behaviour, but there wasn't much more I could do, was there?' Auntie Faye looked at Kate questioningly, as if she had an answer, even after all this time. 'So I just went home again and left them to it. Then your father came back and maybe that brought everything to a head. There was a huge fight and Sophie shot through.'

Kate took a deep breath. 'Do you know where she went?'

'Next door, of course,' replied Auntie Faye promptly. 'Moved in with Thomas.'

Now Kate *was* shocked. 'Next door? They lived next *door*?'

'For a while anyway. But your uncle made it so hard for her, seeing young Angie and all, that they just gave up. Shifted away.'

'Hang on.' Kate put up a hand. 'Are you saying that while they lived next door, Sophie saw Angie? Like with child access?'

'That's right. You see, she was supposed to have her every weekend. But, as I said, your uncle made it so difficult. He was a bit bitter, I suppose.' Auntie Faye made a snorting noise at this before continuing. 'Plus there was a lot of talk around town of course, and feelings were running pretty high against them. Once someone even threw fruit at the house, smashed a window. Another time, the windshield of their car had eggs tossed at it.'

'How awful.' Kate stared at Auntie Faye, aghast, as she tried to imagine what life must have been like for the young couple. Sophie would only have been in her very early twenties. About the same age as Shelley was now, with little Emma.

'So she just gave up. And don't ask me why she didn't try to take Angie with her. I've never been able to understand that bit, but I think she felt guilty for deserting Frank. I'll tell you a secret. *I* think leaving the baby with him was like a penance.'

Kate nodded slowly, trying to take it all in. 'Didn't Thomas only have one eye?'

'Oh, yes. He was always a card, that one.' Auntie Faye's face wreathed with a fond smile, as if the mere possession of a single eye was the epitome of amusement in itself. 'She should have just married him in the first place, saved a lot of bother. You see, he'd pop it out when he'd had a few drinks and put it in your glass. You'd pick it up and it'd be floating there, staring at you! Oh, you'd nearly die of fright!'

'I can imagine,' replied Kate with sincerity.

'Lost it when he was just a boy. One of those kiddie air rifles. You know, the ones where they always say to be careful, otherwise you'll lose an eye? Well, young Thomas was the proof in the pudding, so to speak.'

Kate sipped at her now tepid coffee while she threaded these discoveries together and then tried to determine any loose ends. She looked across at Auntie Faye, who seemed to be rather lost in thought. 'Did you ever know my mother?'

'Your mother? Hmm . . . well, just a bit. Met her once or twice.'

'What was she like?'

For the first time Auntie Faye appeared reluctant to hold forth. She busied herself with topping up her coffee and then glanced at Kate as if hoping she wouldn't be still waiting for an answer. 'Well . . . I don't know that I could really comment, honey. I only met her a few times.'

'But you must have formed an impression at least?'

'Hmm. Let me see . . . well, she was very *neat*,' said Auntie Faye slowly. 'Oh, and she was always *busy*. Even when she was sitting down she'd be fidgeting away and you could tell she was thinking of what was next. Lively! That's a good word for your mother. Lively. Wish I could tell you more but you see I'd hate to give you the wrong notion about your own mum. Not when I'd only met her the few times.'

Kate smiled her appreciation, even as she recognised that the older woman's reluctance spoke as much, if not more, than words could have. Another one who didn't like Rose Kimber.

'Now your father I knew quite well,' continued Auntie Faye with more enthusiasm. 'Lovely man. We were all quite surprised when he got married, always thought him more the bachelor type. Bit shy, liked his own company.' She paused, and then smiled. 'You used to call me Attila the Bum, you know. When you were little. Oh, you could be a bit of a terror.'

Kate grimaced. 'Sorry.'

'Not a problem. I always thought Frank put you up to it anyway. He never really forgave me for knowing about the affair. Which was a bit hypocritical given the way that man carried on. More coffee, honey?'

'Do you mean – no thanks,' Kate put a hand over her mug. 'Do you mean that Uncle Frank was also being unfaithful during the marriage?'

'God, yes! That man couldn't help himself! Never should have got married in the first place. *I* think he only did it because he had this competitive thing going with poor Thomas. And with James, for that matter. Probably would have cuckolded him too if it hadn't been for the fact that Rose was such a . . .' Auntie Faye petered off and then cleared her throat. 'Such a virtuous woman, is what I meant. Lively, too.'

'Yes, we've established that,' replied Kate dryly.

'Would you like more trifle, honey? You've hardly touched yours.'

'No thanks, I am absolutely full.' Kate patted her stomach to underline her words. 'Thank you so much for the lunch.'

'It was my pleasure. We should do it more often. After all, when was the last time I saw you?'

'I'm not sure. It must —'

'Melissa's graduation probably.' Auntie Faye started stacking the trifle dishes back onto the tray. 'Too long. It's my fault as well, though. You see, I'm getting lazier as I get older. Should make the effort to go down to Melbourne more often.'

'Yes, you should.' Kate surprised herself by meaning it. Even if she had never been as close to Angie's aunt as Angie herself had, the woman was still a link to the past. There weren't many of them left now.

'And I will.' Auntie Faye stood up with the tray and smiled down at Kate, who immediately rose too.

'I'd better leave you to it. And thanks again. I really enjoyed myself.'

'So did I. If it wasn't for the fact I have my pottery class this afternoon, I'd be trying to persuade you to stay longer.'

Kate slung her handbag over her shoulder and then opened the French doors for the older woman to pass through. A wall of cooler air immediately engulfed her and it felt wondrous. 'Can I at least help you with the dishes?'

'Certainly not. You're a guest.' Auntie Faye carried the tray through to the kitchen and then returned, empty-handed. 'And now I'm going to give you a present to take back with you.'

With some apprehension Kate followed Auntie Faye back through the lounge room and up to the front door, where a small semicircular hall table hugged the wall. Auntie Faye bent down with a grunt and then straightened, holding out a garden gnome. 'I made her myself.'

'Why, *thank* you,' Kate took the gnome and stared down at it. 'Her?'

'Of course. Can't you see the eyelashes?'

'Now that you mention it. Yes, I can.'

Auntie Faye smiled proudly as she reached out one finger and traced it along the black, spider-like marks that adorned the area above each of the gnome's beady eyes. 'Hand-painted.'

'Really? Amazing.'

She opened the door and then preceded Kate out onto the small porch, peering upwards. 'Doesn't look like we'll ever get rain, does it, honey?'

Kate shook her head, staring up at the blue, cloudless sky. Then they walked companionably down the driveway and towards the kerb. Hugging her gnome awkwardly, Kate dug around in her handbag and eventually came up with the car keys. She unlocked the door and then turned back to Auntie Faye curiously. 'Would you mind if I ask you one more question?'

'Ask away.'

'Well, it must have been hard for you too. I mean, Sophie was your sister.' Kate stared down at the gnome's eyelashes, feeling discomforted about what she was about to ask. 'So . . . do you miss her?'

'Miss who?'

'Your sister.'

'My sister?'

'Yes, your sister. Sophie.'

Auntie Faye frowned, clearly confused. 'Why would I miss her?'

'Well, because she left.' Kate stared at the older woman. 'You know, shot through. With Thomas Painter.'

'Oh, *I* see!' Auntie Faye's face cleared and she laughed. 'I've given you the wrong end of the stick, haven't I? I don't miss Sophie at *all*, honey, because I'm never given the chance to!' Still laughing, she pointed over Kate's shoulder and then waited until Kate turned. 'I'll tell you a secret. See that road over there? Well, you head down it about three miles and then turn left by the milk bar and Sophie's house is the fourth on the right. So, you see, how can I miss her? I see the woman every other day!'

FIFTEEN

Dear Dad, remember those little diaries that Angie and I would get each Christmas? With the tiny little locks and the keys that could be used to open any of them, if you just jiggled them a little. And remember when I was about ten or eleven and I used my key to open Angie's and then made notes in the margins as a sort of critique? Like boring, *and* if you hate me so much, why don't you just run away? *I got in so much trouble. You even made me leave my own diary on the kitchen table for anyone to read if they wanted. And you said that everyone is entitled to some secrets. It's a basic human right. Only now am I beginning to realise how serious you were.*

Kate arrived home early afternoon on Sunday. She hadn't really planned on getting home so early but simply ran out of things to do. After leaving Auntie Faye's, she had followed the older lady's directions to see for herself. It was a very ordinary-looking house, made of red brick and with striped awnings pulled all the way down to keep out the heat. Confirmation rested with the garden gnome that squatted next to the letterbox, clearly a close relative to the one now in the back seat. Hot and sticky, Kate sat in the car for almost twenty minutes while trying to come to terms with the news. Nobody either came or went. The entire neighbourhood remained quiet and peaceful and immobile.

An extremely unlikely setting for a mystery novel, especially given that this discovery should qualify as the climax. *I'll tell you a secret...*

After she finally left, Kate drove into Ballarat itself and found a public bathroom where she splashed water on her face and reapplied some foundation. Then, rather distractedly, she played tourist for the remainder of the afternoon, browsing the shops along the main street and buying herself some supplies, like a book and some paracetamol. Eventually she went back to the car and headed out of town, driving aimlessly down the Midland Highway while she replayed the lunchtime conversation over and over again like a cassette tape. She arrived in Geelong just as the sun was casting the horizon in a fiery glow that promised yet more sunny weather for the following day, and found a motel with a pleasant view of Port Phillip Bay.

It was a relaxing evening but one that was shadowed by a certain numbness. Kate knew that this was a protective device, a sort of anaesthetic that prevented her from fully acknowledging, just yet, that all of the casual understandings hitherto shoring her life were being eroded, one by one. It wasn't as if she was *refusing* to face anything, just postponing the inevitable. Instead letting segments drip-feed into her consciousness, so that, every so often, she could shake her head and say *Well, isn't that amazing?* rather than dive into the facts and let them consume her.

But the numbness also prevented her from fully enjoying her little holiday, because awareness throbbed just beneath her temples. So that she needed a sleeping tablet to fully switch off on Saturday night, and the next morning, when she sat by the foreshore trying to read her new book, the words blurred together and she had to read each sentence several times. Even then it didn't make sense. *Nothing* made sense.

So it was almost a relief to get back to the unit and shut the front door behind her. The phone started ringing almost immediately, so she dropped her things by the foot of the stairs and hurried to pick it up. 'Hello?'

'*Mum!* How come you gave Jacob that lamp?'

'Pardon?'

'The lamp!' repeated Shelley, her voice climbing in pitch. 'Grandpa's lamp! It's on Jacob's *desk*!'

'Well, it was just that he –'

'You *knew* I loved that lamp! You *knew* it!'

The persistent throbbing that had continued behind Kate's temples fell into rhythm with Shelley's voice. Stabbing with each emphasis. She sat down on the armrest of the couch. 'Look, Shelley, actually I *didn't* know that you loved the lamp. And it just so happened that Jacob was giving me a hand with some of Grandpa's things and he saw the lamp there.'

'But that's not fair!'

Kate shrugged. 'He asked if he could have it.'

'Oh, *I* see,' replied Shelley with sarcasm. 'So all I need to do is *ask*, is that it? And here was I trying to do the right thing by waiting. Well then, can I have Grandpa's secretaire, and his armchair, and all of his pictures?'

'For goodness –'

'Hang on, I'm not finished. I really like that one of his parents he used to keep next to his bed. And can I also have that grandmother clock he used to have in the hallway, and his dressing-table, and his desk?'

'This is ridiculous.'

'So it's ridiculous when *I* ask but not when *Jacob* does?'

'You're being incredibly childish,' snapped Kate, standing up again. 'So unless you're going to be reasonable and stop shrieking at me, I'm going to hang up.'

Shelley's voice dropped to a wail. 'But can't you see how *unfair* it is?'

'What about his desk set?'

'What?'

'His desk set,' repeated Kate. 'The maroon leather one that used to sit on his desk all the time. His father gave it to him for his twenty-first birthday.'

'Really?' asked Shelley slowly, considerably calmer already. 'So it's like a family heirloom? And I could have it?'

'Yes. It's in box number six under the house. Don't make a mess.'

'Okay. Um, thanks.' Shelley paused before continuing quickly. 'And Mum? I'm sorry about before, it's just I saw the lamp there and I couldn't believe it. Like, I *did* love it . . . but it was more having something of Grandpa's. You know?'

'Yes, I know. I really do.' Kate kept her voice flat. 'Listen Shelley, is your dad back yet?'

'No, not yet. And now I'm off under the house. Thanks, okay?'

'Okay. Bye.' Kate hung up the phone and massaged her temples gently. Her mind flicked up to Eildon, where she imagined the boys packing up the car, or maybe enjoying a last beer. But preferably not Sam, as he would be driving. She hoped that they didn't leave it too late to hit the road, as the traffic could be heavy.

Kate shook her head and then stood up, stretching. She was surprised to see that Angie wasn't home, being a Sunday, but not disappointed. Because that was yet another problem. What was she to *do* with this new information? The first step, obviously, was to process it properly. But then would sharing it with Angie become the second step?

She went through to the kitchen and put the kettle on, then leant against the island bench as she waited for it to boil. The problem was that, until now, she had not really perceived Sophie as a *person*. There had been no photos of her around the house as she and Angie had been growing up, and no real mention of her in conversations. She was simply a shadowy figure from the past, possessing no real substance other than the fact she had left behind a mystery.

Therefore it had been relatively easy to begin the research into her story, because that's all it was – a story, which was missing an end. As relevant as a host of other tales that had grasped her imagination, like whatever happened to the little French dauphin, or to Anastasia, the tragic Russian princess. But now it was so much more. Sophie was a real woman, living a real life. She was a silly girl who had been swept off her feet by an older man, she was a wife who had fallen again for her first love, and she was a sister who couldn't lie well. Then she was a young mother, giving up her only child through guilt and duress, and a woman who had been forced to start all over again. She had lived an entire life between then and now, so that her story *had* no end, and no part where everything could be tied off neatly and given closure.

Kate made her coffee and took it, with her laptop, upstairs to her bedroom. There she methodically entered all of the newly discovered facts into her research file. There were several things she should have asked Auntie Faye but hadn't thought to. Like, was Thomas still alive? Had the union between him and Sophie been happy? Kate found herself sincerely hoping that it had been. Sophie deserved at least that much.

'Been home long?'

Kate glanced up at Angie and nonchalantly closed the laptop. 'A while. I didn't even hear you come in.'

'I'm not surprised. You looked like you were in another world. I take it the writing's going well?'

'Not bad.'

'Well, tear yourself away and come downstairs.' Angie's eyes were smiling. 'We're having champagne. I've got news.'

'What news?'

Angie's eyes smiled even further. 'Come down and I'll tell you.'

Kate followed her cousin downstairs curiously. Her pillow and overnight bag were still piled in the foyer, with the garden gnome lying on top. Angie glanced at it on her way past and grinned. 'Auntie Faye must have liked you. She doesn't give those away lightly, you know. So, did you enjoy yourself?'

'Actually, yes. Apart from the heat, and the food.'

Angie opened the fridge and drew out a bottle of champagne. 'Don't tell me she gave you her chicken noodle and seafood soup?'

'Is *that* what it was?' Kate sat down on a dining room chair and shook her head. 'No, it couldn't have been. There wasn't a noodle in sight.'

'She drains them out first. Just uses the stock.'

'Then why on earth doesn't she simply use chicken stock in the first place?'

'Says it doesn't taste the same.'

'That could only be a plus.'

Angie grinned at her and got two champagne flutes out of the high cupboard. Then she levered the champagne cork out carefully and poured the frothy liquid into the glasses. She carried them over to the table and passed one to Kate. 'Ta da!'

'Okay then, what's the big news?'

Angie sat down and took a sip of her champagne. 'Patience, m'dear. Patience.'

'Sometimes I think you haven't grown up at all,' Kate laughed. 'You used to do exactly the same thing then, too. Make me wait whenever you had something to say.'

'I'll give you a clue. What are you that I'm not but would like to be?'

'This sounds more like a Dr Seuss riddle.' Kate took a sip and gave it some thought. 'Um, married to Sam? Grey-haired? Wrinkled?'

'You found *one* grey hair last year and haven't had another since. That doesn't qualify. And I'm fond of Sam, but no thanks. As for wrinkles, I've got my own.'

'Okay, I give up. What am I that you're not?'

'A grandmother,' answered Angie, her grin becoming smug.

'A *grandmother*!' repeated Kate with surprise. 'Since when have you wanted to be a grandmother?'

'That's not the point.' Angie waved a hand impatiently and then raised her eyebrows. 'Come on, where's your thought processes today? Don't you get it?'

Kate frowned, and then her face cleared. She stared at her cousin. 'Melissa?'

'Yep.'

'Oh my god, Ange! Congratulations!' Kate suddenly hesitated. 'It *is* congratulations isn't it? I mean, it's not . . .'

'No, it's very much planned, apparently. Not that she'd told *me* they were trying.'

'So tell me all about it.' Kate leant forward. 'When's it due? Are they going to get married? What's going to happen with her job?'

'Well, the baby's due in early October. They didn't want to say anything until they were sure everything was okay. And, no, I don't think they're planning on getting married. Maybe later. As for her job, I assume she'll take maternity leave.'

'I wish we knew him better,' said Kate. 'I mean, we've only met him the once. When she brought him over. Last June.'

'I know.' Angie fell silent for a moment and then brightened again. 'But he did seem really nice. Very supportive. And *she's* happy, that's the main thing.'

'True . . .' Kate glanced across as something occurred to her. 'Hey, do you think that's why Mel wanted you to come over for a year?'

'I *know* it is. And she asked me again.'

Something in Angie's voice made Kate pause and look at her cousin searchingly. 'And now you're thinking about it, aren't you?'

Angie stared down at her flute, and then turned the glass stem slowly with her fingers. 'Yes, I am.'

'But Ange! What about –'

'I *know*,' interrupted Angie impatiently. 'But it's like this might be my *only* chance. She's already saying that they're just going to have the one, because of their careers and such. And . . . well, I keep thinking about when I had her. I mean, I know I had my aunt around and Oscar's parents, but it's not really the same as having a mother there. *You* know that as well as I do.'

Kate nodded slowly, understanding quickly followed by a flash of guilt that annoyed her. It wasn't as if she had known about Angie's mother back then. She looked at Angie earnestly. 'Look, I *really* wish I could say I'd look after the shop for you. But it's such long hours and . . .'

'Yep, I know.' Angie twirled the glass another ninety degrees and the champagne sloshed inside the glass.

'Maybe you could go for the birth? And I take over for just a month or so?'

'Or maybe . . .' Angie petered off and glanced up at Kate. 'I've been thinking about this all day and, well, maybe I could get someone else to do it for the whole year.'

'Who?'

'Shelley.' Angie held up her hand as Kate's eyes widened. 'Let me finish. Look, she loves working there, *and* she's really good at it. She'd manage perfectly.'

'That's a hell of a lot of responsibility. What if something happened?'
'Like what?'
'Fire. Theft. Terrorism. Some sort of book fungus disease.' Kate shook her head. 'Seriously though, you *know* Shelley. I mean, on the one hand I'd be thrilled for her because she'd love it. But then, also, she's been dying to expand your business ever since she started working there. You leave her alone for a year and it won't be the same. She'll either ruin it entirely or turn it into some sort of global corporation.'

'I know. And that's why I also came up with an alternative plan.' Angie paused momentarily. 'Which is that I just sell her the business.'

'*What?*'

'Hang on, just hear me out. I could sell it without too much trouble on the open market, but I'd really like it to go to Shelley. Not just because she's family, but because she's so damn *keen*. She's like I was when I started. And for her, I *do* think it'd be a great investment. It brings in a living as it is, and she may even improve it.'

'But what about you? When you come back?'

Angie shrugged. 'I don't know. But I think I'd *like* to not know. Firstly because it takes all the pressure off me, and secondly because it'd be nice to float for a while. And by then I'll be able to afford to. You know I've done nothing but think this all through today. And I've been working six days a week for an awfully long time. I'd really like a break.'

'So where would she get the money?'

'From her share of the development, of course.' Angie held up her hand again. 'And before you object, look at some of the positives. She'd have a job she loved and something to focus her energy on. Plus she could take Emma to work with her whenever she wanted. And it *is* a really sound investment, trust me.'

'I do. I can see it's a great opportunity. It's just . . .'

'Look, Kate, I really don't mind. I'm running it by you first, that's all. But I'm just as happy to offer her the managership for a year and, if I still feel the same way, sell it then. To her, or somebody else. It's no skin off my nose.'

Kate took another sip of champagne and thought over the proposal.

She knew she was being overprotective, but it was sometimes difficult to really *perceive* the children as adults. And risk-taking just made her feel uneasy. Although clearly Shelley herself was okay with taking risk, ergo Emma.

'Why don't I leave it with you?' said Angie, watching her cousin's face. 'Mull it over while I'm at Oscar's place, and let me know what you think. I promise I won't mention it to Shelley till I get your feedback.' She waited for Kate to nod and then changed the subject. 'So, what do you think of me as a grannie, hey?'

'It'll take getting used to,' Kate smiled, glad to be distracted. 'I haven't even got used to *me* as a grannie yet.'

'I'll have to buy a rocking chair. Start knitting.'

'Oh my lord!' Kate started laughing. 'Oscar will be a *grandfather*!'

'I'm not sure whether he's as thrilled as I am,' Angie grinned. 'He still sees himself as suave and youthful.'

'Hey! What about the unit?'

'I've thought about that too. I wouldn't be going until about September so it won't affect you. I'd just rent it out for a year, that's all.'

Kate looked across at her cousin, at the familiar scattering of freckles and the wide, generous mouth. 'I'll miss you.'

'Hang on, it's not even certain that I'm going yet!'

'It'll happen.' Kate nodded, suddenly certain. And also sure that it was the right thing for Angie. But, god, would she miss her. Although nowadays, with phone calls and emails, it wasn't as bad as it once would have been. And this was something special. *Family* was something special. She thought about Auntie Faye, and how thrilled the older woman would be with the news. Then she thought about Sophie, and wondered what her reaction would be. She would be a great-grandmother, when she'd hardly been a mother. And suddenly Kate knew that Angie *must* be told, that there was really no alternative. The generations had to be given the chance to expand, in either direction. But now was not the time for such news, and champagne was not really the right accompaniment.

SIXTEEN

> *Dear Dad, I don't know what is upsetting me more – that I've found out so much, or there is so much to find out in the first place! If someone had asked me to describe you, or Uncle Frank, I would have said something like 'what you see is what you get'. But maybe what we see is just what we* want *to see. I don't know.*
>
> *PS: Wouldn't Uncle Frank have been thrilled.*
> *PPS: Life's not bloody well fair.*
> *PPPS: I gave Shelley your desk set.*
> *PPPPS: How am I going to tell Angie?*

Kate heard Angie leave for work the next morning, but rather than go downstairs and say goodbye, she closed the laptop and crawled back into bed, staring at the ceiling as she continued her reflections on how best to explain to her cousin about her sleuthing, and the results. Even though she kept telling herself that she now had at least a week to think about it, the subject, together with the heat, had proved a barrier against sleep for the greater part of the night.

Around three o'clock that morning, Kate had finally come to the conclusion that her first instinct, which had been to simply hand everything over to Angie now, was actually ill advised. Instead what she really needed to do was to fill in some of the gaps *before* presenting the information. Otherwise, she was giving her as many questions as she was answers. And that wasn't fair. She fell asleep with that thought but woke only an hour later, on the heels of a frightful dream where she had been trying to close a door, desperately, but something had been pushing against it. She had lain awake then, damp with sweat, and tried to distract herself by revisiting her dilemma. And finally admitted that filling in the gaps was as much for her benefit as it was for Angie's. Having come this far, she just wanted to finish it and then bestow the whole package, neatly tied together, as a fait accompli.

Six o'clock brought a noisy kookaburra to a nearby tree, and also the rather bitter acknowledgement that she might as well finish the investigation as that was all it was ever likely to be. Because Sophie's story simply wasn't hers to write. Even if she somehow gained Sophie's permission, and Angie's, and Auntie Faye's, it would feel not only larcenous, but also exploitative. Profiting from someone else's pain.

The kookaburra let out a series of echoing, full-throated warbles and then one more, as an encore, while he flew off. Kate rolled over with the sheet tangled around her legs, and hugged the pillow against her chest as she stared at the empty side of her bed. At home, even when Sam wasn't beside her, she could still see the indentations left by his body, or smell his particular smell on his pillow. But here there was nothing except an empty expanse, the sheets still relatively neat and the pillow fluffed and even. Maybe she wouldn't see the whole six months out after all. Maybe she was never *meant* to write a book. Maybe this had never really been about that.

Kate kicked the sheet away with an energy that pulled it out from the other side of the bed and brought a sheen of sweat to her forehead. The humidity on the top floor of the unit already felt thick and heavy, like an extra layer of bedclothes itself. But the change was due through today so that, at least, would soon be over. Kate tucked her sweaty hair behind her ears and then sat on the side of the bed and stared blankly towards her father's desk. Would going home be admitting defeat?

She realised that she was staring at the wedding photo of her parents, which she had placed by the lamp on her desk. So she got up and put it in a drawer out of sight. Then, shedding her clammy T-shirt and knickers, she strode into the ensuite for a much-needed shower.

Fifteen minutes later, and now clad in a loose shift dress, Kate went downstairs for coffee. Her eyes still felt grainy with tiredness but it was far cooler here, with the upper storey acting as a type of insulation from the warmth, so while the kettle came to the boil, she fetched her laptop and set it on the dining room table. She stared at the screen broodingly. There seemed to be three major questions needing answers:

1. Was Thomas still alive?
2. Did he and Sophie have any children?
3. What was Uncle Frank in jail for (and how long)?

Of course, there were other questions, like why hadn't Sophie ever attempted to see Angie later on? Especially after Frank died? After all, the man had been dead for nearly *thirty* years. Kate massaged her temples and then shook her head, mystified, but decided that she had to have *some* limitations, and those more emotive angles needed to be left for Angie to unravel. If she wanted to.

She suddenly realised that she no longer felt bitter that this would never be a book, instead she felt almost *relieved*. As if she had been playing poison ball and had just managed to offload it. She smiled, rather ruefully, and went back to her list. The logical source of answers for the first two was Auntie Faye, but she would have to be careful to ensure that her interest sounded casual, and not investigative. Kate brought up the telephone directory on the screen, put in a search for Faye Wharton of Ballarat and seconds later had the number before her. On a sudden whim, she also entered Painter, with the initials TJ and then tapped her fingers impatiently as she waited. Suddenly there it was – the correct address, with TJ & SM in residence.

So he *was* alive then. Kate's stomach clenched with a shaft of indignation. Her uncle and her father were both gone, but one-eyed, wife-stealing Thomas Painter lived on. She swallowed bile and then took a deep breath, reasoning with herself over the ridiculousness of her reaction. Why shouldn't he be alive? His life, or death, had no impact on what had happened to either of his cousins. It would have happened regardless. She stabbed at the delete key, hard, erasing the first question on her list.

Before she could dwell on this any further, Kate went into the lounge room and picked up the phone, dialling Auntie Faye's number. It went straight to an answering machine but before she could think of an appropriate message the doorbell rang, breaking her concentration. With some relief, Kate hung up the phone and went to open the door. Recognition came slowly as she stared at the rather short elderly woman standing on the porch. It was the mercenary member of the poker-playing set.

Kate smiled politely. 'Hello. Bev, isn't it?'

'That's right,' Bev nodded, clearly rather relieved to be recognised. 'And I'm sorry to interrupt you, but, ah, there's been something on my mind since last week. When we spoke to you.'

'Oh. Okay.' Kate felt her interest tighten. 'Do you want to come in?'

'No, no. Won't take a minute. I was going to wait till tomorrow, when I'm over here with poker anyway but, well, it's been preying on me a bit.'

'Really? About Sophie Wharton?'

Bev shook her head. 'That's the thing, it's not. So it's probably irrelevant but I thought, with you writing a book and all . . . I didn't want to give the wrong picture. Or not the whole picture anyhow. But you mayn't even be interested in that bit.'

Kate's curiosity was now fully roused. 'Why don't you just tell me, then I'll let you know if it's relevant or not?'

'Okay then.' Bev pursed her lips slightly and then continued: 'It's the other one we spoke about. Rose Kimber. The one that married Jimmy Painter.'

'Yes?' managed Kate as she forced her expression to remain politely curious.

'I seem to recall we were quite hard on her. Called her a few nasty names.'

Kate's breath caught. 'And they weren't true?'

'Oh no,' Bev frowned and shook her head. 'They were all true. But there's more to it than just that. So if you were to mention Rose in your book, then I'd hate to think you went with what we said, without the rest.'

'And the rest is?'

'She had a dreadful background.' Bev stared at Kate, the intensity of her gaze giving emphasis to her words. 'A *really* dreadful background. Her father wasn't a terribly big man, but he was an absolute brute. Drank heavily.'

Kate took this in, slowly. 'Oh. But what about her mother?'

'Now she was an odd one. Used to sing to herself while she was walking, I remember that. Just quietly, as if she was in her own world. Not that she went out much. She was a bit slow, see. Not quite all there. But whether she was *always* like that, or whether it was because of the home life, who knows?'

Kate wrapped her arms around herself. 'Any sisters? Or brothers?'

'No, Rose was an only child.' Bev furrowed her brow as she thought. 'She was a few years younger than me but I *seem* to remember my mother once referring to Mrs Kimber as having had a lot of miscarriages. Though I can't really recall.'

'It must have been dreadful for her,' said Kate slowly.

'Yes. Especially in those days. Nowadays there'd be social workers on the case, but then? People just minded their own business.'

'God.'

'So you see that even though there's no denying she was a sly little thing as a child, and she grew into a rather unpleasant woman, well, there was probably good reason for it. And that's what's been preying on me. Just in case you want to mention her, in your book, you need the whole story. Not just the fact she wasn't well liked.'

'I appreciate that,' said Kate, her mind still reeling. 'Absolutely.'

'Good.' Bev took a deep breath, clearly relieved. She gave Kate a quick, tight smile and then turned to go.

'One more thing,' Kate stepped out onto the porch. 'Just out of curiosity, what happened to them? Rose's parents, I mean.'

The older woman pursed her lips and gazed over Kate's shoulder into the past. 'Hmm, not sure, but I think she died young. Certainly she wasn't around by the time Rose got married. But *he* still was. In fact, he was probably one of the reasons they moved. Rose and James Painter, I mean. But God *does* strike in mysterious ways.'

'He does?'

'He certainly does. The old bastard ended up getting exactly what he deserved.' Bev smiled with rather inordinate pleasure. 'Got knocked down by a truck one night right outside the local hotel. Killed instantly.'

'Oh.'

'Actually now that I think of it, probably would have been more fitting if he'd lingered for a while, but there you go. Can't have everything.'

'No, I suppose you can't,' said Kate slowly.

'So if you mention Rose, be sure to mention some of this also.'

'I will. And thank you very much for your trouble,' Kate smiled at Bev, who nodded briskly and pursed her lips again, as if congratulating herself that the task was now done.

Kate watched her walk slowly to her car and then went back to her laptop where, after a few moments, she added another question: *Who was Rose Kimber?* Then she sat, staring at the question and trying to imagine what life had been like for her mother. A father who was a violent drunk, and a mother who was what? Mentally disabled? The product of constant abuse? Or maybe both.

The question seemed to fill the screen. *Who was Rose Kimber?* In its shadow were all the other questions about Rose's life, and how dreadful a childhood it must have been. Especially after her own mother had passed away. No wonder she had been a sly child, it had probably been one of the few measures she could develop to protect herself. While bitterly comparing the horrors of her home life with those of other children around. And all those people, none of whom lifted a finger to help her. Why *wouldn't* she be horrid?

But one of the most compelling questions, for Kate, was how her parents got together. Had it been at a dance, as her father always said, where perhaps the quiet, sensitive man saw through the young woman's prickly exterior? Or maybe a scenario like so many others, where fumbling, frantic lust had taken advantage – or been taken advantage *of*. Then again, like much of reality, perhaps it was neither one nor the other, but a mix of both.

Kate suddenly realised that, as depressingly awful as Rose's background was, it was also, in some strange way, a relief. Because suddenly her mother was comprehensible again. She had *not* sprung forth from a happy, secure, middle-class home as a horrid woman; rather she had crawled from a wreck of a childhood and then probably tried to secure herself a future in one of the only ways she would have known. This new mother might not be the princess of her father's stories, but she had regained her tragic essence – even enhanced it. And that was what Kate had always been used to.

The weather finally broke that afternoon, a brisk, cool breeze heralding a sheet of grey clouds that wrapped their way across the sky. An hour later they released their burden, sending down a drizzle of rain that rapidly became a torrent, beating against the windows with a ferocity that forced Kate to turn the television volume up. She was watching an American talk show, one of the types guaranteed to make even the most pessimistic person more cheerful about their own lives. Today's topic seemed to be: *How my father slept with my wife and then she had a baby who was both my step-child and my sibling.*

Kate watched the show until the credits began to roll, then she turned the volume down and immediately the sound of hammering rain filled the room. She could see nothing through the windows but a greyness pierced by slashes of silver whipping across the glass. It brought a sense of isolation and seclusion that was strangely cathartic. She closed her eyes and, with the absence of sight, the drumming of the rain seemed to fill her head, banishing even reason. She laid her head against one of the cushions and let it massage her head, the repetition becoming almost hypnotic.

The shrill ringing of the telephone jerked Kate roughly awake, and she sat up, feeling dislocated and sodden with sleep. The sound of the rain had eased and a newsreader now filled the television screen, his lips moving wordlessly. The telephone rang again so Kate forced herself to answer it.

'Hello?' She turned her head from side to side, trying to erase the stiffness.

'Hello! Who's this? Angie?'

'No, it's Kate.'

'Ah, hello, honey. You sound tired.'

'Auntie Faye.' Kate made an effort to lift the flatness of her tone. 'How are you?'

'I'm well. Very well. Now, did you ring me? Or was it Angie?'

'It was me. How did you know?'

'Can't get anything past this old bird,' Auntie Faye chuckled proudly. 'You see, the answering machine picked up a call, but no message, so I just pressed a few buttons and voilà! Mystery solved. Ah, the wonders of technology.'

Kate stifled a yawn. 'I was just ringing to say thanks. For lunch the other day.'

'My pleasure. Any time.'

'Well, it's our turn next. You'll have to come down here.'

Auntie Faye laughed. 'Then I'd better make it soon, hadn't I? That is, if Angie goes overseas. What wonderful news about Melissa, hey? I've already rung her to say congrats. Fancy me being a great-aunt! I'll tell you a secret though, I *thought* something like this'd be on the cards. Just had this little feeling. I told Angie that too.'

'Did you?' Kate frowned to herself, but she wasn't sure why. Something jarred. 'So you've spoken to her?'

'Oh, yes. We had a lovely chat this morning.'

'I see. Um, and I suppose you spoke about . . .'

'What, honey?'

Kate chewed her lip, wondering how best to ask the older woman whether she had said anything about their little chat over lunch. Then her eyes widened as she was suddenly struck by an anomaly that had framed the entire conversation. If Angie knew very little about her mother's story, then why hadn't Auntie Faye been more discreet in the first place? *I'll tell you a secret* . . .

'I'm going to have to go in a sec,' prompted Auntie Faye. 'I've got pottery. So . . . ?'

'It was nothing,' said Kate weakly. 'Just wanted to say thanks. That's all.'

'Any time at all, honey. Have a lovely Easter.'

Kate hung up the phone slowly. She could have asked Auntie Faye directly but she wanted to get it straight in her mind first. Besides, that would only have served to emphasis the entire episode. And for all she knew, Auntie Faye suffered from periods of forgetfulness, or downright senility, and had put the whole thing out of her mind. In that case, to mention it now would only serve to remind her. And she may well feel that then she *had* to tell Angie.

But the initial anomaly remained, and Kate shook her head with amazement that it had never occurred to her before. Even while she was revealing particularly personal segments of the family history on Saturday, Auntie Faye had never *once* sounded like she was imparting anything confidential. She had spoken as if all was in the public arena already, and she was merely passing it on. Having a bit of a gossip. Kate thought back over the conversation, especially the last part where Auntie Faye had pointed cheerfully towards Sophie's house. And she realised, with a flash of sudden understanding, that *I'll tell you a secret* wasn't the prelude to a revelation at all. It was just an expression. *I'll tell you a secret*, this potato's actually made from powder. *I'll tell you a secret*, my sister lives just up the road. *I'll tell you a secret*, Angie already knows. Everything.

SEVENTEEN

Dear Dad, have I opened Angie's diary again? If so, I didn't mean to. Could she really *have known about this all along? Kept it a secret from me? I've been thinking about it a bit (there's an understatement), and I've decided it makes little practical difference. If she's in the dark, then it's best that I continue on, prepare as complete a gift as possible. And if – as now seems possible – she* does *know, then I need to catch up. That way, when I confront her, my indignation can be informed (and not marred by curiosity).*

PS: I'll never know the full truth about my mother, will I? Not the things that matter, anyway. Like how did you meet? Did she maybe change after the two of you got married? Did happiness make a difference? I really want to think it did, so I've decided that's what I'm going to do.

The week unfolded like a gift, day after day of a seclusion that was augmented by continuing inclement weather. Kate only went out once, to stock up on a few groceries, but apart from that she hunkered down and thrived within the isolation. She watched a lot of television, read a couple of books, and marked up a few manuscripts that weren't due for a while. It was like a little holiday, unencumbered and wonderfully therapeutic. Better than a writers' retreat, because there was nobody here to judge her.

It occurred to her that this time last year, as her father's condition worsened, she would have done almost anything for free time like this. And in a way she had.

To her surprise, however, thoughts like this did not contain the sharply accusatory edges they once had. Certainly they made her feel saddened, but the actual pain seemed blunter, as if it had worn down with use. She steered clear of exploring what this meant, because the notion that she was becoming desensitised was depressing in itself.

Instead she concentrated on reimagining her mother and building a framework for Angie's. Accordingly, Kate also spent a lot of time on the Internet, trawling through the local library website and some archival pages, in search of any references to those on her list. Wharton, Painter, and now Kimber as well. In particular, she was looking for something that referred to Frank's departure to, or arrival back from, his time spent at Her Majesty's pleasure. Along the way, she was also hoping for some mention of the Kimber family, maybe even something relating to the death of either or both of Rose's parents. But all she found was a 1962 article about severe bushfires in the area that had caused over thirty fatalities, where a Mr F Painter was quoted as saying, 'We thought we was all goners.'

So after hours of investigation, all she discovered was that her uncle hadn't been a particularly dab hand at grammar, which she knew already. She sent a few enquiries to genealogy websites asking about pointers to discover prison records and court documents but left it at that. It was then, late on Friday afternoon, that Kate went to check her emails quickly and found several Happy Easter ones from friends and a funny Easter chain letter from Shelley, with a bunny hopping across the bottom of the screen laying chocolate eggs as he went.

Kate smiled, and then slowly frowned. How soon *was* Easter? Even as she jumped off the couch and hurried towards the kitchen, and Angie's Remarkable Scenes of Australia calendar, her stomach was clenching with unease. Yet this did not negate the disbelief she felt as she stared at the words *Good Friday*, which were clearly marked across the square containing today's date. Kate blinked, but nothing changed.

Certainly she had noticed the array of hot-cross buns and chocolate eggs and oversized rabbits through the stores, but since they began making their appearance shortly after the New Year, she had just become accustomed to their presence. And certainly she had registered the occasional mention of Easter in conversations but, if she had thought about it at all, she had just assumed Easter was approaching sometime in early April, not when it was still March. In her defence, it *was* the earliest Easter for a number of years.

But the really puzzling facet was that there had been no mention of Easter from her family. Especially as this was a time they traditionally spent together, with their annual obeisance to religion being a fish dinner on Good Friday and then, on Sunday, a barbecue and a genial exchange of chocolate eggs. Kate sat down at the dining room table; she felt so hurt that she physically ached. Besides, this was Emma's first Easter! Her *first* Easter!

It was also the first Easter since her father had died. And suddenly Kate thought she knew why nothing had been organised. They had been waiting for her, taking their cue from her actions. And as no actions had been forthcoming, maybe they'd thought she would prefer nothing to be done. But they were wrong. Kate ran upstairs to pack her bag for the weekend. Within twenty minutes she was reversing out onto the road, heading down to Lysterfield. She made two stops on the way, the first at a local supermarket to purchase an assortment of chocolate eggs, bunnies and bilbies, and a large box of chocolate-covered cashews for Sam; and the second to her father's house. Kate didn't stay there long. She strode through to the back, feeling rather embarrassed at what she intended but trying to mask it with brisk pragmatism.

The yard was even more overgrown now, the weeds most abundant over the vegetable patch. Knobbly dull-yellow lemons lay scattered on the ground near the tree, and Kate kicked a few away as she sat down at the old wrought-iron setting. Glancing around self-consciously, she slid a small, caramel-centred egg out of her pocket and put it down on the table. The royal blue silver foil glittered incongruously against the dull grey-white of the table top.

'Happy Easter,' Kate spoke in a low voice and then waited, staring down at the egg. There was no reply, and the silence that followed her words seemed somehow deeper than it had before she spoke. With one finger, she rolled the egg backwards and forwards over the rusted nipple section, while she let the quietness stretch until it moved from painful to almost boring. Then she picked up the egg and carefully wedged it into the empty umbrella hole at the centre of the table. 'Happy Easter,' she said again, but this time she just mouthed the words so that the ensuing silence didn't seem quite so harsh.

It was nearly six o'clock by the time Kate pulled in the driveway and the first thing she noticed was the absence, once again, of Sam's silver ute. She stared at the gap in front of the garage, surprised by the depth of her disappointment, and then grabbed her overnight bag from the back seat and walked slowly up the stairs.

Shelley was curled up with Emma on the couch in front of the television. On the coffee table were the remains of their dinner, which looked like it might have been spaghetti bolognaise. Both glanced across as Kate entered, but Emma, after a toothy smile, went straight back to staring at the television.

Shelley frowned. 'Mum! What're you doing here?'

Kate put her bag down by the doorway, feeling suddenly awkward. 'Um, I just thought I'd . . . it *is* Good Friday, you know.'

'Yeah, of course it is,' Shelley nodded, and then her eyes widened. 'Oh no! Did you think we were having a family dinner?'

'Well, we do *every* year, so I sort of assumed . . .'

Shelley looked down at her empty plate and then back at her mother, clearly dismayed. 'I never thought . . . but I *did* ask you a week or so ago what you were doing, and you didn't answer. Shoot, I feel really bad now.'

'Don't worry about it,' said Kate, making an effort to keep her tone light. 'So where's everybody else?'

'Up at Eildon. Hey, do you want some spag bog? I made heaps.'

Kate was staring at her daughter. 'Eildon? *Again?*'

'Yeah. So, do you want some?'

'I, um . . . maybe later. Thanks.'

'No problem.' Shelley unfolded her long legs and sat up. She undid Emma's bib before lowering her to the floor, where Emma immediately crawled over to the television and sat up again, transfixed by the vivid colours. Shelley picked up the remote control and reduced the volume.

Kate went over to her usual armchair and sat down. 'So . . . why did they go up to Eildon again?'

'Dunno,' Shelley shrugged, and then glanced at her mother's overnight bag curiously. 'Are you staying over?'

'Well, I *was* going to. I thought with Easter and all. Do you know when they're going to be back?'

'Not sure. Maybe tomorrow. I know Dad said we'd have a barbie on Sunday.'

'Oh. Nice.'

Kate looked across at the television, where a cartoon cat was now being disembowelled by a hyperactive mouse. Emma stared raptly, her mouth open. 'Do you think she should be watching this?' Kate's voice was harsher than she intended so she smiled to smooth it down. 'Next thing you know, she'll be decapitating you in your sleep. And you'll only –'

'Have myself to blame,' finished Shelley, looking at her daughter pensively. As if sensing her audience, Emma flopped forward and crawled closer to the television, where she hoisted herself up awkwardly. She batted a hand against the colourful characters for a moment and then, mouth open, leant forward and started sucking the screen, a trickle of drool dribbling down the glass. In front of her, now partially blurred by smeared saliva, the mouse continued his macabre occupation. Kate grimaced and then looked across at Shelley with her eyebrows raised.

'Okay, okay.' Shelley picked up the remote and flicked the channel over. As Emma sat back down grumbling, she sighed and crossed her legs, jiggling one foot in the air rhythmically. 'It's just that it keeps her so *quiet*.'

'I'm not surprised.' Kate made a mental note to buy some child-appropriate DVDs, preferably ones that did not include evisceration amongst their learning tools.

'I'm glad you came round,' said Shelley suddenly. 'I was going to drop in on you this weekend anyway.'

'What for?' asked Kate suspiciously.

'God! *Nothing*.' Shelley looked offended. 'Can't I drop in without ulterior motives?'

'I don't know. Can you?'

'Very funny. Hey, did you hear about Melissa?'

Kate nodded, smiling. 'Yes, great news. Your aunt is thrilled.'

'So am I. Now I won't be the only one in this generation with offspring.'

Kate looked at her curiously. 'Does that bother you?'

'Nah, not really.' Shelley stared at her daughter, who had found a piece of spaghetti under the coffee table and was now occupied with trying to separate it from the carpet pile. 'Well, only when people think I'm a screw-up.'

'What! Who thinks you're a screw-up?' asked Kate, instantly furious.

'Calm down, Mum,' Shelley smiled and finally stopped jiggling her foot as she reached down and took the spaghetti from Emma, flicking it onto a plate. 'Nobody thinks that in *particular*. It's just sometimes when people look at Em, and then me, I can tell they're thinking 'Oh, you silly girl.' You know.'

'Yes, I suppose.'

Shelley kept her eyes on Emma. 'Do *you* think I'm a screw-up?'

'Certainly not,' Kate didn't hesitate. Although she was enormously surprised by the question, she sensed it was important her answer be honest and unsentimental. 'I don't deny I was shocked at the time, and I *did* wish you'd waited until you were in a *really* stable relationship, or more financially secure. But that's life. And I think you're an excellent mother and I also think you're going to land on your feet. I have never once thought of you as a screw-up.'

'Good,' said Shelley, still without looking at her mother.

'Besides, how can anyone have any regrets when they see little Miss Buggalugs here?' asked Kate rhetorically as she leant forward and hoisted her grand-daughter up onto her lap. 'Hey, Em? Who's a beautiful girl then?'

Emma wriggled herself into comfort and then gazed up at her grandmother with an adoring expression. Kate, however, noticed the baby's little finger being crooked expectantly. She took hold of it, just in case.

Shelley stacked Emma's plastic plate on top of her own and then used the discarded bib to clean spaghetti sauce from the coffee table. She glanced over at her mother with a thoughtful expression. 'So what've you got planned for tonight then?'

'That depends. I mean, do you want me to stay?' asked Kate, knowing that she was fishing for affirmation. Emma struggled to free her hand and then splayed her fingers and stared at them, as if searching for marks.

'Absolutely. Except . . .'

'Except what?'

'Well, I *was* going out. Just over to some friends. And Daniel's mum *was* going to have Em, but now she's not well. So-o . . .'

'You'd like me to babysit.'

'*Would* you?'

'So much for not having ulterior motives!'

Shelley jumped up with the plates and then turned to Kate with a grin. 'I'm deeply hurt by that. I'd be pleased you were here regardless. It's just that it's *exhausting* being such an excellent mother, and it's sort of fate that you turned up just when you did. Like I *know* you're probably disappointed that we weren't having a family dinner, but this way you get the house to yourself and that *has* to be nice. You must admit it's all sort of serendipitous, hey?'

Kate smiled wryly. 'Yes, serendipitous indeed.'

EIGHTEEN

> *Dear Dad, remember that time Angie borrowed her father's hairbrush to make roads for a Fisher-Price village we were building in the front yard? I think she must have been around six or seven. Anyway, she put it back afterwards but that night he was getting ready to go out and next thing he's standing in the kitchen furiously shaking the hairbrush at us. With dirt sprinkled all over his shoulders like dandruff. I can still see the expression on Angie's face. Wide-eyed innocence, but with a certain furtiveness that hovered just behind. Covert knowledge. And now that it seems possible that she knew about her mother, I keep seeing that expression. The fact is that she's* always *been good at keeping secrets, I just never thought she'd keep them from me.*

Sam and the boys didn't arrive home until late Sunday afternoon, by which time Kate was nearly out of her mind with boredom. She had never realised just how much time she spent around her home cleaning and, now that was no longer an option, she was left with so much time on her hands that she actually felt weighed down. Kate was well aware of the irony of the situation but that didn't help matters. Admittedly it had been very pleasant spending so much time with Shelley, who arrived home from an outing on Saturday with potato chips and chocolate and borrowed movies. They spent the evening curled up in the lounge room, first laughing at Katherine Heigl in *27 Dresses*, and then crying with Sally Fields in *Steel Magnolias*. But by Sunday, the bonding was wearing thin, especially as most of it was spent with Emma while Shelley 'just dashed' somewhere or other, her version of being 'back in a minute' having no correlation whatsoever with real time.

Kate let the curtains fall as Sam's ute turned into the driveway, and then quickly ran her fingers through her hair and tucked one side behind her ear as she curled into her armchair with a book in hand. Her stomach clenched as she heard them take the stairs noisily and she marvelled at the realisation that she was nervous. Then, before she had time to analyse this reaction, the front door was swinging open.

'Mum! Long time no see.' Caleb dropped an army-style sausage bag at his feet. 'What're you doing here?'

'Well, it *is* my home, and it *is* Easter.'

Jacob materialised in the doorway behind his brother. 'Did'ja bring Easter eggs?'

'Your mother's welcome, with or without eggs.' Sam sent a smile in her direction and then continued down the passageway, laden with sleeping bags.

'Yeah, it's not like we're a fertility clinic,' Caleb grinned, and then frowned. 'Hang on, that sounded better in my head.'

'Distur*bing*,' commented Shelley, arriving in the lounge room from the other direction, with Emma in her arms. 'Now, are we still having a barbie? I'm starving!'

'As are we,' Sam came back, now empty-handed. 'So here's the plan. Caleb, you start the barbecue while I have a quick shower. Meat's in the fridge. Jake, you get the rest of the stuff from the car and just dump it in the laundry for now. Okay?'

Jacob frowned. 'Why can't I –'

'Just do it,' said Sam tiredly as he turned and headed towards the main bedroom. Kate got up and followed him, pushing the door open even as it closed in her face.

'Sorry, sweetheart!' Sam looked at her with surprise. 'I didn't realise you were behind me.'

Kate smiled as she sat down on the bed. 'I'm *always* behind you.'

'My very own stalker. How romantic.'

'Consider yourself lucky, some people have to share.'

'Hmm, I wouldn't mind being shared.' Sam stepped neatly out of his clothes and stood in front of Kate, naked. 'Sometimes I think it's a bit unfair that all this . . .' he gave a little jiggle that made Kate laugh, '. . . is reserved for just one female.'

'Put it away before you hurt someone.'

Sam leered. 'Pain could be your friend.'

Kate crossed her legs automatically. 'Besides, you couldn't handle more than one female.'

'Now *that's* probably true.' Sam's smile faded. 'Not even sure I can handle the one I've got.'

'Practice makes perfect,' replied Kate, trying to ease the conversation again. 'Listen, how come you didn't ring me to make plans? For Easter, I mean.'

Sam looked surprised. 'I just assumed you'd be here. And you are.'

'What about Good Friday then? Our fish dinner?'

'Fish?' Sam grimaced. 'I hate bloody fish, you know that. Hey, while I'm having a shower, do you want to put a salad together? There's stuff in the fridge.'

'But what about Eildon? What's with all the trips there?'

Sam shrugged. 'Just having a break.'

Kate looked at him searchingly. 'But we haven't been up there for ages, then suddenly you go up two weekends in a row?'

'Good Lord, woman. I didn't realise this was going to be an interrogation. If you have to know, we went up last weekend on the spur of the moment and had such a good time that we decided to go again. Why all the questions?'

Kate shrugged lightly. 'Just checking you're not having an affair, that's all.'

'You've guessed my secret.' Sam put a hand on his chest melodramatically. 'I've been having an affair with a buxom country wench called Bertha and, just to add some spice, I've been taking the boys along each week as an audience.'

'You're a sick man, mister.'

'Yes, but Bertha has taught me a thing or two to add to my repertoire. So if you want to hang around, little lady, I'll fill you in.'

Kate started laughing again. 'Is that a pun? If so, it's *really* bad.'

'That's me. Bad to the bone.' Sam wiggled his eyebrows suggestively and then stepped over his clothes and went into the ensuite, leaving the door open. A few seconds later the shower started and then, just as Kate was getting off the bed, he poked his head around the doorframe. 'Want to join me? You can wash my back.'

'If you wanted your back washed, you should have brought Bertha with you.'

'Good idea. I'll remember that for next time.' Sam nodded and then disappeared again.

Kate grinned towards the empty doorway, feeling considerably lighter after the easy, flirtatious conversation. Sam certainly didn't seem as if he was harbouring any grudges, which meant the Eildon trips may well have been exactly what he said – just well-deserved breaks. It still didn't explain why he hadn't asked *her*, or even told her about the barbecue, but everything seemed fine. And she decided to accept it at face value for now. Sometimes it was better *not* to peel the onion.

Kate went out into the kitchen and opened the fridge in search of salad. It was almost empty. At the back of the vegetable crisper she found some yellow-edged lettuce, a tomato and a couple of rather soft carrots, so she piled them on the counter and stared at them critically. Clearly salad vegetables were not a priority any more.

'Are you using the power of your mind?' asked Shelley, coming in from the decking. 'If so, no wonder the lettuce is wilting.'

'Yes, and if you keep it up, I'll turn it on you.' Kate got out a bowl and started slicing the tomato into segments.

Shelley put her hands up in mock fright and then took a tray from the top of the fridge and began loading it with plates and cutlery and condiments. The pungent, charcoaled smell of barbecue wafted in from the decking and Kate felt her stomach rumble in anticipation. She tossed the tomato into the bowl and then added the green sections of the lettuce, throwing the rest into the compost container below the sink. Then she started grating carrot. Shelley finished loading her tray and took it outside.

'Wanna hand?' Jacob wandered in and leant against the bench, gazing at the tossed salad with a marked lack of enthusiasm.

Kate looked at him critically. 'Maybe you should have had a shower too?'

'Whatever,' Jacob shrugged and then fished a lettuce leaf out of the bowl and held it up. The lettuce drooped. 'Yum.'

'Damn it,' Sam came in, his hair wet and spiky at the crown. 'I meant to grab some salad things on the way back.'

The sliding door opened and Shelley hurried through to grab the highchair. 'Caleb says the meat's almost ready.'

'Just do what you can.' Sam waved a hand dismissively at the salad and then headed outside. Jacob flipped his lettuce back into the bowl and followed his father.

'Do what you can,' repeated Kate sarcastically as she removed Jacob's lettuce and threw it into the compost. Having seen the boy's fingers, she wasn't about to take the risk. She opened a tin of corn and scooped two spoonfuls into the bowl and then added her grated carrot and a splash of French dressing that wasn't too far past its use-by date. Then she tossed the lot with salad servers and took it through to the decking.

Sam had taken over the barbecue and was now piling the meat onto a plate held by Caleb. They were being watched hopefully by Hector, who had been summoned by the scent of food even though he had been fed only half an hour before. Jacob was already sitting at the table and Shelley was securing Emma into the highchair.

'You would have started back at uni by now, wouldn't you?' Kate asked Caleb as she put the salad down and slid into a seat. 'How's it going?'

Caleb brought the plate of meat over and sat down. 'Brutal. I'm glad it's my last year. I've had enough.'

'Well, it'll all be over soon,' said Sam, turning off the barbecue.

'Unless I fail, that is.'

'You won't fail,' commented Jacob expressionlessly.

Kate glanced at him and then sighed, quietly so that nobody else could hear.

Sam came over and stared at the table. 'Bread! Wine!'

'And having spake, thus they appeared,' intoned Caleb. 'While you're at it, could we have the miracle of the loaves and fishes?'

'I'll give *you* the miracle of the loaves and fishes,' said Sam, heading back inside.

Caleb looked around as his father disappeared. 'Isn't that what I just asked for?'

'I would have thought you'd have got plenty of fishes,' commented Kate lightly, helping herself to some steak. 'You know, up at Eildon.'

'Nah, too busy. Doing other stuff.'

'Yeah,' added Jacob helpfully.

Kate looked at them both curiously and then focused on Jacob as her best chance. 'Like what, honey?'

'Like just relaxing,' said Sam, shutting the sliding door and then coming over with a bottle of wine and a basket of bread. 'Jake, can you grab some glasses for me?'

'Sure. Why not.'

Kate helped herself to some of the limp salad and piled it by her steak. Hector wandered underneath the table and settled by her feet, so she reached down and scratched his neck absently. There was something distinctly odd about these Eildon trips but it was clear she wasn't going to get any more information with Sam here. She would just have to come back during the week.

'Great news about Mel, isn't it?' asked Caleb.

'Sure is, and we'll toast her in a second.' Sam levered the cork from the wine bottle and then, as Jacob returned with the glasses, starting filling each one and passing it over. When everybody had a glass, he raised his. 'To Melissa and . . . what's his name?'

'Brad,' said Kate.

'To Melissa and Brad!'

They all repeated the toast and then raised their glasses and drank. Kate put her glass down and started slicing her steak. 'Did you know Angie's thinking of going over there now? To stay for a year or so?'

Sam raised his eyebrows. 'Really? Good for her.'

'Hang on,' Shelley frowned. 'If she goes over there, what happens to the shop?'

Kate hesitated. 'Um, I'm not sure. Nothing's definite.'

'But she won't be able to run it then.'

'I'm sure she'll have a plan,' said Sam soothingly.

Jacob glanced at his sister. 'Maybe she'll sell it.'

'She can't sell it!'

'Actually she can,' corrected Jacob. 'It *is* hers, after all. And what choice would she have? It's not like she's got anybody *responsible* there.'

'God, you're an arsehole!' spat Shelley.

Sam dropped his cutlery with a clatter and glared at Jacob. 'Now listen, I'm only going to say this once –'

'Promises, promises,' replied Jacob, staring down at his plate.

'That's it! Take your damn –'

'Yeah sure,' interrupted Jacob, standing up with burger in hand. 'I'm going.'

Emma, who had been watching this exchange with stunned fascination, suddenly reached a clasping hand towards her uncle. 'Jate, Jate!'

Jacob stopped by the sliding door and stared back at her, his burger dripping splotches of sauce onto the decking. 'Did you hear that! She said my name!'

'Say it again, Em!' Shelley grabbed her daughter's outstretched hand, her anger gone in an instant.

'Come on, Emma!' added Kate encouragingly. 'Say *Jake!*'

Emma pulled her hand from her mother's and gazed around at her audience. Then she pursed her lips and blew a saliva bubble. It burst against her lips and she chortled proudly before trying again, but this time frothy spittle just ran down her chin.

'She takes after your side of the family,' observed Sam, glancing at Kate.

'Actually, that's the exact same expression you had when you told me about Bertha.'

'Who's Bertha?' asked Caleb.

'Your father's mistress.'

'Sounds like a cow.'

'Don't you knock Bertha,' said Sam. 'She's the salt of the earth.'

Caleb raised an eyebrow. 'You'll probably get an STD. Like mad cow disease. Or foot in mouth.'

'*Foot* in mouth? That sounds like a fetish, mate, not an STD.'

While this banter continued, Kate glanced across to the sliding door, but Jacob had gone, leaving the door half open.

'Fancy her saying Jacob's name first.' Shelley was staring at her daughter critically. 'He's probably been spending hours coaching her.'

'So what made you suspect Dad and Bertha, Mum?' asked Caleb with a grin.

'All those trips to Eildon, of course. I wasn't born yesterday, you know.'

'*That's* stating the obvious,' said Sam.

'Watch it!'

'Do you think she'll *really* sell the shop?' fretted Shelley, drumming her fingers against the table. 'Like she'd *have* to, wouldn't she? If she left?'

Kate stared down at her empty plate, cross with herself for having mentioned Angie's plans. She laid her cutlery down and stood up. 'I brought dessert. Back in a moment.' She went back into the house and fetched her bag of Easter eggs from the main bedroom. Then, going down the passage, she paused outside Jacob's bedroom before knocking lightly.

'What?'

'It's only me. I've got something for you.' Kate pushed open the door and went inside. With the blind pulled down, the room was mostly dark except for the computer screen, which glowed before Jacob like some sort of futuristic altar. He had swivelled around in his chair and was staring at his mother. She pulled a couple of eggs and a large chocolate rabbit from the bag and held them out. 'Happy Easter.'

'Thanks.' Jacob grinned and took the chocolates.

Kate hesitated. 'Why do you do it?'

'Do what?'

'Deliberately bug your sister like that. You know how it always ends.'

'With Dad sticking up for her, you mean?'

'No,' Kate shook her head. 'With you storming off.'

'Actually I was *ordered* off.'

'Can you blame him?'

The side of Jacob's face was luminous in the reflected light. He shrugged. 'Sure I can. Why not?'

Kate shook her head again. 'I don't understand you.'

'Nobody does,' said Jacob melodramatically, but without changing expression.

'Well . . . happy Easter.'

'Yeah. Thanks, Mum.'

Kate closed the door gently and sighed again. It was difficult to help somebody who was their own worst enemy. Even more difficult when you suspected, deeply, that they were miserable. With some effort, she put Jacob to one side for now and took the bag outside to the decking, tipping it onto the table. 'Happy Easter.'

'Excellent!' Caleb put out a hand to stop a gold-foiled egg from rolling off the table.

Sam stared at them and then glanced up at Kate. 'I didn't get you anything.'

'That's okay,' replied Kate lightly. 'I'm sure you were busy. At Eildon.'

'He certainly was,' said Caleb.

'There you go.' Kate passed the cashews over. 'For you to share with Bertha.'

Sam smiled, rather flatly. 'Not a chance. She can get her own.'

'Thanks, Mum.' Shelley picked up a smaller egg and unwrapped the foil from it. Then she passed the chocolate over to Emma, who grabbed it eagerly. 'Here you go, Em. You know what this is, don't you?'

'Has she already had some?' asked Kate.

'Daniel gave her one yesterday. With a big soft rabbit. Really cute.' Shelley stood up. 'Would you mind watching her for a minute? I've got to make a phone call.'

'You're ringing Angie,' stated Sam, pushing his plate to one side. 'Can't you just leave it for now?'

'No! I can't!' Shelley's voice rose in pitch. 'I *love* that job!'

'Okay, okay. We'll watch her.' Kate wondered how Angie would handle this, and whether she would stick to her promise not to offer Shelley the business, just yet.

'Hey, what's the deal with all Grandpa's stuff?' asked Caleb suddenly.

Kate looked at him defensively. 'What do you mean?'

'Well, the great hand-out. Jake's got the lamp, Shelley's got the desk set. What about me?'

'You're giving out your father's things?' Sam stared at her, clearly astounded.

'You can have the carriage clock if you like,' said Kate quickly, but with a sense of weariness. 'You know, the little gold one that used to sit near the candelabra. Or you can have the candelabra. Or both. I don't care. They're in the same box that Shelley got the desk set from. Ask her.'

'Okay. Thanks.'

Sam was still staring at her, but his surprise had given way to a sort of wary gratification. They made eye contact and he looked away, picking up the bottle of wine and topping up their glasses. He held it enquiringly over Caleb's. 'More?'

'Nah, I've got some study.' Caleb stood up, grabbing a few Easter eggs. 'I'll just take some supplies to help me along.'

Kate watched him leave and then turned back to Sam and stared at him narrowly, daring him to say something.

'So . . . just you and me then?' Sam leant over and plucked a piece of lettuce out of the salad bowl. The lettuce dangled limply and Sam had second thoughts, dropping it back in again.

'Seems that way.'

'What're we going to do about Jake?'

'What?' Kate frowned, confused by the sudden shift.

'Jacob. You know, the kid who sleeps till lunchtime and then spends the rest of the day, and half the night, on his computer. Eating everything in the fridge. That one.'

'I know which one,' snapped Kate. 'Why?'

'Because he can't go on like this,' said Sam, with annoying patience. 'Don't get me wrong, I *know* he's good at computers, but if he wants to make a living out of it then he needs to be realistic. Go to university or something.'

'He's not going to do that,' replied Kate with certainty. 'That'd put him in competition with his brother.'

'It would be totally different courses!'

Kate sighed. 'Which makes no difference and you know it. Just give him time, Sam. And support. Something will come up sooner or later. Especially as *he's* getting really sick of the whole thing, I can tell.' She paused to give a half-smile. 'You'll probably laugh about it one day.'

'Yeah, when they cart me off to the asylum, I'll be laughing hysterically.'

'Hope you don't expect many visits. I've never been keen on manic laughter.'

Hector emerged from underneath the table and rubbed himself against Sam's chair like an overgrown cat. Sam reached down and gave his neck an energetic ruffle, then he looked across at Kate. 'Listen, I need to talk to you about what's next. With the land. The development.'

'No,' Kate's face shut down. 'I don't want to know.'

'But you need to be –'

'No,' repeated Kate. 'Look, I *know* we've all agreed, and I *know* it has to be done. But I just don't want to talk about it, okay?'

'Okay, sweetheart.' Sam gazed over her shoulder at the house and then took a gulp of his wine. 'Well then . . . so how's the writing going?'

'Good, good.'

'That's what you always say. But does that *really* mean good, or does it mean lousy but you don't want to admit it?'

Kate suddenly felt tired, drained. 'Bit of both.'

'Want to talk about it?'

'Not really.'

'Do you want to talk about *anything*?'

Kate glanced across at him and then at Emma. The baby was holding tight to her Easter egg with chocolate-covered fingers and had managed to suck a gummy hole right at the top. This was the part she was concentrating on, pressing her face against the egg and smearing chocolate in a circle around her mouth.

Sam followed her gaze. 'I think the kid likes chocolate.'

'I think so,' agreed Kate, turning back to face him. She paused for a moment. 'I *was* going to write about Angie's mother.'

'Angie's mother? Didn't she shoot through?'

'Yes. Left when Angie was a baby.'

'Maybe she just needed some space.' Sam looked at her expressionlessly. 'Maybe she wanted to write a book or something.'

Kate stared at him narrowly. 'Very funny. And very wrong. She actually ran off with the one-eyed next door neighbour.'

'Which shows she wasn't shallow at least.' Sam regarded her thoughtfully. 'So you've changed your mind?'

Kate picked up her glass and tilted it slightly, watching the liquid undulate until it settled at an angle. 'Yes. See, at first it just seemed like a challenge. Almost abstract. Then when I started finding out things, it became more personal. More real.'

'What'd you find out?' asked Sam curiously.

'For starters, Angie's mother was engaged to that neighbour that she ran off with. Before she married Frank, that is. And that's why he bought the land, to settle down with her. But she jilted him and married Frank instead. Then later on they had an affair.'

'So he kept an eye on her, did he?'

'Very funny. The point is that they're *still* together. Living in Ballarat.'

Sam frowned and then looked at her searchingly. 'Hang on. You know this how?'

'That's the bit that started me changing my mind about the whole thing. See, I spoke to Angie's aunt, and it turns out Sophie, that's Angie's mother, and her bloke are just living around the corner from her. And have been for years.'

'Good god,' Sam raised his eyebrows. 'And how's Angie taking all this?'

Kate glanced across at Sam, knowing she looked sheepish but not being able to do anything about it. 'Well, I haven't exactly told her what I know.'

'You *what?*'

'Hang on, it's not like I was keeping secrets,' exclaimed Kate defensively. 'Well, not deliberately. Not after the first bit, anyway. I was always *going* to tell her. Then it sort of snowballed. Bloody hell! I never expected the damn woman to be *alive*, did I?'

'In that case, I'd be writing a letter of complaint if I was you. Extremely selfish of her.'

'Don't be a smart-arse,' snapped Kate. 'And for all I know, Angie's known everything all along and not told *me*.'

'Well, that'd be her choice, wouldn't it? Did you even tell her that her mother was going to star as your main character?'

'Um . . . no.'

Sam shook his head. 'Well, come on then, Kate. You must admit it's a bit audacious. How would you feel if someone decided to write about *your* mother without mentioning it?'

'Whatever.' Kate shrugged, knowing she sounded just like one of her offspring. She thought of all she had discovered about her own mother: the abused child, the pregnant bride, the horrible woman. She glanced back at Sam. 'Did my father ever talk about my mother to you?'

Sam looked puzzled. 'No, why?'

'Nothing about the sort of person she was? Or her background?'

'Not really. Just that they had a great marriage and all that.'

Kate reached for the wine bottle and topped up her glass. 'While I was finding out all this stuff about Angie's mother – and despite what you may think, it *did* just snowball – I also found out some pretty amazing stuff about my own mother. Her childhood. Things like that.'

'Write about her, then,' said Sam promptly.

Kate grimaced and then took a sip of wine as the idea floated down, and then settled. Far more comfortably than she would have expected.

'But you *are* going to tell her, aren't you?'

'Of course I am. And for god's sake, it's not like I've known for *years*.' Kate glared at him, her irritation inflated by guilt. 'It just sort of happened. And there's no need for you to smirk either. It's not all *that* often I stuff up.'

Sam pushed his chair back suddenly and stood up. 'I'm getting a camera.'

'*Christ*, you can be a jerk. I only . . .' Kate petered off as she followed his gaze. Emma, having now finished the body of the Easter egg, had her face down on the highchair tray as she vacuumed up every little bit of chocolate she could find. The result was a gooey mess of spittle and chocolate smeared across the tray, her bib, and her hands, even her wrists. As if sensing the audience, Emma paused and looked up, beaming. Chocolate covered her face, plugging one nostril and clumping over her eyebrows.

'My god,' said Kate. She started laughing.

'Back in a second.' Sam grinned at her as he jumped up and went inside.

'Is that nice, Em?' asked Kate, still laughing.

'Num, num!'

'Very num num, it seems.'

The door of the bungalow could be heard slamming and then shortly afterwards Shelley appeared, running up the path. 'Guess what!'

'What?' asked Kate, already knowing the answer.

Shelley arrived at the bottom of the stairs and leant against the railing, peering up at her mother while she caught her breath. 'Auntie Angie! The shop! Mine!'

'Am I supposed to fill the gaps?'

'She says. That I . . .' Shelley took another breath. 'She says that if she goes overseas I can either manage the shop all by myself or I can – get this! – I can *buy* it!'

Despite a flash of annoyance at Angie, Kate couldn't help but smile at her daughter's enthusiasm. 'That sounds great, Shell, but promise me we'll talk it through before you make up your mind? Discuss the pros and cons? I mean, it'll be a *lot* of responsibility.'

'I *know*!' Shelley came up the steps. 'My *very* own business! And I already know what I want to do with it. For starters, it *has* to be computerised. Totally. Then I need to extend into that little back room that's a total waste of space when there's so much stock. Then I need to –' Shelley glanced over at her daughter and her eyes widened.

'Yes. Your father's gone to get a camera.'

'A facecloth would be more effective,' commented Shelley, rather wittily for her.

The sliding door shot open and Sam stuck his head out. 'Have you seen my glasses? And where's the camera?'

'No, and try the middle drawer of the desk,' replied Kate as Sam's head disappeared again.

'I'm going to tell Dad.' Shelley hurried across the decking past her chocolate-covered daughter and through the sliding door before it was closed again. Kate could hear her clearly as she followed Sam into the house, telling him the news.

She finished off her wine and then leant back. The silvery-grey of the sky had now started to deepen to a pewter colour, as the mostly invisible sun set beyond the thick clouds. The overcast weather, together with the encroaching dusk, should have lent the backyard a gloomy façade, but Kate thought it looked almost magical, with corners darkened by mystery. And she felt snug and secure, sitting on the decking with warm swathes of light cascading from the windows behind her.

She thought about Angie, and what her reaction would be to her mother's proximity. Or whether, indeed, she already knew. Then she thought about Sam's rather accusatory suggestion that she write about her *own* mother. This time she allowed the idea time to expand, and realised that it actually made sense. After all, strangely enough her mother had turned out to have the more *compelling* story. Heartbreak and triumph, intrigue and tragedy. And it was wrapped up with a sense of ownership that meant it was hers to do with what she wanted. With *this* story there were no other stakeholders. Maybe, if she worded it right, when she told Angie she could even infer that this was what she had intended all along.

As the idea gained traction, Kate shook her head in sudden denial. It was like many other impromptu ideas, great in theory alone. Every single thing that she had discovered about Rose had brought with it an ache. And these were details that she had uncovered by *accident*. To deliberately focus on something that brought pain even in a peripheral state would be foolish indeed. And she had enough to cope with already without asking for more.

NINETEEN

Dear Dad, I was cleaning the filing cabinet out at home and I found some of the rosters I'd written up last year, when you were sick. Towards the end. For people to drop in, or bring a meal when the meals on wheels weren't coming, or just make a cup of tea. They have all the timings included. Not just for home help and the nurse, but for all of us. Then there's the one I was working on at the end. With twenty-four-hour coverage, sleepovers included. Trying to buy a bit of time. You never saw these because we didn't want you to think you were a burden, even though I know you did anyway. But now I'm thinking maybe we should have shown you, to demonstrate how many cared. And how much.

PS: But actually they're not just about you, are they? I suppose they also speak volumes about us, as a family. But I didn't see it that way then. Not at all.

There were several messages on the answering machine when Kate got back to the unit late Monday afternoon. She had fully intended to return in the morning but had been roped into babysitting Emma again, who had come down with a bad case of diarrhoea and been unable to attend crèche. Kate took her bag upstairs and then made herself some tea and sat down on the armrest of the couch to listen to the missed calls. They began with Oscar, sounding rather petulant.

I've left a message on your mobile and I've also tried ringing home, so could you please ring me back if you can find the time? I just want to know how the house is going? Any nibbles? Thank you.

Hello there, honey. Oh, did I speak before the tone? Was that the tone? I'll start again. Hello there, honey. It's Auntie Faye. I just got your message but I'm a bit confused. Did you say you were coming up on Easter Sunday? Be lovely if you are. Ring me and let me know so I can make something special. Bye!

Auntie Angie? Are you home? It's Shelley. I just wanted to talk to you about . . . something Mum said. About the shop. Anyway, I'll try you on your mobile.

Hello there Kate, it's Angie. Just ringing to see how you're going. Hope you had a nice Easter. Mine was . . . interesting. Very interesting indeed. Perhaps we'll talk about it when I get back on Tuesday. The shop's still shut that day so maybe we can do lunch? Anyway, see you.

Hello? Angie? What's the point of having a mobile if you don't answer it? It's Monday morning now and I'd really like a call by tonight if that's not too much trouble. I'll be back tomorrow. Oh, and Happy Easter. Hopefully, I'll speak –

Kate pressed fast forward and Oscar's voice sped into a high-pitched Donald Duck whine for a few seconds before the tape stopped with an emphatic click. She pressed delete, wiping all the calls, and then let herself slide down onto the couch. *Very interesting indeed* – what did that mean? Even as she asked the question, Kate knew that the answer was already there. Auntie Faye.

Angie was clearly referring to the conversation that Kate had had with her aunt, so this was confirmation then. She *had* already known the content. Otherwise she would have sounded far more emotional. Ergo she had discovered nothing new, except for Kate's involvement. So much for not keeping secrets. This thought had barely formulated before it was followed by an awareness of the inherent hypocrisy. Kate smiled at herself, but without humour. It seemed there were only two possibilities: one where everybody had a secret except Angie, and the other where everybody had a secret except Kate. Until recently, that is.

Kate was just putting away her things from the weekend when she heard the front door slam. She froze for a moment, frantically trying to remember if there was any chance she had left the door open, and then rushed from the room. Immediately coming face to face with Angie.

'*God!*' Kate put a hand up to her chest. 'You gave me a heart attack!'

Angie grinned. 'I have that effect on people. It's my overwhelming personality.'

'Wait a second.' Kate could feel her heart still beating rapidly underneath her hand. She took a deep breath. 'I though you weren't back till tomorrow?'

'Yeah, but I've spent a week there and nary a burglar in sight. So I've called it quits.'

'Oscar's rung for you. Twice.'

Angie rolled her eyes. 'I know. I spoke to him before. He's just panicking about the house. Now, to more important things, are you hungry?'

'What are the choices?'

'Well, yes,' said Angie slowly, but with a smile. 'Or no. Just the two, I'm afraid.'

'Very funny. I mean what did you have in mind?'

Angie turned and started walking down the stairs, talking over her shoulder. 'Fish and chips and a bottle of wine. To celebrate Easter.'

Kate followed her. She could feel her heart still throbbing but suspected it was now more apprehension than surprise. On the bottom step sat Angie's handbag, a bottle of chardonnay and a loaded shopping bag. They carried them into the lounge room where Angie unpacked a fat parcel wrapped in butcher paper and a tub of coleslaw.

'Dig in!' she announced, opening the chardonnay. 'And note that the fish is grilled not fried. Much better for the waistline.'

Kate grinned. 'But of course.'

They ate in silence, pausing every so often to smile companionably or to take a sip of the wine. It started to rain lightly, bringing a rhythmic patter that seemed to enclose the house within its beat. Kate knew that she was postponing the inevitable, that the subject had to be broached at some stage, but for now welcomed the food as an excuse.

'Want to go in the spa?' asked Angie suddenly.

Kate stared at her. 'Are you serious?'

'Of course I am. Come on, it'll be fun!'

'But it's raining!'

'So? The spa's enclosed anyway. Where's your sense of adventure?'

Kate waited a moment, half expecting Angie to renege, and then nodded reluctantly. After all, if this was what it took to relax Angie, then it would be worth it. Ten minutes later they had both changed; Angie into bathers, over which she wore a loose purple and pink striped singlet top, and Kate into a white T-shirt and black bike shorts. They brought along the bottle of wine, glasses and a towel each. Angie also carried her handbag.

'What are you bringing that for?' asked Kate, nodding towards the bag.

'You'll see.'

It was quite cool outside, the drumming of the rain considerably louder against the perspex roof of the enclosed area. Kate shivered. 'You're mad.'

Angie grinned. She folded back the spa cover and then tugged it off. Warm steam rose from the surface of the water, enhanced by the chill of the early evening. Kate hung her towel over the back of a chair and then sat down on the edge of the spa and gingerly lowered one foot into the water. It was immediately enveloped within liquid warmth. She put the other one in and then sat there, sipping her wine as she watched the ripples settle.

Angie went over to the table and started rummaging through her handbag. 'And now for our Easter present.'

'If it's chocolate, I'm afraid I'll have to pass. I couldn't eat another thing.'

'No, not chocolate.' Angie's voice bubbled with humour so Kate glanced over curiously just as her cousin held up a small plastic zip-lock bag about one-fifth full of what looked like dried oregano. She waved it from side to side. 'Ta da!'

Kate's mouth fell open. 'Is that . . . ? No, it can't be.'

Angie beamed proudly. 'Found it in Mel's old room, at the house. How long has it been since you had any of this, hey?'

Kate was finding it hard to move beyond her amazement that Angie was standing before her waving around a zip-lock bag of marijuana. 'I didn't know Melissa was into . . . that.'

'I don't think she is, not really. Otherwise it would never have been left there.'

Kate looked at the bag dubiously. 'How old is it?'

'I don't know. Couple of years, I suppose.'

'Then how do you know it's okay?'

Angie held the bag higher and pretended to examine it. 'Well, it doesn't have a use-by date so it must be fine. Come on, show some enthusiasm!'

'Well, I'm sorry.' Kate shook her head and started smiling. 'It's just that you've never given me weed as a gift before, so I was taken a little by surprise. I mean, *most* people give chocolate eggs.'

'Huh!' Angie removed a small packet of Tally Ho cigarette papers and some matches from her handbag and then laid everything down on the cobble-stones as if playing show and tell. 'I even stopped off and bought these. How organised am I?'

'Scarily organised.' Kate put down her glass and reached for the bag, holding it up. She remembered the dull green-brown colour, but not the slightly yellow tinge. Or maybe that was her imagination. 'Hmm. I suppose I'm game if you are.'

'Excellent!' Angie topped up both glasses and then lowered her feet into the water beside Kate. She pulled a cigarette paper from the packet and laid it flat on her palm.

'Two, Ange. You need to double it.'

'Who's the expert then?' Angie laughed as she extracted another one and passed them both over. 'In that case, you can roll it.'

Kate took the papers and then joined them together before opening the little bag and removing a large pinch of marijuana. She placed this on the papers and then picked out the larger bits and flicked them back into the bag, which she placed to one side. Next she started lightly rolling the papers between her fingers, until she had a thickish cylindrical shape.

'I'm impressed,' commented Angie, watching with interest.

'My misspent youth. Have you got a business card or something?'

'Sure,' Angie jumped up and went over to fetch her handbag.

Kate carefully licked the glued edge of the joined papers and sealed the joint. Angie sat back down and dropped the handbag, passing over a bookseller's business card which Kate read quickly and then laughed. '*Mary Jane Books*? How appropriate!'

'I thought so.'

Kate tore a strip across the card lengthwise and rolled the thin strip between her fingers, fashioning it into a coil that she then slipped into one of the open ends of the joint as a filter. She held up the finished product smugly. 'Would you look at that?'

'I always said you had a memory like an elephant,' said Angie, passing the matches over.

'Here goes.' Kate held the joint in her mouth with the tips of her thumb and index finger as she lit it and inhaled deeply, the end glowing fiery red as the marijuana crackled within. The drawback shot straight down her windpipe and immediately filled her lungs to capacity. She coughed and then coughed again as smoke spewed out of her mouth and nose only to be drawn back in as she gasped helplessly.

'So much for being impressed,' said Angie matter-of-factly, taking the joint. She put it to her mouth and took a mild, experimental puff before taking another, slightly deeper one. 'Mmm. Try not being so greedy.'

Kate took a gulp of wine, feeling the liquid wash away the smoky residue. She gave one last barking cough and then wiped her watery eyes. 'Great present, Ange. What's for next year? Arsenic?'

'A bad workman always blames his tools.' Angie took another drag and closed her eyes as she held the smoke. Then she expelled it gently from her nostrils.

'Show-off.' Kate took it from her and tried again. This time she was more restrained and felt the smoke travel sedately down to her lungs, where it wafted for a few seconds before journeying back. In a far more civilised fashion.

'So . . . are we going to talk about it?' asked Angie, still with her eyes closed.

'Talk about what?'

'You know. My mother.'

Kate turned to stare at her. 'So you *did* know.'

'In a manner of speaking.' Angie opened her eyes again and looked at Kate. 'But what I *don't* know is why you suddenly asked Auntie Faye about her.'

Kate took another slow drag, buying some time. 'It wasn't exactly like that. The conversation just sort of headed in that direction. And I was curious.'

'*Very* curious from what I hear.' Angie took the joint from Kate and flicked some ash off onto the decking. 'Do you know, it feels a bit like you went behind my back.'

'*I* went behind your back! How do you think *I* feel, finding out you've known for . . . well, how long *have* you known, anyway?'

Angie passed the joint back over. 'Almost thirty years, I suppose.'

Kate froze, staring at her. 'Thirty *years*! But that makes it –'

'When Dad died. That's right.' Angie took a sip of wine and then reached for the little zip-lock bag. 'I'll make another . . . whatever they're called now. Joint? Reefer? Are you feeling high yet?'

'Not really.' Kate was aware of a slight buzzing sensation in her head, but didn't think that was the marijuana. *Thirty years!* She sucked on the joint, this time *feeling* the smoke as it permeated. Her buzz expanded and she realised she wasn't so much cross as she was curious. 'So you went to Ballarat for Easter? To Auntie Faye's?'

Angie shook her head. 'Not the whole of it, just Easter Sunday. I was staying with a friend over at Bendigo but I kept thinking about something Auntie Faye said, about you, when I rang to tell her about Melissa. So I decided to pop over there and find out what was going on. You could have just asked me, you know.'

'Okay then, I'm asking you now. Tell me about it.'

'In a second.' Angie slipped a badly rolled joint into the bag and put it aside. Then she took another sip of her wine and clambered down into one of the spa seats, immersing her body up to the chest.

'Shall we turn the jets on?' asked Kate, her hand hovering over the control panel.

'Nah. Too noisy.'

Kate nodded agreeably and then took a drag before passing the last of the joint to Angie. She puffed to fire it up and then did the drawback, the end suddenly burning rapidly, right down to her finger and thumb. Angie flinched and jerked her hand back, flinging the butt into the air at the same time. It spun for a split second, sparks flying, before plummeting down into the water with a soft hiss and immediately disintegrating.

'Pick it up!' laughed Kate, waving her feet towards the remains through the water, which immediately separated even further.

Angie grinned, reaching out to pluck some stringy, half-burnt marijuana bits from the water. She flicked them over towards the side of the spa, a spray of droplets marking their path. One piece didn't even come close to making it, instead falling back into the water only inches from Angie's still raised hand.

Kate pointed at it, her laughter building. She tried to say something sarcastic but couldn't stop laughing long enough to articulate the words. It suddenly seemed like the funniest thing she had seen for a long time.

'Oh god,' said Angie, wiping her eyes.

Still laughing, Kate lowered herself from the side of the spa into one of the seats by Angie. The water, which had seemed warm around her feet, was gloriously hot once more of her was immersed. Kate's laughter finally started to falter into the occasional giggle as she let her arms float through the water. 'Okay, *now* I'm hot.'

'Who's got tickets on themselves, then?'

Kate started to laugh again but soon petered off as she remembered what they were supposed to be talking about. She looked at Angie accusingly. 'Your mother.'

'My mother,' repeated Angie. 'But before I begin, let me just remind you that I'm not the only one who keeps things to themselves. So don't be a hypocrite, okay?' She paused as she glanced over at Kate's face and then took a deep breath. 'All right then, I'll start from the beginning. And no interruptions.'

'Stop procrastinating.'

'I'm not. Although don't you think that word sounds dirty? Like masticating,' Angie put on a stern voice. 'Don't know *what* I'm going to do with young Johnny. If he's not masticating, he's procrastinating. Damn kid's gonna go blind.'

'You're doing it again.'

'Yes, but . . .' Angie caught sight of Kate's face and her grin faded. 'Okay, okay, I'll get started. Do you remember how I went up to live with Auntie Faye for a while after Dad died?' Angie waited for Kate to nod before continuing. 'Well, that's when I met her. And I don't know whether it was *because* Dad was dead, or whether it would have happened sooner if I'd ever stayed with Auntie Faye before. But she always used to visit *us*. Maybe that was Dad's doing. I don't know.'

'But why didn't you ever *tell* me?'

'Let me finish. I'd been there a day or so and suddenly Auntie Faye says we're having company for lunch. And in comes this middle-aged couple.' Angie stopped suddenly and reached behind for her glass of wine. She took a sip and then glanced over at Kate. 'They were so *ordinary*! Both short and plump and . . . just boring. I remember we had that bloody chicken and seafood soup and they both kept staring at me.' Angie hesitated again and took another sip of wine. 'In fairness to him, he had this weird eye thing happening, so it probably wasn't his fault.'

'When did they tell you?'

'I guessed.' Angie put her glass down again and then leant back again with a sigh. 'For starters, even though Auntie Faye called me Angie, the woman kept calling me Angela, like she had some sort of *investment* in the name. Then there was this *familiarity* between her and Auntie Faye. More than if they were just friends. And of course there was the fact her name was Sophie. That was a bit of a giveaway. Mind you, by half-way through the lunch it was more a case of me praying that I *wasn't* right.'

Kate frowned. 'Why?'

'Oh, a number of things. *Her* mainly. She hardly had a word to say for herself, sort of deferring to him instead. Calling him lover boy all the time. At one stage Auntie Faye chipped in with something or other and *she* said –' Angie put on a high-pitched, babyish voice, ' "– Please don't interrupt, Faye. Go ahead, lover boy." I thought I was going to vomit.'

'God,' Kate grimaced. 'But didn't she ask about *you*? And your life?'

'Not really. Oh, a little bit later on, I suppose.'

'And what about her leaving and all that?'

Angie waved a foot gently through the water, watching the ripples expand. 'Well, after lunch they did the big announcement and I just nodded and didn't really say much. So Auntie Faye took him into another room and left us alone. That was the first time *she* really spoke to me. Asked me how I was going and what my plans were. But, do you know, I don't think she was really that interested. She did say how sorry she was but that apparently she'd had no choice. Then she went on about what a bastard Dad'd been. Which I can tell you went down really well given he'd just died.'

'But did she say why she married him in the first place? And not Thomas?'

'Not really. Auntie Faye was the one who filled in the finer details for me. But do you know what? I don't think she was really that fussed about leaving me anyway. Not particularly maternal. In fact, it may have been a relief.'

'Oh, Ange, that's probably –'

'I'm not being maudlin,' interrupted Angie, shaking her head to add sincerity. Her wet hair flipped around her face. 'I *really* think that. She never had any other kids either, so she may have learnt her lesson. No, there was only room for him anyway. You should have *seen* her with him.' Angie kicked her foot against the water with a little more force. 'Then when they were leaving, he did the big magnanimous father thing and pulled out his wallet. Handed me fifty dollars and then patted me on the head. On the *head*!'

'Oh, Ange.'

'And she was all fluttery. Saying how wonderful he was and how generous. But even then she was saying it to *him*, not me.'

'Fifty dollars was a hell of a lot back then,' remarked Kate pragmatically.

'She even said how lucky I was! *Lucky!*' Angie kicked her foot out once more, this time creating a wave. The water hit the other side of the spa and then splashed back towards them. 'My father had just died and I was lucky! Just because this one-eyed dropkick gives me fifty fucking dollars!'

Kate looked at her cousin sympathetically. 'I'm so sorry, Ange. I just wish you'd told me. Why on earth *didn't* you?'

Angie stared at the rippling water for a moment and then glanced across at Kate. 'Let's have the other joint.'

'Okay.' Kate reached to the side and extracted the second, rather lumpy joint. She lit it and passed it straight to Angie. 'Not quite as good as mine, but here. Enjoy.'

Angie took a long drag and held the smoke down. She closed her eyes and tipped her head back until she could hold her breath no longer, then released it with a rush. 'I found this stuff after I'd spoken to Auntie Faye yesterday. And I thought it would make it so much easier to tell you. If I was a bit high, you know. Relaxed.'

Kate glanced at Angie's spare hand, which was clenched into a fist that was lightly punching the water on her other side. 'Any more relaxed and you'd be scary.'

'And you wonder why I didn't tell you?' Angie took another, shorter drag and passed it over. '*Your* mother was always held up as being perfect. You even named that princess doll you had after her. And the way Uncle James spoke about her was, oh, like she was amazing. *My* dad hardly ever spoke about mine, all *I* had was this mystery thing. But at least with that I could pretend she was *anything*.' Angie turned and looked at Kate, her expression tight. 'Then to find out she was just this ordinary middle-aged woman, who chose this ordinary middle-aged *jerk* over me . . . well, I didn't *want* to tell you. Because I suppose I didn't want it to be true.'

Kate spoke slowly. 'You preferred the mystery.'

'Yep. And then afterwards, when it didn't bother me as much, well there never seemed a reason *to* tell you.'

'Hmm.' Kate took a short puff of the joint. 'Did you ever see her again?'

'I've run into her a couple of times at Auntie Faye's.' Angie shrugged. 'But I haven't sought her out and she certainly hasn't bothered. Which, to be honest, is a bit of a relief. I just get angry when I think about *then*, when I met her. I was feeling so lost after Dad died, she could have really made a difference. I suppose a psychologist would say I've got unresolved issues, but so what? I don't think they affect me too badly so I'll just stick with them.'

Kate leant back, letting this all filter through her mind. It was hard to reconcile this new image of Sophie with the one she had built up. So how much harder would it have been for Angie? She took another drag and handed the joint across. 'At least I can help you with one thing. My mother wasn't any princess, not by a long shot. Apparently she was a bit of a bitch.'

'I know.'

'You *know*?'

'Well, I didn't *know*. Not for certain. But Dad used to give this sort of shudder whenever her name was mentioned, and he also said once that his mother couldn't stand her. I don't think Auntie Faye got on with her either. So I suspected she wasn't the angel your father made out.'

'But it wasn't entirely her fault, you know.' Kate felt defensive. 'Apparently she had a dreadful childhood. Her father was a real bastard, and her mother was a bit simple. It was pretty horrid, by all accounts.'

'That's terrible.' Angie passed the joint back, as if in sympathy.

'And my parents *had* to get married.' Kate took a deep drag, feeling the smoke fill her lungs, and her head. 'I was born in April, you know.'

'I thought as much. Having been to every one of your birthday parties.'

'Smart-arse. I mean they were married in January and I was born in April. You do the maths.'

'Oh, god. Do I have to?' Angie paused for a moment and then nodded slowly. 'Well, well. I must say I'd never have picked Uncle James as someone who'd jump the gun. He never seemed particularly . . . well, *sexual*. No offence.'

'I know what you mean.' Kate blew smoke out and then watched it drift apart. She had a sudden thought. 'Angie! What was your father in jail for?'

'My father was never in jail.' Angie turned her hand over and gazed at the palm. 'Although he did get charged once, when he was in the army.'

'He was in the *army*?'

'Yes, in Korea. You know that.'

Kate stared at her cousin, open-mouthed. Now that it was mentioned, she *did* have a vague memory of Uncle Frank having spent time in the army. Certainly he had never spoken about it much. But could *that* have been where he was? Kate felt laughter bubble in her throat because it suddenly seemed hugely amusing.

'I've got all his military stuff. Medals and all. From Korea.' Angie held her hand higher and frowned at it. 'Have you noticed that my hand is getting all wrinkly?'

'It's called age.'

Angie turned her hand over slowly, and wiped the back of it dry with the other one. 'Look at this. See the hairs? And the dimples when I do this?' She flexed her hand and then straightened it. 'I'm just realising that I don't know it at all. And if I don't know the back of my own hand, then what the hell *do* I know?'

'Dunno,' said Kate slowly, seeing the dilemma. Then Kate started to laugh again because it seemed almost as comical as thinking her uncle had been in jail, when he'd really just been in the army. Angie looked up, frowning, and then her face relaxed into a smile before she began to laugh also.

'I think we're high.'

'I think you're right.' Kate stopped laughing long enough to take another drag. The tip of the joint glowed even brighter and she suddenly realised that it was almost dark. The rain had stopped also, with just the occasional patter as water slid from nearby trees.

'Sometimes I think my Auntie Faye liked your dad. I mean, *really* liked.'

'Are you serious?'

'Unrequited love,' Angie nodded. 'But I think she also accepted the fact he wasn't interested. Sometimes I think it's rather sad that he never even tried to find someone else after your mother, but maybe that's the sort of person he was anyway.'

'You mean solitary?'

'Yeah. And if the marriage wasn't altogether happy, then that just sort of verified it for him. He was like a confirmed bachelor, just one who had a kid along for the ride.'

'I like that image,' said Kate. 'But I think I'll merge it with a somewhat happy marriage, for my mother's sake.'

'Fair enough. Do you know how much I miss him?'

'Yes. Me too.'

'No,' Angie frowned. 'I mean, do you know how much *I* miss him? Because sometimes you act like you're the only one.'

'No, I don't,' said Kate defensively. 'I *know* you miss him. I know everybody misses him.'

'And you must admit you've been a little hypocritical,' continued Angie, as if Kate hadn't spoken. 'Having a go at me for not telling you about my mother, when you haven't exactly been a font of information yourself.' Angie ran her finger over the ash at the end of the joint and grey flakes floated down to the water. 'Although, to be honest, you started closing down even before Uncle James died. I mean, sure most of the hard yards were left to you. Hospital visits, organising the home help, that sort of thing. But I did try to do what I could. I went there every day after work. But it still felt like you shut me out. Especially at the end.'

Kate felt her anger blossom. She took a gulp of wine. And then another.

'Remember a conversation we had a week or so ago? About Sam using avoidance? Well, I think you do too. Not for the little things, but for the really huge ones. Almost as a coping mechanism. Then again, maybe we all do.'

'Hmm.'

'I'm not trying to start an argument,' said Angie, watching her now. 'And I'm not trying to make it a competition. It's just sometimes I think you're hurting so much that you lose sight of the fact the rest of us are too. Me in particular.' She turned away again. 'But let's change the subject. I don't want to be depressed tonight. Besides, methinks it's time for a top-up.'

As Angie clambered out of the spa, Kate stared at the water, at the way the filtered light played across the ripples. She took a deep breath and then released it, with some of her anger. The rest she tucked away for later. Behind her she could hear Angie rummaging through her handbag.

'Where the hell's a pen? You'd think amongst all these odds and ends I'd have a pen.'

'Is a pen an odd or an end?' asked Kate, turning around to watch her.

'Both.' Angie held one up with a flourish. 'You top up our drinks and I'll use this to make the perfect joint.'

Kate hoisted herself up into a kneeling position. Water cascaded from her shoulders, rushing to re-enter the spa. She watched it, fascinated by the seamless fusion, and for some reason suddenly thought of Shelley. She pointed a finger at Angie. 'You! You told her! After you said you'd wait!'

Angie paused, with the pen poking out one end of the half-made joint. 'Well, you started it by telling her I was leaving. You left me no choice.'

Kate thought about this. 'Hmm. I suppose so.'

'Voilà!' Angie carefully pulled the pen out and then screwed that end of the joint closed. 'Bugger your fancy filters. *This* is the way to roll a joint.'

'Pleb,' replied Kate critically. 'Besides, they're not called filters, they're called roaches.' She reached over and grabbed the bottle, refilling their glasses with the last of the wine. She passed one over to Angie, who was lighting the joint. 'Here you go. Something to whet your fancy.'

Angie trickled smoke from her nostrils. 'Hmm, a wet fancy. Not sure that's what I'm aiming for, right now.'

'You know what I mean.'

'Either whet my appetite or tickle my fancy, I'm guessing.' Angie manoeuvred herself forward and sat down on the side of the spa with her towel still wrapped around her shoulders. 'I should get back in, because it's pretty cold out here.'

'Why don't you, then?'

'Not sure.'

Suddenly thirsty, Kate drained her glass and then reached behind and laid it down on the side of the spa. 'I am definitely high.'

'Have you ever heard that theory of testing breast sag?' asked Angie suddenly, holding the pen out. 'You put this underneath your boob. Or you can use a pencil.'

'What *are* you talking about?'

'Look, I'll show you.' Angie passed the joint over and then pulled her T-shirt forward before pushing the pen down behind it and her bathers. She frowned as she made a few awkward adjustments and then looked back at Kate, beaming. The ends of the pen stuck out visibly as two tiny tents on a purple stripe either side of her right breast. 'See?'

'Don't you think it'd be easier just to buy a pencil case?'

'No, you twit. This is to measure breast sag. If you're all pert, then the pen would just roll out. You couldn't hold it at all. But if you're not, then you have to see how many pens you can hold. That tells you how saggy you are.'

'So how saggy are you?'

Angie peered down, considering. 'I'd say I'm a two pen girl nowadays.'

'That's all?' Kate looked at Angie's chest doubtfully.

Angie reached inside her clothing and pulled the pen out. 'Ouch! God! But here's a handy hint: if you try this at home, remove it slowly. Do you want a go?'

'I think not.' Kate turned back to face the water and took a drag of the joint. She could see the outside light of the next door unit and wondered what Mrs Jarvis was doing and how she would react if Kate climbed the fence and made some surreptitious vampire-type sounds in her backyard. She giggled.

'I'm hungry.' Angie sounded surprised.

'Me too.' Kate took another drag and passed it behind to Angie.

'Auntie Faye sent some of that soup down,' said Angie. 'D'you want me to heat it up for you?'

Kate looked at her suspiciously. 'And what'll you be having?'

'I'm going to order pizza. Bugger the diet, I deserve a break.'

'Then, as tempting as the soup sounds, I think I'll give it a miss and join you.'

'I should make you have it, as a penance.'

'Just the thought is penance enough.' Kate brought her hand gently back towards her through the water. 'This must be what it's like in a womb.'

'And so the conversation comes right back to my mother.' Angie sounded annoyed but when Kate turned, concerned, her cousin was grinning.

'Hey, Ange?'

'Yes?'

'I'm sorry about your mum. And I understand why you didn't tell me.'

'Me too.' Angie took a drag and held it. Then she blew the smoke out past Kate's shoulder. 'Have I told you lately that I love you?'

'You don't have to,' replied Kate, facing the water again. 'But ditto.'

'Pizza?'

'Yes, *please*.'

'Coming right up.'

Kate stretched an arm out along the spa either side and leant back. She could see a scattering of stars through the perspex roof, like the lit ends of thousands of joints, only incandescent white instead of red. She smiled lazily, then closed her eyes so that she could be *enveloped* by the buzz within her head. She imagined it was like a tide, moving stealthily downwards all the way to her toes. She wiggled these and the euphoria immediately seemed almost alive, an entity of its own.

She could hear Angie faintly, from inside the house, ordering the pizza. And Kate realised she wasn't just hungry, she was *ravenous*. She opened her eyes and began scissoring her legs gently, loving the ripples that spread across the water. If she blocked out Angie, then the gentle tide and her own shallow breathing were the only sounds that existed. Life wasn't just good, it was marvellous. Past, present and future. And there was nothing that couldn't be grasped within her hand if she so chose. Kate swam her fingers through the water before lifting them to clench at the substance of the air, of *life*, as droplets trickled down her arm. There, it was done.

TWENTY

> *Dear Dad, I've been thinking about what Angie said and maybe she's right. Although if I did shut her out last year, it wasn't on purpose. And it's not like talking was going to change anything. Nothing was. As you said after the diagnosis, it's a done deal. So I probably did use avoidance but, to be honest, I think I was protecting myself. Whether that worked is another matter! But the thing is it was so incredibly draining. Yet it felt selfish to even feel that way. Let alone say it.*
>
> *But surely I can now? Okay – I HAVE NEVER BEEN SO MIND-NUMBINGLY EXHAUSTED IN ALL MY LIFE. Mentally, emotionally and physically. Not just by the illness, but by everything. Trying to be superwoman, but not succeeding. Anywhere.*

The next day was a hangover, from start to finish. Kate knew it wasn't so much the marijuana but everything else that was doing the damage. The chocolate eggs during the day, the fish and chips, the bottle of wine, the plate of nacho corn chips with melted cheese and sour cream that Angie had made while waiting for the pizza, and then the pizza itself because even though they were now full, it seemed a shame to let it go to waste. Nor the bottle of soft drink that came with it, which they had diluted with scotch because it had just seemed right, at the time.

All merged overnight to create a potent mixture that sat uncomfortably within, every now and again sending up bubbles of indigestion that left a sour taste in their wake.

She and Angie passed each other at odd times throughout the day, mostly silent in their suffering except for the odd sociable phrase, like: 'This is all your fault' or 'Just kill me now'. And every time Kate would see in her cousin's face what she knew was mirrored in her own. Bloodshot eyes, pale clammy skin, and a furrowed brow that was born of a persistent headache. And the knowledge that it was all self-inflicted.

After that, Wednesday started off as a wonderful day. Kate emerged from beneath her doona and realised that the world seemed fresh and clear once more. She showered with a euphoria that felt almost drug-induced itself and threw on tracksuit pants and a T-shirt so that she could catch Angie before she headed off to the shop. She found her standing at the sliding door, staring outside at the courtyard.

'Feeling better?' asked Kate with a smile.

'*God*, yes.'

'Me too.'

'Did you know we left the stuff outside?' Angie pointed to the side of the spa, where the zip-lock bag could be seen lying on the cobblestones with the matches and Tally Ho papers beside it.

'I'll clean it up today. But for a purveyor of illegal substances, you're not very hip with the terminology,' commented Kate. 'You should call it weed, or dope, or even pot. Speaking of which, has the kettle just boiled?'

'Yep.' Angie turned around. 'Sam rang yesterday. Did I tell you? He left a message on the answering machine. I think it's about the development.'

Kate nodded as she tipped hot water into her mug and added milk.

Angie watched her. 'God. Do you know, I only ever tried the stuff a few times when I was young, but I *never* felt like I did yesterday. I thought I was going to die.'

'I think that was all the crap we ate. And the alcohol. Not the marijuana.'

'Well, I'm too old for it whatever. But...' She paused and then grinned. 'It *was* fun, wasn't it?'

Kate grinned back, with interest. 'The best.'

'Although next year I think I'll stick to chocolate.'

'You'll probably be in England. Playing grandma.'

'Then you'll have to come visit. And definitely don't try bringing that with you.' Angie gestured outside. 'I don't want to visit you in some dingy prison. And you'll be all po-faced because of the internal search.'

'Believe me, if I was threatened with an internal search, I'd be handing over all contraband before they could even get their gloves on. And keeping my legs crossed.'

'With that image etched on my consciousness, I'm off to work.'

'Nice to know you'll be thinking of me, then.'

Angie rolled her eyes and then grabbed her handbag from the table and headed outside, the front door slamming behind her.

Kate sat down at the table. Even with yesterday's fallout from their little mind-altering sojourn, she had no regrets. Apart from a very enjoyable evening, she had managed to resolve the whole mother issue with Angie quite marvellously. And the additional information only served to reinforce her early decision to discard Sophie as writing material. The mysterious scarlet woman had metamorphosed into a middle-aged woman whose ordinariness eclipsed her past. Besides, whenever her mother was mentioned, a slither of bitterness had slid through Angie's speech. A book based on her mother's life, detailing the abandonment of Angie herself, would be like stabbing her in the back. Again.

She thought about the other discoveries. That her uncle had never been a jailbird, just a soldier. Which made the whole Sophie thing even more understandable. There she'd been, little more than a teenager, engaged to responsible young Thomas who was busily putting down roots, when along came the older, handsome rake of a man, complete with army uniform emblazoned by medals from the Korean War.

Kate smiled, warmed by contented relief. She thought about her father, and Angie's theory that he was a confirmed bachelor, regardless of his brief marriage. Kate liked this image; it made sense, and transformed his whole life into something eminently more satisfying. For her as well as him. She suddenly realised that it had been some time since she had last *really* visited the house. And that it was exactly what she felt like doing right now.

Kate grabbed a banana for a quick breakfast. She peeled it as the engine warmed up and then held it between her teeth as she reversed up the driveway and out onto the road. The day was not quite as overcast as it had been lately, but it was still cloudy and the sun kept disappearing, so that one minute the road was dappled with sunlight and the next it was strewn in shadows. Kate stopped at a café around the corner to buy a cappuccino. She fitted the plastic lid on tightly and balanced the disposable cup on the passenger seat as she drove the rest of the way.

Later she was to wonder, with a sort of masochistic curiosity, how long it was before she realised exactly what was wrong. At the time, though, she was feeling so damn content that it didn't register. *Couldn't* register. The leap was just too big. Instead she coasted to a halt by the kerb and then slowly frowned, twice glancing towards the neighbouring properties, thinking that she had made some ridiculous mistake and was parked outside the wrong place. Each time her gaze was brought back again and nothing had changed. Except everything.

Because the whole house was gone. Completely. Missing from the foundations up, with not even a piece of roofing or a weatherboard plank to mark where it had once stood. All that was left was a patchy piece of dirt, which stood out starkly amongst the weeds.

Kate turned off the ignition, almost automatically, and then sat with her hands on the steering wheel and stared. Although she could see it was gone, she was having enormous difficulty actually registering this as fact.

Kate got slowly out of the car and walked up onto the footpath. She felt stiff, like an old woman. Now that she was closer she could see the grey stumps upon which the house had once rested. And she could also see the more practical evidence of obliteration. Long trench marks scarred the gravelled driveway, and then veered off to loop around the dirt itself, leaving an almost decorative pattern of tyre-tracked mutilation.

Kate walked over to the driveway and up along the side of the trenches. At the top she stopped for a moment to stare at the rhododendron bush that had edged the kitchen window. It sat torn and crushed, rippled with the herringbone pattern of heavy tyres.

There was a rubbish pile by the back fence, with the Hills hoist on top, one arm jabbing drunkenly towards the sky like the mast of a stricken ship. And, right by the fence, on top of the foliage from the lemon tree, was the wrought-iron setting from the backyard.

Kate stared at it numbly. The table lay on its side, two legs bent inwards where it had landed. The still-green flamboyance of the lemon tree lent it the lie of life, even when they were damned themselves. Underneath was a tiny scrap of bright royal blue, incongruous amidst the dirt. It was the Easter egg, now flattened into an oval pancake oozing chocolate from the seams.

Kate walked away quickly, then stopped where the side gate had once stood, where not even a fence post now remained, and stared over at the compacted dirt again. Suddenly, as the sun came out from behind a cloud, everything was illuminated as if within a spotlight. Just as quickly though, the sunlight disappeared behind another cloud bank and it seemed even darker than before.

The stumps delineated the layout of the house, but Kate didn't need them. She tracked from hallway to lounge room, kitchen to laundry, bedroom to bedroom. She hesitated outside her father's bedroom and then retraced her steps. Over and over and over, walking in the front door, standing at the kitchen window, gazing around the lounge room, staring down the passage.

Now her mind was full of noise. The radio in the kitchen, the television in the lounge room, the sound of the bath being run, Angie playing somewhere. And everyone talking, laughing, interrupting, shouting at once so that, finally, she had to get out just to be able to think. Back over to the driveway, where the clamour was only a distant memory. And as the echo faded, Kate suddenly realised that her eyes had filled with tears that were now tracking wetly down her cheeks. And the numbness had started to recede. To be replaced by a white-hot anger so pure and absolute that it was painful in itself.

The anger continued unabated through the drive back to the unit. Beside her, on the passenger seat, the cappuccino tipped sideways and the plastic lid flipped off, tepid coffee gushing over the seat and down beside the door. As Kate pulled into the space before the unit, her mobile phone rang but she ignored that also. Because *that* wouldn't do, it was too small, too delicate.

She got out of the car and slammed the door, hard, before heading inside. Straight to the phone.

'Hello?'

'It's me.'

'Kate! I just tried to ring you.' Sam's voice was deep with relief. 'Now, I know –'

'I've just been there.'

'Oh. Well, I tried –'

'How *dare* you. How fucking *dare* you,' Kate spat the words like bullets. 'You *arsehole*. You *knew* how I felt, and yet you went ahead and –'

'Just a bloody minute.' Sam's voice suddenly veered towards anger itself. 'You knew what was going to happen. We discussed all of this.'

'You mean *you* discussed it. You *railroaded* me.'

'No, I pointed out options. And you agreed. As did Angie.'

'But I wanted to *leave* the house! Build the units *around* it!'

There was a pause before Sam replied, more gently, 'You know that was impossible. We went through all this. There wasn't enough room on either side for a driveway that met council specifications.'

'So you *destroyed* my father's house? It's *gone*!'

'And you *knew* it would be. I tried to give you fair warning but *you* said you didn't want to know.'

'I can't believe you did this.' Kate's words were clipped with fury.

'And I tried to ring you yesterday when it got brought forward. You didn't even bother answering my call!'

'Well, get used to it. *Arsehole*!' Kate slammed the phone down and then stood staring at it, her lips a thin line of rage. After a few minutes she realised she was still holding the spiralled cord with her other hand, so tightly that her knuckles were protruding whitely against her skin. She unclenched her hand painfully, and the cord bounced back into neat, compact coils.

She felt like screaming *It's not fair!* as loudly as she could, but at the same time was unwilling to release any of her anger. It felt almost wholesome in its righteousness, fuelled by a deep sense of injustice, and betrayal, and severance. That house had been one of the few remaining anchors to her childhood, and to her father. It had framed her early life, grounding her even as she moved away. She would never again see that solid façade, never walk through the rooms, never draw strength from the occasional visit.

Over the next few hours Kate's anger, without losing any intensity, gradually contracted until it was like a white-hot laser with a singular focus – Sam. His lack of sensitivity, his greed, and his willingness to hurt her all framed him like a kaleidoscope of sins. There was a small part of her that acknowledged she was not being wholly fair but it was shouted down by the fact the house was gone, demolished. And Sam had been responsible. Even when they had all spoken about what to do with the property, way back in July last year, he had been the one who had come up with the idea of development. Then he had been the one behind it from that point on. Organising, drawing up plans, obtaining council permission, arranging temporary finances. And yet he was the one who should have been *most* supportive of her feelings, not the one so eager to ignore the obvious – that she was just *not ready*.

Kate held her rage until she saw it as an entity in itself. A fluorescent-white orb of statically charged fury that could be marginalised without any reduction in intensity. So that as she began to function once more, she could shift it into the background where its maintenance was only betrayed by a sudden thinning of the lips.

But an unintentional side-effect of this concentration was that, in order to preserve it, Kate had little emotion left for anything else. So that by mid-afternoon, she was able to explore the destruction of the house as if it was an abstract theorem, without causing any particular angst at all. She could even say the words: *my father's house has been destroyed. It's gone.* And they were almost intriguing. Whilst the word *Sam* shot from her like venom.

The phone rang just as Kate had finished picking the remains of the burnt marijuana from the spa filter, so she wiped her arm down with a towel and went inside. She waited until Shelley's voice sounded on the answering machine before she picked up. 'Hi, Shell.'

'Oh good, you *are* home.' Shelley's voice had a tremor of excitement. 'Screening your calls, hey?'

'Something like that. Aren't you supposed to be at work?'

'I took today off,' replied Shelley impatiently. 'Guess what? I'm going to buy Angie's shop with a *partner*.'

Kate frowned. 'A partner? Who?'

'Jacob.'

'You have to be kidding.' Kate almost laughed. 'Jacob? And you?'

'I *know* it sounds stupid but it actually makes sense if you hear me out,' Shelley spoke with eager rapidity. 'He's going to be in charge of the computer side of things. See, we're going to branch into online selling as well. It's a *huge* market nowadays. Jake's going to computerise all the stock.'

'Yes, that sounds like a good idea,' said Kate slowly, sitting down on the armrest of the couch. 'But . . . well, you two don't get on very well, do you?'

'Oh, that's just because we've never had anything in common,' replied Shelley airily. 'Now we will. Besides, he's not that bad. And Mum, it's like a win-win situation. An extra source of revenue *plus* I get to share the workload. *And* the risks!'

Kate tried to get her head around the proposal. 'What about Jacob? Is he *really* keen on this?'

'Absolutely. In fact, he was the one who brought it up. See, I was telling Dad all about my ideas yesterday and I mentioned about going online when I get time. Then Jacob just sort of suggested he come on board. I was pretty stunned at first, but when you think about it, it makes sense. And Dad thought it was a *great* idea.'

'Really.'

'Yes. And so did Auntie Angie. That's why I took a sickie today. I just *couldn't* wait till Friday. So I spent all morning at the shop talking to her and she thought it was an *excellent* idea. And that it'd be really good for Jake too.'

'I suppose so.' Kate wound the cord around her finger as she tried to imagine the two of them working together, and although the picture failed to materialise, she realised that this *could* be a good thing, both for the business *and* for their relationship with each other.

'D'you reckon you might be a little more enthusiastic?'

'I am, really,' Kate injected her voice with sincerity. 'It'll just take a bit of getting used to. No, I think you may be on to something. Really. Listen, Shell . . . did you know about the house?'

'What house?'

Kate felt instantly wounded. 'Doesn't matter.'

'D'you mean Grandpa's house? About it being gone now?'

'Yes.'

'Yeah, I knew. Caleb and I went round to say goodbye to it yesterday.'

'Did you?' Kate was pleased that they had done this, and resentful that she hadn't.

'It's sort of sad, but good at the same time, if you know what I mean. Because if it wasn't for the development, Jake and I wouldn't be able to afford the shop. Don't you think Grandpa would be pleased?'

Kate frowned for a moment and then her face cleared. 'Actually . . . yes. I think he'd be thrilled.'

'I better go anyway, Mum. I'm meeting Bronte at the play centre.'

'Okay. Have fun.' Kate hung up the phone. She replayed Shelley's words several times: *Don't you think Grandpa would be pleased?* And felt suddenly floored by the realisation. It had simply never occurred to her to think about it like that. Shelley was right, her grandfather *would* be pleased. Both that he was able to leave them such an inheritance, and that they were using it to improve their lives.

Kate realised that her father would be *glad* that the house was gone, just as he would be furious with her inability to let it go. Where she saw an anchor that protected, he would have seen an anchor that held back. Where she saw severance as a tragedy, he would have seen it as a necessary evil, and the first step to freedom. Certainly he would have been horrified that, over nine months later, she was still clinging to the past. Not only because it was such a self-defeating gesture, but because he would have felt responsible. That what he had required at the end was the reason she was stuck. The guilt would have killed him.

The irony of this made Kate smile, despite herself, even as tears welled in her eyes. She missed him so *much*. His insight, his support, his wisdom, his presence. Her grief was, she knew, exacerbated by the manner of his death. And pretending a connection by jotting down random thoughts and memories each day was simply a link to herself, not him. He wasn't listening or reading them or even at the house, waiting for her visits. And never would be either. He was gone.

Kate was still sitting on the armrest when Angie's car turned into the carport half an hour later. She jumped up and hurried into the bathroom where she washed her face and then patted it dry, peering at herself in the mirror. Her eyes were a trifle swollen but apart from that there was nothing to really indicate the emotional rollercoaster she had ridden. She heard the front door open and close as she smoothed on some foundation and then ran a brush through her hair.

Angie was at the island bench opening mail as Kate came through and she looked up with a smile that quickly turned into a frown. 'Have you been crying?'

'No.' Kate pulled out a chair and sat down. 'Well, yes. Just a bit.'

'Why? What's wrong?'

'Did you know about the house?'

'Ah.' Angie pushed the mail to one side. 'I gather it's gone then?'

'So you didn't know?'

Angie took a deep breath and then let it out before answering. 'I knew it was soon. Sam told me. But I didn't really want to know when or say goodbye or anything.' She picked up an empty envelope and started pleating one corner. 'Because I didn't want to remember it like that anyway, all empty and rundown. I'd rather just remember the way it was, before.'

Kate considered this, and then nodded. 'At least you had the choice.'

'Do you mean he didn't tell you?' asked Angie, clearly surprised. 'Hang on, what about when he tried to ring yesterday? Maybe that was it?'

'Maybe.'

'You're angry with him.'

Kate felt her fury invigorate, and looked away to hide it. 'Yes. I am.'

'Angry about you not knowing? Or angry about the whole thing?'

'Everything.' Kate kept her gaze averted and her voice even.

'But that's not really fair.' Angie scrunched the envelope up and tossed it on top of the other letters. 'It wasn't only Sam, we *all* agreed. Just because he's the one –'

'Doing the demolition?' finished Kate. Her head pounded but she stretched her mouth into a smile. 'Anyway, let's talk about something pleasant. I gather my daughter paid you a visit today?'

Angie frowned for a moment before deciding to go with the flow. 'Yes, she certainly did. So you've heard the news? About Jacob?'

Kate nodded. 'So what do you think?'

'Do you know, I think it's brilliant. At first I was a bit taken aback, but the more I think about it, the more it makes sense. She's going to need help, and he needs something to motivate him.'

'What about the online selling idea? Is it feasible?'

'Absolutely,' Angie didn't hesitate. 'Big business nowadays. I've just never bothered because it's not my forte and it will take a lot of work. But it'll pay off.'

'And all this means you're definitely going?'

'I don't think I've got a choice now!' Angie laughed. 'Shelley would never speak to me again if I changed my mind!'

'I think you should go anyway. It'll be good for you. Branch out.'

Angie gazed at her steadily. 'You know none of this would be possible without the development? Shelley and Jacob buying the business. Me going overseas.'

'I know. And I also know that Dad would be pleased. Uncle Frank too.'

'They would be, wouldn't they?' Angie inserted her fingernail into the top of another envelope and slid it across with a tearing sound. Then she put it down without opening it further and looked back at Kate.

'I must say you're taking all this better than I expected. I thought you'd be a wreck when the house went.'

'No, not at all.' Kate tucked her fury securely to one side so that she could smile, unencumbered. 'Onwards and upwards as they say.'

Angie gazed at her searchingly for a moment and then smiled back. 'That's a huge relief. And maybe this'll be really good for you in the long run. Allow you to move on more easily.'

'Definitely.'

'I've been quite worried about you, you know.'

'Really?'

'Yes. Ever since it happened.'

'Well, I don't know why. I'm fine.'

'Oh sure.' Angie rolled her eyes. 'Do you have any idea what you've been like for the past year?'

Kate felt herself tense. 'Actually, it's been nine months. And of course I have.'

'You think you've been, well . . . reasonable?'

'Must we have this conversation now?' asked Kate, staring at her cousin.

'No, of course not.' Angie suddenly looked contrite. 'I'm sorry. Bad timing.'

Kate nodded, without answering. She laid her hands on the table and entwined her fingers, making the skin around her knuckles pouch loosely. She flexed, watching the skin tighten and then relax once more, and remembered what Angie had said, the night they were stoned, about not even knowing the back of her own hand. 'Do you realise he was going to ring you? That night.'

'Was he?' Angie spoke carefully. 'You never told me that.'

'I never told you anything.'

'No. You didn't.'

Kate glanced up suddenly. 'Do you resent me for that?'

'Actually . . . yes. Even though I do understand. But it's like you cut me out. And . . .'

'And what?'

'Well, you talk about not having a chance to say goodbye to the house. I suppose I would have liked a chance to say goodbye to him.'

'But you *knew* it was going to happen.' Kate felt wounded.

'Yes. But still . . .'

Kate stared at her. 'I never realised. I'm sorry.'

'That's okay.' Angie shrugged. 'I know it wasn't deliberate.'

'It's not like I was expecting it that particular day. It was all pretty sudden.'

'I said it was okay.' Angie gave her a half-smile for emphasis. 'But you said he wanted to ring me. Why didn't he?'

Kate hesitated. 'I can't remember.'

'Oh.'

'I'm going to write it all down,' said Kate suddenly. 'And then I'll show you. It'll be easier that way.'

'I'd appreciate that. I really would. It'll be like . . . closure.'

Kate smiled. She realised that she felt good, almost philanthropic, as if she was about to bestow the perfect gift. It might be a consolation prize but it was all she had to give. 'Do you think sometimes that he thought he had no choice? That because he talked about doing it so much, he had to go through with it? That maybe, even, he was doing it for us?'

Angie was silent for a long time. 'I don't think so. Because if he was thinking so rationally, then he would have managed, somehow, to do it without you being there. I think, to be honest, the pain made him selfish. So he was one hundred percent doing it for him. It was his choice.'

Kate nodded, wanting to believe.

'And I also think that you should see someone. To talk all this through.'

'Maybe.' Kate shrugged. 'It was a shit of a thing, wasn't it?'

'Yes,' replied Angie without hesitation. 'Absolutely.'

'He deserved better.'

'He certainly did.'

Kate glanced up at her cousin and saw, without much surprise, that Angie's eyes were brimming. She laid her hand across the table and, after a moment of hesitation, it was taken. The physical contact brought tears to Kate's eyes also, and she blinked, squeezing them out to trickle damply down her cheeks. He *had* deserved better, but then again, so had she.

TWENTY-ONE

She saw the rifle, its barrel gleaming dully in the fading light, as soon as she turned into the passageway leading to her father's bedroom. She came to an abrupt halt, and stared, disbelief shoved aside by mushrooming distress. For as long as she could remember, that rifle's existence had been betrayed only by a flash of walnut stock or a glimpse of blackened metal deep in the recesses of her father's wardrobe; but now it was out in the open. And she understood the implications immediately.

The rifle was propped in the only corner of the bedroom that she could see from where she now stood, and she knew there was significance in the placement. To see the rest of the room she would have to continue up the passage and through the doorway, then turn to face the matching twin beds, and her father, and a choice that had clearly been made. But instead she remained where she was, unwilling to move forward in either space or time. And she suddenly reasoned that the events waiting to unfold could not begin without her, that she was the linchpin, and therefore as long as she remained on the periphery there could be no conclusion. But even as she clutched at this reasoning, the rifle casually mocked her with its presence. And she knew that, really, she was nothing more than a bit player. She could only postpone, not prevent, whether she liked it or not.

Her feet moved forwards, almost mechanically, as if they belonged to someone else. And part of her was able to marvel at this, to glance down and think, Look at that, how funny, I'm walking and I didn't really mean to. *Even while her mind started to protest, becoming louder and louder as she slowly neared the doorway. Until she was only a few metres away and it was* yelling *at her not to go closer. Now she could see how the wooden stock of the rifle gleamed, as if it had recently been polished. And this thought spiralled into the noise within her head until it was no longer yelling, it was* screaming. *And so was she. But not because of the rifle, or the doorway, or what lay beyond, but because the house was shaking, vibrating, from the* thunderous *noise of bulldozers shuddering through the walls. And she just wanted it all. To. Stop.*

Kate's eyes flew open and she stared up at the darkened ceiling, her heart thumping. For a moment she wasn't sure where she was and she reached out a hand, automatically, towards Sam's side of the bed. Realisation that he wasn't there came at the same time as remembrance that she didn't want him anyway. Not at all. She took deep breaths until her heart steadied. *In*, two, three, out. *In*, two, three, out. Then she rolled over to check the time: 3.23 am.

Curling into the foetal position, Kate allowed herself to go through the dream before it faded. Already the pure intensity of emotion was rather blunted, although a dull sense of foreboding remained, even though she already knew that the worst had happened. Whether or not she chose to go through the doorway wouldn't change a thing now. But this dream had been extraordinarily vivid. She could still see the passage walls on either side of her, the doorway ahead, the rifle in the corner. She paused, and took an imaginary step forward, and then another. And another. When she was so close that she could have reached out her hand and touched the wood of the doorframe, she stopped and wrapped herself around the image, holding it tight. Then, without allowing herself to think about what she was doing, she got out of bed and went over to the desk, turning on the laptop.

The screen glowed in the darkness but Kate didn't bother turning on the overhead light. She sat down and immediately started typing out her nightmare which, apart from the bulldozers, hadn't been a nightmare at all. Not in the true sense anyway. She used third person, to maintain distance, and her fingers flew across the keys, suddenly desperate to turn thought into text. They only slowed as she reached the part that matched the image she still held tight. Standing at the doorway, poised to go forward.

Kate leant back in her chair, no longer in such a hurry. She read through what she had written and suddenly realised that, despite the subject matter, she felt proud. Even though she had yet to turn the corner, she had accomplished *something*. Which was good. And when it was finished, and it *would* be finished, she would package it up and give it to Angie to read, and understand, and share.

She stared at the patiently blinking cursor and thought about the earlier conversation with her cousin, warmed by the *validation* it had brought in its wake. It was not as if she hadn't always realised Angie was there, more that it had simply all seemed too hard. Too hard to start, too hard to finish. Nor had some sort of miracle now occurred, whereby everything was suddenly effortless and uncomplicated; that only seemed to happen in the movies. But things did seem a little bit clearer and Kate supposed that a psychologist would have some clinical term for it all. But terminology wasn't nearly as important as results, and she *knew* that she felt lighter.

Not that this absolved Sam of culpability. Kate's eyes narrowed even at the thought. Her orb of anger was still very much intact. Regardless of yesterday's watershed moments, he had betrayed her by his actions. The end did not justify the means. And what that meant for their marriage remained to be seen.

For now though she kept that to one side so that she was able to concentrate on other matters. Kate stared at the screen, at the patient cursor, and was reminded of a Latin phrase her father would use when turning over a new garden bed. *Tabula rasa*, a blank slate. She knew, from later studies at university, that it actually referred to infant humans, rather than organic vegetables, but nevertheless it had stuck as a term for new beginnings. This could be her *tabula rasa*. An opportunity to come to terms with the past, package it up neatly and then put it away. It was time to finish his story, so that she could continue with her own.

TWENTY-TWO

She walked slowly forward, her stomach tight, and passed through the doorway. Her father's eyes flew open as soon as she entered and she knew he had been waiting for her, battling sleep. She sat down on the bed opposite and watched as he slowly levered himself into a sitting position and then swung his legs to the floor, pulling his chequered dressing-gown over his shoulders. He looked no different from yesterday, or the day before. Yet unimaginably different from last year.

Olive skin now pale, with fleshy pouches that cradled deep-set eyes. A network of lines that once spoke of hard work and ready smiles, but were now cemented with pain. Grey hair kept short all over except for a few strands vainly covering his balding pate. A body once lean and strong, but now with the muscles so eroded that the skin hung like curtain swags between the jutting bones. The room had a sickly-sweet smell, a cloying mix of old man, illness and mind-numbing boredom. Their eyes caught and she looked down, unwilling to acknowledge the subject that hung, like a tangible entity, in the air between them.

'How do you feel?'

'Shithouse.' His breath rasped and he adjusted his position awkwardly. As he did so, the bedspread moved and she glimpsed, beneath the bed, a bottle half-full with urine. She closed her eyes briefly against the pain. Throughout her entire childhood she had never even seen him semi-naked. Now disease had accomplished what temperament could not: it left him exposed.

'I got the rifle out, but I couldn't get the other stuff.' The words punctuated the silence like bullets themselves.

She inhaled deeply, forcing the air into her lungs and holding it there until it seared, then letting it go with a rush that broke the silence. Only then did she glance across at him. 'Are you absolutely sure?'

'Yes.'

'And it has to be now? You can't wait?' Anything to postpone.

'No. Enough's enough.'

'Then I'll get them for you.' She rose slowly to her feet. 'What about everyone else? They'll want to see you. First.'

He began shaking his head before she even finished the sentence. 'No. I can't. Just say that . . . whatever. Do what you have to.' He shrugged as he avoided her gaze and she realised that he was almost beyond caring, yet paradoxically still capable of feeling a measure of guilt. But relief was more meaningful than the solace of others.

Suicide had first been given a voice about five months ago. But the voice, until recently, had been compassionate, caring, thoughtful. Sharing with everybody, not keeping secrets, raising questions and exploring options based on mutual concern. And then discussing them endlessly – so endlessly that there had been times, many times, that she had wished he would go ahead and do it. Just do it.

But that was then – and now everything was different. He had deteriorated rapidly over the past few weeks and was now in constant pain. Motor neurone disease warred with chronic bronchitis that placed pressure on the inoperable aneurysm near his heart. He simply no longer had the strength to be anxious about others. He just wanted out.

She went to the glass-fronted secretaire in the lounge room. Purchased at an auction years before for the princely sum of ten shillings, and now jammed behind his Jason recliner, it had always been a place for him to keep his coin collection, old keys and a myriad of odds and ends – including the bolt from his rifle, and a choice of two different types of ammunition.

When she returned, he was lying down again and at first she thought he was sleeping. But he opened his eyes and fastened them on what she held *in her hands with an anticipation that made her blood run cold. She sat back down as he struggled to rise and immediately reached out for the bolt and two boxes of rounds. He cradled them gently, his calluses a roughly hewn red against the pewter sheen of the rifle bolt.*

'Do you want a cup of tea?' She asked the question automatically, grasping at the mundane. Deflecting the inevitable.

'No, love,' he smiled at her for the first time as he shook his head ruefully. 'I just couldn't stomach it.'

She went over to the corner and picked up the rifle, pausing for a moment to breathe as she felt the cool weight press against her hands. Then she took it over and leant it against his bed. He had put on his thick-rimmed glasses and was examining the boxes of rounds with an interest that stood in stark contrast to his previous apathy. She turned away and wandered aimlessly around the room, glancing at the cluster of framed photographs with their nostalgia strangely at odds with what was happening. She paused on her paternal grandparents, captured in a brief moment of time when they had eyes only for each other. They ignored her sternly. What was she doing? Why was she doing it? Sacrilege, sacrilege.

He was suddenly racked by a vicious coughing fit. It lasted for a minute or so, rattling the box of rounds in his hand, before finally fracturing into a series of dry, hacking gasps. Putting the rounds down, he reached for a jar of tablets on the bedside table and extracted several, washing them down with a glass of water.

'I'm going to use rat shot, makes less mess.'

'But isn't . . . I mean, won't that be more risky?' Even with her limited knowledge of ammunition, she was fairly sure that solid shot was a safer bet. Momentarily, she replayed this conversation and realised that she was sitting here, discussing with her father *the best type of bullet to use in order to end his life. Her mind recoiled from the absurdity and she filed it away under things to deal with later. Much later.*

He inserted the bolt and then loaded the rifle clumsily with the chosen rounds. 'Could be, but this is better . . . less mess,'

'Are you absolutely sure?' She had to be certain, really certain.

'I've never been surer of anything.' He leant the rifle carefully by his leg

and stared at her, demanding eye contact. 'If I wait any longer, I won't be able to stay here. You know that. And I'll still be in bloody agony. I can't breathe, can't eat, can't keep anything down. It's a done deal. And I'll tell you something for nothing, love, I've had a gutful.'

She tried desperately to think of something that could steal a few more precious moments, rescue a semblance of normalcy. But there was nothing left. 'Do you want me to stay?' *Please say no, please, please, please.*

'No!' His horror was automatic and she was washed with relief, and a strange sense of comfort that he could still be protective. Even now.

'I love you.' She couldn't think of anything else to say, so she moved across to his bed and sat beside him. They hugged, and she could smell his illness and his desperation, but most of all she could sense an overwhelming feeling of regret, threaded with relief. But maybe that was just hers.

He broke off the embrace first, probably not because he wanted to but because it was simply too painful for him to remain in one position for long. He looked at the phone. 'D'you reckon I should ring Angie?'

She stood up, surprised at the question, and by a flash of jealousy. 'Well, I suppose if you want to. It's up to you.'

'Nah,' he shrugged. 'Just tell her . . . you know.'

She nodded. 'I know.'

He reached out suddenly and clasped her hand with a firm grip that made his knuckles stand out as the flesh folded in around. 'Love you . . . and thanks.'

She left the room and walked down the passageway and into the kitchen. There she stood at the window and gazed blindly through the net curtains. Long minutes passed and she began counting under her breath. Five, four, three, two, one . . . she could hear the occasional car on the road outside and it seemed a world away.

As the minutes ticked by, she started to panic, drumming her fingers painfully against the countertop. Maybe he was having second thoughts. Maybe he was even hoping that she would stop him, take control, call it off – and unless she went back in now, right now, he would be forced to go through with it to save face. Maybe he desperately wanted someone, anyone, HER, to call his bluff, take the rifle, confiscate all knives, forbid him to do anything. Maybe her grand sacrifice was nothing more than a grand betrayal.

She had just turned away from the window when the rifle shot cracked across the silence, leaving behind an echo that belied its finality. It was almost immediately accompanied by a thin, high wail so full of pain that she thought she would vomit just from hearing it. She didn't pause to think, just raced back through the house and into the bedroom. Then she came to a shuddering halt as she took in the scene before her.

The wail had stopped and, on the bed, her father lay full-length with the rifle on his stomach, his hands clutching the trigger guard and the barrel just short of his mouth as if it had popped out with the recoil. And his mouth . . . it gaped and glistened with the sheen of blood while his eyes stared at the ceiling. Until, that is, he realised she was there and then they suddenly, swiftly, swivelled around to meet her own and she realised at once that they were conveying an urgent, desperate message. He was just as horrified, horrified at her entry, horrified at her presence, he was telling her, beseeching her, screaming at her to get out, get out, for God's sake don't look at me like this, GET OUT!

She got out. She ran back to the kitchen where she froze, her hands clenched in desperation. They had stuffed it up. She needed to call an ambulance. He would be a vegetable, brain-damaged, worse off than before. She needed someone to tell her what do to. Somebody. Anybody. Sam.

After about five minutes of mind-numbing indecision, she forced herself to walk slowly, quietly back up the passageway, but stopped short of entering the bedroom. She never, never, wanted to see those eyes again. And that was when she realised she could still hear his breathing. Big, strong gulps for breath, desperately gasping, rasping, agonised labouring, frantic inhalations. Oh god, why couldn't he just die?

She leant with her back against the doorframe, put her hands over her ears, and slowly slid down until she was squatting on the floor. Silently screaming, shouting, pleading, begging, until her head was thick with noise. And there she stayed, rocking backwards and forwards, for what seemed like hours before she forced herself into stillness and took her hands away from her ears. Then all she could hear was someone muttering 'Oh god, oh god, oh god', over and over and over again. Moments later she realised that the litany was hers, and the breathing had stopped.

Afterwards, when she checked the little carriage clock, she realised that it had taken him fifteen minutes to die. For her, it would always feel like time froze and yet stretched simultaneously. Somehow. Even when she registered that she could no longer hear the ragged breathing, it was a long while before she could enter the room. And when she did, she moved very slowly. She saw her paternal grandparents endlessly gazing at each other, she saw her father's medi-alert lying nearby and she saw a full cup of cold tea that he must have attempted earlier in the day. She saw his dressing-gown folded at the end of the bed, she saw his yellowed dentures placed neatly next to the glass of water – and she saw him.

In all the months that have passed since that day, this is the image that has remained clear. It requires a deliberate effort to picture her father as the man he once was, to see him at work or at play, a grandchild on a knee, or a meal before him. Yet it requires no effort to remember how he looked at the end. Like an indestructible photograph – a hideous moment carved in time. His final gift to her. That she need only close her eyes in order to see him again, and again, and again.

The peripherals are slightly blurred, but he himself is quite clear, striped pyjamas shrouded by a floral bedspread, lying flat on his back, with his legs looking rather longer than they should. His hands are no longer clutching at the rifle but have fallen away and lie limply, one at his side and the other on his concave belly. The rifle itself lies snugly along the length of his body, with the muzzle now innocently pointing at the wall behind. But these are incidentals, and it is always the face that compels. His neck is slightly arched and his head is tilted back so that it is necessary to take another step forward in order to see the expression – and it is awful. Forever frozen in a last paroxysm of agony, silently screaming for eternity. Yet totally vacant. The spirit has fled, the vessel depleted. Tabula rasa. His mouth still gapes but is now black and cavernous. And his eyes . . . they are already dull and marbled, no longer accusing, they now just stare blindly at the ceiling.

But he was right, there's hardly any mess.

TWENTY-THREE

April slid past with pleasant, incremental speed. The uncommonly hot March was forgotten as the weather bowed to the inevitable and wholeheartedly embraced the congenial vagaries of autumn. This meant mild, steadily cooler temperatures and an occasional wind that stripped the trees and gusted annoyingly at night.

Whilst finishing her father's story hadn't brought Kate definitive closure, where a clear line is drawn between then and now, it had been a surprisingly agile leap in the right direction. Rather than feeling merely drained, she felt *purged*, and there was a world of difference. Alongside this was a sense of personal achievement, having finally written *something*, and a huge sense of relief that the chronicle now existed somewhere else other than inside her head. That gave it a life of its own, which was no longer dependent on her for survival, and the subsequent distance brought an objectivity that was liberating in itself.

Kate developed the habit of reading it each evening, just before going to bed. Initially she treated this as a matter of professional pride, a desire to polish the story to perfection before passing it to Angie. But she also accepted that the gesture had an undercurrent of masochism; and a reluctance to actually finish and let go. Imperceptibly, however, this all changed. With nightly readings, the words that scrolled down the screen gradually became so familiar that she developed a sort of cathartic desensitisation, which enabled her to crawl into bed afterwards and simply dismiss the story from her mind.

Towards the end of April, Kate even faced the fact that the narrative required no more polishing. So she printed out five sheets of A4 paper and slid them into a large envelope marked with Angie's name. But it certainly wasn't the sum of her creativity that month. Rather, and much to her surprise, her father's story had almost immediately heralded a surge of productivity. It was as if the act of forcing herself to actually *write*, for more than just an hour or so, had reawakened something despite the subject matter. Something with an insatiable appetite that craved more, and would not be content with five pages that few people would ever read.

And this time she had no problem coming up with an idea.

Kate had always expected that these six months, for her, would be full of change and growth and, hopefully, new directions. But she never anticipated that her mother would accompany her on the ride. Much of what she had taken for granted about the woman had been exposed as a façade, created by her father himself. Possibly, Kate now realised, for his sake as much as for his daughter. But simply replacing the idealistic image with a less appealing reality was too simplistic, and too unfair on the long-ago child who had endured such a horrid home life. A home life that may well have governed her later choices, as well as having fashioned the exterior that had so alienated others. Liveliness notwithstanding.

And Kate felt she owed her something. Not a true biography, where everything was laid bare, but a framework of fact wrapped around a fluid centre of fiction. Fashioned out of imagination and compassion. Giving the gentlest of closure to a woman who had been dead for many years, and who had deserved much more than life had offered. Furthermore, it seemed *right* that, having given so much to her father, she should offer this to her mother.

And once she started writing, Kate wondered why it had taken so long. Why on earth she had ever contemplated writing about Angie's mother when her own had been waiting in the wings, crying out for recognition. She didn't bother with any further research, just starting with

Rose as a child and letting her own inventiveness fill in the gaps. After a rather unsteady beginning, the words began to flow and the story soon took on a life of its own. Demanding her attention like a greedy child, taking all she could give and then crying out for more whenever she turned away.

It left time for very little else during those weeks, so that she surfaced only occasionally to touch base with those around. Like Angie, who was soon to take a few months off before leaving for England in September. Which meant that Shelley and Jacob would be taking over the shop at the end of May, with the added advantage of having their aunt around for a while if they ran into any difficulties.

With this Kate slowly realised that she had made one major mistake in her story about her father. Her remembrance of his face at the end had not been his final gift, not even close. Instead, he kept on giving. To Angie, with her trip overseas; to Melissa, who would have her mother's company; to Shelley and Jacob, with a new career; and to her. Especially to her. Amongst everything else, he had given her this journey that had culminated in her writing again. Rediscovering a lost love that had lain dormant for so long. And she knew, instinctively, that she would never let it go again. So Kate erased those lines from his story and then reprinted the whole. And this time she sealed the envelope before placing it by the laptop on her desk.

But there was one glaring absence within her life – Sam. And while Kate was grateful for the occasional visits and phone calls from her children, and being kept up to date, these also served to highlight the fact that she had not been home since her father's house had been demolished. At first she continued to maintain her anger with a religious righteousness. But as she moved from her father's story towards her mother's, the orb began to show signs of fragility. Slowly at first, with hairline cracks spider-webbing the surface, but building in momentum until, at last, it imploded.

She still felt, strongly, that Sam had lacked sensitivity in the way he had handled the demolition. But she also saw that he had been backed into a corner. As the builder in the family, he had been given the accountability for the entire development and then everybody else had virtually backed away. Leaving him to juggle reality and the demands of a work force with the conflicting expectations of those who had charged him with the task. If he had done a less than perfect job, then the responsibility was not his alone and never should have been.

Besides, the time for her to state objections had been last year, when they met to discuss what to do with the house and land. But at the time she had remained mostly silent, instead expecting those around her, and Sam in particular, to pick up on her brittle body language and interpret it. When this hadn't happened, she had simply retreated into the role of the martyr. And the feelings of resentment and bitterness had been a perfect cohort for the overwhelming grief from both her father's death and the dreadful manner of his dying.

But there had been no particular moment when all this had suddenly become clear; rather it had been a slow series of realisations, so it was mid-April before the thought of a visit home had even started to appeal. And by then it was too late.

There had been no word from Sam since she had hung up on him. Not a phone call, or a note, or even a casual message passed on by one of the kids. She knew he was working hard because she had gleaned this information from Shelley, and she also knew that the trips to Eildon had continued. But she didn't know how to end the impasse without a loss of dignity that felt unbearable. However, as April slipped steadily by, Kate started to ask herself what was worse, swallowing her pride or losing Sam, and the answer became both clearer and more insistent.

On the morning of her forty-eighth birthday, Kate woke to breakfast in bed. Fried bacon and eggs, with toast on the side and a mug of fresh coffee. Angie placed the laden tray on the doona by Kate and then sat down on the side of the bed with a grin. 'Happy birthday! I can't believe you were still asleep.'

Kate struggled to a sitting position and put the mug onto her bedside table so that it wouldn't spill. She glanced at the clock. 'Ten past eight!'

'What time did you finish up? I heard you still typing away when I went to bed.'

'About one-ish, I think.' Kate pushed a pillow behind her back and then picked up the tray and balanced it on her lap. 'Thank you! This looks delicious!'

'You're welcome. Just remember to return the favour, okay?'

'And by your birthday, you'll be a lady of leisure so you'll be able to enjoy it.'

Angie plucked a small rasher of bacon off the plate. 'So any big plans today?'

'No. Think I'll just continue with the writing.' Kate sliced into her egg, releasing a burst of thick yellow yolk. 'Actually, maybe I'll go for a drive.'

'When? This morning?'

Kate frowned at her tone. 'No, probably later. Why?'

'Nothing,' Angie shrugged. 'I just thought maybe . . . you'd like to have lunch or something? Then you can go for a drive afterwards.'

'Sounds good. Shall I meet you at the shop?'

'Sure.' Angie took a bite of the bacon and started chewing.

Kate looked at her. 'Well, what time?'

'Oh, say noon?'

'Okay, then.' Kate nodded and turned to her meal. It was a long while since she had last had breakfast in bed. In fact, she suspected it might have been soon after the birth of the twins, when Sam had surprised her one morning with scrambled eggs on toast. And a nearly three-year-old Shelley had scrambled into the bed next to her and they all kept their voices down for fear of waking the occupants of the two nearby bassinets. Whose vocal chords had to be heard to be believed.

'What are you smiling about?' asked Angie.

'Nothing much.'

'Oh well, I'd better get going. Some of us have to work for a living.'

'Hey! I've been working flat out!'

'True. I meant some of us don't have the luxury of staying at home and working in our pyjamas.' Angie peered at herself in the mirror and tried to smooth down her hair. Then she shrugged and turned towards the doorway, pausing as she saw the envelope on the desk. 'Is this for me?'

Kate felt a frisson of what felt almost like panic. Then, as quickly as it had formed, it slid away, leaving just the answer behind.

Angie frowned. 'Well?'

'Actually . . . yes, it's for you. Take it. But don't read it at work.'

'Why on earth not?'

'Because it's personal, that's why.' Kate stared at her for a few moments, willing the message across. She sighed. 'Because it's that thing I promised you. The story. About Dad's last day.'

'Oh.' Angie looked down at the envelope again with sudden understanding and then picked it up gingerly, as if it were precious. 'I see. Okay. Thanks.'

Kate listened to the sound of Angie running down the stairs and felt a knot of anticipation over her cousin reading the story, a feeling of being judged, both for her actions and for her writing technique. The latter admission made Kate smile. I *must* be a writer, she thought, if the words matter as much as the content. Or almost as much.

Nevertheless there was also an unexpected sense of relief at finally passing the envelope over, and thus sharing ownership. Spreading it around. Kate steadied the tray as she put the bacon into her mouth. Breakfast in bed was one of those things that always sounded much better in theory than it played out in practice. Forty-eight years old. She took a deep breath and then shrugged. It was only a number, and it didn't seem quite so important when she felt that she was achieving something. And she was.

If it wasn't for the dilemma involving Sam, Kate knew that she would have been more content than she had been for a long time. Everything else seemed to be coming together, except that – which was falling apart. But maybe today, maybe he would ring. Kate pushed the tray over to the side of the bed and then flung back the doona and padded into the ensuite where she stared at the mirror, trying to see the evidence of her freshly amplified age. It didn't seem too obvious, only some slight indentations running down to her mouth, and a few shadows where once all had seemed smooth.

After showering, Kate pulled on a pair of snug black tracksuit pants that flared over her runners and a lime-green and black striped windcheater jacket with a wide hood. In the kitchen Angie had left the morning paper folded on the bench so Kate curled up in the armchair to bring herself up to date with the news. She had just finished when the phone rang. Immediately her stomach clenched.

'Hello?'

'Happy birthday, Mum!' shouted Caleb, a great deal of noise in the background.

'Thanks, but where *are* you?'

'At uni! Early lecture!'

'So what's all the noise then?'

'Pardon?'

'I said what's all the —'

'Sorry, can't hear you!' yelled Caleb. 'Too much noise! I'll ring back later!'

Kate hung up the phone with a wry smile and it rang again almost immediately. She answered it quickly, before she could start debating who it might be.

'Mum! Happy birthday!'

'Thanks, Shell. How are things?'

'Good, good.' Shelley sounded breathless. 'I'm at the shop today. Took another sickie. Jacob wanted to fit the network cable. For the computer.'

'Jacob's there too?'

'Yeah, hang on.' Shelley's voice faded as she obviously turned from the phone and whispered, rather loudly, 'Mum's on the phone. Say happy birthday.'

Jacob's voice came clearly. 'Happy birthday, Mum!'

'Thanks, Jake. So how's the —'

'It's me again, Mum,' interrupted Shelley. 'So, got a big day planned?'

'Not really, although I'll be down there later.'

'Down where?'

Kate frowned. 'The shop, of course. I'm having lunch with your aunt.'

'Oh, really? Okay, we'll see you then.'

Kate hung up the telephone with the frown still in place. While it was nice for the kids to ring her for her birthday, even if it clearly hadn't occurred to Jacob himself, it was a bit puzzling that not one of them had said anything about catching up. Maybe for a birthday dinner, or at least to give her a present, or even a card. Instead, it seemed that a lunch with Angie was going to be the extent of her birthday celebrations.

She stared at the telephone, willing it to ring again. Just once more. In the background she could hear the clock counting down the minutes. It suddenly occurred to her that only a few months ago she had been desperate for time to decelerate, and now it had. Maybe too much.

But maybe also time had never been the problem, only the symptom. Maybe *she* had been the problem. Thrown out of sync with her surroundings. And whether this lack of equilibrium had been building for years, and had then been hugely exacerbated by her father's death, or whether it had actually been *caused* by her father's death, was really a moot point. As long as it was re-established.

Kate took a deep breath and gazed at the telephone again. She picked up the receiver and re-hung it to check that it had been disengaged properly. And when the *beep* was immediately followed by the tinny melody of the doorbell, she was at first rather confused as to its origin. But then her stomach clenched again, and for a few seconds she just stared up towards the foyer. Then she took a deep breath and made herself walk slowly, steadily, over to answer the door.

'Happy birthday,' said Sam, with a cheerful smile.

She felt suddenly light-headed. 'Thank you.'

'No problem.'

Kate looked at him expectantly, waiting for some sort of acknowledgement of the fact that they'd just spent nearly four weeks not speaking, but he continued to grin. Kate glanced involuntarily down towards his hands. No flowers, no present. Nothing. She kept her face blank. 'Um, would you like to come in?'

'Nah, haven't got time.'

'Oh.' Her stomach went into freefall. What could she say, or do, to make him stay? Or talk? Or *something*?

'D'you want to come for a drive?'

'Yes!' said Kate, much too quickly. She hazarded a smile and this seemed to have an immediate relaxing effect, on her at least. *Sam* had seemed perfectly relaxed from the moment she opened the door.

'Okay then. Let's go.'

Kate's smile widened with relief, as well as the unexpectedness of it all. His nonchalance did more than anything else to diminish her feelings of awkwardness. She glanced at Sam's cargo pants and assumed that casual was fine, so she just grabbed her handbag from the hall table and walked out onto the porch, reaching behind to shut the door.

'Hang on.' Sam put a hand out. 'I have to grab something for Angie.'

'For Angie?'

'Yeah. She asked me to,' said Sam, rather lamely. 'You go ahead and hop in the car. I'll just be a tick.'

Kate frowned as she watched Sam go past her and then run quickly up the stairs, taking the steps two at a time. This was distinctly odd, not only because Angie hadn't mentioned anything about Sam but because if she *did* want something, then why hadn't she just asked Kate? Then she smiled again as she remembered it was her birthday, and distinctly odd was usually *good* on such occasions.

Kate had just opened the passenger-side door when she heard the front door close. She glanced back curiously. Sam was coming towards her carrying a navy blue sports bag which he took straight to the rear of the ute. He unfastened a corner of the black tarpaulin and slid the bag underneath carefully before hooking it back up. He turned to her with a grin. 'Let's rock and roll!'

'Okay.' Kate looked at him suspiciously, but didn't move.

His grin widened. 'Come on, trust me.'

'Hmm,' said Kate noncommittally. But she got into the car and did up her seatbelt. The interior had clearly been tidied recently but the familiar dusty smell remained, reminiscent of brick dust and concrete and countless building sites. Sam slipped into the driver's seat, and turned the key in the ignition. He flicked another grin at her and then put the car into gear and drove up the driveway and out into the road.

'So where are we going?' asked Kate, winding down her window a trifle.

'You'll soon see.'

Kate stared at him for a moment, but when no further information was offered, she looked straight ahead, letting herself enjoy the relief that came from a chance at resolution, as well as the whole mystery of the occasion. They headed up towards the nearby foothills and Kate continued to relax as they drove, aided by a strong sense that the further they went, the more certain they would be able to settle their differences before returning. She sneaked a glance towards Sam and wasn't sure whether to be disappointed that he looked so well, although rather in need of a haircut. He caught her eye.

'So, how do you feel about being kidnapped?'

'Well, it's never been one of my fantasies. But I suppose it depends on where I'm held, and by whom.'

Sam chuckled. 'All will be revealed.'

'That sounds interesting.' Kate moved herself around in her seat so that she was facing him. 'Should I have brought supplies?'

'Nah.'

'What's in the sports bag?'

'You'll find out later.'

'It's not really for Angie, is it?'

'You have to know everything, don't you?' asked Sam mildly. 'Can't stand surprises.'

'I wouldn't say I can't *stand* them. More that they're . . . itchy.'

'Itchy?' Sam glanced at her, with eyebrows raised.

'You know what I mean.' Kate watched him as he drove. 'Anyway, I hope I won't have to rely on one of the kids to ransom me?'

Sam laughed again. '*That* could mean a long stay.'

She stared at the slight shadow along the curve of his jawbone, the fine lines that fanned out from the corner of his eye. She wondered that she had ever been prepared to trade *this* for some notion of freedom. Not when she could have both.

'You trying to make up your mind?' asked Sam lightly.

'No.' Kate looked away. 'Um, I probably should tell you that I'm supposed to be meeting Angie for lunch later.'

Sam lifted one hand from the steering wheel and waved it dismissively.

'Does that mean I'm *not* meeting Angie for lunch later?'

'Just be patient.' Sam coasted to a halt at a traffic intersection and turned to her. 'So what do you think of Shelley and Jake going into partnership, then?'

'Mixed feelings. But I'm feeling a lot better about it all now that Angie's passing the shop over earlier. That'll give them plenty of time to learn the ropes while she's still around. I mean, neither of them has ever run a business before. It's not that easy.'

'I know. But I reckon it'll be good for them. Besides, if and when they split up the partnership, it'll still be something for his resume. Which is better than nothing.'

'I didn't say I wasn't in favour.' Kate pointed towards the traffic lights. 'Green.'

Sam nodded and drove off. 'I can always help them anyway.'

'That's right. Because you keep your *own* business paperwork in such tiptop condition.' Kate looked at him. 'Speaking of which, how *is* everything going?'

'Well . . .' Sam grimaced. 'Actually, it's all just waiting for you. I did try, but I couldn't make head or tail of your system.'

'That's not *my* system, it's the government's. Clearly I'll have to spend some time with you, going over it all.'

'Good. I'm in desperate need of some going over.'

Kate glanced across, both pleased and surprised by how *easy* this all was. 'Play your cards right and we'll see what happens.'

'I'd rather just have a good hand to start off with.'

Kate smiled, slowly. 'Are we still talking about cards?'

'What else?' Sam stopped at another intersection behind a large truck that belched plumes of black smoke from the exhaust pipe. He looked at her for a moment. 'I'm sorry about the house.'

'No, it's not your fault,' said Kate quickly, filled with a sort of exultation that the subject had been raised. 'I should have told you what I wanted. Not expected you to have some sort of ESP.'

'Yeah, but I *did* rush it all a bit. It was just fitting it between other jobs, and I didn't really think.'

Kate looked down at her hands, clasped loosely across her lap. 'But I shouldn't have yelled at you like that. It wasn't fair.'

'Oh, well. It's done now.'

'Yes. All done now,' Kate straightened in her seat, and stared ahead as Sam drove away from the intersection and changed lanes heading towards the blue-grey bulk of Mount Dandenong. Kate wanted to talk about other things, and had actually *expected* the conversation to continue, but silence had suddenly fallen like a blanket. And the longer it went on, the harder it was to shake off. She wound her window down a bit further and leant her head to the side, feeling the air whisk through the gap and blow roughly against her face as she listened to the steady drone of the engine, whipping past in the wind. She took a deep breath and then wound up her window so that she wouldn't have to raise her voice. 'Um, are you not speaking to me?'

Sam looked at her, clearly stunned. 'What?'

'Well, you haven't said a word for ages. Since we spoke about . . . the house.'

'Are you *kidding* me?' Sam shook his head and started to laugh.

'Glad you're so amused,' said Kate stiffly.

'Sometimes I just don't get women.' Sam took one hand off the steering wheel and pointed at her. '*You* think we're not talking, and *I* think we're having a companionable silence!'

Kate stared at him. After a few minutes, she started to laugh as well. 'You did?'

'Absolutely. Why not?'

'Maybe because things are a little . . . well, *awkward*. What with not having spoken for almost four weeks.'

Sam concentrated on the road. 'I thought it best to give you some space. Although I was a bit surprised it stretched out so long. Didn't time fly, hey?'

'Oh, it sure did,' replied Kate, her laughter petering off.

Sam glanced over with concern. 'I thought that's what you wanted? Some space?'

'Oh, it was. And that's what I was doing for *you* too. Giving you some space.'

'What did *I* need space for?'

'You know,' replied Kate airily. She felt tears pricking at the back of her eyes but didn't know why. She took a deep breath and turned to him. 'I've taken a lot out on you lately, haven't I?'

Sam kept his eyes on the road. 'You could say that.'

'I *am* saying that. And . . .' Kate willed him to look in her direction. 'You know when you said I was moving into the unit to . . . well, punish you?'

'Yes. I remember.'

'I think you may have been right. Just a bit.'

'Really?'

'Really. I mean, I *did* want to write a book. You know that. But I don't think I would ever have moved out if it hadn't been for . . . you know.'

'Your father.'

'Yes.'

Sam sighed but still didn't look at her. 'Do you have any idea how hard it is to help someone who won't let you?'

'I know,' Kate nodded. 'But it was difficult. Still is, just maybe not as much.'

'Look, I'm not saying it wasn't a hell of a thing to go through. And I still reckon you should've talked to someone back then. I think it'd still help now, just as a sort of release. But we can talk about that later.'

Kate waited, but he didn't continue. She took a deep breath. 'Maybe. Because I was so . . .' she searched for the right word, but there didn't seem to be one. 'Angry,' she finished lamely. 'So angry.'

'Yeah, I got that.'

'And I don't think I knew what to do with it. So, well, all the stuff about developing the land probably let me channel that anger . . . against you for doing it. Not that I let it show, all that much.'

'Oh no, not at all,' Sam gave a short bark of laughter.

Kate stared ahead and spoke tightly. 'So . . . I'm sorry. Okay?'

Sam didn't answer this and the ensuing silence began to deepen uncomfortably again. This wasn't a companionable silence, not at all. In fact, it was beginning to segue into humiliation. And vulnerability. Then suddenly Sam's hand was on her right thigh, not with so much a smoothly supportive gesture as an awkward thump, but all the more welcome because of that. Kate stared at it for a few seconds, at his square-tipped fingers and workman-like hands, and then put her own on top, entwining her fingers loosely through his.

'Are we okay now, though?' asked Sam, watching the road.

'God, I *hope* so.'

They slowed down as they entered the small town of Yarra Glen and Sam glanced at her, with a quick grin, as he took his hand back. The wind had picked up now and curly brown autumn leaves skittered across the road to dance along the gutters.

Now that she had said what she wanted to say, what she *needed* to say, and it had been accepted, Kate felt queasy with relief. But also, at the same time, warmed by a sense of peace.

'You know, I reckon you've got every right to be angry,' said Sam, almost conversationally. 'Not at me, mind you. But at what happened.'

'Yes.'

'Because it shouldn't have *had* to happen. Not like that. The man made a rational decision months before, and when the time came, he had a right to die with dignity.' Sam reached over with his left hand and held hers loosely. 'There's something wrong when you can be as sick as a dog but the dog's got more bloody rights.'

'You mean to be . . . euthanased. Put down.'

Sam glanced over at her. 'If somebody's in that much pain, and there's no hope, then they should have the choice. And if they decide they want to end it, then that should be bloody well respected. So that they can slip away peacefully, with their family around them. It's only common decency, for god's sake.'

'I agree. One hundred percent.'

'And they should never have to go through what James had to.' Sam hesitated for a moment. 'Or ask relatives to go through what you did.'

Kate stared at him and suddenly realised that he was angry too. Her easygoing, laid-back Sam was angry. 'Do you blame my father . . . for that?'

He hesitated again, a moment too long. 'No, not really. And anyway I've gotten myself sidetracked. What I wanted to say was that I reckon you *should* be angry. Just make sure you point it in the right direction.'

'And what direction would that be?'

'The government. Politicians. All those who know that most of the population would support euthanasia but refuse to put it to a vote.'

'Yes.' Kate looked back out of the window at the grassy, rolling hills that formed a picturesque backdrop for the paddocks that lined the road. She wondered, suddenly, whether one of those lawmakers ever had a relative make the most fundamental of choices, like her father had, and then have to suffer so horribly as a result.

'You're a writer. *Use* that anger. Write about it.'

Kate looked down at their joined hands. 'Actually, I have. But I know what you mean . . . and I'll think about it.'

'Anyway, change of subject.' Sam squeezed her hand and then let it go, putting both his hands back on the steering wheel. 'I hear you've been writing flat out?'

Kate nodded proudly. 'Yes. And enjoying every minute.'

'What's it about?'

'Actually . . . my mother. Sort of.'

Sam glanced at her curiously. 'So you took up my idea then? To write about your own mother instead of Angie's?'

'That's right.' Kate smiled with surprise. 'I'd forgotten about that.'

'That'd be right. I never get the recognition I deserve.'

Kate looked at him pensively. 'No, maybe you don't.'

'Hey, I was only joking.'

'I'm not.'

'In that case, it does go *both* ways, you know. You might take me for granted sometimes, but I do the same to you.'

'True. But then I suppose if we *didn't* take each other for granted every now and again, that'd mean we never really relaxed.'

'Very philosophical of you, my love.'

Kate laughed contentedly, her queasiness almost gone. They passed a sign for the Kinglake National Park and started up a winding road that was thickly bordered by hugely towering trees. After a while, Kate glanced at the clock on the dashboard and saw, with some surprise, that it was getting close to midday.

Sam followed her gaze. 'Do you want to stop for lunch soon? Maybe in Yea?'

'Sure,' Kate nodded and was about to make a comment about Angie, and lunch, when she suddenly realised where they were headed, and immediately marvelled that it had taken so long to occur to her. 'We're going to Eildon, aren't we?'

'God, took you long enough.'

'Maybe I had other things on my mind.' Kate turned to look at Sam curiously. 'Um, why are we going to Eildon?'

'Birthday surprise.'

'Then we won't be driving back again today?'

'Nope.'

'Is the caravan still habitable?' Kate grimaced at the thought. 'And I don't have anything with me. No clothes or anything.'

'All taken care of,' said Sam, with a smug smile.

Kate stared at him. 'The sports bag.'

'Yep. Good old Angie.'

'You mean Angie *knew* about this? And she packed me some things?'

Sam nodded, clearly pleased with himself.

'Don't know if I like being kept in the dark,' said Kate lightly.

'I know the feeling.'

Kate glanced at him quickly to gauge this response, but he grinned at her, taking the sting out of his words. She smiled back until he turned to face the road again, and then she stared out of the window, watching the trees whip past. She knew there was still a bit of work to be done with Sam, to repair the damage done over the last year, but for the first time she felt confident that they were on the right track. And maybe, in the long run, their marriage might even be strengthened by the whole experience. Yet another gift.

A large truck roared past, on the opposite side of the road, with a line of cars trailing behind it as if playing follow-the-leader. Kate watched them zip past, one by one, and thought about how odd it was that one could feel so safe, encased inside a metal cocoon and hurtling along at about one hundred kilometres per hour. It actually defied common sense.

Soon afterwards they stopped in Yea, at a busy roadside café, and bought hamburgers for lunch; then took off again just after one o'clock. Kate expected to drive straight through but, after only twenty minutes or so, Sam pulled off the road and parked diagonally before a small general store. A Streets ice-cream sign on a metal frame swung lazily in the breeze, and multi-coloured plastic strips hung from the doorway. Sam turned to her with a grin and she started to laugh. 'Oh, my god. Yarck coffee, how could I have forgotten?'

'Coming right up.' Sam got out and went inside the store, the plastic strips noisily rearranging themselves behind him.

Kate leant back, still smiling. Over the years, when they had come up here on a regular basis, it had become a sort of tradition to stop in Yarck, just outside Yea, for a coffee-break. Not because the coffee was particularly remarkable, but because all three kids had absolutely loved the name. And the way it could transform any comment. How's your day been? *Yarck*. How's your coffee? *Yarck*. What does a cockatoo say? *Yarck, yarck, yarck*.

Sam came back out, bearing two takeaway cardboard coffee cups. Kate stretched over to open his door for him, and he got in awkwardly, passing her over one of the cups. 'Yarck coffee, ma'am. Specially brewed.'

'Thank you, kind sir. How terribly yarck of you.'

Sam grinned. 'Some things never change.'

'No, some things don't,' agreed Kate. She looked across at him. 'So, are you going to tell me why you've been going to Eildon so much lately?'

'Just having a break, that's all.'

'Don't give me that.' Kate shook her head dismissively. 'We've hardly been up there for ages. Yet now all of a sudden it's your favourite hang-out?'

'Maybe I needed somewhere to have a . . . what did you call your break? A *hiatus*, that's right. So maybe I needed one too?'

'*My* hiatus wasn't a three hour drive away. And why are *we* suddenly going up there?'

'Let me see.' Sam looked pensive. 'Last time we spoke, you inferred that you never wanted to speak to me again, so kidnapping seemed the only option left. And the further away I take you, the less likely you can do a runner.'

'What about Bertha, then?' asked Kate. 'There'll be no threesomes with me involved, mate. It's not *your* birthday.'

'Does that mean when it *is* my birthday, that you'll –'

'Definitely not.'

'Typical. Get my hopes up and then dash them.' Sam finished his coffee and screwed up the cardboard cup before tossing it out of the window into a nearby metal rubbish bin. It landed perfectly. 'Okay for me to get going?'

'Sure.' Kate held her cup tightly as Sam reversed out of the car-park and then waited for a bus to pass by before taking off down the highway. After a while, they passed through Bonnie Doon and over the beautiful wooden bridge that spanned the northern end of Lake Eildon. Kate stared at the water level, so much lower than it had been even the last time she had visited. She sighed, and Sam caught her eye and nodded with tacit agreement.

Fifteen minutes later they finally reached their intersection and Kate felt her stomach tense as Sam slowed and turned off the main highway. They drove down the arterial road for about twenty kilometres, between the occasional new house and tracts of farmland, with lazy cows grazing at nearby fences, before turning onto a smaller dirt road. Clouds of dust now marked their progress as the tyres crunched over the unmade surface. Kate glanced at Sam with a smile as he negotiated a bend and then started up the rise that led to their own driveway.

'First to see the land!' cried Kate, echoing the well-remembered chant of her children from years before. Then she realised her mistake and started to laugh. Their block must be over the next rise, because this one had a house on it. She glanced at Sam, still grinning at her error, but then her grin faded as she saw him flick on the indicator and turn off the road.

Kate frowned at the smirk on his face, and then slowly, almost reluctantly, turned her head as the car coasted to a halt. To stare through the windscreen at the block of land, *their* block of land, and the house that now sat squarely by the driveway where the caravan had once lived. It was strange enough to see a house here, any house, but *this* house – it was unbelievable. And it took her a few minutes to fully acknowledge it, without the rhododendrons, and the side gate, and the whole *context* she was accustomed to.

'I don't believe this.' Kate undid her seatbelt and got slowly out of the car, still staring. The weatherboards were the same dirty-white colour, with mission-brown trim around the windows and the front door with its diamond pane of frosted glass in the centre. The same curtains even hung at the windows. Strangely, though, the whole house seemed lower somehow, and slighter straighter. But there could be no doubting its provenance: it was her father's house, here, in Eildon.

'Surprised?' asked Sam from behind her.

'Um . . . yes,' replied Kate, rather numbly, not really wanting to talk. And anyway, it would be impossible to find the right words.

She walked slowly up the dirt driveway towards the house, trying to tread lightly lest the scrunching of her footsteps break the spell. But the house remained, alien-like within its oasis of grey dirt. No vegetable patch behind, no garden beds in front, no anything – except an oddly gnarled, naked tree to the side with its many-fingered branches grasping at the heavens as if in supplication. Sam came alongside, glancing at her every so often to gauge her reactions. She slowed by the strange-looking tree, a trickle of recognition bringing incredulity.

'It's the lemon tree, from your father's house.' Sam grinned with obvious pride. 'I got an arborist to help me, which is why it's been trimmed so drastically. He said there's a fifty-fifty chance of it taking. But I thought it was worth a chance.'

'Definitely,' replied Kate, running her fingers over the nubbly tip of a branch but staring, once more, at the house itself.

'And it's like it goes with the house, you know? A family tree.'

'Definitely,' repeated Kate. She sent the tree some brisk best wishes through her fingertips and then continued on. When they reached the porch she realised there was only one step up to the front door now, instead of three, which explained why the house appeared lower. She stepped up and then looked back down at Sam, shaking her head with disbelief.

He grinned. 'Happy birthday.'

'This is . . . amazing. Absolutely amazing.'

'You like?'

'I . . .' Kate turned around and looked at the house again. 'I'm in shock. I don't know what to say.'

'Then don't say anything.'

'But how did you *do* this?'

'House removalists,' replied Sam promptly, stepping up onto the porch. 'It got moved in two sections, just after Easter.'

Kate stared at him. 'So when I was screaming at you, it'd already –'

'Been moved,' Sam finished, stepping past to open the front door. He rattled the doorknob several times but it was clearly locked so he turned to her with a slight frown. 'Have you got a key?'

'Have I *what?*'

'Got a key?'

Kate started to laugh, almost hysterically. 'Do you mean to tell me you've moved this whole house, and brought me all the way up here, and you can't get in?'

'We could always try knocking, I suppose,' said Sam, doing just that. The sound of his knuckles against the wood echoed as Kate's laughter abruptly halted. With her mouth still open, she stared stupidly at the door. And then it began to open.

For an awful moment, she was struck by the prospect that her father would be framed in the doorway, smiling at them welcomingly. *What a surprise! Come in, come in, make yourselves at home.* The idea filled her, blocking her throat. But before she even had time to acknowledge the ridiculousness of it, the diamond-framed door swung all the way open and suddenly there were Shelley and Caleb crowding the threshold, with Jacob just behind them. All yelling in unison.

'Surprise!'

'Happy birthday!'

'About time!'

Kate stared at them, absolutely dumbstruck. It was suddenly all too much; it was difficult to actually register their presence, in the *house*. She could see that they were delighted by her bewilderment, and the success of their surprise. And she could hear them still talking at her, and each other. 'Did you guess?' 'How come it took you so long?' 'What do you think of the house?' And she could hear Sam behind her, laughing along with them. And then she felt his hands on either side of her waist, propelling her through the doorway and inside.

Kate found herself being led towards the kitchen. Everything was the same, yet everything was different. It was her father's house, without doubt, and the house she had grown up in, but it was fundamentally altered at the same time. The views through the windows were different, the sounds were different, even the smell was different. And it fleetingly occurred to her that this might be a good thing, the best of both worlds.

Sam guided her towards a kitchen chair and Kate sat, her numbness starting to dissipate in the face of noisy familiarity. Her foot brushed against something soft yet solid underneath the table and she glanced down. Hector lay there, in a mound of ruffled grey-black fur, his back rising and falling as he slept. It was all amazingly unbelievable. The house, the family, the dog. And then she realised that the chair she was sitting on was one of the old ones, which had always sat in this large country-style kitchen, surrounding once again the formica table that had been stored upside down under her own house. In the centre of the table was a chocolate mud cake, with eight candy-striped birthday candles.

'We brought some furniture up last weekend,' offered Caleb, still grinning.

Sam was watching her carefully. 'Just a few bits and pieces to make it livable. You don't mind, do you?'

'Don't mind?' repeated Kate, already shaking her head. 'I don't mind at *all*. In fact . . . no, I don't mind.'

'Hey, guess where we were when we rang you this morning?' said Shelley, pulling out a chair opposite her mother. 'Outside the McDonald's in Lilydale! Already on the way up here!'

'I had no idea.' Kate finally managed a smile. 'What about you, Caleb?'

'I was *inside*, that's what all the noise was. Ordering breakfast. We needed a break because the damn dog kept farting every five minutes. Hell of a trip.'

'So you all knew then? About the house?'

'Oh, yeah.' Shelley waved a hand dismissively. 'We've been helping get it sorted.'

Jacob looked at her with disdain. 'What'd you mean "we"? You've been up here *once*, Caleb and I've been up here nearly every weekend.'

'We had to get the footings dug out,' said Sam to Kate, by way of explanation. 'Before the house was moved. And then there was a bit of work needed after.'

Shelley was staring at her youngest brother. 'I've done my bit.'

'Well, I still can't believe it.' Kate stared around the kitchen, noting each and every familiar object.

'You like?' asked Sam, watching her.

Kate nodded. 'I like.'

'For starters, I've looked after the house while you've been up here,' continued Shelley, still focused on Jacob. 'And then I worked like a Trojan when I was here. Which is more than –'

'God, don't *start*.' Sam sat down heavily and looked from one to the other. 'It's your mother's birthday! How the hell are you two going to go with the bloody shop?'

'Oh, Mum!' Shelley turned to her mother excitedly. 'Shoot! You should *see* the computer program Jake's got going! It's *terrific*.'

Jacob nodded modestly. 'Yeah, it's not bad.'

'I'm actually quite jealous,' commented Caleb, with a grin at his siblings. Jacob stared back with a slight frown, as if he thought he was being teased.

'Where's Emma?' asked Kate, suddenly realising her family was one member short. 'Didn't you bring her up?'

'Asleep.' Shelley lowered her voice. 'In Grandpa's bedroom.'

'Oh.' Kate thought suddenly of Angie, opening the envelope tonight, and felt anew the satisfaction of having handed the story over, as well as a trickle of relief that she wouldn't be there to watch her read it. Later on they could open a bottle of wine and, if Angie wanted to, discuss it a bit.

'We're only staying the one night.' Caleb pulled out a chair and sat down astride it, facing his mother. 'I've got uni on tomorrow.'

Shelley grimaced. 'And I've got work.'

'And I've got all the time in the world,' said Kate, suddenly realising the truth of this. She looked out the window and marvelled again at the strangely familiar view. 'So maybe I'll never go back.'

'And leave me with this lot?' Sam glanced at his children with irritated fondness, although a touch more of the former than the latter. He put his hands down on the table and pushed himself to his feet. 'Coffee? Then you can cut your cake.'

'Thanks. And . . . thanks.'

'I'll have one too, Dad,' said Shelley, standing up. 'I'll just go check on Em.'

Sam filled the electric kettle. 'And you boys can go out and get the stuff from the car. There's my overnight bag, your mother's birthday presents and a sports bag with her things.' He turned back to Kate. 'I even grabbed your laptop out of your room. In case you want to do some writing while you're here.'

Kate smiled, because it was simpler than verbalisation. Through the kitchen window she could see the crest towards the rear of their land, where it dipped down to what was once an out-reaching shore of Lake Eildon. This made for a rather straight horizon, with just the occasional gum tree as a contrast against the sky. No hilly backdrop, or multitude of houses, or fences, or the familiar cat's cradle of electricity and telephone lines.

It was almost surreal to see this view through her father's window. As if the house had been relocated in some sort of Wizard of Oz-style tornado. *Toto, I don't think we're in Kansas any more*. But it was more than just the view, it was the presence of the house itself. Its very *existence*. From overwhelming fury at its demolition, Kate had gradually made her way towards an acknowledgement that the house was gone. But each time the word *forever* had crept across her consciousness, it had been like an emotional assault.

She looked across at Sam and said softly, 'I wonder if you know how much this means to me.'

'Well, I certainly got a hint when I spoke to you on the phone last month.' Sam smiled at her, and then his smile faded. 'But, yes, I think I know.'

'I can't believe you did this. For me.'

'You underestimate how much this house means to us all.' Sam put a mug of coffee in front of her and then sat down, facing her. 'You should have seen their reaction when I suggested this. To be honest, the only thing I was worried about was . . .'

Kate stared at him as he petered off. 'You thought it'd keep bringing back memories for me.'

'Yes.'

'Maybe, maybe not. It's *different* here, so . . . I don't know. Anyway, if it does happen, then I'll just have to deal with it. Or maybe I'll do what you said – channel those memories.'

'Why not?' Sam nodded. 'Bloody well *use* it. I reckon your father would appreciate that.'

'Are you talking about Grandpa?' asked Shelley, coming in with a very flushed Emma whose tousled blonde hair stood up in a mohawk. She wriggled in her mother's arms so Shelley unceremoniously deposited her on Kate's lap.

'Hello there, sweetheart,' said Kate, loving the pliable heaviness of the child. Emma blinked at her and then leant her head sleepily against her grandmother's chest and put her thumb in her mouth.

Jacob and Caleb arrived back, carrying the belongings from the car which they piled haphazardly by the doorway.

'Sustenance!' said Caleb succinctly, staring at the mud cake.

'Just a minute.' Sam frowned as he opened a few drawers. 'I'm sure we brought up some . . . *here* we go.'

'Are we doing presents now too?' asked Shelley, sitting down next to Kate and drumming her fingernails against the table.

'Yeah, the whole birthday thing.' Sam lit a match and held it to one of the candles. As it flamed, Jacob reached across and plucked it from the cake, holding it against other candles while his father used the match.

As her family started singing happy birthday, with a distinct lack of tunefulness, Kate gazed from one to the other, trying to control the smile that was spreading across her face. She still felt numb, but it was a delicious numbness that allowed through a filter of delight and deep appreciation. Halfway through the song, Emma took her thumb from her mouth and started to clap enthusiastically. Kate paused with her eyes on Sam, sitting on the other side of the table. The candle flames were now elongating upwards, casting his face in mottled light and shade. And she suddenly realised that this was as good as it gets. Which was just fine.

ACKNOWLEDGEMENTS

First and foremost I would like to acknowledge my father, Maurice Vivian Evans (1927 – 1988), who was the inspiration behind the nucleus of this story, even though I wish it wasn't the case.

I would like to thank all the rest of the assorted relatives hanging around on my own rather misshapen family tree. Without you lot I would never have been able to write about families – warts and all!

And thanks also to my own little branch: Michael, Jaime and Caitlin. You guys are a never-ending source of weird and wonderful material. Keep it coming but maybe tone it down for a while – just to give me a break!

A big thank you to all the readers (from the website) who emailed to let me know their ideas on the title for this book. And thanks also to the friends and family who weighed in on the debate. We were really stuck for a while there, so your input was invaluable. Hope you all like it.

Thanks also to the real Angie (Storm) for lending me her name (guess who I merged you with?), and thanks to Mr Chris Egan from the titles office, who generously answered all my questions, and also to my agent Rick Raftos and his staff. Finally thanks once again, as always, to everyone at Pan Macmillan, especially Cate Paterson (whose patience is admirable, even when stretched!), Louise Bourke, Jane Novak and now also Julia Stiles (aka Edward Scissorhands), who was able to expertly trim away the dross and reveal the story beneath.

ALSO BY ILSA EVANS IN PAN MACMILLAN

Broken

When some things break they just shouldn't be fixed.

Mattie Hampton's marriage is over. But it seems the games are just beginning.

And so Mattie must draw upon all the strength and courage she has left not to be broken by Jake, the man who promised to love her till death does them part . . .

'terrifying, moving, compelling, important, enlightening, and deeply, deeply upsetting.'
SUNDAY TELEGRAPH

'This book is confronting and will help answer the question "Why doesn't she just leave?"'
CANBERRA TIMES

'This is a compelling and disturbing book, one that delves into the private life of someone who suffers at the hand of the person they love. It's not a world we often read about, but Ilsa Evans delivers a beautifully composed novel that will haunt you for days after you put it down.'
GOOD READING MAGAZINE

Flying the Coop

Once upon a time Chris Beggs and her husband had a dream – to one day own a farm, with cows and poultry and a white fence surrounding a quaint cottage. So what could possibly be wrong with fulfilling that dream 15 years later as a 38-year-old divorced mother of two?

Chris says goodbye to her city life and hello to dawn egg collections, strange noises in the night, a feisty alpaca and poultry named after political figures. Meanwhile, her teenage daughter is bent on world domination, the bookkeeper is out for revenge and the tractor has a mind of its own. And soon Chris realises that the least of her worries is dressing in a chicken suit and learning how to waddle.

With the enthusiastic help of her family, old friends, new neighbours, and a stranger on the end of daily emails, can Chris succeed in making this spur of the moment decision revitalise her life, or has she put all her eggs in the wrong basket?

Each Way Bet

The Broadhurst sisters, book editor Emily and stay-at-home wife and mother Jill, are suffering severe cases of the-grass-is-always-greener syndrome. So, when Melbourne Cup Day rolls around, they decide to have an each-way bet by trading places.

But then they find they have to cope with an elusive pregnancy test, vegetable-flavoured punch, flying carpet bowls, a predatory femme fatale, a foul-mouthed three-year old, and argumentative and accident-prone teenagers.

Spend a madcap Melbourne Cup with the Broadhursts, and find out if the race that stops the nation can get their lives back on track.

Odd Socks

Unlike her best friend Camilla Riley, compulsive list-maker Terry Diamond prides herself on her organisational abilities. Also unlike Camilla, Terry is tall, blonde, curvaceous and self-confident.

However, all this doesn't stop chaos bursting into her life when her daughter not only gives birth on Terry's living-room rug but decides to move home with infant in tow.

Then there are the problems Terry is having with her love life, as she realises her boyfriend – a handyman who wears pink overalls – may not even be Mr Right For Now, and falls in love at first sight with a mysterious stranger who dresses like the father in a 1950s sitcom.

Will all this mayhem make the play-it-safe Terry do what she needs to do to turn her life around?

Drip Dry

Because sometimes coffee isn't nearly enough and you have to take a deep breath, maintain control, and assess the situation . . . Or just reach for the scotch.

The twice-divorced mother of three is back. New, improved and stronger than ever – but still struggling to keep her head above water, even in the bath. And what a week it is in the Riley/Brown/McNeill household. There's one wedding, two babies, three engagements and four birthdays. Then ex-ex-husband Alex's long-awaited return from overseas heralds unexpected results, which in turn heralds the arrival of a most unwanted guest. Meanwhile, Sam wants to join the armed forces, Ben is setting up embarrassing money-making schemes and CJ's wreaking havoc with sharp fairy wands.

Along the way there's an infectious disease outbreak, a mysterious death in the family, a broken nose, a bruised rump and several bruised egos. Can life get more frenetic than this?

Spin Cycle

Ever had one of those weeks when you've been soaked, put through the ringer & hung out to dry?

On Monday morning, this twice-divorced mother of three was bemoaning her boring life that left her feeling deflated and unhappy. By the end of the week she wishes that was all she had to worry about.

In the space of seven days her life is picked up and spun around when she discovers her mother's getting married again (for the fourth time), her older sister is pregnant again (for the fifth time), her younger sister lands the perfect boyfriend (who is very fanciable), her sister-in-law is running a brothel, her new next-door neighbour is going to be her ex-ex husband. Oh, and she's been arrested, her best friend's gone missing and the pets keep dying.

All in the same week she sacks her therapist because she thinks she can work it all out for herself. But can she? And how can she work it all out if she doesn't even know what it is she wants to work out?

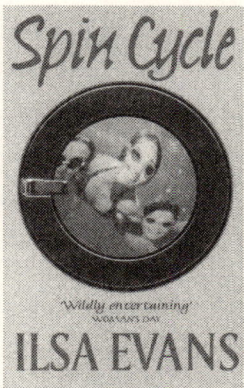